英語閱讀技巧完全攻略

作者 Owain Mckimm / Connie Sliger / Zachary Fillingham / Richard Luhrs　二版
譯者 劉嘉珮／蘇裕承／蔡裴驊　審訂 Helen Yeh

Success With Reading

全英文學習訓練英文思維及語感
可調整語速／播放／複誦模式訓練聽力

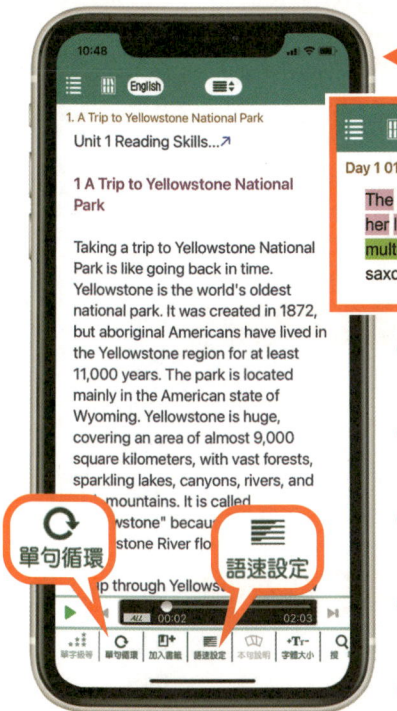

◀ 全文閱讀

單句閱讀色底表示單字級等

◀ 單句閱讀

單句循環
語速設定

- 標示高中字彙、全民英檢、多益字級，掌握難度，立即理解文章
- 設定自動／循環／範圍播放，訓練聽力超有感
- 設定 7 段語速、複誦間距及次數，扎實訓練聽力
- 設定克漏字比率學習，提高理解力、詞彙量及文法
- 睡眠學習，複習文章幫助記憶

快速查詢字義理解文章內容

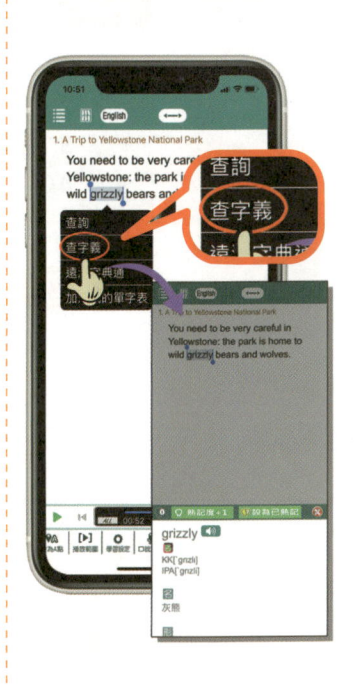

查詢
查字義

課後閱讀測驗檢驗理解力

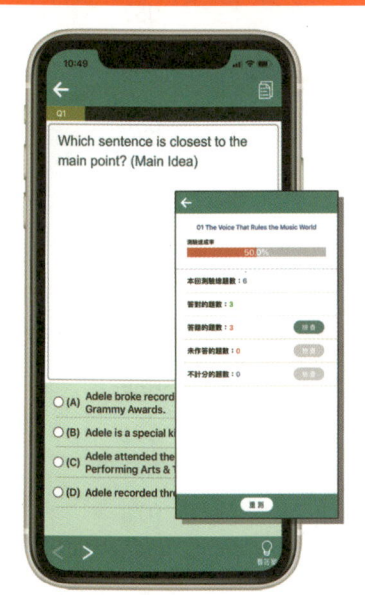

強力口說練習

錄下發音和原音比對辨識，精進口語能力。

單字分析掌握單字力

提供全書總單字量及單字表，掌握單字難易度，針對不熟單字加強學習。

目錄 Contents

簡介 Introduction … 006
使用導覽 How Do I Use This Book? … 010

UNIT 1 Reading Skills 閱讀技巧 … 012

1-1 Main Idea 歸納要旨 … 014

1. Versification With a Voice … 014
2. Hungry Little Hounds … 016
3. Salaried Citizenship … 018
4. Feeling Better, Naturally … 021
5. Dos and Don'ts of a Good Night's Sleep … 024

1-2 Supporting Details 找出支持性細節 … 026

6. The Day a Demon Came Knocking … 026
7. From Graffiato to Hip-Hop … 030
8. For Richer or Poorer, For Better or Worse … 033
9. The Sport Where Brains and Brawn Meet … 036
10. The Emperors' Domain … 039

1-3 Making Inferences 進行推論 … 042

11. Gazing Into the Crystal Ball … 042
12. A Fix for Feral Animals? … 045
13. When Shadows Cover Stars … 048
14. A Different Kind of Dance … 050
15. The Twittering of the Sparrows … 053

1-4 Clarifying Devices 釐清寫作技巧 … 056

16. The European Experiment … 056
17. Frozen Fields … 059
18. Hacking the Human Code … 062
19. Let's Get Rich—in Space! … 064
20. The Choice is Yours! … 066

1-5 Figurative Language 瞭解譬喻性語言 … 068

21. A Globally Unifying Event … 068
22. A Battle Over Bricks … 071
23. Portrait of a Primitive Painter … 074
24. Against Impossible Odds … 078
25. The New Einstein? … 082

1-6 Author's Purpose and Tone 明瞭作者目的和語氣 — 086

26.	Our Glorious Nighttime Lights	086
27.	The Big Hangover	090
28.	Island Purradises	094
29.	Don't Believe Everything You Hear—or Read	097
30.	Thriving With the Slash Effect	100

1-7 Cause and Effect 理解因果關係 — 104

31.	Ditching the Plastic Habit	104
32.	Four Ways to Be Quiet	108
33.	Trouble in the Air—and Under the Ground	111
34.	A Man of Passionate Callings	114
35.	Super Sensitive Souls	118

1-8 Finding Bias 明辨寫作偏見 — 122

36.	Nothing but the Best for Mr. Whiskers	122
37.	Salvaged, Served, Savored	125
38.	Convenience on Every Corner	128
39.	Do You Like Me Now?	131
40.	A Plant-tastic Solution for Global Warming	134

1-9 Fact or Opinion 分辨事實與意見 — 138

41.	Japan's Master of Animation	138
42.	One Story for All Time	142
43.	A Revolution in Convenience	146
44.	The Secret of the Stones	150
45.	Welcome to the Wood Wide Web	153

1-10 Review Test 實力檢測 — 156

46.	Is There Anybody Out There?	156
47.	Kiss, Kiss, Hello!	159
48.	Food Worth Saving: Preserving the World's Culinary Heritage	162
49.	The World's Most Famous Investor	166
50.	Declutter Your House, Declutter Your Heart	169

目錄 Contents

UNIT 2 Word Study 字彙學習 — 172

2-1 Synonyms (Words With the Same Meaning) 同義字 — 174

- 51. Ireland: A Troubled History — 174
- 52. Crop Circles: A Worldwide Enigma — 178
- 53. Bruce Lee: From Trailblazer to Legend — 182
- 54. How to Survive a Plane Crash — 185
- 55. Here Today, Gone the Next — 188

2-2 Antonyms (Words With Opposite Meanings) 反義字 — 190

- 56. Why Do We Forget Things? — 190
- 57. Is Your Smartphone Destroying the Planet? — 192
- 58. Biofuels — 194
- 59. Blinded by Too Much Light — 196
- 60. Saving Up for the Future — 198

2-3 Words in Context 依上下文猜測字義 — 200

- 61. Five-Star Fibs — 200
- 62. The Problem With Pork — 202
- 63. Giants of the Steppe — 204
- 64. Did We All Come From Africa? — 206
- 65. Born Survivors — 208

2-4 Review Test 實力檢測 — 210

- 66. Scammers, Scammers Everywhere! — 210
- 67. Virtually Famous — 213
- 68. Becoming a Bookworm — 216
- 69. Life Lessons From the Ancient Stage — 219
- 70. Deceptive Digestion — 222

UNIT 3 Study Strategies 學習策略 — 224

3-1 Visual Material 影像圖表 — 226

- 71. **Bar Graph:** A Concerning Road Safety Record — 226
- 72. **Line Chart:** Asia's Ticking Time Bomb — 229
- 73. **Map:** Stressing Out Over Water! — 231
- 74. **Pie Chart:** Get Your Priorities Right! — 234
- 75. **Schedule/Timetable:** Try Before You Apply — 237

3-2	**Reference Sources** 參考資料		240
76.	**Table of Contents:** Teaching Haute Cuisine to the Masses		240
77.	**Index:** Keep Your Eyes on the Skies		242
78.	**Menu:** Start Your Day the Right Way		244
79.	**Internet:** Sharpening Your Search Skills		246
80.	**Data Flow Chart:** How to Make Money From Social Media		248

UNIT 4 Final Review 綜合練習 — 250

4-1	Final Review 綜合練習		252
81.	Get in the Cage!		252
82.	A Monument to Flops and Failures		254
83.	Stephen King: The Master of Horror		256
84.	The Shining Spoils of War		258
85.	The Superheroes of the Food World		260
86.	The Woman Who Invented Science Fiction		262
87.	Cactus: The Ultimate Desert Survivor		264
88.	Isis: The Rise and Fall of a Global Terror Network		267
89.	**Table and Bar Chart:** A Shift in Belief		270
90.	**List:** Debit or Credit?		273

課文中譯	276
習題解答	320

簡介 Introduction

　　本套書共分四冊，目的在於培養閱讀能力與增進閱讀技巧。書中共有 90 篇文章，不僅網羅各類主題，還搭配大量閱讀測驗題，以訓練讀者記憶重點與理解內容的能力。

　　本書依不同主題劃分為四大單元。每單元主要介紹一種閱讀攻略。讀者不僅能透過本書文章增進閱讀能力，還能涉獵包羅萬象的知識，包括文化、藝術、史地、人物、科技、生物、經濟、教育等主題閱讀。

主要特色

• 包羅萬象的文章主題

　　本書內容涵蓋各類多元主題，幫助讀者充實知識，宛如一套生活知識小百科。囊括主題包括：

社會學	科學	其他主題
藝術與文學	動物／植物	體育
歷史		
地理與景點	健康與人體	
文化		
政治／經濟		
語言傳播	網路或科技	神秘事件
環境保育		
人物	科學	
教育		

• 全方位的閱讀攻略

　　本書以豐富的高效率閱讀攻略，幫助讀者輕鬆理解任何主題文章的內容。書中閱讀攻略包括：

1 閱讀技巧（Reading Skills）

幫助你練習瞭解整體內文的技巧。此單元涵蓋以下項目：

❶ 歸納要旨（Main Idea）

文章要旨代表的是文章想傳達的大意，有可能是一種想法或事實。文章要旨通常會以主題論述的方式表達。除了整體主旨之外，文章每段內容也有其中心思想，只要清楚每段內容的重點，即可了解整篇文章的意思。

❷ 找出支持性細節（Supporting Details）

支持性細節是作者用來支持文章主題句的說明，例如事實、直喻、說明、比較、舉例等，或是任何能佐證主題的資訊。一篇好文章，一定會以事實、統計數據和其他證據為基礎，堆砌出作者想要表達的主旨。

❸ 進行推論（Making Inferences）

「推論」技巧意指運用已知資訊來猜測未知的人事物。舉例而言，如果朋友開門時看起來怒氣沖沖，你會猜測事有蹊蹺或有事發生。作者同樣會以推論方式，來提點讀者相似的情境。

❹ 釐清寫作技巧（Clarifying Devices）

釐清寫作技巧包括瞭解字彙、片語的應用，以及分辨作者用來讓文章大意與支持性細節更加清楚、更引人入勝的寫作方式。有時候，最重要的釐清技巧就是要能分辨「文章類型」和「作者意圖」。

❺ 瞭解譬喻性語言（Figurative Language）

作者會運用譬喻性的語言來觸動讀者的感受或令人在腦海中產生畫面，讓讀者留下深刻印象。本書會介紹下列幾種譬喻性語言：

明喻會以「like」（像）、「as」（如）或「than」（比……還……）等字比較兩者，例如「她的心比石頭還硬」。**隱喻**會更直接比較兩者，並且將兩者畫上等號，例如「她有一顆鐵石心腸」或「全世界就是一座大舞台」，因此表達效果比明喻更強烈。

擬人法意指將無生物的物體賦予人類特質，例如「太陽漫步於天空」。**成語**屬於不能照字面意思解讀的片語，其意義與拆解各字來看不同。例如

「To let the cat out of the bag.」和貓一點關係也沒有，真正的意思為「洩漏祕密」。

誇飾法意指加油添醋的誇張表達方式，例如「我已經告訴過你一百萬遍了！」

❻ 明瞭作者目的和語氣（Author's Purpose and Tone）

作者寫作皆有目的，可能是提出論點、呈現重要議題，甚或只是想娛樂讀者。為了達到其寫作目的，作者會調整文中的字彙和資訊，來符合文章想呈現出的語氣。

❼ 理解因果關係（Cause and Effect）

事出必有因，所導致的行為或事件就是一種結果。因果之間的關係有時顯而易見，有時卻幾乎不著痕跡。為了更清楚理解因果關係，請仔細觀察具有因果意味的用字，例如「therefore」（因此）、「as a result」（所以）或是「consequently」（因而）。

❽ 明辨寫作偏見（Finding Bias）

作者有其本身的歷練、看法和信仰。混為一談時，就會形成偏見或特定觀點。雖然有時難以看出作者的偏見，但可從作者的用字以及是否公平陳述兩造論點來窺見端倪。

❾ 分辨事實與意見（Fact or Opinion）

大多數文章均含有事實和意見，因此分辨兩者間的差異相當重要。只要是能透過測驗、紀錄或文件來證明真實度的資訊，即屬於「事實」（fact）；「意見」（opinion）則代表作者的信念或主觀評判。有時候「意見」看似「事實」，倘若無法證明其真實性，該資訊還是得歸類為「意見」。

2　字彙練習（Word Study）

能幫助你練習累積字彙量與理解文章新字彙的技巧。本單元涵蓋以下項目：

❶ 同義字（意義相同的用語）（Synonyms: Words With the Same Meaning）

同義字是意義完全相同或非常相近的單字，例如 huge 和 gigantic 就是同義字。英語擁有將近一百萬個字彙，其中許多單字的意義相近。如果能夠辨識這些同義字，將是增進閱讀理解能力的一大利器。

❷ 反義字（意義相反的用語）（Antonyms: Words With Opposite Meanings）

反義字是意思相反的單字，good 和 bad、big 和 small、hot 和 cold，這幾組都是反義字。有時候我們很容易辨別反義字，有時候則需要費點力。記得務必要從前後文當中，尋找可能的線索。

❸ 依上下文猜測字義（Words in Context）

英文單字可能有許多不同的意思。當你遇到可能有爭議的單字時，一定要讀完上下文再決定字義。萬一你遇到完全陌生的單字，也可以從上下文來推斷字義。

3 學習策略（Study Strategies）

幫助你理解文意，並運用文章中不同素材來蒐集資訊，培養查詢資料的基本能力。影像圖表和參考資料等資訊，不會直接呈現出文章的含意，而是以圖片、編號清單、依字母順序編列的清單，和其他方法來展示資訊。本單元涵蓋以下項目：

❶ 影像圖表（Visual Material）

資料有許多種形式，有些難以用文字來表達，這時候就需要使用影像圖表來輔助說明。影像圖表運用了圖片和圖表來傳達資訊，包括了圖表、表格和地圖。運用得當的話，可以化繁為簡，使資料容易理解。

❷ 參考資料（Reference Sources）

百科全書、旅遊指南、網際網路、報紙、食譜等，都是知識的寶庫。但要在如此巨大的寶庫中找到特定的資訊，可不是件容易的事。此時，索引、搜索引擎、節目表等工具即可派上用場。只要學會如何瀏覽這些資料，即可大幅增進閱讀理解力。

4 綜合練習（Final Review）

以豐富的閱讀素材和推敲式問題，幫助你有效複習學過的內容。此單元目的在檢視你對本書所提供之學習資訊的吸收程度。為了檢測你理解內文的能力，請務必於研讀前述單元之後，完成最後的綜合練習單元。

• 最佳考試準備用書

本書適合初學者閱讀，亦為準備大學學測、指考、多益、托福及雅思等考試的最佳用書。

使用導覽 How Do I Use This Book?

全方位的閱讀攻略

每單元主要介紹一種閱讀攻略，幫助讀者更加輕鬆理解任何主題文章的內容。

包羅萬象的閱讀主題

內容涵蓋各類多元主題，包括藝術、地理、歷史、文化與科學，不僅能充實讀者的知識，亦可加強閱讀能力。

010

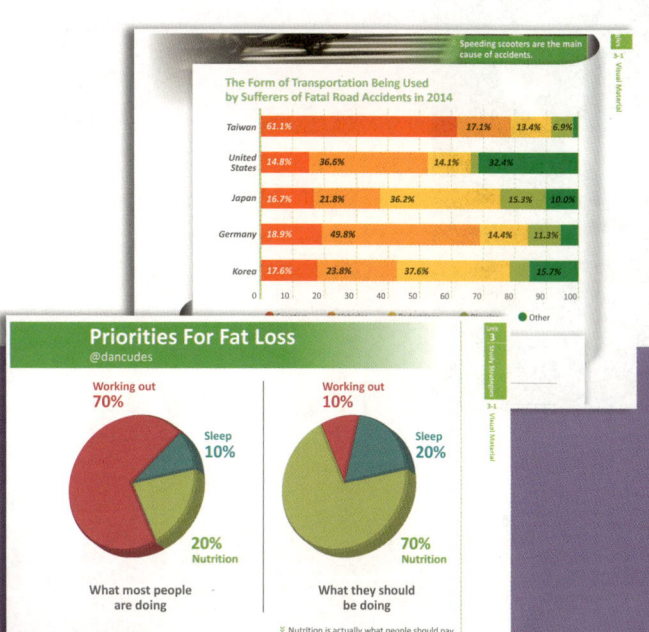

琳瑯滿目的彩色圖表

琳瑯滿目的彩色圖表，有助於讀者學習使用圖表，幫助快速理解文章內容，增加閱讀趣味性。

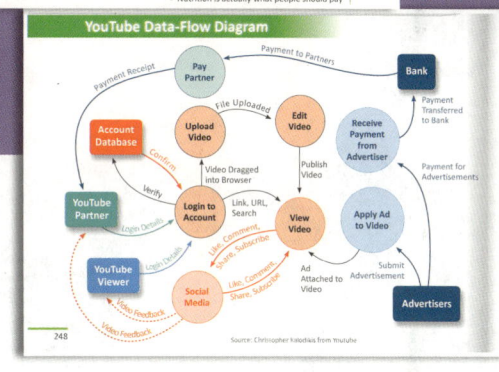

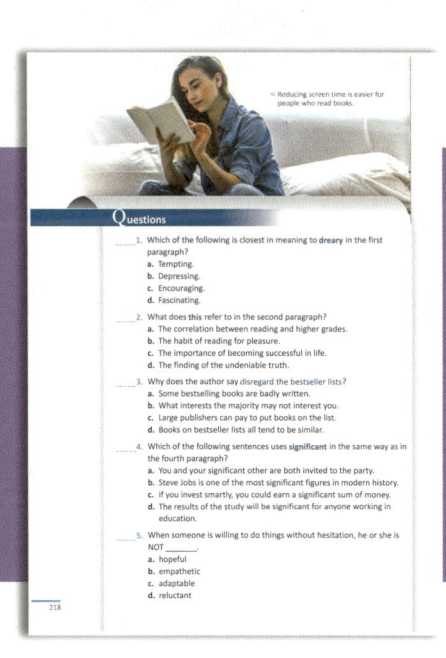

實用的主題式練習題

每篇文章後均附有五題選擇題，用以檢測閱讀理解能力，並加強字彙認知力。讀者可運用此類練習來有效評估自己的程度，以作自我實力之檢測與提升。

011

Unit 1

Reading Skills

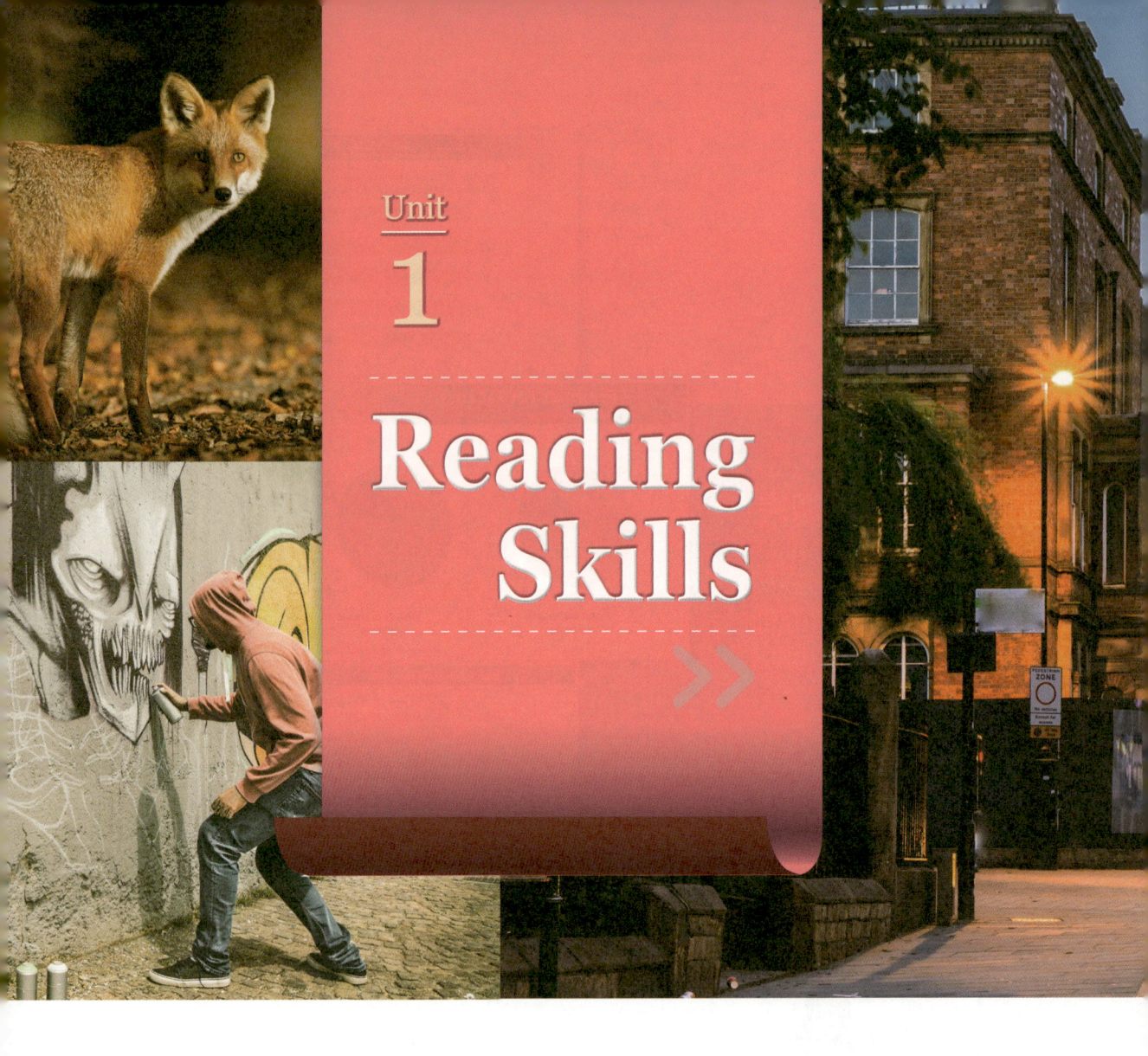

1-1 Main Idea

1-2 Supporting Details

1-3 Making Inferences

1-4 Clarifying Devices

1-5 Figurative Language

1-6 Author's Purpose and Tone

1-7 Cause and Effect

1-8 Finding Bias

1-9 Fact or Opinion

1-10 Review Test

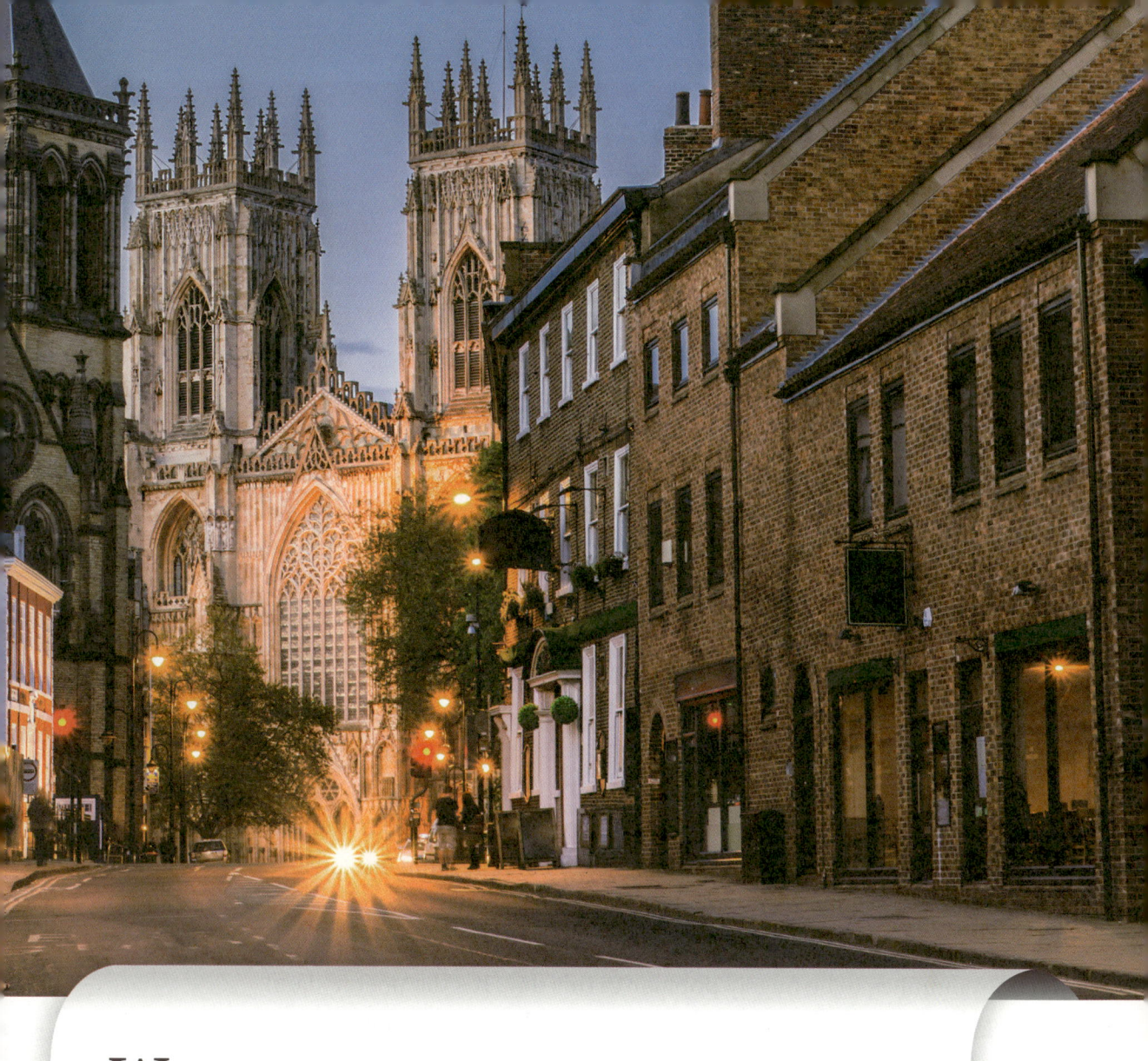

When it comes to understanding a text, knowing what the individual words mean is often not enough. It takes many different reading skills to truly understand what the author is trying to convey. Of course, understanding the literal meaning of a passage is an important first step, but you also need to be able to read between the lines; that is, you should analyze the relationships between ideas, recognize cause and effect, and predict the outcomes of stated events.

At an even more advanced level, you need to be able to recognize the author's persuasive techniques and bias and be able to distinguish between facts and opinions. The reading skills developed in this unit will help you do just that.

1-1 Main Idea

The **main idea** of an article is not always obvious, so when reading, don't forget to ask yourself, *"What point is the author trying to make?"* In addition to the article as a whole having a main idea, each paragraph will also have its own central idea. Once you know the point of each paragraph, you can use that knowledge to make sense of the whole piece.

> Poets at the poetry slam would shift rapidly between volumes and tones.
> (cc by Heinrich-Böll-Stiftung)

> three contestants at the poetry slam (cc by alex lang)

1 Versification With a Voice

1 When we think of poetry, we usually picture words organized into lines and stanzas printed on a page. But poetry was not always confined to paper. In fact, for much of human history, poetry was recited aloud in front of large audiences. Poetic devices such as rhythm, repetition, and rhyme are thought to have developed to aid poets commit these verses to memory. As writing emerged and became universal, poetry gradually fell out of this oral tradition. However, in the United States in the 1980s, a form of poetry competition emerged that revitalized interest in poetry performance, and it continues to be hugely popular to this day. It's the poetry slam!

2 The structure of a poetry slam was devised by construction worker and poet Marc Smith from Chicago, who believed that modern poetry had become far too academic and stuffy. Smith wanted a medium that was looser, freer, and that could directly engage an audience. In a poetry slam, members of the audience are chosen by a host to act as judges for the event. After each poet performs, each judge awards a score to that poem. The highest scorers advance to the next round, where they compete again, until eventually a winner is declared.

3 The broad range of voices, styles, and approaches on show at poetry slams makes each event unique and full of surprises. Some poets make radical use of their voice, shifting rapidly between volumes and tones. Others use their entire body to convey the meaning of their poem and employ

> A U.S. Coast Guard Academy cadet participates in a poetry slam. (cc by US Coast Guard Academy)

highly choreographed, emphatic movements, and even dance. Topics tend to be political and provocative—race, gender, discrimination—which are perfect for triggering emotional and vocal responses from a live audience (something that is vital in order for the poet to gain a competitive edge over his or her opponents).

4   Some critics of the poetry slam cite this emphasis on pleasing the audience as the movement's great flaw, proclaiming that the competitive "tournament" element has made slam poetry more like a sport than an art form. Others, however, point out that for those frustrated with the stuffy reputation of written poetry and traditional poetry readings, which take place in hushed, reverent rooms, the poetry slam is a place for poets to scream, shout, and sing their verses to the world. What's more, it allows the world to respond, with heckles or cheers, creating a moment of poetic dialogue between poet and audience that is impossible to replicate with words on a page.

Questions

1. What is the author's main point in the first paragraph?
   a. When people think of poetry, they often think of words on a page.
   b. Poetic devices were originally used to aid in memorizing poems.
   c. Performing poetry aloud has made a resurgence in recent years.
   d. For much of human history, poetry was performed aloud to large groups.

2. Which of the following could be a suitable heading for the second paragraph?
   a. The Origin and Structure of Poetry Slams   b. The Problem With Modern Poetry
   c. The Creator of the Poetry Slam   d. How do You Win a Poetry Slam?

3. Which of the following statements can summarize the third paragraph?
   a. Some slam poets combine reciting their poems with exaggerated movements and dance.
   b. Politically charged topics are often the subjects of the poems performed at slams.
   c. Poetry slams are both highly surprising and entertaining for members of the audience.
   d. Slam poets use a variety of techniques and provocative topics to emotionally engage audiences.

4. What is the author's conclusion in the final paragraph?
   a. Despite some criticism, slams provide a unique experience for both poets and audiences.
   b. Poetry slams are often criticized for making poetry more like a sport than an art from.
   c. Poetry slams are an excellent venue for poets frustrated with traditional poetry readings.
   d. Poetry slam audiences aren't afraid to voice their opinion of a poet's work.

5. Which of the following could be an alternative title for the passage?
   a. The History of Poetry in the United States   b. The Return of Performance Poetry
   c. The Poetry of Marc Smith   d. Poetry Competitions in the 1980s

small breed dog

large breed dog

2 Hungry Little Hounds

1 Congratulations! You've adopted a new puppy. You are soon going to find out, though, that as well as being super cute, your puppy is also super *hungry*, and as a responsible pet owner it's up to you to provide your puppy with food that contains all the proper nutrition needed to help it grow into a happy, healthy adult dog.

2 However, contrary to what you might think, feeding a puppy a diet supercharged with every nutrient in the book isn't the answer. Many dogs are at risk of health problems that are particular to their breed or size. Thus, they need a very specific balance of nutrients when developing in order to counter those potentially dangerous conditions. Larger breeds, for example, are at high risk of developing skeletal and joint problems, particularly if they get too much calcium and potassium in their diet. Only by buying puppy food designed specifically for your type of dog can you ensure their diet contains the optimal mount of each required nutrient.

3 Something that surprises many first-time puppy owners is just how much food puppies eat. Puppies do most of their growing in the first five months and so need enough calories to support that initial spurt—about double the amount

≫ dog food

≪ Buying food designed especially for your type of dog can ensure their diet contains the optimal amount of each required nutrient.

016

an adult dog of the same breed would need. However, you will need to adjust this amount as the puppy grows, and this can be done with the help of a feeding chart that comes with most brands of puppy food. And how long do you need to keep this up? A puppy needs to be on this special puppy diet until it reaches about 90% of its expected adult weight, and while small breeds may reach this in around 9 months, large breeds need special feeding until 18 months of age.

4 However, though puppies may be comparable to food vacuum cleaners, happy to hoover up anything in sight, you must be careful not to overfeed them. It is actually normal for a healthy 8- to 10-week-old puppy to look fairly thin, and too much body fat is a sign that the dog should cut back; otherwise, it might be at risk of becoming obese. If you are feeding your puppy correctly, the signs should be obvious: plenty of energy, a thick shiny coat, and well-formed, brown feces. These are all indicators that your puppy is getting the diet it needs to thrive.

Questions

_____ 1. Which of the following could serve as an alternative title to this article?
   a. The Joys of Owning a Pup
   b. Keeping Your New Dog Entertained
   c. A Healthy Diet for Puppies
   d. Danger—These Foods Are Not for Dogs

_____ 2. What is the author's main point in the first paragraph?
   a. Puppies are incredibly cute and make wonderful first-time pets.
   b. It is a pet owner's responsibility to ensure a new puppy gets properly fed.
   c. It is better to adopt a puppy than to buy one from a pet store.
   d. Puppies are very hungry creatures, a fact that surprises many first-time owners.

_____ 3. Which of the following is the author's main point in the second paragraph?
   a. You should buy food designed specifically for your puppy's breed or type.
   b. Larger dog breeds have a high risk of developing skeletal and joint problems.
   c. Feeding puppies a nutrient-infused diet isn't the best way to ensure their health.
   d. Many dogs are at risk of health problems particular to their breed.

_____ 4. Which of the following would make a suitable heading for the third paragraph?
   a. Foods to Avoid
   b. Which Brand Is Best?
   c. The Signs of a Healthy Pup
   d. How Much and for How Long?

_____ 5. Which of the following best summarizes the author's main point in final paragraph?
   a. Signs such as coat quality and fat levels can help confirm a correct diet.
   b. Overfeeding is actually normal and doesn't need to be avoided.
   c. Owners shouldn't worry if their puppy appears lean as this is actually normal.
   d. Puppies eat so much they can be compared to vacuum cleaners.

"Universal Basic Income" is the concept that citizens get paid by the government regardless of whether they have a job.

Robots are replacing human workers in factories around the world.

3 Salaried Citizenship

1 A new policy concept is gaining traction around the world. It goes by many names, including "basic income," "universal basic income," "citizen's income," and even "freedom dividend." But the substance is always the same: citizens get paid a certain amount of money every month, regardless of whether or not they have a job.

2 Many people might be thinking: "Free money? That's insane . . . but I like it."

3 The idea of a universal basic income (UBI) is considered extreme by some people, but it stems from equally radical changes to the global economy. Automation is replacing human workers with robots in factories around the world. And advances in artificial intelligence mean that white collar positions will soon be next. There are fewer and fewer jobs, and the jobs that remain are subject to intense competition from desperate workers. The end result is lower wages and higher poverty.

4 Here's where the universal basic income comes in. It's not necessarily designed to *replace* a working wage, but to *supplement* it. For example, if every citizen received $500 a month, it would allow them to accept part-time positions without jeopardizing their overall

» Swiss activists organized a performance to force the government to hold a referendum on whether to incorporate basic income.

˅ Basic Income Summer Forum held in Dublin in 2015
(cc by stanjourdan)

economic well-being. It would also allow more people to work the job they want, like starting a small business or pursuing the arts, rather than the job they need.

5   In theory, the UBI provides some major benefits. For one, it helps reduce inequality and poverty. It also puts more money into the pockets of the lower and middle classes, which spurs consumer spending and boosts the economy. Finally, it can save the government time and money by simplifying or eliminating preexisting welfare programs for poor people.

6   However, a universal basic income also has drawbacks. Paramount among them is the cost of such a program. One US study by the National Bureau of Economic Research found that a UBI of $12,000 a year would add a whopping $3 trillion to the government budget. There are also expensive government programs that wouldn't be replaced by new UBI spending, such as health care.

7   The idea is still generating a lot of buzz among young people and governments around the world, from Taiwan to the United Kingdom. Canada and Finland have already instituted limited trials, and Indian politicians are increasingly advocating UBI as a way to alleviate rural poverty. Supporters of UBI are hoping that these voices only get louder as time goes on.

Universal Basic Income

Unconditional   **Automatic**   **Individual**   **As a Right**

↑ the concept of universal basic income

Questions

1. What is the main idea of the third paragraph?
   a. UBI is an extreme idea.
   b. The nature of work is changing around the world.
   c. Automation couldn't replace human workers.
   d. Poverty is getting worse around the world.

2. What is the fourth paragraph about?
   a. UBI will impact the way we work.
   b. The UBI amount must be set very low to be successful.
   c. Everybody wants to start their own business.
   d. Part-time jobs are increasingly common in the modern economy.

3. What is the main idea in the fifth paragraph?
   a. Inequality and poverty are getting worse around the world.
   b. There are lots of ways to increase economic prosperity.
   c. Welfare programs are important to poor people.
   d. UBI has a variety of benefits.

4. What is the main idea of the sixth paragraph?
   a. UBI has more drawbacks than it has benefits.
   b. Healthcare programs wouldn't be replaced by UBI.
   c. UBI would be very expensive to implement.
   d. Studies are being conducted on UBI in the United States.

5. What is the main idea of the final paragraph?
   a. UBI is a hot topic around the world.
   b. India is about to implement a UBI program.
   c. Young people like the idea of UBI.
   d. Support for UBI is decreasing.

≫ depression

4 Feeling Better, Naturally

1 Depression is one of the most widespread and debilitating of all diseases, affecting countless millions of people the world over. It can range from a temporary inability to overcome sadness to a clinical disorder in which feelings of loss, frustration, anger and/or sorrow extend over a long period, requiring medical intervention.

2 There are many pharmaceutical antidepressants available, and many patients respond well to them. Some sufferers, however, do not wish to risk the danger of side effects or addiction. It can also take time to find the right medication for a depressed individual.

3 Fortunately, studies have shown that natural remedies can be effective alternatives in treating mild depression. Better yet, they can be tried *before* seeking help from a psychiatrist, who may prescribe more extreme treatments.

4 The following are some natural remedies to help people cope with depression.

❶ Get enough exercise. Exercise raises the level of serotonin in the brain, and serotonin improves one's mood.

❷ Maintain a healthy diet. Nutrition plays a key role in mental health. Eat fresh fruits and vegetables, and take vitamin and mineral supplements.
❸ Avoid alcohol. While many people drink when they feel depressed, alcohol is itself a depressant and can make bad feelings even worse in the long run.
❹ Enlarge your circle of friends, and spend more time with them. The more close friends you have, the less likely you are to get depressed. Also, get closer to your family members. It is important to be able to share your feelings with people you can trust.
❺ Become a volunteer. When you stop focusing only on yourself, it is difficult to stay depressed. Also, it will help you to see that others have problems, too, and you will feel good about aiding them in hard times.
❻ Occupy yourself with activities that you are good at. When you see your accomplishments, it will give your spirits and your self-esteem a boost.
❼ Relax, meditate, and get enough sleep. Meditation helps to alleviate tension. Relaxation and rest are imperative for a sound mind.

⌃ Get exercise.

⌃ Do activities you're good at.

⌃ Meditate.

⌃ Keep a daily journal.

» Enlarge your circle of friends.

❽ Keep a daily journal. This will help you keep track of your depression from the beginning, so that you can see what is causing it, and control it before it controls you.

5 Many of the keys to a psychologically healthy life are also what will keep you physically healthy. If, however, you still find that you are unable to return to a normal level of happiness, do not hesitate to seek professional help.

⌃ Become a volunteer.

Questions

1. What is the main idea of this passage?
   a. Medication is not the only way to combat depression.
   b. Depression is a serious health problem everywhere.
   c. Seeing other people's problems will make you feel better.
   d. Eating the right foods will keep you from getting depressed.

2. Which of the following best expresses the main idea of the first paragraph?
   a. Depression can occur in many different forms.
   b. Depression can extend over a very long period.
   c. Depression is one of the world's most serious health problems.
   d. Medication is usually required to treat people with depression.

3. What is the main idea of the second paragraph?
   a. Many antidepressant medications are available.
   b. Many patients respond well to antidepressants.
   c. Not all depressed people want to take medication.
   d. Antidepressant medications can have side effects.

4. Which of these best expresses the main idea of the third paragraph?
   a. Many studies of depression have been done over the years.
   b. Natural remedies can be helpful in fighting depression.
   c. People should try natural remedies before seeing a doctor.
   d. Doctors generally prescribe extreme treatments for depression.

5. What is the main idea of the final paragraph?
   a. Physically healthy people don't suffer from depression.
   b. Natural remedies will always cure depressed people.
   c. Maintaining a normal level of happiness is difficult.
   d. One should consult a doctor if other remedies don't help.

5 Dos and Don'ts of a Good Night's Sleep

> Your body must replenish itself by getting enough good sleep.

1 Night after night, your body must replenish itself by getting enough good sleep. If not, daytime sleepiness can negatively affect your work, studies, relationships, and socioeconomic condition. This article provides a few handy "dos and don'ts" for achieving a good night's sleep.

2 Sometimes the culprit behind your incessant tossing and turning is simple: the body's natural clock is unsettled. This might be due to schedule changes; for instance, you start a new job and your body needs a period of adjustment. It could also be because you are too physically active right before trying to get some precious shut-eye. While it is a great idea to get around 30 minutes of physical exercise every day, never do it too close to your bedtime!

3 Just like with exercise, mental overexertion can also leave you wide awake and staring up at the ceiling in the dead of night. Avoid doing work or watching television in bed; instead, give yourself about a two-hour period of mental calm before sleeping. One trick that many people try is to keep a personal journal, which allows you to write down all of the problems and stresses that you might face the next day, instead of lying awake and thinking about them all night.

4 Don't neglect your pre-bed bathroom ritual. Try taking a hot shower or bath, or even visiting the sauna, around 90 minutes before going to bed. Your body temperature increases in the shower, but it will start to gently fall by bedtime, helping you get the deep and relaxing sleep that you need. And don't forget to go to the bathroom right before bed, so that you are less likely to get up during the night.

> Caffeine can cause insomnia.

> Don't drink alcohol before bedtime.

> crackers and peanut butter

5   It is important to know what to avoid eating, for certain things can cause havoc in your digestive system and keep you awake. Allergies to foods cause congestion and an upset stomach, and being too full can cause sleep apnea. Caffeine may lead to insomnia if you consume it in the afternoon, because it does not metabolize efficiently. In addition, don't drink alcohol before bed, because it keeps you from achieving a deep sleep. The ideal is to eat a small portion of high-protein food, such as a small plate of crackers and peanut butter, several hours before bedtime. This helps the essential amino acid L-tryptophan produce melatonin, a hormone that controls sleep.

Take a hot bath as a way of getting ready for bed.

Questions

_____ 1. What is the main idea of the article?
   a. Sleep is the most important thing in someone's life.
   b. There are a few things you can do to get the sleep you need.
   c. Your body needs sleep to replenish itself.
   d. Certain foods will help you get a good night's rest.

_____ 2. Which statement best expresses the main idea of the first paragraph?
   a. Sleep is something all of us do.
   b. Sleep can negatively affect your work.
   c. Sleep helps to replenish the body.
   d. Sleep is extremely important to all of us.

_____ 3. Which statement best expresses the main idea of the third paragraph?
   a. Mental overexertion can leave you wide awake.
   b. Avoid doing work or watching television in bed.
   c. Give yourself a two-hour period of mental calm.
   d. Write down all of the problems and stresses that you might face.

_____ 4. What is the main idea of the fourth paragraph?
   a. Most people have their own pre-bed bathroom rituals.
   b. Don't forget to shower and go to the bathroom before bed.
   c. Lots of people get up in the night to go to the bathroom.
   d. Your body temperature increases after a bath or shower.

_____ 5. What is the final paragraph trying to say?
   a. High-protein foods help produce essential amino acids.
   b. Caffeine is difficult for the body to metabolize.
   c. Most people eat a lot before going to bed.
   d. What you eat can affect how you sleep.

1-2 Supporting Details

A good article is always built on a foundation of facts, statistics, and other kinds of evidence that help to develop the author's main idea. These are called **supporting details**, because they "**support**" the author's argument. So if you were to write an article on how cold it is in Russia, a good supporting detail would be temperature statistics.

↑ a young man wearing a horned mask and a straw cape (cc by kanegen)

6 The Day a Demon Came Knocking

1 Children have always been scared of monsters lurking in the darkness. More often than not, their fear stems from an overactive imagination. But in one region in northern Japan, the threat is all too real.

2 For the kids of Oga, in Akita prefecture, there's one day in particular
5   when they're on guard: New Year's Eve. At any time, they could be visited by a group of rowdy demons. When they arrive, the demons will shout: "Are there any bad kids here?" And thus the terrified children are scared into being good boys and
10   girls for another year.

↑ Namahage's face (cc by kyu3)

« Adapting Namahage to modern tourism is a way to ensure the survival of Namahage. (cc by kyu3)

026

⌃ people dressed as Namahage (cc by 掬茶)

3   This is all part of an age-old cultural tradition in Oga, where demons, or Namahage, come to visit local kids. The demons are young men wearing elaborate, horned masks and straw capes, all of which are made by hand.

4   Like many rural traditions, the Namahage practices fell on tough times during Japan's rapid economic rise after World War II. As more people moved to the major cities in search of education and jobs, there were fewer young people left behind in Oga. Without young people, there were no kids to scare and no demons to do the scaring. In 1989, Oga had 120 Namahage troupes. By 2015, the number had fallen to 85.

5   Thankfully, the Namahage ritual has seen a reversal of fortunes in recent years. One reason for this is its addition to UNESCO's Intangible Cultural Heritage list, which has drawn new outside attention to it. Another is an increase in efforts to bring the Namahage experience to foreign tourists.

6   Adapting Namahage to the realities of modern tourism represents some unique challenges. There are a few different cultural events in Oga that involve the Namahage troupes. Some, like the demon visits to children on New Year's Eve, are hard to adapt into a tourist experience. These visits take place in over 80 communities, and the demon troupes don't follow any set route. However, there are some other aspects that are more accessible to tourists. For example, there is the Sedo Festival in February, where a procession of torch-bearing demons hikes down a mountain. This event has been growing in popularity in recent years. In 2019, it drew 7,600 tourists, up from the 6,100 recorded in 2018.

7   The local government intends to use tourism to ensure the survival of Namahage traditions, all while carefully maintaining their original character. Everyone is hoping that they succeed; that is, except the traumatized children of Oga.

⌄ Namahage Museum in Oga

▽ Namahage masks　　　　　　　　　　▽ Namahage souvenir

Questions

_____ 1. Who does a Namahage target on New Year's Eve?
   a. Children who are not well behaved.
   b. Tourists from foreign countries.
   c. The local government.
   d. People who do not have any children.

_____ 2. Which of the following statements about the Sedo Festival is true?
   a. It is an adaption of a fairytale.
   b. It doesn't take place anywhere near Oga.
   c. It is not accessible to local children.
   d. It is increasingly popular with tourists.

_____ 3. Which of the following is true about the Namahage troupes?
   a. They have been banned in Oga.
   b. They numbered 120 in 2015.
   c. They have been declining over the years.
   d. Only children are allowed to participate in them.

_____ 4. What do we learn from this passage?
   a. Only children are allowed to make Namahage masks.
   b. People don't celebrate New Year's Eve in Oga.
   c. The Namahage rituals have been recognized by UNESCO.
   d. The Namahage troupes are very dangerous.

_____ 5. Which of the following is true about Oga?
   a. More and more young people are leaving it.
   b. Namahage is the only cultural event there.
   c. The local government is against tourism.
   d. It had over 1,000 Namahage troupes back in 1989.

▲ graffiti

7 From Graffiato to Hip-Hop

1   Many people think of graffiti as vandalism, and laws prohibiting it are enforced in many places. What most do not realize, however, is that graffiti has been around for a very long time. In prehistoric times, images of wildlife and hunting excursions were scratched onto the walls of caves. With the development of written language, messages containing public and personal information began to be chiseled on boulders, monuments, and stone walls. These included such things as notices announcing where herds were allowed to graze, laments for people who had died, declarations of love, and even advertisements for prostitutes. Examples of such early graffiti date back at least as far as the 8th century BC and have been found throughout the Middle East, in Greece, and in various parts of the Roman Empire.

2   The word "graffiti" comes from the Italian *graffiato*, meaning scratched. These scratched-out statements and symbols give us hints about past civilizations and their ways of life. Taking a closer look, one might find that not much has changed in terms of human nature after all these centuries, for those who have taken to the streets as modern-day graffiti artists have likewise done so to get their messages across to the masses.

↟ graffiti zone in Taipei, Taiwan
(cc by Everlong)

↟ "approved" graffiti in Germany
(cc by Kai Hendrik Schlusche Lörrach Germany)

3   Many graffiti artists have gained infamy, but the father of modern graffiti is Cornbread, the nickname of artist Darryl McCray. In the late 1960s in Philadelphia, McCray began his legendary "tagging," writing his nickname in his own style on city buildings, train cars, and buses. Tagging has since spread to every corner of the globe and become a worldwide cultural phenomenon.

4   Graffiti is now widely regarded as a vibrant part of hip-hop culture, like rapping and break dancing. Hip-hop's creative environment has been credited with helping to reduce inner-city gang violence by replacing it with artistic battles centered on graffiti and dancing. Graffiti competitions may sometimes include themes of political or local rivalry, but they are safe, nonviolent ways for young people to express themselves. Some create extremely detailed masterpieces which can be appreciated by almost anyone.

5   The value of graffiti artists and their work today is proven by the fact that some cities have gone through the trouble of installing makeshift walls especially for graffiti, which can later be taken down or moved. At the same time, an ever-growing number of small urban businesses are utilizing the skills of street artists to create eye-catching murals for purposes of advertising.

⌄ A street artist is painting colorful graffiti on a public wall.

▲ graffiti truck in Paris

Questions

_____ 1. Which of the following statements is not true, based on the article?
   a. Graffiti existed before the creation of written language.
   b. "Tagging" is a common practice all over the world.
   c. Graffiti competitions generally lead to gang fights.
   d. People have different ideas about the value of graffiti.

_____ 2. Where did the modern graffiti movement get its start?
   a. In the Middle East.
   b. In ancient Greece.
   c. In the Roman Empire.
   d. In Philadelphia.

˅ Graffiti can be an art form.

_____ 3. Which of these would probably not be found among ancient examples of graffiti?
   a. A person's nickname written in his or her own style.
   b. A message of mourning for a deceased family member.
   c. An announcement of a new local property law.
   d. A love letter from a young man to his girlfriend.

_____ 4. What is one reason why some people think graffiti is a good thing?
   a. It has been around for a very long time.
   b. It makes walls and buses more beautiful.
   c. It reduces violence among young people.
   d. It reflects the basic facts of human nature.

_____ 5. Which of the following statements is true?
   a. Laws prohibiting graffiti exist everywhere in the world.
   b. No one knows who started the modern graffiti movement.
   c. Some cities have designated areas for graffiti artists to work.
   d. Business owners never like to have graffiti outside their shops.

8 For Richer or Poorer, For Better or Worse

1   Wedding customs vary greatly throughout the world, and most couples follow the nuptial traditions in which they were raised. Increasingly, however, individual stamps are put on time-honored practices, as people make their weddings personal rather than cultural statements.

2   A long, trailing white dress and veil is the image normally associated with a Western bride. The origins and connotations of these two garments, however, are quite different from what most people believe. The veil and dress train date back to ancient Rome, when brides were wrapped in body-length red shrouds to scare away evil spirits. The white dress, meanwhile, only arrived in 1840, when Queen Victoria wore one to her own wedding—not to symbolize purity, but just because she liked white. Western grooms, meanwhile, still sometimes don tuxedos and bow ties for the big event, though any dark-colored suit will generally suffice. While churches remain popular locations for European and American weddings, almost any place that holds significance for the couple can be used.

» Western-style wedding ceremony

A white gown and veil are images associated with a Western bride.

[3] Adornment is important in many wedding traditions. The night before an Armenian wedding, the groom's family brings the bride's veil and shoes—along with perfume, jewelry, and other potentially useful items—to her family in beautifully wrapped boxes. At a Czech wedding, the bride wears a rosemary wreath made by her bridesmaids to symbolize love and wisdom. The bride and groom at an Indian wedding exchange floral garlands.

[4] The future of the married couple is another major concern. This is apparent in China, where wedding dates are carefully chosen according to the birth dates and zodiac signs of the bride and groom to ensure happiness and prosperity. One Dutch wedding custom is to make a "wish tree" on whose "leaves" guests write wishes for the couple's future. Before a German wedding, the bride and groom break dishes into pieces and clean them up together to prepare them for life's trials.

[5] All of these customs are still observed at many weddings. It is also now common for couples to write their own wedding vows, design their own ceremonies, and otherwise personalize this most important occasion of their lives. The growing trend of same-sex marriage will no doubt bring with it a slew of entirely new wedding traditions as well. Wherever and whenever people join hands in matrimony, it is certain they and their guests will make the event one to remember.

rosemary wreath

Questions

1. Which of the following statements is not true?
   a. Czech bridesmaids make a wreath for the bride to wear at her wedding.
   b. Some people design their own wedding ceremonies.
   c. Queen Victoria's wedding date was chosen according to her birth date.
   d. The ancient Romans worried about evil spirits at weddings.

2. Which of these things would an Armenian groom's family be likely to bring to his bride's family the night before their wedding?
   a. A pair of earrings.
   b. Broken dishes.
   c. A floral garland.
   d. A dark-colored suit.

3. How did the custom of Western brides wearing white dresses get started?
   a. Wearing white was a way for brides to show her purity before marriage.
   b. The ancient Romans believed white scared away evil spirits.
   c. Guests wanted to write their wishes on the bride's dress.
   d. A famous queen wore one to her wedding because she liked white.

4. Which is not likely a reason why many couples get married at churches?
   a. Because it is traditional to do so.
   b. Because weddings are often considered religious ceremonies.
   c. Because it is required by law in many places.
   d. Because churches are associated with special occasions.

5. Which of the following would likely be considered important in planning a Chinese wedding?
   a. The location of the wedding.
   b. The bride's and groom's birth dates.
   c. The quality of the groom's suit.
   d. The number of guests invited.

≫ In Germany, the bride and groom break dishes and then clean them up together.

≫ A Dutch wedding custom is to create a "wish tree" where guests write wishes for the couple. (cc by ellajphillips)

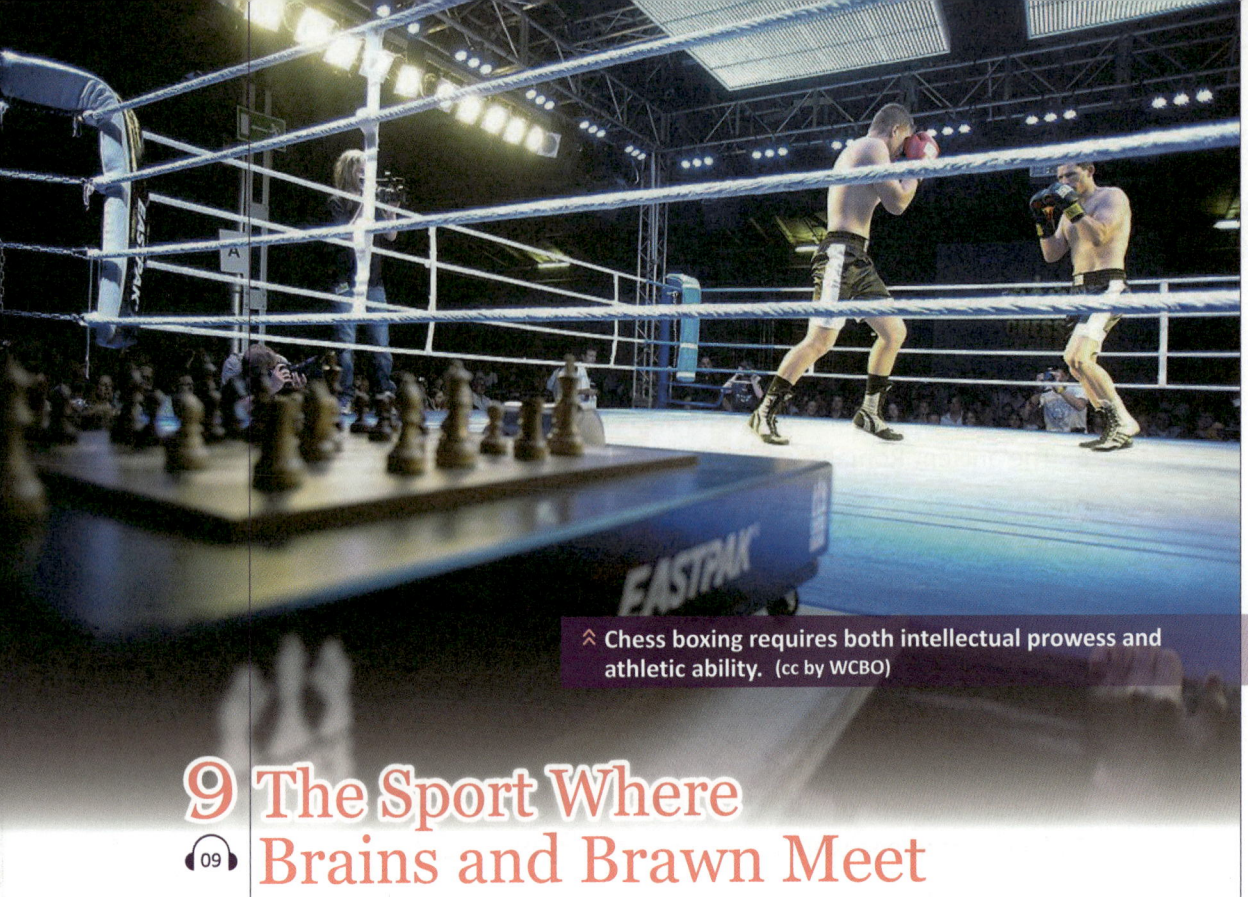

Chess boxing requires both intellectual prowess and athletic ability. (cc by WCBO)

9 The Sport Where Brains and Brawn Meet

1. They say that opposites attract in matters of the heart. But what about in sport? The rise of chess boxing would suggest that the maxim still applies.

2. Chess boxing merges two opposing ends of the spectrum of human endeavor: intellectual prowess and athletic ability. It's not exactly a natural combination and, unsurprisingly, it was born of an artistic whim. Back in 1992, the French artist Enki Bilal portrayed a world chess boxing championship in his comic *Froid Équateur*. In 2003, a Dutchman named Iepe Rubingh was inspired by the comic to make the sport a reality and established the World Chess Boxing Organization (WCBO).

3. The rules of chess boxing are simple. Matches have up to eleven alternating rounds in total, with each round lasting three minutes. The chess segment is six rounds, so each fighter has a total of nine minutes on the clock. To win, a player must either achieve a knockout, a checkmate, or be deemed victorious by the judge's decision. A player can also prevail if their opponent exceeds the time limit during the chess rounds.

4. For some people, chess boxing is a gimmick. They just want to see fighters stand up from a chess board and start punching each

« two chess boxing players during the chess segment

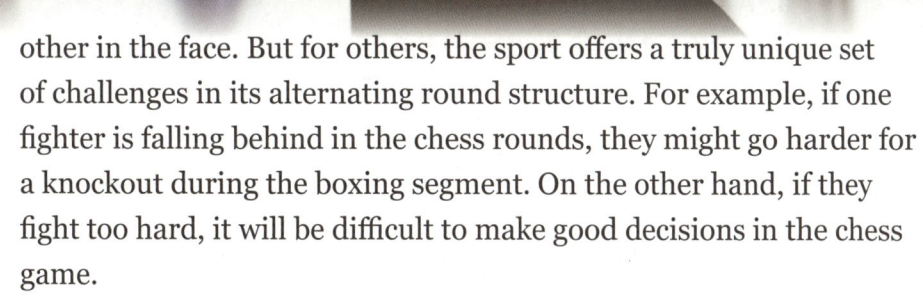

other in the face. But for others, the sport offers a truly unique set of challenges in its alternating round structure. For example, if one fighter is falling behind in the chess rounds, they might go harder for a knockout during the boxing segment. On the other hand, if they fight too hard, it will be difficult to make good decisions in the chess game.

5   Regardless of what attracts people to chess boxing, it's clear that there's ample interest in the sport. The first fight took place in Amsterdam in 2003, and it was attended by over a thousand curious people. One year later, the first chess boxing club was formed in Berlin. By 2019, the sport had gone global, and the WCBO now has members in China, Iran, Italy, Russia, Germany, Mexico, Spain, and the United States. It has proven particularly successful in India, where at least 10 state-level associations have been established. It's also popular with both genders, as one third of Indian chess boxers are women. Just how high can chess boxing go? Its most ardent supporters believe that one day it will even become an Olympic sport.

↑ a knockout during a boxing match

Questions

_____ 1. Which of the following is true about the invention of chess boxing?
   a. Iepe Rubingh was inspired to create the WCBO by a close friend.
   b. The sport was first thought up by French artist Enki Bilal.
   c. The first chess boxing match was organized as a practical joke.
   d. The sport was first invented in the United States.

_____ 2. Which of the following is true about a chess boxing match?
   a. A knockout is the only way to win.
   b. There are three fighters in the ring.
   c. The chess segment is five rounds.
   d. There are eleven rounds in total.

_____ 3. Which of the following is NOT true about the rise of chess boxing?
   a. The first chess boxing match was attended by over 1,000 people.
   b. The first chess boxing club was founded in Berlin.
   c. The sport has been particularly popular in China.
   d. The WCBO had over seven members in 2019.

_____ 4. What is one of the sport's success stories identified in the article?
   a. The legalization of the sport in the United States.
   b. The growing popularity of chess boxing in India.
   c. The first chess boxing fight taking place in Amsterdam in 2003.
   d. Germany being added to the WCBO.

_____ 5. How much total time does each fighter get on the chess clock during a match?
   a. Nine minutes.
   b. Six minutes.
   c. Three minutes.
   d. Five minutes.

038

10 The Emperors' Domain

1   Just north of Tiananmen Square in Beijing, the Palace Museum is both the world's largest palace and home to the largest collection of preserved wooden structures. The museum, boasting no fewer than 980 buildings over an area of 72 hectares, was the imperial palace for half a millennium during the Ming and Qing Dynasties. It is known as the Forbidden City from the Chinese name Zijin Cheng, meaning Purple Forbidden City. The purple here refers to the North Star, traditionally regarded as the home of the Celestial Emperor. Being as it was the home of the mortal emperor, the City was considered the star's earthly equivalent, forbidden because no one was allowed to enter or leave it without the emperor's permission.

2   Today, the City is most certainly not forbidden, and it is open to tourists and researchers from all corners of the world. Its artistic and architectural treasures are appreciated by an estimated 15 to 16 million visitors a year, none with imperial permission but all bearing tickets issued by the Chinese authorities. Small wonder, then, that UNESCO has listed the Palace Museum as a World Heritage Site.

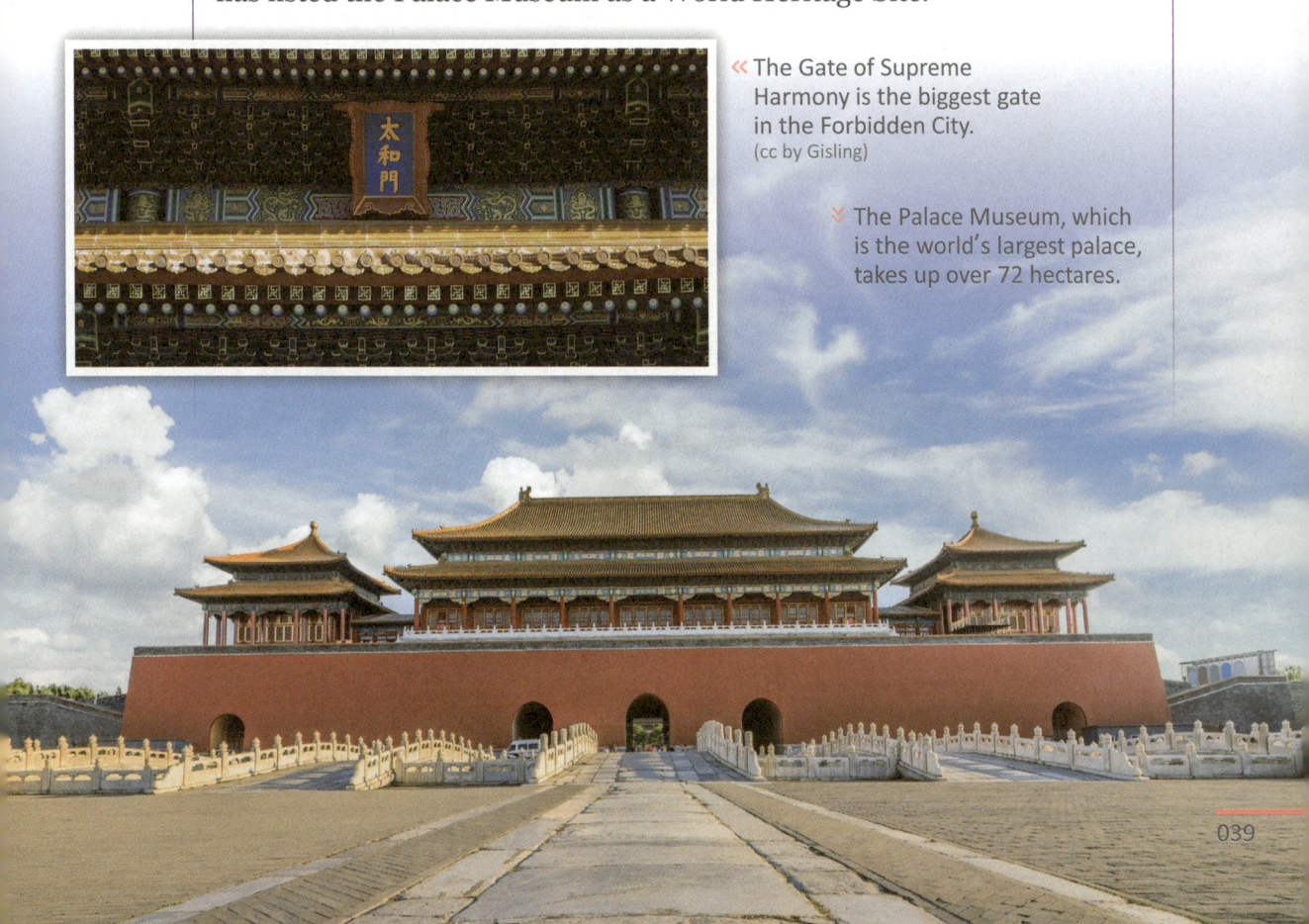

« The Gate of Supreme Harmony is the biggest gate in the Forbidden City.
(cc by Gisling)

⌄ The Palace Museum, which is the world's largest palace, takes up over 72 hectares.

3   The vast complex was constructed between 1406 and 1420. Over one million workers, including one hundred thousand skilled artisans, are said to have been drafted into hard labor to complete it. Marble was quarried from nearby, and tremendous amounts of precious timber and other building materials were freighted in from throughout the empire.

4   Yellow is the predominant color of the palace, for it is the color of the imperial family. The interior decoration is mostly yellow, and all but two roofs (those of the library and the crown prince's residences) are made of yellow glazed tiles. Even the floors of the most important areas are paved with yellow "golden bricks."

5   The Forbidden City consists of an outer court and an inner court. Fourteen Ming and ten Qing emperors ruled China from the Outer Court while living with their families in the Inner Court. The last Qing emperor, Pu Yi, was evicted after a coup in 1924. In 1933, Japan's invasion of China resulted in countless treasures' hasty removal from the palace to places of safety. Though some were returned at the end of World War II, many others found their way to Taiwan, and they can be seen today at the National Palace Museum in Taipei.

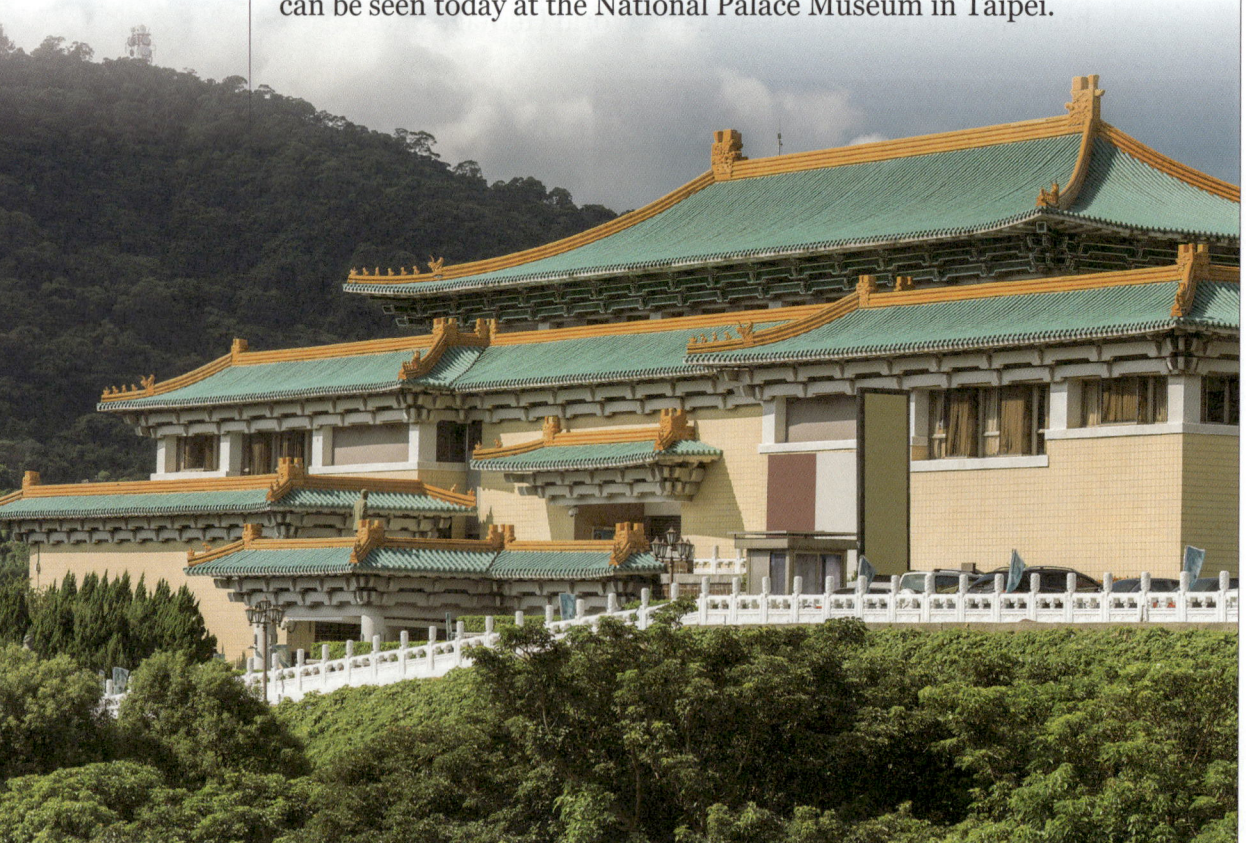

⌃ the National Palace Museum in Taipei

» the bronze lion in the Forbidden City

Questions

_____ 1. Which of the following statements is true?
   a. The Forbidden City is the largest collection of buildings in the world.
   b. The Forbidden City can be seen in Taipei.
   c. The Forbidden City was destroyed when Japan invaded China.
   d. The Forbidden City is the largest palace in the world.

_____ 2. Why was the color purple chosen as part of the Chinese name of the Forbidden City?
   a. Because purple is the color of the imperial family.
   b. It refers to the North Star, home of the Celestial Emperor.
   c. Most of the decorations in the Forbidden City are purple.
   d. There are many different opinions concerning the reason for it.

_____ 3. Why was the Forbidden City built?
   a. To serve as a museum where people could view great works of art.
   b. To serve as a residence and seat of government for Chinese emperors.
   c. To serve as a religious center where people could worship the Celestial Emperor.
   d. To serve as a fort and castle for a war against the Japanese.

_____ 4. How many people did it take to build the Forbidden City?
   a. Over one million.
   b. Between 15 and 16 million.
   c. One hundred thousand.
   d. Twenty-four, including Pu Yi.

_____ 5. Which of the following statements is not true?
   a. China's emperors lived in the Forbidden City for 500 years.
   b. The last emperor to live in the Forbidden City left it in 1924.
   c. China's emperors and their families lived in the outer court of the Forbidden City.
   d. No one could enter or leave the Forbidden City unless the emperor said so.

041

1-3 Making Inferences

Inference is when we guess at something we don't know using the information we do know. For example, if a friend looks angry when she opens the door, you can guess that something is wrong or something bad has happened. Authors also use this kind of inference to make similar suggestions to their readers.

⌃ fortune-teller with a crystal ball

11 Gazing Into the Crystal Ball

1 Though we all wonder what the future will bring, some of us just can't wait to find out. For these people, the solution is to consult a fortune teller. Fortune telling, or "divination" as it is sometimes called, is a booming business around the globe. It can also be interlocked with many religions and cultures, and for this reason, it is a prodigious part of everyday life in various societies.

2 In Europe, however, the opposite is true. Both the church and state declared fortune-telling to be a sin several centuries ago, and laws still prohibit its practice in some places today. It is, therefore, not held in high regard publicly. Mainstream religions in the United States also uphold this view, though one may be surprised at how many people there, from the very rich to the very poor, do consult fortune-tellers of all kinds. After all, aren't horoscopes also a form of fortune-telling?

⌄ crystal sphere

3 Techniques for telling fortunes stem from the roots of a civilization. Those who claim an ability to see future events do so with the passed-on knowledge of many before them, using whatever means available at the time. Some techniques that have been practiced in Europe and in North and South America are: tarot reading (by cards), tasseography (by tea leaves), chiromancy (palmistry), and crystallomancy (by a crystal sphere).

4 In Asia, many kinds of divination originated from the Chinese concept of *suan ming*. One of the most popular of these fortune-telling systems is the "Eight Characters." The method was devised by taking a person's birth year, month, day, and hour and displaying them as four columns, or "pillars," consisting of two characters each. The four pillars have eight characters altogether, thus the name Eight Characters.

5 The "casting," or throwing, of bones, stones, shells, leather strips, or pieces of wood is the most traditional method of telling fortunes in Africa. The techniques fall into one of several categories: casting marked objects and numerically counting up how they fall according to their markings or whether they touch each other, and casting a set of symbolic bones or articles to signify, for instance, travel, pregnancy, etc.

6 As expected, fortune-telling by any method is controversial. It is not surprising that scientific investigations have concluded that divination is impossible and that fortune-tellers are really just experts in reading body language and making general statements that seem specific to the situation.

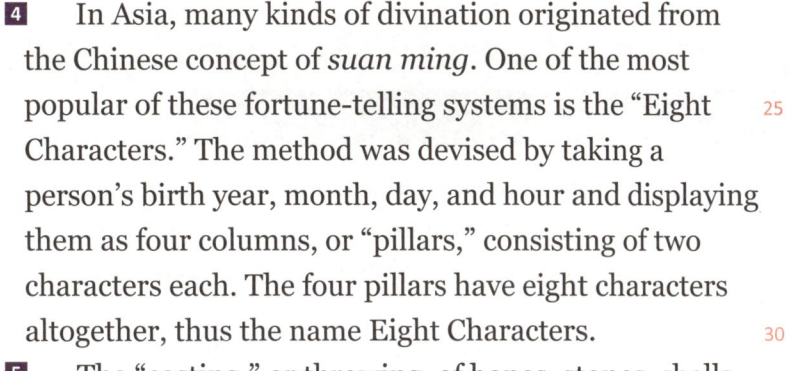

⌃ tasseography

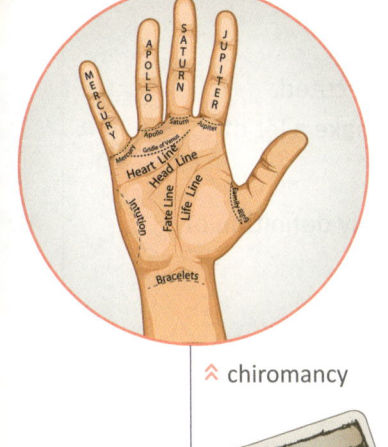

⌃ chiromancy

⌃ tarot reading

« the casting of stones

⌃ suan ming (Chinese fortune-telling)

Unit 1 Reading Skills
1-3 Making Inferences

043

Questions

1. Which of the following statements would the author likely agree with?
   a. Horoscopes are not an example of fortune-telling.
   b. Fortune-telling should only be practiced by those who have a special gift.
   c. Fortune-telling is popular around the world, but it is also fake.
   d. Europe was wrong to ban fortune-telling centuries ago.

2. What is probably true about the history of fortune-telling in Europe?
   a. It was reserved for kings and church leaders.
   b. It was never practiced in Europe until the modern era.
   c. If you were caught telling fortunes, you could be executed.
   d. If your fortunes were always accurate, you would make a lot of money.

3. According to the third paragraph, what is the most likely definition of the Greek word "mancy"?
   a. Someone who sees.
   b. Someone who harms.
   c. Someone who grows food.
   d. Someone who provides justice.

4. Which of the following is probably true about fortune-telling in Africa?
   a. It remains banned until this day.
   b. It is very popular and comes in many forms.
   c. It is only practiced in one small community.
   d. It is a totally new phenomenon.

5. According to the second paragraph, what is the most likely definition of a horoscope?
   a. A type of lens that people can use to see the past.
   b. A book describing some of the most famous fortune-tellers throughout history.
   c. A linguistic term describing a certain type of future tense.
   d. A broad prediction of future events based on people's birthdates.

12 A Fix for Feral Animals?

1   There's nothing more heart-warming than seeing a well-cared-for dog or cat looking happy and healthy at home with their human companions. Unfortunately, there is a huge population of cats and dogs, some 300 million by some estimates, that are stray or even feral—that is, either born on the streets or having been without human contact for so long that they have become fearful of human contact. In the past, in order to control the stray and feral population, these animals may have been exterminated, often using cruel and brutal methods.

2   Thankfully, we live in an age where such practices are considered in most countries as barbaric. However, this still leaves us with the question of what humane methods can be employed to reduce the number of strays. In the case of dogs in particular, strays can often form large packs and be a danger or menace to communities.

3   One widely accepted solution is trap-neuter-release, or TNR. This involves capturing stray animals, desexing them, and then returning them to their territory. Over time, the stray and feral population will decrease due to the absence of breeding. And the fewer feral animals there are, the less pressure there is on animal shelters to euthanize due to overcrowding, and the greater chance there is of rehoming these rescued animals. Furthermore, the lack of sexual desire among the animals, particularly the dogs, makes them far less aggressive and, therefore, far less of a problem. In many countries, TNR programs are sponsored or funded by the government, and all have witnessed a marked decline in their feral animal population.

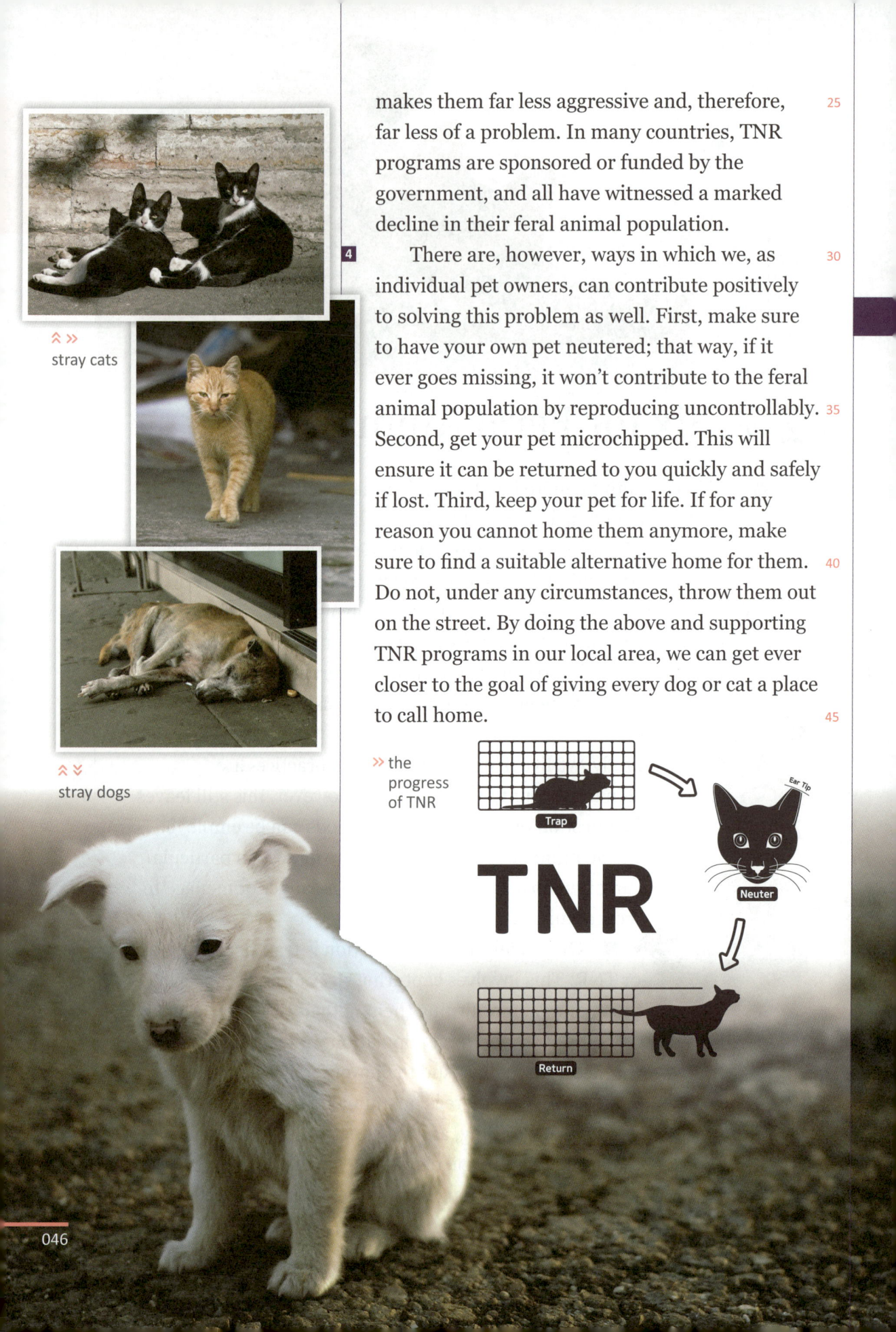

There are, however, ways in which we, as individual pet owners, can contribute positively to solving this problem as well. First, make sure to have your own pet neutered; that way, if it ever goes missing, it won't contribute to the feral animal population by reproducing uncontrollably. Second, get your pet microchipped. This will ensure it can be returned to you quickly and safely if lost. Third, keep your pet for life. If for any reason you cannot home them anymore, make sure to find a suitable alternative home for them. Do not, under any circumstances, throw them out on the street. By doing the above and supporting TNR programs in our local area, we can get ever closer to the goal of giving every dog or cat a place to call home.

stray cats

stray dogs

» the progress of TNR

» dog shelter

Questions

_____ 1. Which of the following can be inferred from the first and second paragraphs?
   a. There are still some countries in which barbaric means of controlling feral animal population persist.
   b. There is no humane solution to the problem of feral animal population control.
   c. Most animals that now live on the streets once had a permanent home and human owners.
   d. Groups of feral cats are often more of a community nuisance than feral dogs.

_____ 2. Which of the following can be inferred from the third paragraph?
   a. TNR leads to a higher number of animals in animal shelters.
   b. TNR is an effective and humane method of reducing feral animal populations.
   c. TNR programs are often criticized as being cruel and outdated.
   d. TNR programs seldom achieve funding as they are incredibly costly.

_____ 3. What can we infer from the sentence beginning "And the fewer feral animals there are . . ." in the third paragraph?
   a. Animal shelters often suffer from a lack of volunteer staff and require more funding.
   b. Animals in overcrowded shelters are often euthanized before they can be rehomed.
   c. Feral dogs are twice as easy to re-home as feral cats.
   d. It is very uncommon for people to adopt feral dogs and cats from animal shelters.

_____ 4. What can we infer about the author of this passage?
   a. He is strongly in favor of euthanizing feral animals.
   b. He is strongly opposed to pet owners neutering their pets.
   c. He believes pets are better off on the streets than in a home.
   d. He is strongly opposed to people abandoning their pets.

_____ 5. What can we infer about feral dogs from the third paragraph?
   a. They often gather in people's back gardens.
   b. They might attack people, but only when hungry.
   c. They can be aggressive if left un-neutered.
   d. They are fairly easy to trap and catch.

047

13 When Shadows Cover Stars

[1] When the Moon moves directly between the Sun and Earth, it casts a shadow upon Earth, and anyone standing in that shadow momentarily stops seeing the Sun. We call this an eclipse, and throughout history solar eclipses have been viewed as mysterious, spectacular, and sometimes ominous events.

[2] In the 7th century BC, the acclaimed Greek poet Archilochus wrote that Zeus, supreme god of Greek mythology, had made midday turn into night. In ancient China, a solar eclipse was a dreadful matter, for the Chinese believed that the sun had been eaten by a dragon. What a truly distressing event that must have been!

[3] Not everyone is lucky enough to witness a total eclipse of the Sun, for they don't occur often enough in the same locations or during times of the right atmospheric conditions. In fact, it is only with great luck that one can witness a total solar eclipse at all. As nature would have it, though, while the Moon is approximately 400 times smaller than the Sun, the Sun is approximately 400 times farther away from Earth, so they look the same size from our perspective—just right for the Moon to completely "cover" the Sun during an eclipse.

[4] The other kind of eclipse is a lunar eclipse, during which Earth moves between the Sun and Moon, thereby casting a shadow on the latter. The Moon shines because it reflects the Sun's light, but when an eclipse occurs, Earth obstructs that light. During some lunar eclipses, the Moon takes on a reddish hue and is nicknamed a blood moon, which is associated with magic in many cultures.

[5] Both solar and lunar eclipses are infrequent, but solar eclipses do occur at least twice a year in small areas. The reason for this infrequency is that while Earth's orbit around the sun is constant, the Moon's

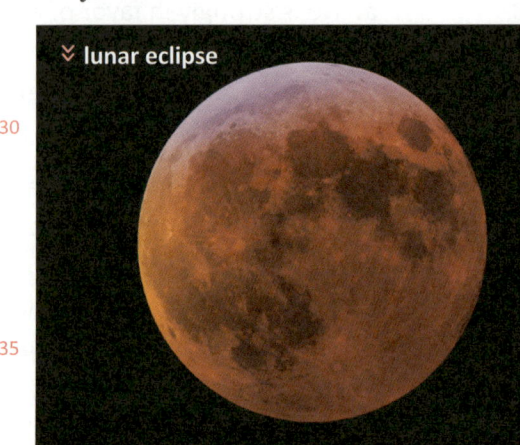

solar eclipse

lunar eclipse

orbit around Earth is not. The Moon's orbit is tilted and deviates very slowly, so it doesn't often pass in a straight line between Earth and the Sun. While the order of the heavenly bodies may be right, therefore, the Moon's orbital tilt must also be in line. For both solar and lunar
40 eclipses, the process is the same: when the Sun, the Moon, and Earth are all in a straight line, the globe in the middle projects
45 a shadow. As the outer globe moves into that shadow, an eclipse occurs.

↑ lunar eclipse over city

Questions

_____ 1. What can be inferred from the information in the first and second paragraphs?
   a. Archilochus was the greatest of all ancient Greek poets.
   b. People who witness a solar eclipse will go blind.
   c. Dragons actually lived in ancient China.
   d. Ancient people did not understand how eclipses happened.

_____ 2. What can the reader infer about a solar eclipse?
   a. It can only be explained by reference to Greek mythology.
   b. It is caused by the distances of the Sun and the moon from Earth.
   c. Only a few very lucky people will ever get to see one.
   d. It can only be experienced in a few locations on Earth.

_____ 3. Which of the following statements is true about a "blood moon"?
   a. It is the result of a solar eclipse.
   b. It is the result of magic.
   c. It sometimes happens during a lunar eclipse.
   d. It occurs at least twice a year in small areas.

_____ 4. What is the reason for the infrequency of eclipses of both types?
   a. The sun's reflected light.   b. Earth's orbit around the sun.
   c. The moon's orbit around Earth.   d. The order of the heavenly bodies.

_____ 5. What is most likely true about people's attitudes toward the phenomenon of eclipses?
   a. People have wondered about it for a long time.
   b. Scientists have explained it, so now it's boring.
   c. Greeks and Chinese disagree about what causes it.
   d. Everyone can enjoy it at least twice a year.

flamenco dancers

14 A Different Kind of Dance

1 The term "flamenco" conjures up vivid imagery: a dancer, arms over their head, stamping their feet to the rhythm of guitar music. The dancer's expression is always one of sheer emotional intensity. Most importantly, they are from Spain, because flamenco is as Spanish as bullfighting.

2 But the history of flamenco is actually more complicated than that—at least, what we actually know of it. The story seems to begin all the way back in the 8th century, when southern Spain was conquered by invaders from Africa. These Moors brought their own musical instruments and types of dance with them, and they were soon joined by other new arrivals. The Romani people, who originated from northwest India, settled in waves following the Moorish conquest. The musical traditions of both groups blended with those of the Christians and Jewish people already living in the area. The result was the synthesis of folk musical and dance traditions that would one day become flamenco.

3 This dance didn't even have a name until the late 18th century. For hundreds of years, the music and dances were merely a part of life, something you'd see at a marriage ceremony or friendly gathering. When the Romantic era descended in the late 18th century, flamenco

flamenco shoes

exploded in popularity. Cafés opened that specialized in flamenco performances, and it suddenly became popular with the upper classes of society. In 1939, the dictator Francisco Franco came to power and made flamenco Spain's national dance. He would go on to use flamenco to promote tourism, even as he oppressed the very Romani people who had helped create it.

4 The cross-cultural nature of flamenco is still alive today. In the latest phase of its evolution, flamenco is now going global. Young people from around the world are coming to Spain to study the dance, and some are bringing it back to their home countries. These people have helped support local teachers and academies, even as interest in flamenco has waned in Spain. They have also produced a boom in overseas schools. For example, there are now more flamenco academies in Japan than there are in Spain.

5 Perhaps it's this dynamism that makes flamenco so compelling. In the words of Yinka Graves, a British student studying the dance in Seville: "Flamenco is about feelings, not blood." Whatever the case, though the art form originated in Spain, it's now a celebrated and important part of global culture.

Flamenco dances require emotional intensity.

flamenco dancer, Yinka Graves (cc by Festival de Cine Africano – FCAT)

051

» traditional flamenco dresses

Questions

_____ 1. What's probably true about the history of flamenco?
   a. It was written by Spanish Christians.
   b. It is not very clear before the 18th century.
   c. It has always been ignored by the Spanish public.
   d. It was banned during the Franco era.

_____ 2. What is probably true about bullfighting?
   a. It is more popular than flamenco music.
   b. It is considered a safe sport.
   c. It is a popular sport in Spain.
   d. It was invented by the Romani people.

_____ 3. What kind of art forms were probably favored during the Romantic era?
   a. Those that were expensive and out-of-reach for regular people.
   b. Those that were emotional and enjoyed by everyone.
   c. Those that were new, and only invented recently.
   d. Those that were based on religious teachings.

_____ 4. What is probably true about flamenco in Japan?
   a. Flamenco is one of the most popular dances in Japan.
   b. Flamenco is good for Japan's tourism industry.
   c. Flamenco training is so expensive that few Japanese people do it.
   d. Japanese people dislike the outright emotionality of flamenco.

_____ 5. Which of the following would Yinka Graves probably agree with?
   a. "Flamenco is the most important thing in life."
   b. "Master Spanish before you try to study flamenco."
   c. "Flamenco music is boring."
   d. "Anyone can study flamenco."

> Mahjong is an ancient Chinese game.

a pair of dice

tokens

15 The Twittering of the Sparrows

1   Mahjong, a very popular table game, originated in China sometime before the late 19th century. The Chinese call it *ma que*, which means sparrow. It is played by four people using 144 beautifully designed little ivory blocks, or tiles, which vaguely resemble dominoes. The object of the game is to put together sets of like tiles, or what are called winning hands. The complete game set also includes a pair of dice, tokens used for keeping score, and a rack for each player to stand their tiles upright and keep their faces hidden from opponents.

2   The origins of mahjong are unclear, but one myth suggests that Confucius created it sometime around 500 BC. This is because the game is thought to have first appeared around the time and place of the great sage's travels to spread his doctrines. The three dragon tiles in mahjong represent the cardinal virtues of benevolence, sincerity, and filial piety taught by Confucius. He was also very fond of birds, which may explain the name sparrow. Many historians, however, believe that mahjong is derived from card games that were popular during the Qing Dynasty. The oldest known mahjong tile sets date from around 1870, while the earliest surviving references to the game are from the following decade.

↑ Mahjong set

[3] Mahjong has spread to many Asian countries, including Japan, Korea, and Vietnam. In those places, as in Taiwan, it is often played as a gambling game with local variations. The American J. P. Babcock brought Mahjong to the West around 1920. As a result of Babcock's devising a set of rules and a complete terminology for English-speaking players, the game became a popular pastime in the United States. Such is mahjong's longevity that it has even entered the world of technology and can now be played as a type of solitaire on the Internet.

[4] In 1998, the All-China Sports Federation produced a standardized set of rules for competition mahjong (known in Chinese as national standard mahjong) to dissociate it from illegal gambling. The principles of this new, "wholesome" version of mahjong are no

« Mahjong being played in China
(cc by Romain Guy from Lyon, France)

⌄ students in the United States learning how to play Mahjong
(cc by Charles Nguyen)

gambling, drinking, or smoking during play. Players are often grouped in teams to emphasize that mahjong is now officially considered a sport. The World Mahjong Organization was established in 2005, and the first World Mahjong Championship was held in Chengdu, China, in 2007. Since then, the championship has become a periodic event, with participants from all over the world.

« Mahjong tiles

Questions

_____ 1. What can the reader infer from the passage about the beginnings of mahjong?
   a. Confucius probably created the game about 2,500 years ago.
   b. An American named J.P. Babcock created mahjong around 1920.
   c. Mahjong was most likely invented during the Qing Dynasty.
   d. The game was invented by the All-China Sports Federation in 1998.

_____ 2. What is suggested about people who play mahjong?
   a. They often smoke, drink, and gamble while playing.
   b. They all play by exactly the same set of rules.
   c. They only live in Asian countries.
   d. They are always grouped in teams.

_____ 3. What can be inferred from the fourth paragraph?
   a. The Chinese thought there were too many variations of mahjong.
   b. The World Mahjong Championship is held every year.
   c. People from all over the world made the rules for competition mahjong.
   d. Mahjong had acquired a bad reputation in China by the late 1990s.

_____ 4. What is probably true about people who play mahjong online?
   a. They play it as a gambling game.
   b. They play by J. P. Babcock's rules.
   c. They usually play it by themselves.
   d. They don't smoke or drink while they play.

_____ 5. What does the author suggest about the tiles used in mahjong?
   a. They look exactly like dominoes.
   b. They have particular meanings.
   c. They were introduced in 1998.
   d. They aren't used in some countries.

055

1-4 Clarifying Devices

Writers strive to make their work both interesting and clear. They do this by using various **techniques**, **words**, and **phrases** that give the writing order and structure and that draw the reader's attention. To identify these devices, you'll need to be able to deconstruct a piece of writing structurally and recognize the tricks of the writer's trade.

People in London march to call for a final vote on the United Kingdom's relationship with the EU.

16 The European Experiment

1 Since the European Union's creation more than six decades ago, Europe has enjoyed a time of peace and prosperity unheard of in its long and often bloody history. The EU's freedom of movement policy has given its 500 million-strong population the right to live, study, and work in any of the 28 member states. And the single market has made the EU one of the biggest trading powers in the world.

2 However, as it continues to expand, the EU is seen as increasingly out of touch with the desires of many of its key member states. Furthermore, its highly bureaucratic institutions and complex decision-making procedures remain baffling and frustrating to many.

3 Worse still, the EU's ambitious single-currency experiment—the euro—has resulted in poor economic growth and widespread dissatisfaction among those members hit hardest by the 2008 financial crisis. Greece, for example, has had to be repeatedly bailed out of debt by

European Union flag, of which the 12 golden stars stand for unity, solidarity, and harmony among the people of Europe

European Union country

≪ Migrants fleeing towards Germany, 2015

other EU members. Other countries, too, such as Italy and Spain, have felt pressured into taking austerity measures to boost their failing economies and prevent a currency collapse. This economic divide within the EU has deepened resentment between its member states.

4 A perhaps even bigger rift emerged in the EU following the 2015 migrant crisis, which saw hundreds of thousands of refugees fleeing conflicts in Iraq and Syria attempting to enter Europe. Though Germany opened its doors to the migrants, other countries were reticent to do so, and attempts by Germany to force other nations to accept refugees were met with hostility. This resulted in a rise of xenophobia and nationalistic politics in many EU countries.

5 Angry over issues such as immigration and the perceived lack of control over their own laws, the people of the United Kingdom voted in 2016 to leave the union for good. The EU, once united over the common purpose of peace and prosperity in Europe, seems increasingly unable to speak with one voice.

6   What the future holds for the EU is uncertain. In many ways, the EU has been a triumph, bringing peace and stability to a once highly divided Europe. But as recent events have made clear, it is far from perfect. With much-needed reform and a greater level of transparency, the EU may still be able to address the issues that are driving its member nations apart. The great European experiment could yet prove itself to be a lasting success.

Questions

_____ 1. What form does the passage take?
   a. A personal narrative.
   b. A retelling of a myth.
   c. A balanced analysis.
   d. A biased opinion.

_____ 2. How does the author treat his subject matter?
   a. With seriousness.
   b. With humor.
   c. With fear.
   d. With disapproval.

_____ 3. Which of the following best describes the third and fourth paragraphs?
   a. An analysis of a famous quotation.
   b. A list of causes and their effects.
   c. A series of steps in a process.
   d. A series of difficult questions.

_____ 4. How does the author end the fifth paragraph?
   a. With a contrast.
   b. With a simile.
   c. With a joke.
   d. With an example.

_____ 5. How does the author end the passage?
   a. With a warning for the future.
   b. With a personal memory.
   c. With a hopeful resolution.
   d. With an emotional appeal.

⌄ Euros

17 Frozen Fields

≈ glacier

≈ freezing rain

1   Glaciers are enormous, moving streams of ice that have existed for anywhere between a century and millions of years. They cover approximately 0.5 percent of Earth's surface and are formed by the accumulation of snow, which over time compacts into what is called neve.

2   Neve constitutes the grainy outer layer of a glacier that has already survived one or more melting seasons. Substantial accumulations of neve become large ice crystals that are very dense and slightly blue in color.

3   Avalanches, freezing rain, and wind drifts are all important in maintaining a glacier. Glaciers lose snow to erosion, thawing, evaporation, and "calving," or a sudden separation due to breakage. The two most common types of glaciers are continental and valley glaciers.

4   The sheer mass of a glacier is sufficient for gravity to set it in motion. Glaciers move slowly down valleys and mountainsides. They are normally found at high latitudes and altitudes, where they tend to gain more snow in winter than they lose in summer. Although most of the world's glaciers are located near the Poles, they can be found on every continent except Australia.

« avalanche

≫ iceberg

5   What sculpts the land around a glacier? Abrasion. The hardness of the debris at a glacier's base, the presence and amount of water in the area, and the thickness of the glacial ice are the key factors. If the debris is harder than the rock beneath it, that rock will be significantly defaced. Water can have an erosive effect because it results in a greater velocity of glacial movement. Thicker ice creates more pressure, which naturally deforms the surrounding land.

6   Glaciers have had a tremendous impact on how land is used. Crop farming is far easier and more successful on land which glacial activity has made uniform in texture and rich in mineral deposits. Road gravel and concrete are readily obtained from areas with large amounts of sand and crushed rocks. Glacial deposits also serve as storage areas for water, peat, and natural gas.

7   But the world's glaciers are in danger, and their rapid dwindling is perhaps the most overt indication of global warming. There are roughly 198,000 glaciers on Earth, containing nearly 70 percent of the world's fresh water between them. Most have been shrinking for over a century at this point, with the melt rate drastically accelerating since the mid-1990s. These invaluable sources of fresh water just might be eliminated one dark day.

≫ valley glacier

≫ blue ice crystal

060

˅ continental glacier

Questions

____ 1. What does the author do in the first paragraph of this passage?
   a. Tell a personal story.
   b. Make a comparison.
   c. Provide examples.
   d. Introduce the topic.

____ 2. What is the function of the second paragraph?
   a. To explain how glaciers are formed and maintained.
   b. To define a term that is unfamiliar to most people.
   c. To provide some historical background on the topic.
   d. To convince the reader that glaciers must be protected.

____ 3. What does the first sentence of the fourth paragraph do?
   a. Tell the reader where glaciers are generally found.
   b. Explain the process by which glaciers begin to move.
   c. Describe how glaciers gain and lose their snow.
   d. Express the author's personal opinion of glaciers.

____ 4. Why does the fifth paragraph begin with a question?
   a. So the author can answer it in the next sentence.
   b. Because the author actually doesn't know the answer.
   c. To emphasize the impact of glaciers.
   d. To emphasize just how mysterious glaciers really are.

____ 5. What is the main purpose of the final paragraph?
   a. To tell the reader how many glaciers there are in the world.
   b. To give examples of the ways in which glaciers are helpful.
   c. To explain the vulnerability of glaciers to climate change.
   d. To persuade the reader to join an environmental organization.

human genetic engineering

18 Hacking the Human Code

1   Imagine a future populated by humans who are free of all diseases, who stay young for longer, and whose bodies and minds are stronger, faster, and more finely tuned than anyone alive today. This is a future that could be possible with modern advances in gene editing technology—the ability to make changes to specific parts of a living creature's DNA. However, though human gene editing presents many exciting possibilities, many fear that without proper care and vigilance, this dream could quickly become a nightmare.

2   Until very recently, genetic engineering was considered clumsy, inefficient, and prohibitively expensive. In the early 2010s, however, a gene-editing technology called CRISPR-Cas9 emerged which was faster, cheaper, more accurate, and more efficient than any other existing technique. Scientists couldn't wait to play with their new toy, and the fruits of their animal experiments—super dogs with bulging muscles, cutesy miniature pigs, and disease-resistant goats, to name a few—began to appear thick and fast. The question on everyone's minds, however, was how CRISPR-Cas9 could be applied in humans. The tool could be used to edit out harmful genes or even imbue newborns with beneficial traits such as disease resistance, stronger bones, and more robust hearts.

3   Fearing that this technology could easily be abused, many countries have strict rules in place regarding the use of human gene editing. Others, **though**, are not so strict. In November, 2018, a Chinese researcher announced the birth of two babies whose DNA he had edited to lower their risk of contracting HIV. The news

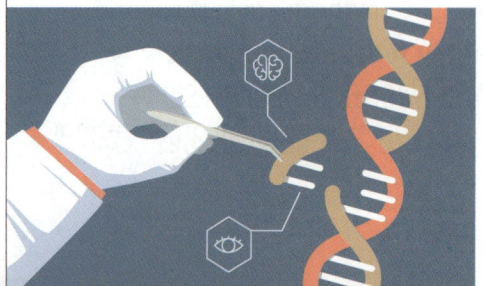

« CRISPR-Cas9

shocked the global medical community and created a huge debate around the medical ethics of human gene editing, particularly in unborn babies.

[4] Concerns about encouraging a trend of "designer babies" available only to the rich and powerful are already well established; however, a more pressing concern is the fact that we do not know enough about the possible side-effects of gene editing to perform it safely. Changing a gene often has more than just one effect, and a seemingly beneficial edit may cause unforeseen problems elsewhere. Some rabbits, for example, modified to produce leaner meat, also grew enlarged tongues; goats modified to grow longer cashmere wool grew too large in the womb for natural births.

[5] Though the issue is both scientifically and ethically complex, human genome editing is, it seems, an inevitable part of our future human journey. Our best hope is that we don't make too many mistakes along the way.

Questions

1. How does the author capture the reader's attention in the first sentence?
   a. By asking a thought-provoking question.
   b. By citing a shocking statistic.
   c. By vividly describing a historical event.
   d. By appealing to the reader's sense of wonder.

2. What does the dash (—) in the second paragraph introduce?
   a. A contrast.   b. A series of examples.
   c. A definition.   d. A conclusion.

3. What does the author accomplish by using the word **though** in the third paragraph?
   a. He creates an ominous shift in tone.
   b. He introduces his own contrasting opinion.
   c. He signals that the preceding facts may be inaccurate.
   d. He introduces an alternative possibility.

4. How is the fourth paragraph organized?
   a. As a series of events narrated in chronological order.
   b. As a common question and expert answer.
   c. As a series of steps in a process.
   d. As a statement followed by supporting evidence.

5. How does the author end the passage?
   a. By relating the past to the present.
   b. By endorsing one solution over another.
   c. By expressing a hope for the future.
   d. By stating a scientific fact.

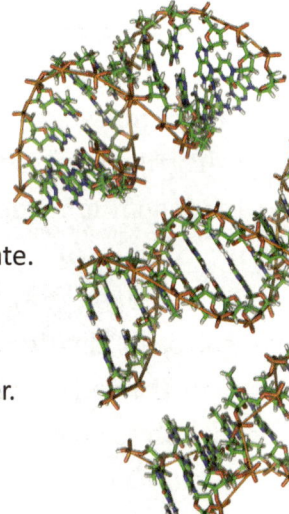

⌃ DNA strands

19 Let's Get Rich—in Space!

[1] In 1848, gold was discovered in California. Over 300,000 people poured into the state looking to make their fortune. Now, almost 200 years later, a new kind of gold rush is on the horizon. But this time, it's not taking place in the hills of California. Rather, it will take place in the vastness of space. For floating around in the void are thousands upon thousands of asteroids—giant space rocks packed full of valuable metals such as iron, nickel, platinum, and gold.

⌃ Space rocks may contain valuable metals.

[2] Several large companies are already making plans to take advantage of this untapped resource in our solar system, pouring huge sums of money into research and development. You might well ask, is all that investment worth it? Let's look at some figures: It is estimated that there are about 18,000 asteroids currently orbiting near Earth. Some of these could contain more platinum than has ever been obtained from all the mines on Earth in history. That's hundreds of billions of dollars' worth of precious metal. Others contain enough iron and nickel to cover the needs of Earth for the next 3,000 years. One asteroid alone—named 16 Psyche—contains a quantity of iron worth around US$10,000 quadrillion. For comparison, all the money on Earth is currently estimated at just $75 trillion.

⌄ Asteroid mining is a new form of investment that may change our future.

⌃ 16 Psyche (cc by ASU/Peter Rubin)

3 **Furthermore**, asteroid mining would not only take care of our resource-scarcity problems on Earth. It would also form a key part of human beings' future colonization of space. Mining resources that can be used as fuel for spaceships and then making them accessible in space would significantly improve our planet-going capabilities. A trip to Mars, for example, would be much easier if we could refuel and resupply along the way. Indeed, many experts believe that asteroid mining is the only way to support permanent space development, making it the foundation on which our future space industry will be built.

4 While you may say all this sounds more like science fiction than fact, in reality asteroid mining will be up and running far sooner than you might expect. Some companies have plans to begin mining as early as 2030. And though the true extent of asteroid mining's impact on our future society is difficult to predict accurately, one thing is for certain—for those who do strike it big in space, the money will be out of this world!

▲ A trip to Mars may be easier if we can refuel and resupply along the way.

Questions

_____ 1. How does the author create interest in the first paragraph?
   a. By comparing the past and the future.
   b. By referring to documents.
   c. By using exotic language.
   d. By exaggerating.

_____ 2. What does the second paragraph largely consist of?
   a. Dates of important events.   b. Evidence to back-up a point.
   c. A series of causes and effects. d. A series of logical steps.

_____ 3. What does the use of the word **furthermore** at the beginning of the third paragraph indicate?
   a. The author is setting up a contrast with the previous paragraph.
   b. The author wants to digress from his main point.
   c. The author wants to return to an earlier point.
   d. The author intends to build upon what was said in the previous paragraph.

_____ 4. The first sentence of the last paragraph aims to do which of the following?
   a. Correct a possible misapprehension. b. Mislead the reader.
   c. Make the reader laugh.   d. Suggest a course of action.

_____ 5. Which of the following best describes the passage?
   a. A personal anecdote.   b. A balanced argument.
   c. An informative article.   d. A historical examination.

065

» "Bandersnatch" has 10 endings that viewers can choose from.

20 The Choice is Yours!

1   In December 2018, the dark science-fiction TV series *Black Mirror*, which airs on Netflix, released a special episode entitled "Bandersnatch" that got the whole world talking. Why? Because unlike most TV episodes where the story unfolds without the viewer's control, "Bandersnatch" allowed viewers to make real-time choices that influenced how the story would unfold and ultimately end.

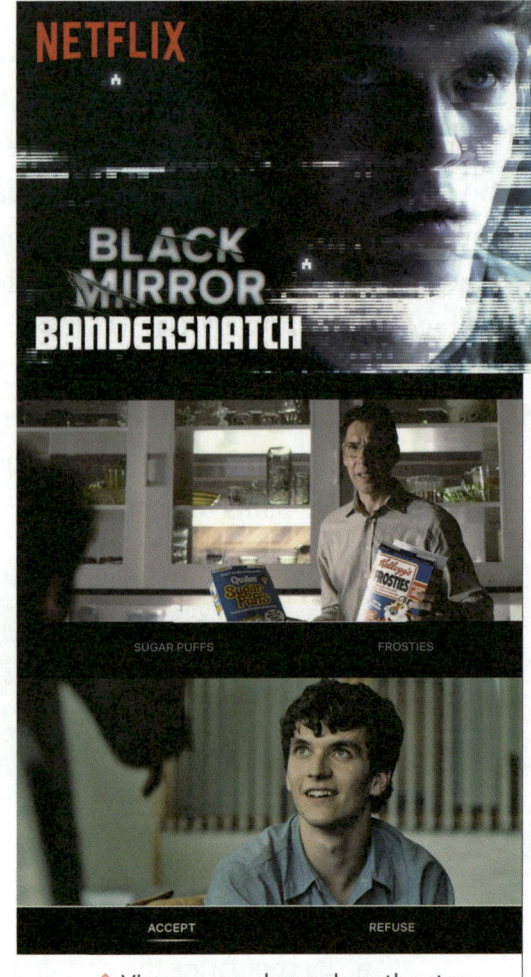

2   The idea of a story that allows you to choose your own path isn't a new one. During the 80s and 90s, Choose Your Own Adventure books were immensely popular. At the end of a page, the reader would be presented with a choice (e.g., *enter the cave*, or *explore the forest*). The reader would then turn to the corresponding page number and continue the story. These gamebooks, as they became called, had multiple endings, and readers/players would often read the book repeatedly in order to experience a different story each time.

3   As video gaming began to take off, these interactive books gradually fell out of mainstream popularity. Though many wanted to transfer the idea to television, the technology just wasn't up to the task—until "Bandersnatch" that is. **Now**, a whole range of possible "choose-your-own-adventure" TV shows lies before us: murder mysteries where you guide the detective to solve a terrible crime, romantic comedies where you get to choose who the protagonist falls in love with, creepy

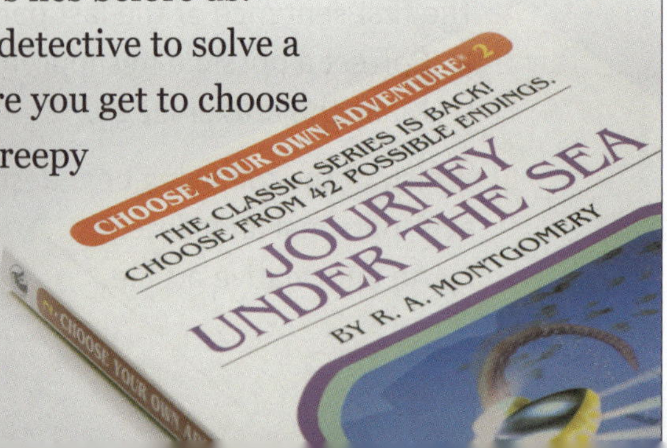

⌃ Viewers can choose how the story progresses. (photo credit: engadget, UPROXX)

⌃ the poster for *Black Mirror*

» *Choose Your Own Adventure* books let readers decide on the endings.

066

tales where viewers can choose how a group of teens survive a night in a haunted house. The possibilities for great storytelling are endless.

4 However, there's another reason that producers are eager to make their TV shows more interactive, and that is data gathering. In "Bandersnatch," for example, early on in the show, the viewer is asked to choose what cereal the main character should have for breakfast. Choices like these can be stored and used by advertising companies to better target-market their products. People's choices also demonstrate their personality—do they choose more violent courses of action or more thoughtful ones? All these choices can be collated into a personal profile that will be used to tailor marketing towards you, whether it's for products or show recommendations. It's interesting to think that the more control we seem to gain over our entertainment, the more control we're in fact giving to big companies who will gather our data and use it to control what we watch and buy.

5 So, will you participate in the interactive entertainment revolution? The choice is yours. . . .

⌃ Netflix logo

Questions

_____ 1. How does the author create interest in the first paragraph?
   a. By describing something in great detail.
   b. By providing a definition.
   c. By highlighting an exciting development.
   d. By employing a shocking statistic.

_____ 2. What is the second paragraph mostly devoted to?
   a. Giving historical background.
   b. Providing evidence to support a theory.
   c. Explaining the steps in a process.
   d. Comparing and contrasting.

_____ 3. What does the word **now** in the third paragraph emphasize?
   a. The need to do something immediately.
   b. The importance of the present moment.
   c. A particular length of time.
   d. A break with the past as the result of a recent event.

_____ 4. What does the author do with the first sentence of the fourth paragraph?
   a. Introduce an unexpected point.
   b. Mislead the reader.
   c. Summarize the content of the passage.
   d. Provide some comic relief.

_____ 5. Why does the author end the article with a question?
   a. To convince the reader of the author's opinion.
   b. To provoke a strong emotional response.
   c. To make the reader think.
   d. To leave the reader in a state of awe.

1-5 Figurative Language

Writers use **figurative language** to invoke feelings or create images that leave a deep impression on the reader. Here are some examples of the figurative language that you will encounter in this section.

Similes compare one object with another using the words "like," "as," or "than" (e.g., "Her heart is harder than stone."). **Metaphors** make more direct comparisons and usually equate one thing with another (e.g., "She has a heart of stone," or "All the world's a stage.") and are therefore more powerful than similes.

Personification is when a nonhuman object is given human qualities (e.g., "The sun strolled across the sky."). **Idioms** are phrases that should not be taken literally and have a meaning other than those of the individual words (e.g., "To let the cat out of the bag" has nothing to do with cats, but instead means "to reveal a secret."). Finally, **hyperbole** is an exaggeration that is used for added effect (e.g., "I've told you a million times!").

21 | A Globally Unifying Event

1 What exactly are *asteroids*? Some people think of them as comets or "shooting stars," but in fact the two differ greatly in composition. Scientists believe asteroids are leftover matter from our solar system's beginnings that couldn't collide to form a planet because of the interruptive gravity of Jupiter. They number in the thousands, and altogether would be about half the size of Earth's moon. The largest, Ceres, actually qualifies as a dwarf planet, and at nearly 1,000 kilometers in diameter accounts for roughly one third of the total mass inhabiting the "asteroid belt" that stretches between Mars and Jupiter.

2 Meteoroids, on the other hand, are basically extraterrestrial gravel, and although they usually burn up upon hitting Earth's atmosphere, not all of them do. Even a meteoroid can prove deadly if a person happens to be standing in the wrong place at the wrong time!

3 While most asteroids are **content** to stay in their vast domain between Mars and Jupiter, "near-Earth objects" (asteroids) can wander far closer to our planet. Currently

≪ Jupiter

≫ Mars

⌃ asteroids

there are no such "minor planets" believed to be threatening humanity. This is good because a collision with an asteroid only 300 meters in length would result in a global year of winter, while being hit by one a kilometer in length would cause unspeakable destruction worldwide.

4 On March 4, 2009, NASA reported that an asteroid had just missed Earth the previous Monday. Named 2009 DD45, the asteroid had maneuvered to within about 78,000 kilometers of Earth's surface. That's only twice as far as some telecommunications satellites to Earth's surface and very close when one considers the absolute disaster it could have caused.

5 2009 DD45 was about the same size as the asteroid that hit Siberia in 1908 and destroyed 2,000 square kilometers of forest—an area larger than London! What's more disturbing yet is that the asteroid was noticed only 48 hours before it (barely) passed Earth, even though its impact would have been akin to that of a nuclear explosion. And we cannot sigh with relief just yet, for 2009 DD45 could still return if it is captured by Earth's gravitational pull.

6 Perhaps the most terrifying thing about near-Earth objects is that we can do nothing whatsoever about them. Here is a danger utterly beyond the power of any statesperson or scientist to solve, a pure and indiscriminate force of nature. Thus, one NASA asteroid expert has labeled a potential collision "a globally unifying event."

» building of Nasa

Questions

____ 1. The phrase "in the wrong place at the wrong time" in the second paragraph is an example of what sort of figurative language?
   a. Alliteration.   b. A metaphor.   c. A cliché.   d. A simile.

____ 2. Which of the following is an example of an idiom?
   a. Shooting stars.
   b. Leftover matter.
   c. Extraterrestrial gravel.
   d. Minor planets.

____ 3. In the third paragraph, the writer says most asteroids are **content** to stay between Mars and Jupiter. What is this an example of?
   a. Hyperbole.   b. A simile.   c. Personification.   d. A metaphor.

____ 4. Identify the example of hyperbole from the choices below.
   a. Threatening humanity.
   b. Unspeakable destruction.
   c. Near-Earth objects.
   d. Nuclear explosion.

____ 5. "Here is a danger utterly beyond the power of any statesperson or scientist to solve" contains which figure of speech?
   a. Metaphor.
   b. Onomatopoeia.
   c. Personification.
   d. Alliteration.

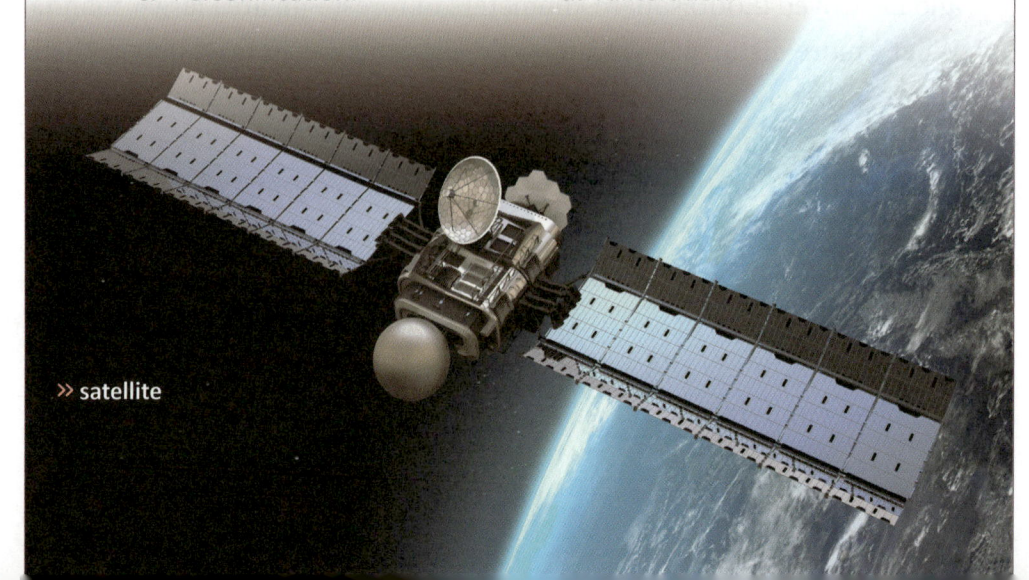

» satellite

22 A Battle Over Bricks

> the Wailing Wall, Jerusalem

1   All religions share the concept of hallowed ground. This refers to locations that are the scenes of special rites and celebrations or to the remembrance of important events. One such place, however, is less an example of religions' *sharing* hallowed ground than fighting over it. That place is the Wailing Wall in Jerusalem.

2   The Wailing Wall is actually only a small portion of the western wall of the Second Jewish Temple, which was extended by King Herod the Great around 19 BCE. First appearing in English literature in the 19th century, the term "Wailing Wall" originates from the Jews' tradition of walking to the wall like mourners to weep over the temple's destruction in 70 CE. Successive Christian and Islamic empires limited or completely forbade Jewish access to the wall, which was only fully restored with the establishment of British rule in 1920.

3   Over the following decade, disputes over rights to the wall hit the ceiling between Jews and Arabs, with the latter believing the wall to be the place where Muhammad tied his sacred steed,

> Mecca

al-Buraq, following his night journey to Jerusalem. In addition to having been the tethering post of *al-Buraq*, it is now part of the *Al-Aqsa* Mosque, Islam's third-holiest site. Muslims believe that Muhammad led prayers here after his arrival from Mecca on *al-Buraq*. Part of the mosque has risen upon the ruins of the Second Jewish Temple, and is considered by Muslims to be the holiest place in Jerusalem.

4 Jews, for their part, maintain that the Wailing Wall (which they call the Western Wall) is the only part of their second temple to have escaped demolition by the Romans under the emperor Vespasian. They come to it to mourn their people's suffering and pray for blessings or guidance. While some consider this place the so-called "Holy of Holies," where the Ark containing the Ten Commandments was supposed to be kept, it is in fact a retaining wall for the elevated platform on which the temple stood.

5 In recent years, the Wailing Wall has become a popular superstar hangout. Two of the last three popes visited the site, and then-US presidential candidate Barack Obama traveled to it during his election campaign in 2008. Meanwhile, Muslims and Jews are restricted to their respective sections of the area, and this bit of ground long sacred to two faiths continues to divide rather than unite them.

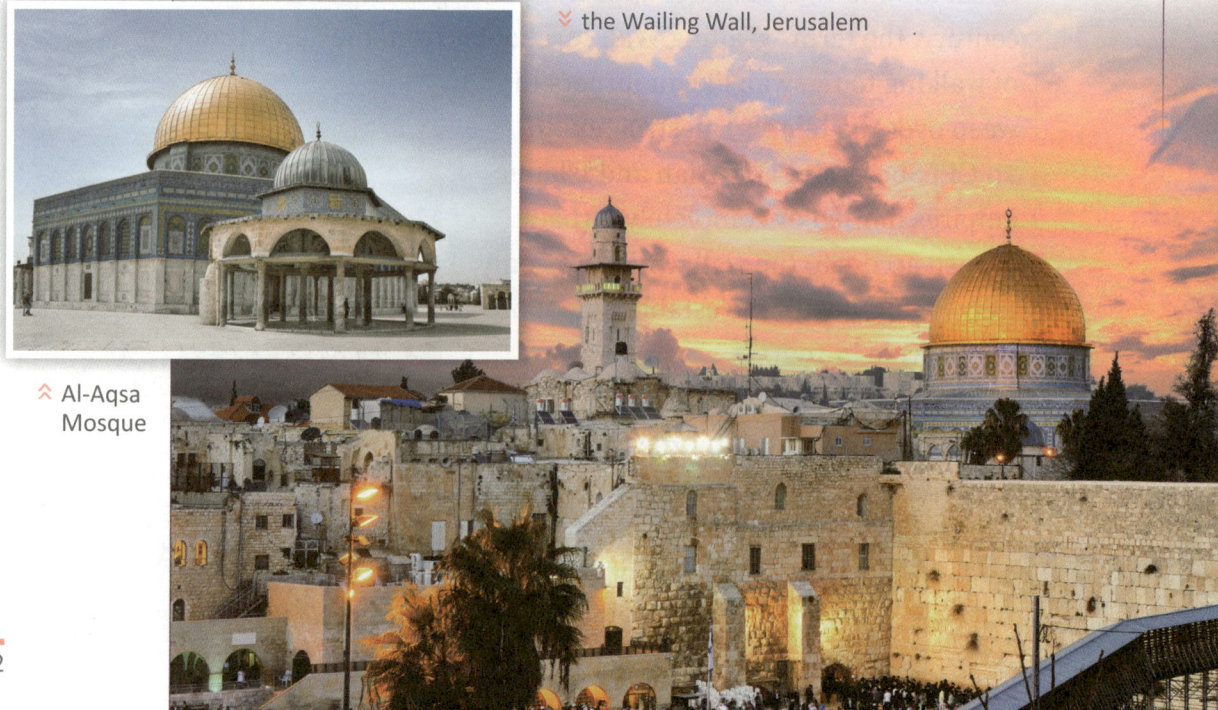

» Pope Benedict

⌄ the Wailing Wall, Jerusalem

⌃ Al-Aqsa Mosque

» Muslim

Questions

_____ 1. "One such place, however, is less an example of religions' *sharing* hallowed ground than fighting over it" is an example of what type of figurative language?
   a. Hyperbole.   b. Personification.   c. Metaphor.   d. Simile.

_____ 2. Which of the following is an example of a simile?
   a. "The Wailing Wall is actually only a small portion of the western wall of the Second Jewish Temple, which was extended by King Herod the Great around 19 BCE."
   b. "The term 'Wailing Wall' originates from the Jews' tradition of walking to the wall like mourners to weep over the temple's destruction in 70 CE."
   c. "Successive Christian and Islamic empires limited or completely forbade Jewish access to the wall, which was only fully restored with the establishment of British rule in 1920."
   d. "Jews, for their part, maintain that the Wailing Wall (which they call the Western Wall) is the only part of their second temple to have escaped demolition by the Romans under the emperor Vespasian."

_____ 3. "Over the following decade, disputes over rights to the wall hit the ceiling between Jews and Arabs" would be an example of what type of figurative language?
   a. A simile.   b. A metaphor.   c. Personification.   d. Hyperbole.

_____ 4. Which of the following contains an example of personification?
   a. "The Wall has great significance for Muslims for two reasons."
   b. "Muslims believe that Muhammad led prayers here after his arrival from Mecca on *al-Buraq*."
   c. "Part of the mosque has risen upon the ruins of the Second Jewish Temple."
   d. "It is considered by Muslims to be the holiest place in Jerusalem."

_____ 5. "In recent years, the Wailing Wall has become a popular superstar hangout." What does this metaphor probably mean?
   a. Many superstars can be seen giving performances at the Wailing Wall.
   b. The Wailing Wall is where many rich people take their vacations.
   c. Many movies are filmed in the area around the Wailing Wall.
   d. Many major world figures want to be seen at the Wailing Wall.

073

23 Portrait of a Primitive Painter

›› Paul Gauguin (1848—1903)

›› Tahitian Women on the Beach (1891)

1	Born in Paris in 1848, Paul Gauguin is considered one of the most important artists of the Postimpressionist era. He was responsible for countless paintings, sculptures, drawings, prints, engravings, and ceramics. His acknowledged masterpieces include *Vision after the Sermon* (1888) and *Tahitian Women on the Beach* (1891).

2	From 1871 to 1882, Gauguin made a successful living as a stockbroker while also dabbling in the art market. Both careers were brought to an abrupt end by the collapse of the Paris stock market.

⌃ *Vision After the Sermon* (1888)

» *The Sorcerer of Hiva Oa* (1902)

˅ *Where Do We Come From? What Are We? Where Are We Going?* (1897)

˅ *Woman With a Flower* (1891)

[3] Following a brief period in Copenhagen with his Danish wife and their five children, Gauguin returned to Paris in 1885. Having painted as a hobby since 1873, he now decided to pursue art as a career. Many of his friends were painters, including the Postimpressionist masters Pissarro, Cezanne, Monet, and Van Gogh.

Although he enjoyed some success as a Postimpressionist painter, Gauguin felt frustrated by what he saw as the imitative and conventional quality of European art. A stay on the Caribbean island of Martinique in 1887 proved stimulating, and Gauguin painted perhaps a dozen canvases there, despite bouts of dysentery and malaria.

[4] Back in France, Gauguin's newfound style and subject matter (the daily lives of Martinique's natives) were quite successful among both the artistic community and its patrons. Continuing to seek inspiration in exotic locations, Gauguin left for Tahiti in 1891. Over the next two years he painted and

I Raro te Oviri
(1891)

Les Alyscamps
(1888)

Gauguin's grave in Atuona

sculpted extensively, and notably took a 13-year-old Tahitian native girl as his wife. His art became progressively more primitive and colorful, and he made greater use of religious imagery.

[5] Migratory bird that he was, he returned to Paris in 1893 and continued painting and sculpting on Polynesian themes. His work was generally unsuccessful, however, and by 1895 he had to accept the charity of friends so that he could set sail for Tahiti once more, never to see Europe again.

[6] Gauguin spent the next six years in and around the Tahitian capital of Papeete, sculpting and painting for an expanding market of patrons. His most famous painting, *Where Do We Come From? What Are We? Where Are We Going?* (1897-8), dates from this period, which unfortunately was also one of increasing ill health for the artist. He settled in the Marquesas Islands in 1901, convinced that even Tahiti was no longer "primitive" enough to satisfy his ambitions, and met his maker due to syphilis in 1903 at the age of 54.

Questions

_____ 1. The title of this passage is an example of what sort of figurative language?
   a. Alliteration.
   b. Simile.
   c. Personification.
   d. Hyperbole.

_____ 2. Which of the following contains an example of hyperbole?
   a. He "is considered one of the most important artists of the post-Impressionist era."
   b. He "made a successful living as a stockbroker while also dabbling in the art market."
   c. "He was responsible for countless works of art including paintings, sculptures, drawings, prints, engravings, and ceramics."
   d. "Following a brief period in Copenhagen with his Danish wife and their five children, Gauguin returned to Paris in 1885."

_____ 3. "The collapse of the Paris stock market" is an example of what?
   a. A simile.
   b. A metaphor.
   c. Alliteration.
   d. Personification.

_____ 4. Which of the following is a metaphor?
   a. Gauguin "notably took a 13-year-old Tahitian native girl as his wife."
   b. "Migratory bird that he was, he returned to Paris in 1893. . . ."
   c. "He had to accept the charity of friends so that he could set sail for Tahiti once more."
   d. "Gauguin spent the next six years in and around the Tahitian capital of Papeete. . . ."

_____ 5. "He . . . met his maker. . . ." is an example of what?
   a. Hyperbole.
   b. An idiom.
   c. Alliteration.
   d. A simile.

≽ *Self-portrait* (1893)

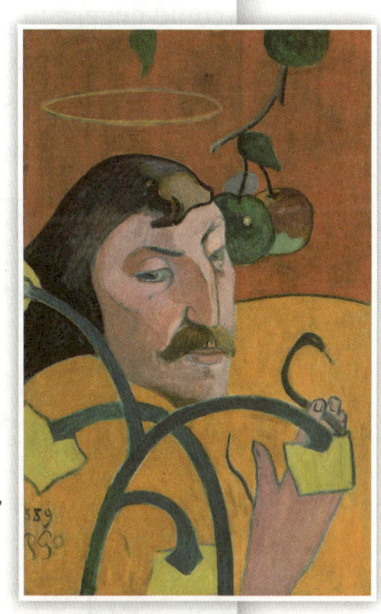

≽ *Self-portrait* (1889)

077

24 Against Impossible Odds

1. In 486 BCE, Xerxes succeeded his father Darius as King of Persia. The Persian Empire had by then swallowed two thirds of the known world; only Europe remained free. For the Persians, Greece was the gateway. Darius had tried to conquer Greece once but was famously defeated at Marathon. Xerxes inherited his father's aspirations and set out to succeed where Darius had failed.

2. Xerxes spent six years preparing the most massive fighting force the world had ever seen. Estimates range from 100,000 to over a million soldiers. Greece, on the other hand, was neither unified nor ready for war. It was a loose collection of small city-states, each with its own laws and government. Indeed, some Greek city-states were already at war with each other.

3. Nevertheless, it was **do or die**, and so King Leonidas of Sparta led a 1,200-man unit to face the might of Persia. The other Greek city-states sent a combined total of about 6,000 soldiers. This paltry group met the colossal Persian army in a narrow mountain pass called the Hot Gates, or Thermopylae. Funneling the Persian army into this **bottleneck** severely limited the number of soldiers who could engage in combat. The Greek forces, few as they were, could not be surrounded.

4. Though the Spartan contingent was miniscule, they had each been trained in warfare from the age of seven and did not work at any other trade. They were the most heavily armed soldiers in the world at that time, each

« Xerxes (519 BC—465 BC)
⌄ Persian soldiers (cc by Keyvan Mahmudi)

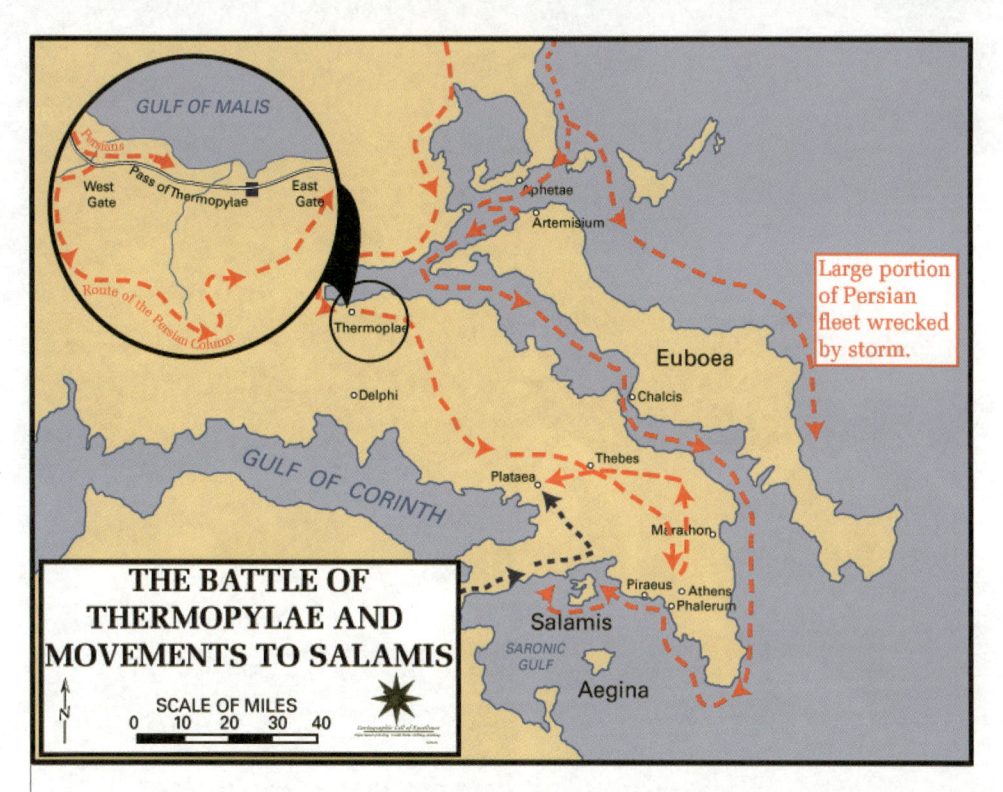

THE BATTLE OF THERMOPYLAE AND MOVEMENTS TO SALAMIS

wearing a sculpted bronze breastplate and carrying a bronze-plated solid oak shield, a short sword, and a 2.4-meter steel-tipped spear. What gave them the passion to fight, however, was neither their training nor their equipment; it was the ideal of freedom for which they fought.

5 When a Greek traitor showed Xerxes a path he could use to surround the Greeks, Leonidas, knowing the battle could not be won, sent most of his allies home to minimize losses. Though Xerxes' forces did surround the few remaining Greeks, they had to resort to raining arrows on their enemies (who fought to the very death) to finally capture the pass.

6 The Spartans have left us no monuments. They are remembered only for their inspiring actions during those two crucial days, when, like one of their own shields, they were all that stood between the European mainland and a ruthless conquering force. The Battle of Thermopylae was truly one of history's most pivotal battles.

« Statue of Leonidas in Sparta, Greece

▽ *Leonidas at Thermopylae*

Questions

1. "The Persian Empire had by then swallowed two thirds of the known world" is an example of what sort of figurative language?
   a. Personification.
   b. Hyperbole.
   c. Metaphor.
   d. Alliteration.

2. Which of the following is an example of a metaphor?
   a. "Xerxes inherited his father's aspirations."
   b. "Greece was neither unified nor ready for war."
   c. "For the Persians, Greece was the gateway."
   d. "Xerxes succeeded his father Darius as King of Persia."

↟ the hot springs from which Thermopylae takes its name

≫ Bas relief of Darius

↟ **Leonidas monument** (cc by vaggelis vlahos)

____3. The phrase "**do or die**" combines two kinds of figurative language. What is it?
   a. A hyperbolic metaphor.
   b. A personifying simile.
   c. An onomatopoeic idiom.
   d. An alliterative cliché.

____4. The reference to Thermopylae as a "**bottleneck**" in the third paragraph is an example of what?
   a. A simile.   b. A cliché.   c. A metaphor.   d. An idiom.

____5. Which of the following is an example of a simile?
   a. "The most heavily armed soldiers in the world."
   b. "Like one of their own shields."
   c. "The ideal of freedom for which they fought."
   d. "One of history's pivotal battles."

≪ the site of the battle of Thermopylae today (cc by Fkerasar)

≫ Persian Immortals

Unit 1 — Reading Skills — 1-5 Figurative Language

081

25 The New Einstein?

1 Sabrina Pasterski, a first-generation Cuban-American born and raised in the suburbs of Chicago, is only in her mid-twenties and already has a résumé that would put many older academics to shame. She has been called the new Einstein by Harvard University, where she completed her PhD in physics, and her papers were even cited by the great scientist Stephen Hawking. In an area of study traditionally dominated by men, Pasterski serves as an inspiration for young women to embrace the sciences and to **make their mark** on the field.

2 Her own passion for science was kindled when she took a flying lesson at age nine. Over the following years, that **flame** grew stronger

Sabrina Pasterski (cc by Cambridge02138)

Albert Einstein (1879–1955)

Sabrina Pasterski has been called the new Einstein. (cc by Cambridge02138)

and stronger, and at thirteen, she succeeded in building her own airplane and even piloted a solo flight. It wasn't always plain sailing for her, though. At sixteen, Pasterski applied for early entry to both Harvard and MIT but was rejected from both. However, some months later, two MIT professors saw a YouTube video she had made documenting the construction of her airplane and their jaws dropped. Recognizing her potential, they offered her a place, and in just three years she graduated MIT with a perfect 5.00 GPA.

3 An engineer at heart, Pasterski's original goal was to work for an aerospace company building spacecraft. However, while studying at MIT, she **caught the bug** for learning the physics behind flight. Several years down the line, this passion for figuring out the secrets behind phenomena we take for granted every day has led her to study some of the most complex issues in science. And her research into the nature of black holes, gravity, and space-time is set to challenge our understanding of just how the universe works.

˅ Sabrina Pasterski has built a website to record her physics research.
(retrieved from PhysicsGirl.com)

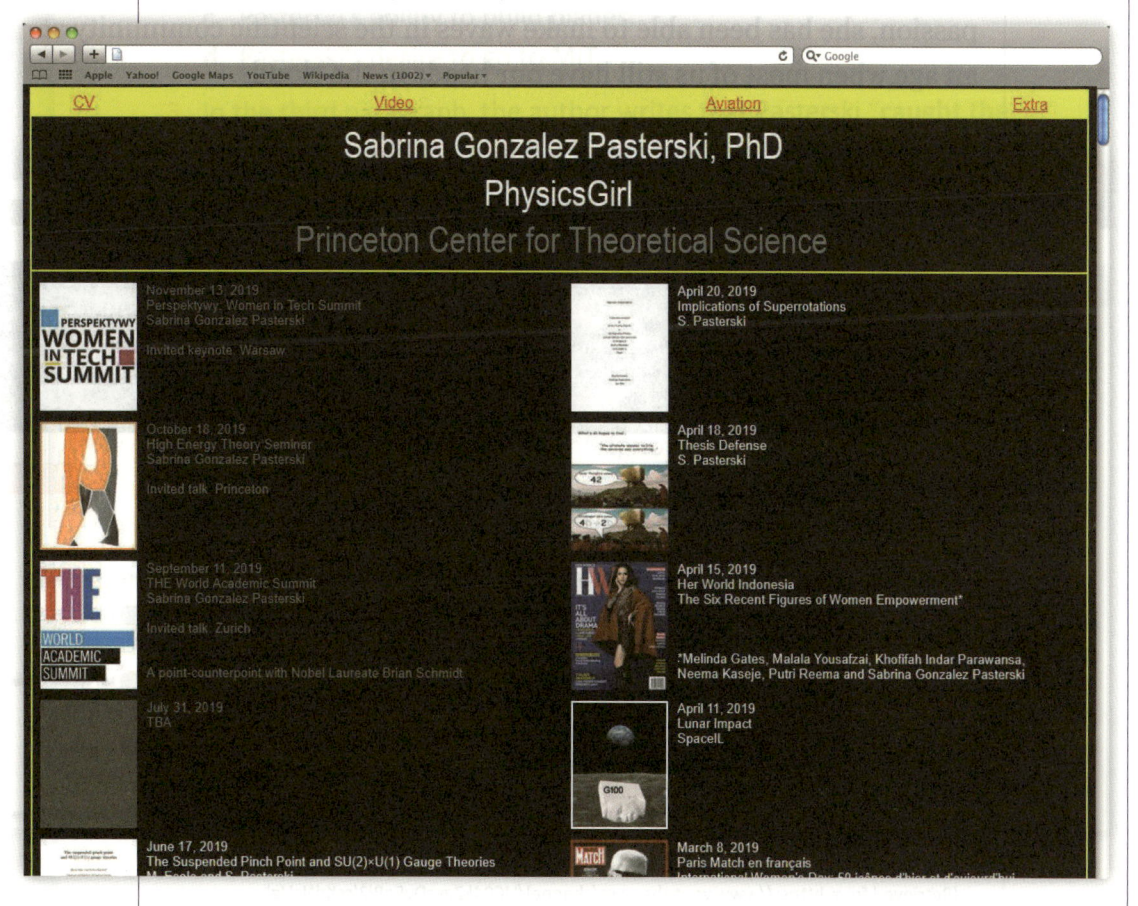

1-6 Author's Purpose and Tone

An author always has a goal in mind when he or she writes something. The *goal* might be to argue a point, to present an important problem, or even just to make the reader laugh. To achieve this goal, the author will adapt the vocabulary and the information presented, affecting the *tone* of the article.

aurora australis captured by NASA's IMAGE satellite

26 Our Glorious Nighttime Lights

All night long the northern streamers shot across the trembling sky;
Fearful lights that never beckon save when kings and heroes die.

—W. E. Aytoun

1   Such was the opinion of Scottish poet William Aytoun in the 1800s, for the aurora borealis is indeed a glorious sight. This magnificent display of dancing light and color can sometimes even resemble draperies hanging in the glowing nighttime sky. One of the most impressive of natural phenomena, it gets its name from that of the Roman goddess of dawn, Aurora, and boreas, the Greek word for north wind. It is also popularly known as the northern lights.

2   Unbeknownst to many admirers of the aurora borealis, however, their famed lights have a counterpart in the Southern Hemisphere. This is the aurora australis, or southern lights, with "australis" being the Latin word for "of the south."

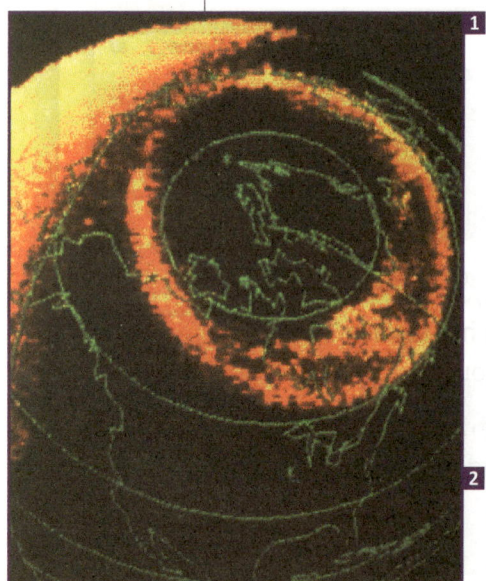

diffuse aurora observed by satellite

images of the aurora australis and
aurora borealis from around the world

▽ red and green auroras, Norway
(cc by Arctic light Frank Olsen, Norway)

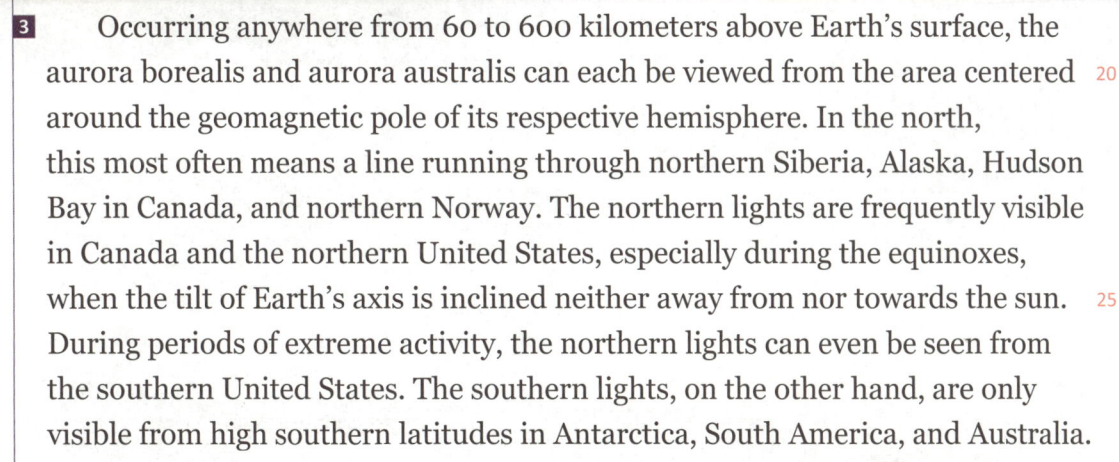

(cc by Samuel Blanc)

3   Occurring anywhere from 60 to 600 kilometers above Earth's surface, the aurora borealis and aurora australis can each be viewed from the area centered around the geomagnetic pole of its respective hemisphere. In the north, this most often means a line running through northern Siberia, Alaska, Hudson Bay in Canada, and northern Norway. The northern lights are frequently visible in Canada and the northern United States, especially during the equinoxes, when the tilt of Earth's axis is inclined neither away from nor towards the sun. During periods of extreme activity, the northern lights can even be seen from the southern United States. The southern lights, on the other hand, are only visible from high southern latitudes in Antarctica, South America, and Australia.

4   Even in our age of highly advanced scientific investigation, many still wonder what causes these splendid natural displays. None other than the American inventor and statesman Benjamin Franklin was the first to publicly theorize that they were dense collections of electrical charges in the Arctic and Antarctic areas intensified by the condensation of water.

[5] The actual answer, however, is a bit more complex. We know now that the auroras are the results of encounters with electrically charged particles from the sun which enter Earth's atmosphere and collide with air molecules. These particles are trapped in radiation belts high above Earth and transmitted toward the polar regions by their magnetic fields. The ensuing collisions cause luminosity, and the result is a dramatic performance of colorful banners of light. Having been fortunate enough to witness the aurora borealis firsthand, I can assure readers that our glorious nighttime lights do indeed inspire one to reflect upon the many natural marvels of this wondrous planet.

(cc by Brocken Inaglory)

(cc by Arctic light -Frank Olsen)

(cc by Jerry MagnuM Porsbjer)

▲ aurora borealis over the gulf of Finland

Questions

___ 1. Why did the author write this passage?
   a. To review the work of a Scottish poet.
   b. To describe a natural phenomenon.
   c. To inform the reader about a trip he took.
   d. To give instructions for a scientific experiment.

___ 2. What is the author trying to achieve in the second paragraph?
   a. Compare and contrast the aurora borealis and the aurora australis.
   b. Teach the reader some simple Latin words and phrases.
   c. Present information that might surprise some readers.
   d. Explain that no one knows anything about the southern lights.

___ 3. What is the author's main purpose in the third paragraph?
   a. To explain what causes the northern and southern lights.
   b. To relate a personal story involving the aurora borealis.
   c. To tell the reader where the auroras can be seen from.
   d. To inform the reader about what happens during an equinox.

___ 4. Why does the writer begin the second sentence of the fourth paragraph with "None other than. . . ."?
   a. To make sure the reader knows exactly whom he is writing about.
   b. To show that there is some confusion or controversy about this point.
   c. To introduce a character who will be very important in the passage.
   d. To introduce someone that the reader may already know about.

___ 5. How can the author's tone in the final sentence of the passage best be described?
   a. Awestruck.   b. Reassuring.   c. Skeptical.   d. Reflective.

089

27 The Big Hangover

1. *Prost*! That is German for "Cheers," and you will certainly want to learn it if you are attending Oktoberfest, the world's biggest beer party.

2. Oktoberfest began in 1810 in Munich, Germany, to celebrate the wedding of Crown Prince Ludwig (later King Ludwig I) and Princess Therese of Saxe-Hildburghausen. The royal couple graciously invited Munich's citizens to their wedding reception, which lasted an impressive 16 days. This inspired the idea to hold a similar festival at the same time every year thereafter. Despite its name, Oktoberfest is held mostly in September, and ends during the first weekend of October.

3. In any case, Oktoberfest is now the world's largest fair, boasting an attendance of over six million people each year. Even more impressive than the number of participants, however, is the amount of beer they consume. In 2018, a record-setting 7.5 million liters of frosty German *bier* were drunk during what was, at just 16 days, a relatively short Oktoberfest. A special type of beer, known as *Oktoberfestbier*, is brewed for the fair and served in oversized glass mugs called *biersteins*. The accompanying traditional dishes include

sausage, chicken, cheese noodles, oxtail, and sauerkraut, finely shredded cabbage that has been fermented. There are also plenty of the enormous pretzels for which the festival is known.

[4] All of this food and drink is served in huge tents that hold thousands of people. In fact, a single tent can seat over 8,000 guests simultaneously! In 2018, approximately 280,000 sausages, 550,000 roasted chickens, and 124 roasted oxen were served to hungry festivalgoers!

[5] With so many people wanting to take part, and so much money to be made, it is no surprise that Oktoberfest is no longer exclusively a German event. Other countries throughout the world have added their own flavors to the Oktoberfest celebration. In Mexico City, the German-Mexican population offers amusement park rides and a craft fair. In Blumenau, Brazil, 18 days of music and dancing help Brazilians pay their respects to all their German ancestors. And in the United States, literally hundreds of Oktoberfest celebrations are held, with the largest being in Cincinnati, Ohio.

[6] While Oktoberfest is still a fairly new idea in Taiwan, local German business owners have begun to observe it and, needless to say, the local population has responded enthusiastically. As this most German of traditions continues to go global, who knows where it will wind up being celebrated next?

>> waitress with Hacker-Pschorr, one of the traditional beers allowed to be served at Oktoberfest (cc by Markburger83)

» Oktoberfest rides and roller coasters
(cc by Michael.chlistalla)

Questions

_____ 1. What is the purpose of this passage's opening paragraph?
   a. To give the reader a sense of the fun nature of the topic.
   b. To teach the reader proper German manners.
   c. To persuade the reader to attend a festival overseas.
   d. To advise the reader about appropriate behavior at Oktoberfest.

_____ 2. What is the author's purpose in the second paragraph?
   a. To provide brief biographies of a German king and queen.
   b. To provide relevant information about the city of Munich.
   c. To provide a historical context for the festival under discussion.
   d. To provide the precise starting and ending dates of Oktoberfest.

˅ Oktoberfest at night

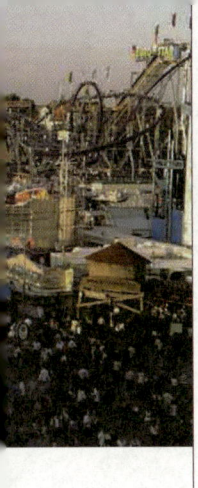

» mugs of beer

_____ 3. How might the author's tone in the third and fourth paragraph best be described?
   a. Scholarly.
   b. Mocking.
   c. Concerned.
   d. Enthusiastic.

_____ 4. What does the author do in the fifth paragraph?
   a. Describe different traditional festivals in countries around the world.
   b. Expand the idea of Oktoberfest from a German to a global event.
   c. Express amazement at the widespread popularity of Oktoberfest.
   d. State that the German Oktoberfest is better than those in other places.

_____ 5. With what sort of tone does the writer conclude the passage?
   a. Disappointed.
   b. Curious.
   c. Worried.
   d. Argumentative.

» sauerkraut

ˆ German sausages with sauerkraut

« floats at the annual Oktoberfest Opening Parade in central Munich
(cc by Poco a poco)

093

> A cat is resting on the street on Aoshima island.

28 Island Purrradises

[1]   Being a cat lover in Japan is like being a kid in a candy store. Cat temples, lucky cats, Hello Kitty, cat cafés—the nation appears to be obsessed with the furry creatures. There are some places in Japan, however, that take this obsession to another level entirely. The nation's eleven "cat islands"—islands off the Japanese coast where, in many cases, the cats outnumber the people, are the ultimate destination for anyone with a more than normal fondness for felines.

[2]   One of the most famous of these cat islands is Aoshima, a 1.6 km long island located 30 minutes by ferry off the coast of southern Japan. Approximately 20 people live on Aoshima, but there are well over 100 cats, who spend their days curled up in the island's abandoned buildings or prowling about the harbour hunting for fish. After pictures of the island went viral online, the number of tourists visiting Aoshima has risen dramatically. The island is not exactly tourist friendly, though, with no cars, hotels, restaurants, or even vending machines, and the current human residents are mostly elderly people who make a simple living by fishing. Indeed, cats were originally introduced to the

⌄ Aoshima island in Ehime prefecture of Japan

Tourists feeding the island's cats can lead to overpopulation.

TNR (trap-neuter-return) is a way to control the number of cats on the island.

island in order to help control the rats and mice that hung around the fishing boats. But as the population of the island dwindled over the years, the cat population rapidly took over.

3 The increased awareness and subsequent popularity of these cat islands have, however, brought problems. On the tiny cat island of Ainoshima, for instance, the abundance of food provided by tourists for the hundreds of local cats has led to serious overpopulation. This in turn has led to stress, violence, and disease among the cats, who often die in fights over territory on the crowded island.

4 Therefore, while visiting one of these islands may be a must for any cat lover, it's important to do whatever is possible to minimize the negative impact that tourism can bring. While many islands are now implementing trap-neuter-return programs to help control their feline populations, visitors must do their part, too. When visiting, tourists must refrain from feeding the islands' cats, no matter how hard it might be to resist those heart-melting feline eyes! Only by doing this can we ensure that these islands remain heavens for both visitors and the cats themselves.

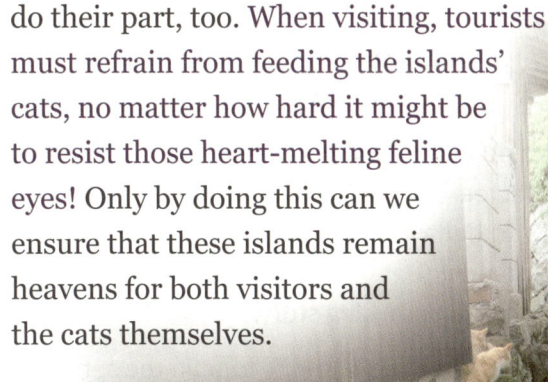

> There are over 100 cats on Aoshima island, which outnumbers the residents.

» Tourism may cause stress, violence, and disease among the cats.

Questions

_____ 1. What is the author's purpose in writing this passage?
   a. To warn the reader about a danger.
   b. To convince the reader of his opinion.
   c. To inform the reader about a place.
   d. To describe a series of events.

_____ 2. What tone does the author take in the first paragraph?
   a. Melancholy.
   b. Apathetic.
   c. Outraged.
   d. Enthusiastic.

_____ 3. Which of the following describes the author's tone in the third paragraph?
   a. Nostalgic.
   b. Mocking.
   c. Grim.
   d. Arrogant.

_____ 4. What does the author aim to do in the final paragraph?
   a. Describe a person or character.
   b. Advise the reader on how to behave.
   c. Criticize a popularly held idea.
   d. Entertain the reader by telling an amusing story.

_____ 5. Which of the following best describes the author's tone in the sentence "When visiting, tourists must refrain. . . ." in the last paragraph?
   a. Serious, then playful.
   b. Frustrated, then awestruck.
   c. Cheerful, then solemn.
   d. Angry, then ironic.

▲ Urban legends are modern genre of folklore.

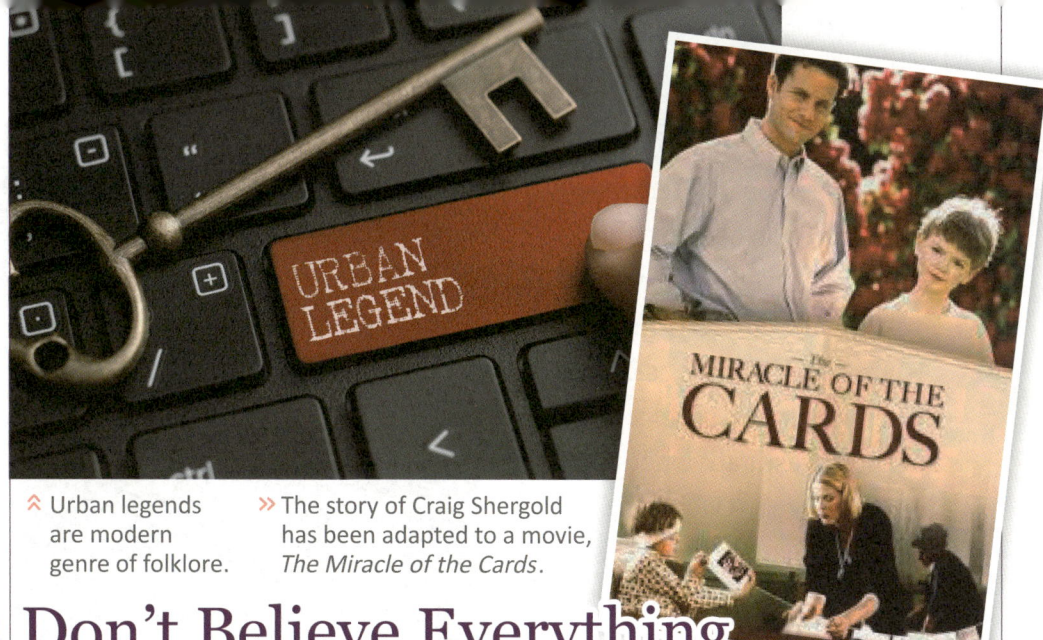

» The story of Craig Shergold has been adapted to a movie, *The Miracle of the Cards*.

29 Don't Believe Everything You Hear – or Read

1   According to Wikipedia, an urban legend is "a modern genre of folklore rooted in local popular culture, usually comprising fictional stories that are often presented as true, with macabre or humorous elements." Some urban legends are outright horror stories meant to scare people. They are explicit in their warnings of government conspiracies, attacks by criminals, and so forth. Others are ridiculous graphic tales intended to shock. An urban legend may be based on reality, but over time it can take on the outlandish proportions of myth.

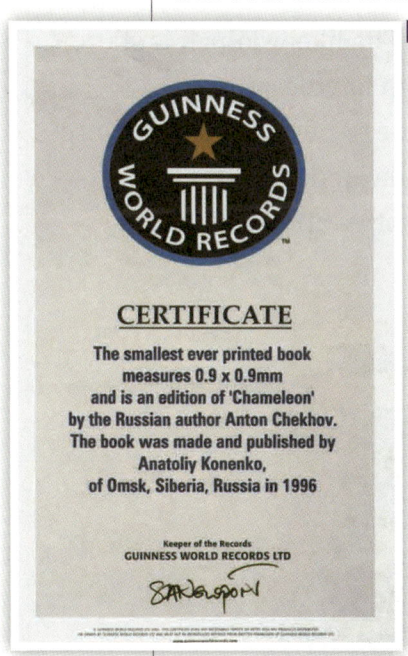

2   While the term "urban legend" dates back to at least as far as the late 1960s, the advent of the Internet has massively increased both the number and range of urban legends. Two that regularly pop up are the "email tax" and the story of Craig Shergold. The email tax legend says that the US Postal Service is going to impose a five-cent tax on every email sent to make up for lost postage fees, since people now send electronic mail instead of using the postal system. The Shergold legend, for its part, was initially true. It tells of a young British boy with a cancerous brain tumor who wanted to enter the Guinness Book of World Records by way of a chain letter campaign. Although notice was given that the boy was cured in 1991, he was still receiving thousands of letters and business cards as late as 2013.

▲ Guinness World Records certificate

3   **Needless to say**, many people have been affected by urban legends because they're gullible and get embroiled in stories with fantastic themes. Attempting to serve as definitive sources of truth, several urban legend investigative bodies have emerged. Two of the better known are the website Snopes.com and the television program *MythBusters*. While Snopes generally limits itself to research, *MythBusters* conducts entertaining experiments to test the veracity of myths old and new.

4   Some urban legends are so convincing, however, that laws are enacted because of them. One example is the falsehood that using a cell phone while pumping gasoline can ignite the fumes. Fire department testing and other experiments have proven this is not true. The likely culprit is static electric discharge when people touch the metal pump handles.

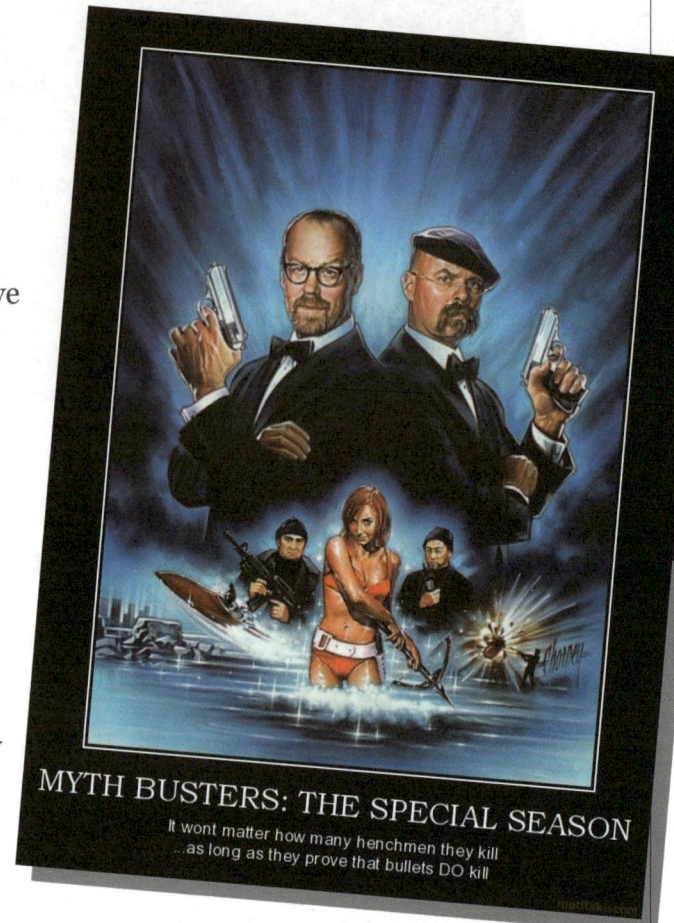

5   There's no doubt that urban legends will continue to permeate our culture and shape our world. Nevertheless, the efforts of dedicated truth-seekers may help keep us rooted in reality despite our instinctive attraction to the sensational.

MythBusters poster

« Snopes.com (retrieved from www.snopes.com)

« Former president Barack Obama records an episode of the television show *MythBusters* with co-hosts at the White House.

Unit 1 Reading Skills

1-6 Author's Purpose and Tone

Questions

_____ 1. What is the author's purpose in writing this passage?
   a. To spread some popular stories that aren't true.
   b. To prove that some popular stories aren't true.
   c. To create a new story and make people believe it.
   d. To make people more careful about believing stories.

_____ 2. What attitude does the author take toward urban legends in the first paragraph?
   a. He believes all of them.
   b. He thinks they are all ridiculous.
   c. He is generally skeptical of them.
   d. He finds them very frightening.

_____ 3. What is the purpose of the second paragraph?
   a. To explain the origins of the term "urban legend."
   b. To persuade people to use the postal system more often.
   c. To provide some famous examples of urban legends.
   d. To tell people to stop writing letters to Craig Shergold.

_____ 4. Why does the author begin the third paragraph with the phrase "**Needless to say**"?
   a. Because the information following the phrase is so obvious.
   b. Because he doesn't want to inform the reader of something.
   c. Because he is worried the reader will repeat what comes next.
   d. Because he doesn't see any point in writing the paragraph.

_____ 5. What tone does the author take in the final paragraph?
   a. Doubtful.
   b. Hopeful.
   c. Enthusiastic.
   d. Concerned.

099

> Having multiple careers is becoming increasingly popular among modern workers.
> (cc by Clip Art by Vector Toons)

30 Thriving With the Slash Effect

1 The nature of work is undergoing a fundamental shift. It used to be that you'd work for the same company for your entire life, fulfilling the same tasks and relying on the same skills. Now companies come and go like the changing of the seasons. Just consider the fact that popular careers like social media manager and mobile app designer didn't even exist 15 years ago!

2 The modern worker must change, too, or risk being left in the dust. This is where the "slash effect" comes in. The slash effect is a term coined by *The New York Times* columnist and former lawyer Marci Alboher. It refers to the multiple skill sets and identities—or "slashes"—of many

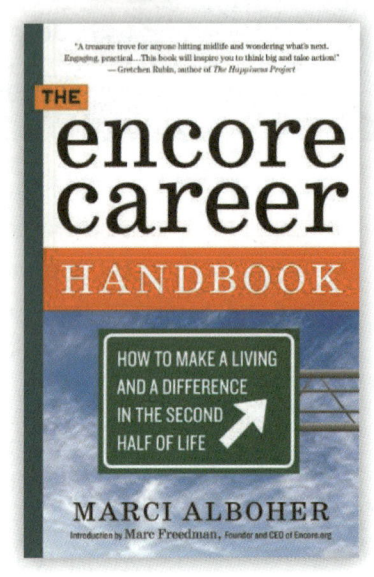

↟ "Slash" comes from the book *The Encore Career Handbook* written by Marci Alboher.

↟ The job mobile app designer didn't exist 15 years ago.

⌃ a slashie, who is a sales representative and photographer at the same time

modern workers. Alboher identifies herself, for example, as an author/speaker/coach.

3 The slash effect applies to a variety of scenarios. It could mean someone who changes their career, like a journalist who decides to become a social worker. It could also refer to a self-employed person engaged in multiple careers at once, like a writer/editor/translator. In a broader sense, it could mean the different identities and roles required by modern life, like CEO/Mom. Or maybe it's just someone who's pursuing a creative talent like photography by night while working an unrelated day job. Eventually this individual might be able to survive on their art alone, but until then they still need to pay the bills.

⌄ a social media manager

101

4 What skills are the most valuable in this new economy? First and foremost is adaptability. Slashing requires constant evolution and change over different roles in the course of a lifetime. Those with a lifelong passion for learning and self-improvement will thrive, and those who can't adapt risk being left behind.

5 There are some significant drawbacks to this new economic reality. In some ways the slash effect is a symptom of the growing precariousness of working life. We don't always seek out new careers because we want to, but because we have to. Some of the positive aspects of lifelong employment with a single company are also increasingly rare, like health and retirement benefits.

6 However, there are plenty of perks as well. Young people can now follow their passions and develop new skills over time. They can also nurture their creative side without putting themselves at serious financial risk. So what are you waiting for? Get out there and get slashing!

⌃ Being a YouTuber has become a common career path in today's economic reality.

⌄ Slashing requires a life-long passion for learning and self-improvement.

Questions

____ 1. What's the author's purpose in this article?
   a. To present two historical examples.
   b. To offer a solution.
   c. To introduce a new trend.
   d. To state a problem.

____ 2. Which of the following best describes the author's attitude toward the slash effect in the fifth paragraph?
   a. Skeptical.   b. Joyful.   c. Angry.   d. Inspired.

____ 3. How can the author's tone be described in the first paragraph?
   a. Grim.   b. Excited.   c. Confused.   d. Indifferent.

____ 4. Why does the author ask the question "What are you waiting for?" in the final paragraph?
   a. To state an opinion.
   b. To ask for an answer.
   c. To give a personal example.
   d. To be humorous.

____ 5. What is the author's purpose in the third paragraph?
   a. To present several relevant examples.
   b. To provide a historical background.
   c. To express doubts.
   d. To offer several personal opinions.

103

1-7 Cause and Effect

A **cause** makes something happen, and an **effect** is the resulting action or event. The link between causes and their effects can sometimes be obvious; other times they are more subtle. To make identifying these relationships easier, look out for words that expressly imply a **cause-effect relationship**, such as "therefore," "as a result," or "consequently."

People can have numerous plastic products in their kitchen and bathroom.

31 Ditching the Plastic Habit

1   We've been told a thousand times that we should cut back on plastic. The problem is no longer a lack of awareness—it's that plastic shows up in so many everyday products. What's needed now is practical advice about easy, affordable alternatives to plastic.

2   Sure, you probably already take a cotton bag to the supermarket. (More than 90 countries now ban or impose a charge on plastic bags, following Bangladesh's example in 2002.) Maybe you even bring your own cup to the coffee shop and refuse plastic drinking straws. But if you really want to make a difference, it's time to go beyond this.

A trip to the supermarket may consume plenty of plastic bags.

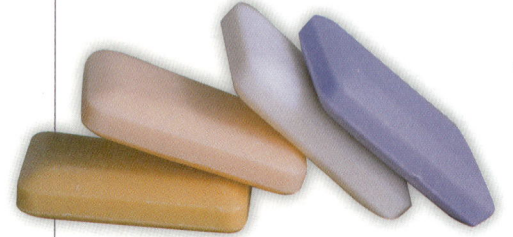

bars of soap

cotton handkerchiefs

104

⌄ potato chips

⌄ nonstick pan

3   Think back to your last supermarket trip. How many of your purchases were wrapped in plastic? Processed food (e.g., candy, potato chips, and instant noodles) is the worst offender, but even whole foods like bananas or rice often come in plastic packaging. What's the use of filling a cotton bag with plastic containers? Buy your groceries from the supermarket, bakery, or independent stores, and take your own boxes, jars, and cloths to hold them in.

4   You can also replace commercial cleaning products and cosmetics with natural alternatives. Instead of harsh household cleaners, try a mix of water and vinegar. Ditch packets of tissues for cotton handkerchiefs, bottles of body wash for bars of soap, and deodorant for baking soda. It really works, and you can make it smell attractive by adding essential oils like lavender. Plain baking soda can also be used for washing dishes, and it leaves them just as shiny as liquid from the store.

⌄ The plastic bottle we use may ultimately end up in the ocean.

5   What about the common items in your kitchen? So many pans these days are "nonstick," which usually means they're coated with Teflon. When heated, this plastic can release toxic chemicals. Therefore, go back to metal pans, like Mom and Dad used to use. Don't be tempted by cheap plastic utensils, either, as they inevitably have a short shelf-life. Invest in quality wooden spoons and metal implements that will last for decades.

6   But the truly frightening thing is how many products, from tea bags to chewing gum, contain invisible plastics. That's right: to freshen your breath, you're chewing on plastic. (A zero-waste solution is to eat fennel seeds, as is common in India.) These indigestible "microplastics" are the hardest to avoid. But by changing your overall lifestyle, and questioning everything you put in your cart, you'll slowly learn which products are planet-friendly.

⌃ baking soda

» Bringing our own bags to the supermarket is a good way to cut down on plastic use.

⌄ We can use our own cutlery and water bottles to replace disposable ones.

Questions

___ 1. Why do so many people still use plastic, according to the article?
   a. People are not aware of how harmful it is.
   b. Alternatives to plastic tend to cost more.
   c. A lot of common products contain plastic.
   d. Plastic is the most practical everyday material.

___ 2. What was the result of Bangladesh's plastic bag ban, according to the article?
   a. People made their own cotton bags.
   b. Other countries copied the idea.
   c. Some shops had fewer customers.
   d. More plastic goods were banned.

___ 3. What is produced by adding lavender essential oil to baking soda?
   a. Cleaning fluid.
   b. Deodorant.
   c. Dishwashing liquid.
   d. Body wash.

___ 4. Which of these items can cause an unpleasant chemical reaction?
   a. Nonstick pans.
   b. Metal implements.
   c. Plastic utensils.
   d. Wooden spoons.

___ 5. Which action will lead to greater understanding of the plastic problem, according to the article?
   a. Copying the behavior of Indian consumers.
   b. Refusing to eat products containing microplastics.
   c. Considering everything you buy carefully.
   d. Making small, slow changes to your lifestyle.

32 Four Ways to Be Quiet

[1] Which Saturday night plan do you find more appealing: a party with lots of new people, or milk and cookies in front of the TV? If you prefer the party, you are probably an extrovert—someone who gets their energy from socializing. But if you'd opt for the sofa, chances are you're an introvert—someone who needs time alone to recharge.

[2] In the past, introversion was thought of as a mild social disability. Introverts would force themselves out of the house to avoid being mocked as boring. Thankfully, these days, introversion is understood as a difference rather than a handicap. It is being studied and written about more than ever. And experts today are even suggesting introversion is not a single "condition," but it comes in four types.

[3] The first type of introvert that's been identified is social. Social introverts are reluctant to spend time in large groups. Contrary to traditional definitions, social introverts don't hate people or insist on permanent solitude. They just prefer to have deeper relationships with fewer friends. Once a social introvert is comfortable around you, they may keep you talking for hours!

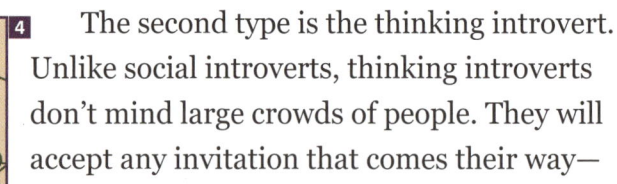

[4] The second type is the thinking introvert. Unlike social introverts, thinking introverts don't mind large crowds of people. They will accept any invitation that comes their way—

« Anxious introverts don't enjoy being with people.

Extroverts may prefer going out to parties while introverts might opt to stay home and watch TV.

then spend the event lost in their own thoughts. They are imaginative people; writers and artists often fall into this category.

5 The third type of introvert, perhaps the toughest kind, is anxious. Most of the time anxious introverts really don't enjoy being with people, as they worry they are doing something wrong. Even when they get home, they replay their perceived mistakes during interactions with others. Anxious introversion can be an uphill struggle for those who suffer from it.

6 The fourth and final type of introvert is restrained—people who like to reflect before speaking or acting. They are probably quiet during noisy debates, but that doesn't mean they are confused or uninterested. Restrained introverts just take a while to warm up, like a car on a cold morning.

7 Do you recognize yourself as one of these types? If so, psychologists say you should take your introversion and own it! Educate your more extroverted friends if the topic arises. And as Susan Cain said in her book, *Quiet: The Power of Introverts in a World that Can't Stop Talking*: "Don't think of introversion as something that needs to be cured . . . Spend your free time the way you like, not the way you think you're supposed to."

Quiet: The Power of Introverts in a World that Can't Stop Talking

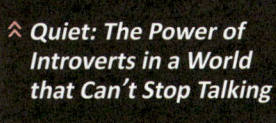

Susan Cain
(cc by Gage Skidmore)

109

» Nowadays, introversion is understood as a difference rather than a handicap.

Questions

_____ 1. Why did introverts in the past go to social events when they didn't want to, according to the passage?
   a. They didn't want to be teased.
   b. They were never given any choice.
   c. They wanted to make their friends happy.
   d. They enjoyed the events when they arrived.

_____ 2. Which of these is the most likely effect of social introversion?
   a. Spending most weekends alone.
   b. Being quiet around other people.
   c. Talking too much when nervous.
   d. Having a small circle of friends.

_____ 3. Why might a thinking introvert be "lost in their thoughts" at a party?
   a. They get stressed when surrounded by people.
   b. They are coming up with creative ideas.
   c. They need be sure of themselves before they speak.
   d. They don't like to answer silly questions.

_____ 4. Why does the author suggest anxious introverts have a particularly hard time?
   a. They don't have anyone to support them.
   b. They find it hard to switch off mentally.
   c. They tend to stay at home most of the time.
   d. They find it impossible to start a conversation.

_____ 5. Which of these factors could lead to silence from a restrained introvert?
   a. Being asked about their personal life.
   b. Being in a group of unfamiliar people.
   c. Being asked to give an opinion immediately.
   d. Being in a group with people speaking loudly.

33 Trouble in the Air – and Under the Ground

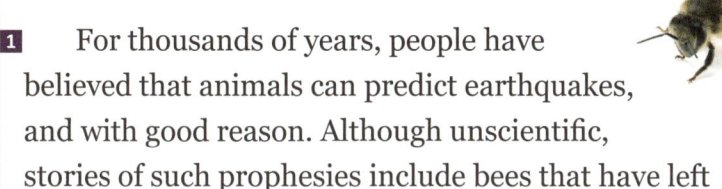

1   For thousands of years, people have believed that animals can predict earthquakes, and with good reason. Although unscientific, stories of such prophesies include bees that have left their hives in swarms as though in a panic, chickens that have stopped laying eggs, catfish that have swum about violently, and dogs, cats, and caged birds that have become noticeably restless.

2   In the case of wild animals, news reports documented that three days before the 2008 Sichuan earthquake in China, thousands of toads appeared on the streets of Mianzhu, a city where 2,000 people were subsequently killed. On the day of the earthquake, some 965 kilometers from the epicenter at a zoo in the city of Wuhan, zebras anxiously banged their heads against a door, elephants swung their trunks wildly, and lions and tigers, usually asleep during the day, paced in their cages. Five minutes before the quake, the zoo's peacocks started screeching.

3   Such accounts go back a long way. As early as 373 BC, historians wrote that droves of snakes, weasels, rats, and centipedes left the city of Helike, Greece, days before an earthquake and tsunami devastated it.

111

centipede

catfish

4 Exactly what such animals sense is a mystery. Some theories are that they feel movements, or weak "shocks," in the earth before humans do; that they become aware of gases being released; or that they hear "infrasound," audio frequencies below the range of human hearing, from sources such as earthquakes and volcanoes. Animals also use Earth's magnetic field to navigate during migration, so they are very much in tune with it. Therefore, one belief is that animals can detect electrical signals caused by electromagnetic field variations, which alert them that an earthquake is about to happen.

5 The US Geological Survey states that no consistent connection between the occurrence of a quake and a particular behavior on the part of animals exists and, therefore, no concrete evidence can be obtained. American seismologists are likewise skeptical. They allege that animals may exhibit strange behavior at any time for other reasons—because they are hungry, to defend their territory, to face a predator, or because it is their mating season. Other researchers, however, have not given up on the idea. They continue to follow the anecdotal evidence, especially in earthquake-prone areas such as Japan, India, and China. They hope that one day what they have learned will prove invaluable in predicting earthquakes more accurately, thus saving millions of lives.

weasel

peacock

Questions

_____ 1. According to the author, what have some birds been known to do before an earthquake?
   a. Fly far away from the epicenter.
   b. Suddenly stop laying eggs.
   c. Bang their heads against doors.
   d. Fill the streets of affected cities.

_____ 2. What is said to have happened just before the 2008 Sichuan quake?
   a. Many animals left the city of Helike in Greece.
   b. Zoo animals in Wuhan began acting strangely.
   c. Two thousand people were killed in Mianzhu.
   d. Catfish began to swim about violently.

_____ 3. Why might some animals exhibit unusual behavior before an earthquake strikes?
   a. They see other animals acting in unusual ways.
   b. It makes them more nervous about predators.
   c. There is less food available at such times.
   d. They can feel the earth moving before people do.

_____ 4. Why do American seismologists doubt that animals can sense quakes in advance?
   a. Because animals may act strangely for other reasons.
   b. Because they don't trust scientists from other countries.
   c. Because the US Geological Survey says it's impossible.
   d. Because they don't care about people dying in earthquakes.

_____ 5. What is one possible result of the research being done on animals' behavior before earthquakes?
   a. Zookeepers will have fewer problems.
   b. People's pets will stop being so nervous.
   c. Fewer people will be killed by quakes.
   d. Earthquakes will stop happening.

» King with President Lyndon Johnson in 1966

34 A Man of Passionate Callings

1 Martin Luther King, Jr. was the most celebrated activist of the 1960s American civil rights movement. Born Michael King in Atlanta, Georgia in 1929, he was renamed Martin Luther King at age five by his father in honor of the initiator of the Protestant Reformation. Like his namesake, King became a man of passionate callings with the courage to answer them.

2 Growing up in the segregated south, King experienced racism firsthand throughout his early life. An excellent student, he graduated college at 19 before going on to religious studies at Crozer Theological Seminary. He became a Baptist minister in 1954 and earned a doctoral degree in theology from Boston University the following year. King felt the church answered his "inner urge to serve humanity" and hoped to deliver sermons which would be "a respectful force for ideas, even social protest."

3 King's ideas about race and religion stemmed from his relationships with people of like minds and beliefs. One was Howard Thurman, an educator, civil rights leader,

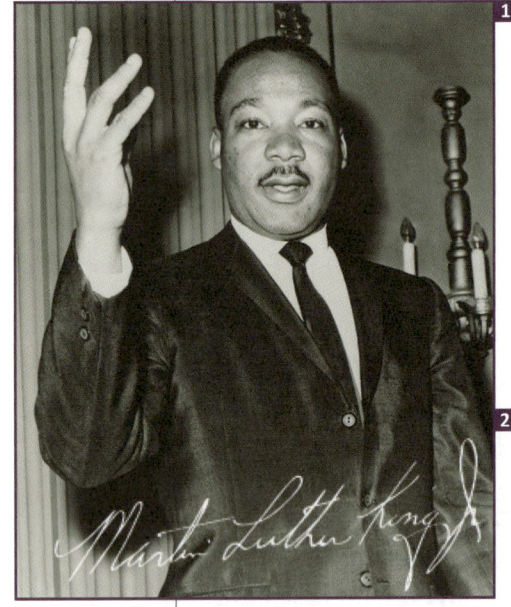

∧ Martin Luther King, Jr. (1929—1968)

» President Johnson signs the Civil Rights Act of 1964. Among the guests behind him is Martin Luther King Jr. (Wikipedia)

> King is most famous for his "I Have a Dream" speech, given during the 1963 March on Washington for Jobs and Freedom.

King at the Civil Rights March on Washington, D.C., 1963

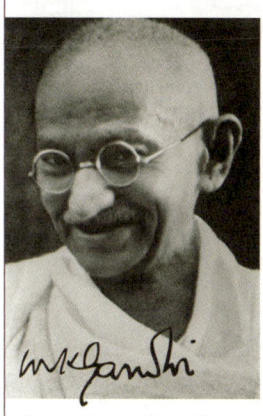

Martin Luther King was greatly inspired by Gandhi.

and theologian at Boston University, who taught King about the nonviolent activism of Mahatma Gandhi. King once stated that he was "convinced . . . that the method of nonviolent resistance is the most potent weapon available to oppressed people in their struggle for justice. . . . "

4 In 1957, King helped found the Southern Christian Leadership Conference (SCLC). The SCLC organized and led marches for desegregation and worked to secure blacks' voting and labor rights. King led the SCLC until his death, and was arrested numerous times for his participation in its activities.

5 During the March on Washington for Jobs and Freedom in 1963, King delivered his famous "I Have a Dream" speech at the Lincoln Memorial before an estimated 250,000 people. The 17-minute speech is widely considered to be one of the most inspiring of all time.

6 In 1964, King was awarded the Nobel Peace Prize for leading non-violent opposition to racial prejudice in the United States. As a result of the civil rights movement spearheaded by the SCLC, the Civil Rights Act of 1964 and the Voting Rights Act of 1965 were enacted into law.

7 On April 4th, 1968, while standing on the balcony of his motel in Memphis, Tennessee, where he had gone to support black sanitary public works employees, King was shot and killed by an assassin. The previous evening, he had delivered his "I've Been to the Mountaintop" address, saying, ". . . we, as a people, will get to the promised land."

» Martin Luther King Jr.'s tomb, located on the grounds of the Martin Luther King, Jr. National Historic Site in Atlanta, Georgia (Wikipedia)

Questions

1. What is the most likely reason Martin Luther King, Jr. first became interested in social protest?
   a. He was named after a famous Protestant reformer.
   b. He learned about it at Crozer Theological Seminary.
   c. He personally experienced racism while growing up.
   d. He was a great admirer of Mahatma Gandhi.

2. What did King do as a result of his desire to serve other people?
   a. He became a minister.
   b. He earned a doctoral degree.
   c. He made many speeches.
   d. He excelled at his studies.

» Martin Luther King, Jr. and Malcolm X, March 26, 1964

˅ The Civil Rights March, Alabama in 1965 (Wikipedia)

» Protestors at the 2012 Republican National Convention display Dr. King's words and image on a banner. (Wikipedia)

_____ 3. Who gave King the idea to use nonviolent methods of protest?
   a. Martin Luther.
   b. His father.
   c. Howard Thurman.
   d. Lincoln.

_____ 4. Why was the Civil Rights Act of 1964 made into a law?
   a. Because Martin Luther King, Jr. was arrested many times.
   b. Because King's "I Have a Dream" speech was so inspiring.
   c. Because of the influence of the civil rights movement.
   d. Because King had won the Nobel Peace Prize.

_____ 5. What is the most likely reason for King's assassination?
   a. Memphis, Tennessee, is a very dangerous city.
   b. King had worked to secure equal rights for black people.
   c. Someone disliked the "I Have a Dream" address.
   d. Someone was jealous of King's prominence.

« King speaking to an anti-Vietnam war rally at the University of Minnesota, 1967 (Wikipedia)

117

» A highly sensitive person feel things more deeply.

35 Super Sensitive Souls

1 My friend Jenny has a kind of superpower—she feels things more deeply than others. She can enter a room and sense the mood instantly. She can empathize with anybody, as if absorbing their feelings. When she walks in the countryside, she notices birds singing, colors changing, tiny fluctuations in temperature. She's a painter and a poet, and she thinks deeply about her own experiences and ideas. She dreams vividly every night. Jenny, like about 15 percent of all human beings, is an HSP—a highly sensitive person.

2 The brain of an HSP is wired differently from that of most people. Certain genes possessed by HSPs affect the way their brains respond to neurochemicals, how active certain neurons in their brains are, and how sensitive certain areas of their brains are to emotional stimuli. This means that HSPs feel not only positive emotions and physical sensations more intensely but also stress, pain, and negative stimuli such as loud noises or uncomfortable clothing. Overstimulation of this sort can lead to HSPs feeling quickly overwhelmed or drained by situations that less sensitive

« HSP may feel physical sensations more intensely than others.

people would find perfectly ordinary or easily bearable. Timed tests, being criticized, conflict at work, even getting a new job or promotion—all these can be extremely uncomfortable and stressful for an HSP, even making them feel physically sick. Too much of this too often can actually cause an HSP to succumb to mental illness such as depression or anxiety.

3 Doesn't that mean that having such a high level of sensitivity is more of a curse than a superpower? Not necessarily. There are several things HSPs can do to manage the more negative aspects of their super sensitivity.

4 HSPs are advised to reduce the number of intense stimuli in their environment—such as noise-making appliances, rough furniture, or bright wallpaper. They are also encouraged to focus on one task at a time to avoid becoming overwhelmed. Exercising their creativity, by writing, painting, or drawing can also help declutter their thoughts and help with their habit of overthinking. For their low pain tolerance, meditation can be highly beneficial, helping them to detach from any negative physical sensations.

5 An HSP can be a wonderful friend, who understands you better than anyone else. But they need care, too. So spare a thought for any HSPs in your life and make an effort to be considerate to their needs. After all, having more attentive, sensitive people functioning in our society will certainly make it a more pleasant place for everyone.

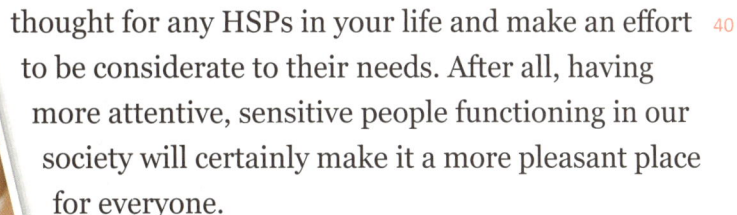

«∨ Timed tests and conflict at work can be very stressful for an HSP.

HSP can exercise their creativity by writing, painting, or drawing

Questions

1. What is stated as the root cause of an HSPs unique brain function?
   a. Negative stimuli.
   b. Certain genes.
   c. Fluctuations in temperature.
   d. Positive emotions.

2. Which of the following does NOT result from having a highly sensitive brain?
   a. Having a high level of empathy.
   b. Dreaming vividly.
   c. Having a low pain tolerance.
   d. Making loud noises.

3. Which of the following does the author think will result from people being more considerate towards HSPs?
   a. A more pleasant society for us all.
   b. More HSPs being promoted at work.
   c. An increase in mental illnesses among HSPs.
   d. A rise in the number of HSPs.

Are You Highly Sensitive?

Copyright, Elaine N. Aron, 1996

Instructions: Answer each question according to the way you personally feel. Check the box if it is at least somewhat true for you; leave unchecked if it is not very true or not at all true for you.

If you are a parent trying to evaluate your child, please use the test "**Is Your Child Highly Sensitive?**"

- ☐ I am easily overwhelmed by strong sensory input.
- ☐ I seem to be aware of subtleties in my environment.
- ☐ Other people's moods affect me.
- ☐ I tend to be very sensitive to pain.
- ☐ I find myself needing to withdraw during busy days, into bed or into a darkened room or any place where I can have some privacy and relief from stimulation.
- ☐ I am particularly sensitive to the effects of caffeine.
- ☐ I am easily overwhelmed by things like bright lights, strong smells, coarse fabrics, or sirens close by.

⌃ There are tests to see if one's a highly sensitive person.
(designed by Elaine N. Aron, 1996) (retrieved from https://hsperson.com/test/highly-sensitive-test/)

_____ 4. Which of the following would NOT cause high levels of stress for an HSP?
   a. Taking a timed test.
   b. Getting a new job.
   c. Meditating.
   d. Being criticized.

_____ 5. Which of the following sentences suggests a cause-and-effect relationship?
   a. "The brain of an HSP is wired differently from most people."
   b. "Overstimulation of this sort can lead to HSPs feeling quickly overwhelmed. . . ."
   c. "An HSP can be a wonderful friend, who understands you better than anyone else."
   d. "Jenny, like about 15 percent of all humans, is an HSP—a highly sensitive person."

Unit 1 Reading Skills

1-7 Cause and Effect

121

1-8 Finding Bias

Writers have their own experiences, opinions, and beliefs. When you add all these together, they form a bias, or a particular point of view. Discovering a writer's bias can sometimes be difficult, but a good place to start is the language used and whether or not the writer portrays both sides of an argument fairly.

36 Nothing but the Best for Mr. Whiskers

The pet industry has been growing at a rate of 14 percent per year.

1 Once relegated to the roles of house guards or pest catchers, pets are increasingly being treated as part of the family. If, like me, you're one of those people who love to spoil their pets rotten, you are probably a large contributor to the growing pet economy. This industry based around our four-legged friends is currently undergoing a massive boom—particularly in Asia, where it's growing at a rate of around 14 percent per year.

2 In order to cater to this growing number of relatively well-off pet-focused consumers, high-quality pet products are becoming ever more readily available. And with people caring more about their pets' health and therefore the quality of their food, branding has become vitally important, with a focus on building consumer trust. In some cases, local food scandals have led pet owners to abandon local brands and pay a premium for food produced in countries with higher food safety standards. You can never be too careful when the health of your pet is concerned.

» different kinds of pets

» More and more people treat their pets as part of the family.

3   Indeed, with such a large new customer base to cater to, many companies are scrambling to adapt to the modern marketplace. Once upon a time, we all did our shopping at our local pet store. Now, with the proliferation of e-commerce, the pet economy has been forced to migrate online. Some large pet-product brands, however, still lack a strong online presence. But with customers such as myself preferring the convenience of online order and delivery rather than trekking back and forth to the pet store, they'd better shape up if they want to stay competitive.

4   And it's not just pet products that are booming. Once a niche market, pet services such as grooming, pet spas, and training are also more in demand than ever. This trend, though good for the pet economy, is one that many passionate pet owners rightly frown upon, as it cultivates an idea of pets as objects to be owned and shown off on social media, like handbags or jewellery, rather than as beloved family members.

5   That aside, for those of us who just want the best for our pets, the growth of the pet economy is something of a godsend. And while some of the products can be expensive, we don't complain. For us, being stingy towards our pets just isn't an option.

» Pet services are also more in demand than ever.

123

» Some people prefer doing shopping at a local pet store.

Questions

_____ 1. Which of the following does the author show bias against?
   a. Spoiling pets.
   b. Buying expensive goods for pets.
   c. Treating pets like objects.
   d. Treading pets like members of the family.

_____ 2. Which of the following does the author show bias towards?
   a. Paying more for trusted brands.
   b. Raising pets in the city.
   c. Buying pet food at a local store.
   d. Taking pets to a pet spa.

_____ 3. What kind of statement is "for us, being stingy towards our pets just isn't an option," in the final paragraph?
   a. One of argument.
   b. One of fact.
   c. One of bias.
   d. One of prediction.

_____ 4. Which of the following is a biased word?
   a. Undergoing.
   b. Branding.
   c. Preferring.
   d. Building.

_____ 5. Which of the following best represents the author's bias in the passage?
   a. " . . . for those of us who just want the best for our pets, the growth of the pet economy is something of a godsend . . ."
   b. ". . . with such a large new customer base to cater to, many companies are scrambling to adapt to the modern marketplace."
   c. "Now, with the proliferation of e-commerce, the pet economy has been forced to migrate online."
   d. "Once a niche market, pet services such as grooming, pet spas, and training are more in demand than ever . . ."

37 Salvaged, Served, Savored

1   "Don't waste your food! There are people starving in the world!" I, like doubtless many others, had these words shouted at me as a child whenever I felt too full to finish my dinner. As a child, I never really took those words to heart, but after growing up and learning more about food production, my eyes have been well and truly opened. According to the UN, around 30 percent of all food produced globally is wasted. That's almost a third—a truly terrifying statistic!

2   Customers prefer the prettiest products, so a lot of the "uglier" food is dumped even before it gets to our supermarkets. Shame on us for being so shallow. After all, doesn't a crooked carrot taste the same as a straight one? And if the food makes it to the supermarket, what do you think happens to it if it isn't sold by the end of the day? It goes straight in the dumpster for not being "fresh" and is eventually burned. This practice wastes not only food but also money and energy. It even causes harm to the atmosphere. The thought of it really makes my blood boil.

▲ Around 30% of all food produced globally is wasted.

3   Thank goodness some people are doing something about it. In many countries around the world, charitable organizations exist that work tirelessly to salvage perfectly edible food that would otherwise be wasted. This food, collected from restaurants, grocery stores, and farmers' markets, is often donated to food banks and homeless shelters, so that people who know the true value of food can enjoy it. In fact, we should all be tucking in to salvaged food, not just the homeless and hungry. If restaurant customers would get over their snobbishness, they could go a long way to cutting food waste by a huge margin. One organization in the Netherlands, called Instock, is already doing sterling work in this area. The organization collects surplus food from 160 grocery stores across the Netherlands, which it then uses in one of its three fashionable restaurants. The hope is that by serving salvaged food in a high-end restaurant setting, the stigma of rescued food will finally disappear for good.

4   In the future, I hope we'll live in a society where no edible product ends its life in an incinerator. After all, with all the potential for consuming salvaged food, there is absolutely no good reason why it ever should.

⌃ Instock restaurant in Netherlands, which collects surplus food from grocery stores and uses it.

▽ Some food may end up in the dumpster for not being beautiful enough.

Questions

____ 1. In the passage the author shows a clear bias against which of the following?
   a. Food salvage.
   b. Food waste.
   c. Fashionable restaurants.
   d. The Netherlands.

____ 2. Which of these sentences from the passage does NOT show bias?
   a. "Shame on us for being so shallow."
   b. "The thought of it really makes my blood boil."
   c. "If restaurant customers would get over their snobbishness. . . ."
   d. "According to the UN, around 30 percent of all food produced globally is wasted."

____ 3. "The organization collects surplus food from 160 grocery stores across the Netherlands." What kind of sentence is this?
   a. One of fact.
   b. One of bias.
   c. One of opinion.
   d. One of argument.

____ 4. The sentence "After all, doesn't a crooked carrot taste the same as a straight one?" demonstrates the author's bias against which of the following?
   a. People who dislike carrots.
   b. People who buy crooked vegetables.
   c. People who only buy "beautiful" vegetables.
   d. People who eat meat.

____ 5. What kind of tone does the writer have towards people who waste food?
   a. Tragic.
   b. Understanding.
   c. Hostile.
   d. Formal.

Unit 1 Reading Skills
1-8 Finding Bias

127

38 Convenience on Every Corner

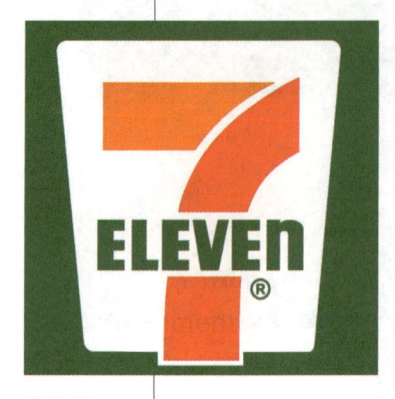

1 For anyone in Taiwan, 7-Eleven is far more than just the island's largest convenience store chain. It has been such a big part of Taiwanese life for so long that chances are you cannot even remember when the first one opened in your neighborhood.

2 Who among us doesn't appreciate the easy access, quick service, and fair, uniform prices of 7-Elevens everywhere? Our stomachs can be filled with an array of packaged meals ready to be microwaved at the counter. Our utility bills and parking fees can be paid right to the cashiers. We can buy bus, train, and movie tickets from an in-store machine which also enables us to print, scan and/or fax documents on an adjoining photocopier. We can even send and receive packages when a trip to the post office is too . . . well, inconvenient. And if we don't have enough money on us to pay for all of this, an ATM is just a few feet away.

3 7-Eleven's fabulous success story began in 1927, when Joe C. Thompson of the Southland Ice Company in Dallas, Texas, began selling milk, bread, and eggs on Sundays and evenings when grocery stores were closed. Thompson eventually bought Southland with the aim of opening small convenience stores to sell commonly needed items. These shops were originally called Tote'm stores, as customers toted away the items they had purchased. In 1946, Thompson

↑ 7-Eleven logo

» 7-Eleven in Squamish, Canada

7-Eleven in New York

« 7-Eleven in Hong Kong

» We can buy movie tickets from an in-store machine as well as print a document on an adjoining photocopier. (cc by Desmond Chieng)

extended the stores' operating hours, from 7:00 a.m. till 11:00 p.m., and changed their name to advertise this fact. Today, the name is still the same, but the stores are now open around the clock.

4 By the end of 2018, there were 67,480 7-Eleven stores in 17 countries, including over 5,200 in Taiwan. The company has seen dramatic growth in Asia in recent decades and is, in fact, now Japanese-owned. It is worth noting that 7-Elevens in the United States offer none of the extra services available at their counterparts in Asia, though it seems to me that they certainly should!

5 Unsurprisingly, many people now want to run 7-Eleven franchises. For new franchisees, six weeks' training is provided at local training centers. After "graduation," the company's support continues with evaluations, periodic newsletters, business meetings, safety and security information, a toll-free phone line, and purchasing collaboration. It's no wonder 7-Eleven is so prosperous; besides being invaluable to customers, it takes good care of those who choose to join its ranks.

« inside a 7-Eleven

» Many 7-Elevens are equipped with an ATM.

↑ 7-Eleven in Denmark

Questions

_____ 1. In this passage, the author displays a bias toward which of the following?
  a. Grocery stores.
  b. Post offices.
  c. Supermarkets.
  d. Convenience stores.

_____ 2. Which of the following is a biased word?
  a. Packaged.   b. Adjoining.   c. Fabulous.   d. Available.

_____ 3. In the passage, the author displays a bias against which of the following?
  a. People who work at 7-Elevens.   b. Asian 7-Eleven stores.
  c. American 7-Eleven stores.   d. People who shop at 7-Elevens.

_____ 4. In the final paragraph, the author writes "It's no wonder 7-Eleven is so prosperous." What kind of statement is this?
  a. One of bias.
  b. One of fact.
  c. One of argument.
  d. One of explanation.

_____ 5. Which of the following excerpts best represents the author's bias in this passage?
  a. "For anyone in Taiwan, 7-Eleven is far more than just the island's largest convenience store chain."
  b. "Who among us doesn't appreciate the easy access, quick service, and fair, uniform prices of 7-Elevens everywhere?"
  c. "Thompson eventually bought Southland with the aim of opening small convenience stores to sell commonly needed items."
  d. "By the end of 2018, there were 67,480 7-Eleven stores in 17 countries, including over 5,200 in Taiwan."

39
Do You Like Me Now?

≈ the like button

[1]   Hitting the "like" button on a post you approve of has become almost like second nature for most of us who belong to a social media site. A "like" here, a "like" there—pretty harmless, right? In fact, this seemingly innocuous act provides data miners with more than enough information to build an entire picture of who you are, whether you want to share that data or not.

[2]   A 2013 study revealed that by using computer programs to look for connections between seemingly unrelated things, such as having a high IQ and a love for curly fries, data miners could infer all sorts of information about an individual just from what he or she had "liked" online. The scope of the inferred information was shown to be truly broad—not just relatively simple things like age, gender, or political leanings, but also things like whether someone used addictive substances and even whether an individual's parents would stay together until the person turned 21 years old. It's enough to send shivers down your spine!

[3]   Most of us have by now had the experience of being targeted by ads that seem to know exactly what we want before we've even shared our desires with those closest to us. I once received targeted ads for a trip to Europe before I'd even mentioned the idea to my partner! Is it any wonder, then, that advertisers seem to have such uncanny predictive

˄ Modern people are used to using social media.

˄ The social interactions we have on social media determine the types of advertisements we see.

powers if all they need to know what we most deeply want and think is revealed to them in our easily accessible, publicly available likes?

[4] And while you might be fine with advertisers knowing so much about you, what about government agencies or malicious groups? What if interested parties could use this data to influence not just what you buy but also how you think about key issues, even how you vote in elections!

[5] The more you think about it, the more sinister the possibilities become. But is there anything you can do about it? Going into your privacy settings and finding an option that disables third-party access to your data might limit some of the damage, but in reality, social media sites have become so open to data exploitation that really the only way to keep your information safe is to remain inactive. It's a question only you can answer: what's of greater value to you, your personal data or your social media presence?

˅ Different kinds of social media.

Web Promotion
Social Media Marketing

» Businesses use social media to advertise to their target customers.

▲ Data miners collect information on users' tastes and habits from social media sites.

Unit 1 — Reading Skills
1-8 Finding Bias

Questions

1. In the passage, the author shows bias against which of the following?
   a. Voting.
   b. Privacy.
   c. Exploiting personal data.
   d. Online shopping.

2. Which of the following is the author in favor of?
   a. "Liking" posts.
   b. Abandoning social media.
   c. Targeted ads.
   d. Influencing votes.

3. Which of the following is a biased word?
   a. Sinister.
   b. Accessible.
   c. Simple.
   d. Unrelated.

4. Which of the following is a biased statement?
   a. "The scope of the inferred information was shown to be truly broad. . . ."
   b. "Hitting the 'like' button on a post you approve of has become almost like second nature. . . ."
   c. "It's enough to send shivers down your spine!"
   d. "Most of us have by now had the experience of being targeted by ads. . . ."

5. What kind of tone does the author create in this passage?
   a. One of enthusiasm and support.
   b. One of being under threat.
   c. One of intense sadness.
   d. One of optimism for the future.

133

40 A Plant-tastic Solution for Global Warming

1   Some willfully blind sceptics aside, most of us by now have accepted that global warming is a fact—and a very worrying one at that. Further, there is overwhelming evidence that global warming is caused by human activity, or more specifically, the releasing of greenhouse gases—which trap the sun's heat and reflect it back towards the earth—into the atmosphere. The most efficient way to combat greenhouse gases would be for humans to reduce their carbon emissions—ideally by 50 percent. However, with a growing global population, this is not looking very likely.

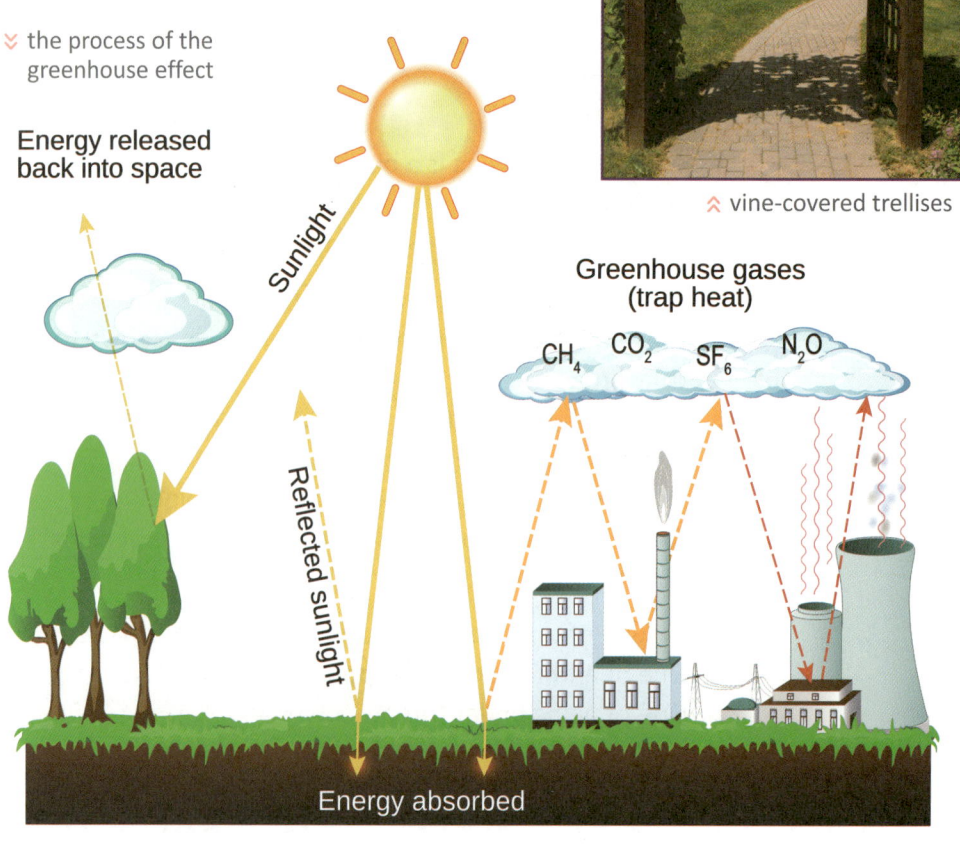

⌄ the process of the greenhouse effect

Energy released back into space

Sunlight

Reflected sunlight

Greenhouse gases (trap heat)

CH_4 CO_2 SF_6 N_2O

Energy absorbed

⌃ vine-covered trellises

▲ Plants could help reduce the amount of CO2 in the atmosphere.

Perhaps the problem can be solved in a different way: by removing large amounts of greenhouse gases, carbon dioxide (CO2) in particular, from the air and then keeping it safely locked away.

2   One of our greatest allies in this mission to trap CO2 is plants. As part of their food cycle, known as photosynthesis, plants absorb CO2 from the atmosphere. In this increasingly CO2-rich atmosphere, plants are actually becoming more efficient in processing CO2. Better photosynthesis helps them grow bigger, which in turn allows them to store even more carbon away. Should this increase in plant efficiency continue, it could actually help offset a large amount of our human carbon emissions. But many farsighted experts believe that this increase in plant efficiency will not continue indefinitely and will probably level out before it can save us all from dying of heat.

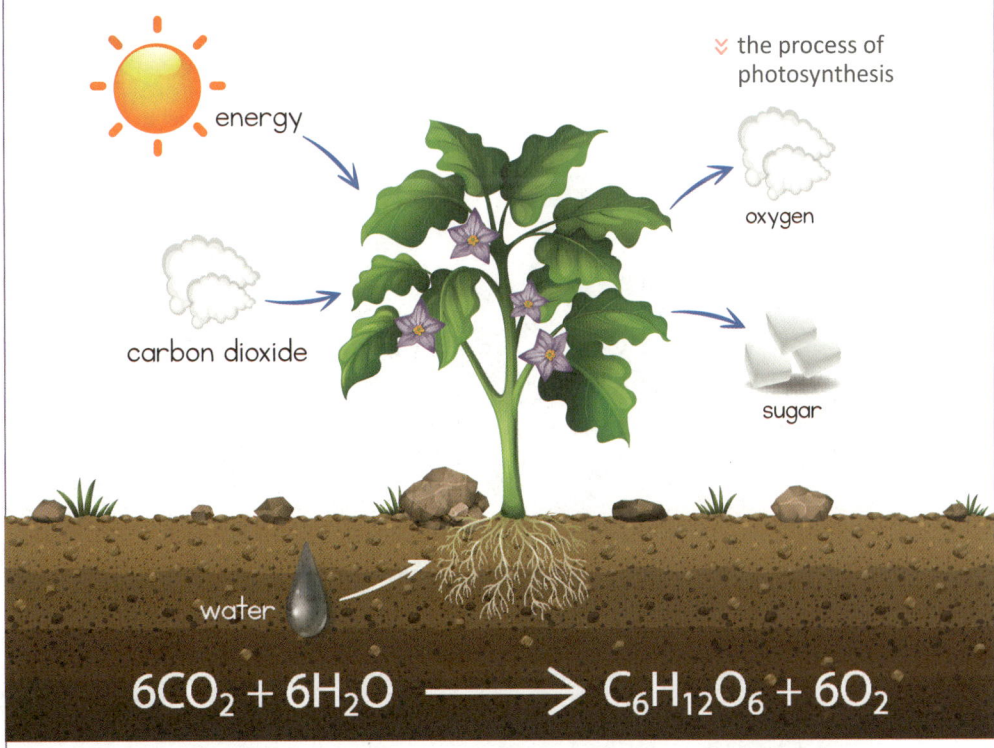

˅ the process of photosynthesis

energy

carbon dioxide

oxygen

sugar

water

$6CO_2 + 6H_2O \longrightarrow C_6H_{12}O_6 + 6O_2$

3 All is not lost, however. Pioneering researchers at the Salk Institute for Biological Studies in California are attempting to create, through a variety of genetic engineering techniques, the "Ideal Plant"—a plant that can be widely grown and has the capability of storing large amounts of carbon dioxide in its root system. In one mustard-like plant, *Arabidopsis*, scientists identified genes that would trigger the development of a deeper root system, increase root mass, and make them resistant to decay. Now the scientists' job is to find and activate similar genes in agricultural plants such as corn, wheat, and rice so that the plan can be carried out on a large enough scale to make an impact.

4 According to the researchers, with a little luck, the solution could be in our fields within a decade. We may not be out of the woods yet, but it seems that plants—and the scientists working on the project—might just be humanity's saving grace.

Arabidopsis

Increased vegetation can help cool local climates.

Questions

_____ 1. In the first paragraph, which of the following does the author show bias against?
   a. People who deny the existence of global warming.
   b. People who want to remove greenhouse gases using plants.
   c. People who are trying to reduce their own carbon emissions.
   d. People who doubt humans can sufficiently reduce their carbon emissions.

_____ 2. Which of the following sentences from the article contains authorial bias?
   a. "As part of their food cycle . . . plants absorb CO2 from the atmosphere."
   b. "In . . . *Arabidopsis*, scientists identified genes that would trigger the development of a deeper root system. . . ."
   c. "Pioneering researchers at the Salk Institute for Biological Studies in California are attempting to create . . . the 'Ideal Plant'. . . ."
   d. "Better photosynthesis helps them grow bigger, which in turn allows them to store even more carbon away."

_____ 3. Which of the following is a biased word in the article?
   a. Farsighted.   b. Mustard-like.   c. Resistant.   d. Bigger.

_____ 4. Which of the following sentences from the article does NOT contain biased language?
   a. ". . . the scientists working on the project . . . might just be humanity's saving grace."
   b. "Some willfully blind sceptics aside, most of us by now have accepted that global warming is a fact. . . ."
   c. "Further, there is overwhelming evidence that global warming is caused by human activity. . . ."
   d. "Now the scientists' job is to find and activate similar genes in agricultural plants such as corn, wheat, and rice. . . ."

_____ 5. Which of the following statements best describes the author's bias in the article?
   a. Developing plants that absorb large amounts of CO2 is going to save the world.
   b. Developing plants that absorb large amounts of CO2 is a complete waste of time.
   c. Scientists are arrogant people who don't know what they're talking about.
   d. People reducing their carbon emissions is the most effective way of stopping global warming.

1-9 Fact or Opinion

Most pieces of writing contain a mixture of facts and opinions, and it's important to be able to differentiate between the two. **Facts** are things that can be proved to be true—whether it be through tests, records, or documents—while **opinions** express the author's beliefs or judgments. Sometimes an opinion may read like a fact, but if the truth of it cannot be proved, it remains only an opinion.

⌄ Hayao Miyazaki (b. 1941)
(cc by Natasha Baucas)

41 Japan's Master of Animation

⌃ In 2005, *Time* magazine included Hayao Miyazaki in the "*Time* 100 Most Influential People."

1   Tomoyuki Sugiyama, founder of Digital Hollywood and author of the book, *Cool Japan*, believes that Japan's culture of cute has evolved as a result of a love for natural harmony. To him, "the Japanese are seeking a spiritual peace and an escape from brutal reality through cute things." The very gifted animation film director 5
Hayao Miyazaki exercises this modern global image better than anyone else. His fantasies are of profound, vibrant characters in carefully contrived stories, featuring anti-war and power-of-love themes, as well as being socially, politically, and environmentally conscious. Moreover, his characters are masterfully created, 10
infused with his own style—not like the huge-eyed characters with brightly colored, wild hair that Japanese animation is famous for, but rather with more realistic proportions found in the country's traditional artistry.

2   Hayao Miyazaki's love of art helped shape his life. Born on 15
January 5, 1941, in Tokyo, Japan, Miyazaki was raised in a nurturing family by two interesting parents: his father was director of Miyazaki Airplane, and his mother was an avid reader who doubted what was normally accepted by society. From his father, Hayao formed a love

138

« *Scarlet Pig* (1992)

» Miyazaki is the co-founder of Studio Ghibli.

スタジオジブリ
STUDIO GHIBLI

for aviation and expressed that love by drawing airplanes, thus cultivating his artistic talent.

[3] Miyazaki's thoughtful upbringing helped fuel a long and illustrious career. Besides being a director and filmmaker of animated films, Miyazaki is a screenwriter, character designer, and co-founder of Studio Ghibli, a production company and animation studio. In 1999, Miramax, a subsidiary of Walt Disney Company, released his *Princess Mononoke* in the United States, which brought him outstanding recognition in the West. Additionally, *Princess Mononoke* garnered the highest revenue in Japan until *Titanic* was shown, and it was the first animation to win "Picture of the Year" at the Japanese Academy Awards. But his most memorable film by far was 2008's *Ponyo on the Cliff by the Sea*, which he drew freehand with watercolors rather than using computer generated imagery, thereby producing a delightful aesthetic effect. His greatest visual achievement, 2001's *Spirited Away*, won him the Oscar for Best Animated Feature Film, Best Film at the Japan Academy Awards, and the 2002 Berlin Film Festival's First Prize.

[4] After finishing *The Wind Rises* in 2013, Miyazaki announced his retirement from making films, but a mind this creative can't remain inactive for long, and he is said to be working now on a new movie set for release in 2021.

⌃ *Kiki's Delivery Service* (1989)

» *Howl's Moving Castle* (2004)

⌄ *The Wind Rises* (2013)

Unit 1 Reading Skills

1-9 Fact or Opinion

139

Questions

_____ 1. 1. Which of the following is a fact?
   a. Miyazaki's fantasies are profound.
   b. Miramax released *Princess Mononoke* in 1999.
   c. A creative mind can't remain inactive for long.
   d. Miyazaki is a very gifted animation film director.

_____ 2. Which of the following is an opinion?
   a. *Spirited Away* won Best Picture at the Japan Academy Awards.
   b. Miyazaki was born on January 5, 1945.
   c. Miyazaki's father was the director of Miyazaki Airplane.
   d. *Ponyo on the Cliff by the Sea* is Miyazaki's most memorable film by far.

_____ 3. "Besides being a director and filmmaker of animated films, Miyazaki is a screenwriter, character designer, and co-founder of Studio Ghibli." This is an example of a(n) _____.
   a. fact
   b. opinion

Miyazaki's characters are unlike typical huge-eyed, colored-haired anime characters. (cc by Danny Choo)

⌃ *Spirited Away* (2001)

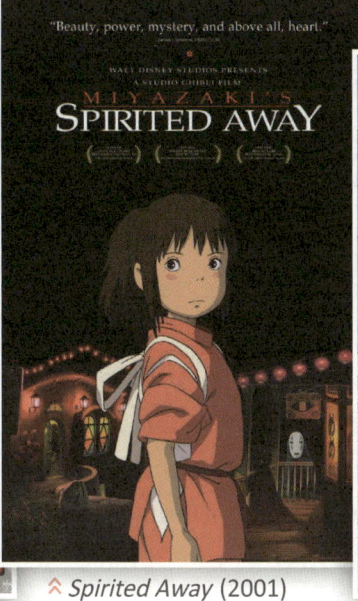

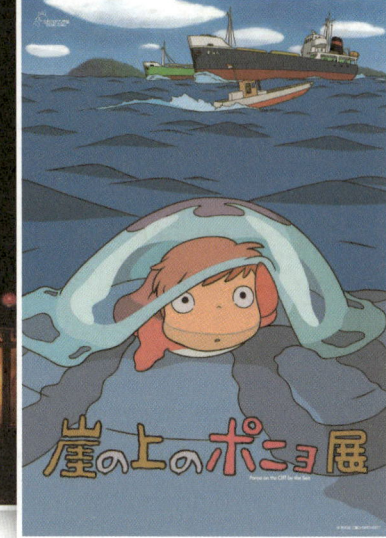

⌃ *Princess Mononoke* (1997)

⌃ *Ponyo on the Cliff by the Sea* (2008)

_____ 4. "His greatest visual achievement, 2001's *Spirited Away*. . . ." This is an example of a(n) _____.
   a. fact
   b. opinion

_____ 5. ". . . which he drew freehand with watercolors rather than using computer generated imagery. . . ." This is an example of a(n) _____.
   a. fact
   b. opinion

⌄ The store Donguri Kyouwakoku has a wide selection of Hayao Miyazaki animation toys.

141

42 One Story for All Time

1   What do *Star Wars*, the legends of King Arthur, *The Hobbit*, *The Wizard of Oz*, the Harry Potter series, and the Greek myth of Odysseus all have in common? They are all wonderful stories that have enchanted millions of readers and viewers, of course, but there's more. These stories, along with countless others throughout history, all share a common structure—the Hero's Journey.

2   First described by the mythologist Joseph Campbell in his seminal book *The Hero with a Thousand Faces* (1949), the Hero's Journey is a story pattern commonly found in works both ancient and modern. Though the name may be unfamiliar, the pattern itself will almost certainly be recognizable to you from many of your favorite stories.

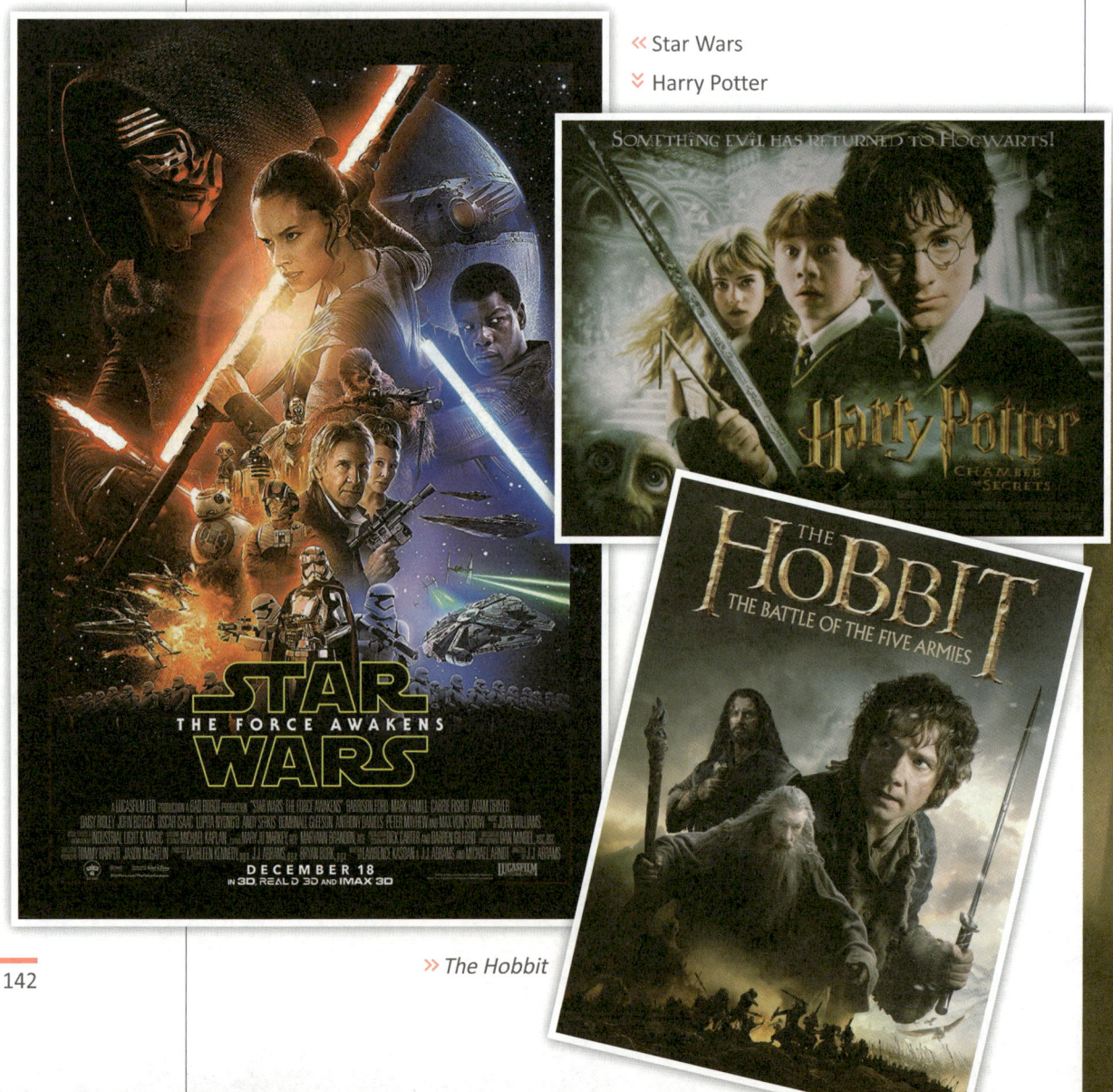

« *Star Wars*

⌄ *Harry Potter*

» *The Hobbit*

Campbell wrote that at its most basic, the Hero's Journey can be condensed into to three stages: "Departure," where the hero leaves the familiar world behind; "Initiation," where the Hero undergoes trials and proves themselves worthy; and "Return," where the hero returns home victorious. Within these three stages, Campbell identified seventeen possible plot elements, though other scholars since Campbell have created their own variations of the Hero's Journey with slight differences to Campbell's original. Most stories will include at least a handful of these elements, though the best stories will often include most if not all of them in some form or other.

3   One common element is the "Herald," who approaches the hero with a "Call to Adventure." Another, "Crossing the Threshold," is where the Hero enters a dream-like realm with strange topsy-turvy

⌄ The hero encounters challenges and ordeals on his journey.

⌄ *The Hero With A Thousand Faces* by Joseph Campbell

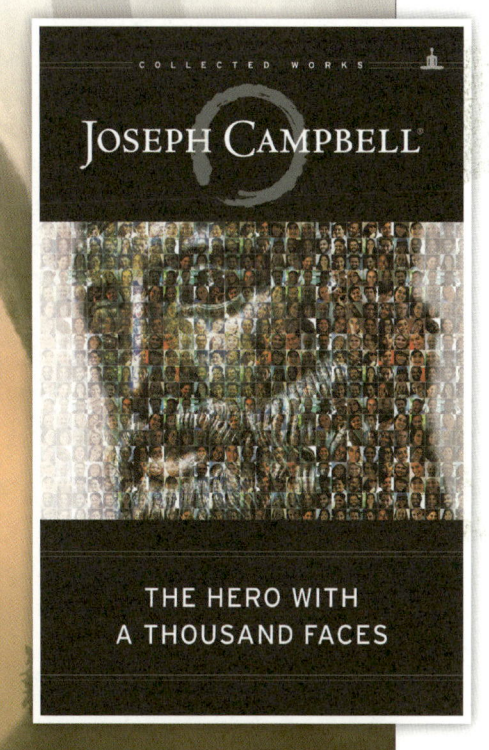

rules (Harry Potter experiencing the magical world of Hogwarts for the first time is a good example). The final "Ordeal," often a life-or-death confrontation with the main villain, is another common element in the Hero's Journey.

[4] But why is the Hero's Journey such a popular story structure? It is because this type of story connects with audiences on a deep psychological level, tapping into our own desire to become better versions of ourselves and showing us that personal growth is possible. This desire—common to all humanity—is what makes the Hero's Journey so universal and, in turn, such a powerful tool for storytellers. By mirroring the fundamental aspects of our own personal human journeys, the Hero's Journey creates stories that are able to cross both cultures and time, remaining relevant long after their authors are dead and gone. The Hero's Journey is so connected to what it means to be human that writers will undoubtedly be using it, consciously or unconsciously, for thousands of years to come.

⌄ The stages of the hero's journey

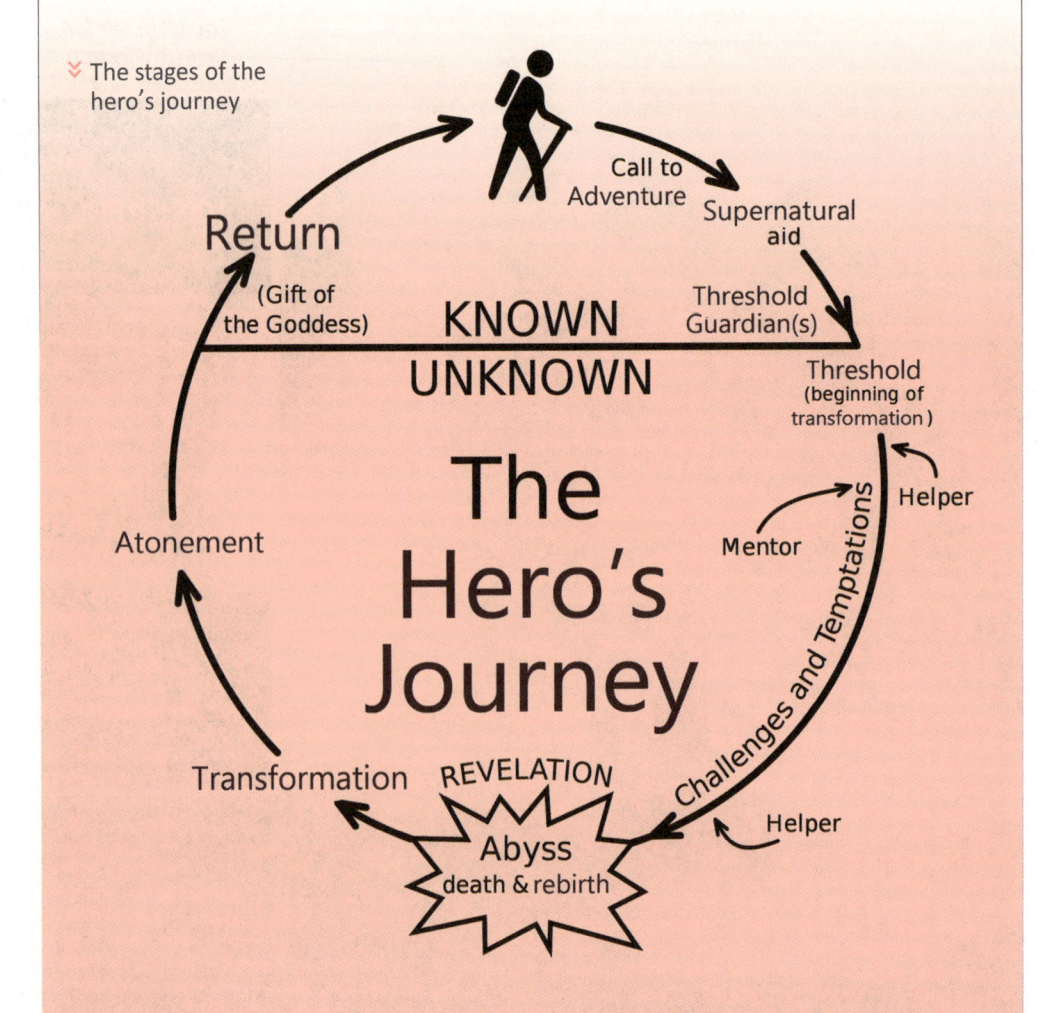

⌃ The legend of King Arthur follows the structure of the Hero's Journey.

Questions

_____ 1. Which of the following is the author's opinion?
   a. The Hero's Journey was first described by Joseph Campbell in 1949.
   b. The best stories use most if not all of the Hero's Journey's plot elements.
   c. "Crossing the Threshold" is a possible element in a Hero's Journey story.
   d. Campbell identified seventeen possible plot elements for the Hero's Journey.

_____ 2. Which of the following is NOT the author's opinion?
   a. Several writers other than Campbell have written about the Hero's Journey.
   b. The Hero's Journey connects with audiences on a deep psychological level.
   c. Harry Potter experiencing Hogwarts for the first time is a good example of "Crossing the Threshold."
   d. Star Wars and the Greek myth of Odysseus share a similar plot structure.

_____ 3. Is the statement "Though the name may be unfamiliar, the pattern itself will almost certainly be recognizable to you from many of your favorite stories" one of fact or opinion?
   a. Fact.   b. Opinion.

_____ 4. Is the statement "Campbell wrote that at its most basic, the Hero's Journey can be condensed into to three stages" one of fact or opinion?
   a. Fact.   b. Opinion.

_____ 5. Which of the following statements is a factual one?
   a. Writers will be using the Hero's Journey structure for thousands of years to come.
   b. According to Joseph Campbell, the Hero's Journey is a story pattern commonly found in works both ancient and modern.
   c. The Hero's Journey is an incredibly powerful tool for storytellers.
   d. Stories that use the Hero's Journey remain relevant long after their authors are dead.

> Amazon Go in Seattle, Washington

43 A Revolution in Convenience

1 Imagine going into a store, taking whatever you need, and then walking out without paying anyone. No, this isn't a crime being committed. Rather, it is a revolutionary new shopping concept from the US company Amazon. The stores are called Amazon Go, and if you haven't heard of them yet, you are definitely going to be hearing about them soon.

2 Unlike the online shopping platform that Amazon is famous for, Amazon Go is a real, brick-and-mortar location that customers can visit. The stores offer a variety of delicious treats to nibble on. There are ready-to-eat meals for breakfast, lunch, and dinner. You will also find basic groceries like bread, milk, cheese, and chocolate. And for those who love to cook, the stores sell kits with all the necessary ingredients for a full meal.

3 What you buy is the boring part, but how you buy it—now that is the real thrill! Every customer at an Amazon Go store must install a special app on their smartphone. When

> the Amazon Go app

⌄ inside an Amazon Go

shoppers arrive, they use the app to enter the store. Then it is simply a matter of finding what they need. When a customer takes something off the shelf, weight sensors will detect what it is and add the item to their virtual shopping cart. Should they put it back, the item will be removed from the cart. And when they leave the store, their Amazon account will be charged. The app keeps track of all the purchases; no cash or credit card is required!

4 As of early 2019, Amazon Go is still in the early testing phase, with just 10 locations spread out across Seattle, Chicago, and San Francisco. But there are plans to expand to as many as 3,000 stores by 2021. Before long, Amazon Go convenience stores might be as common as 7-Eleven or Family Mart branches.

« The weight sensor will detect the product when customers take something off the shelf.

5 Some people are concerned about Amazon Go and similar technological advances that minimize human labor. They argue that cashier and salesperson are two of the most common jobs, and eliminating them could trigger mass unemployment. But these people are completely misguided. There are still some human workers at Amazon Go locations, like the chefs who prepare the meals. And no one should stand in the way of progress. Change is coming; it has been since the invention of online shopping. So I say the sooner there's an Amazon Go in my neighborhood, the better.

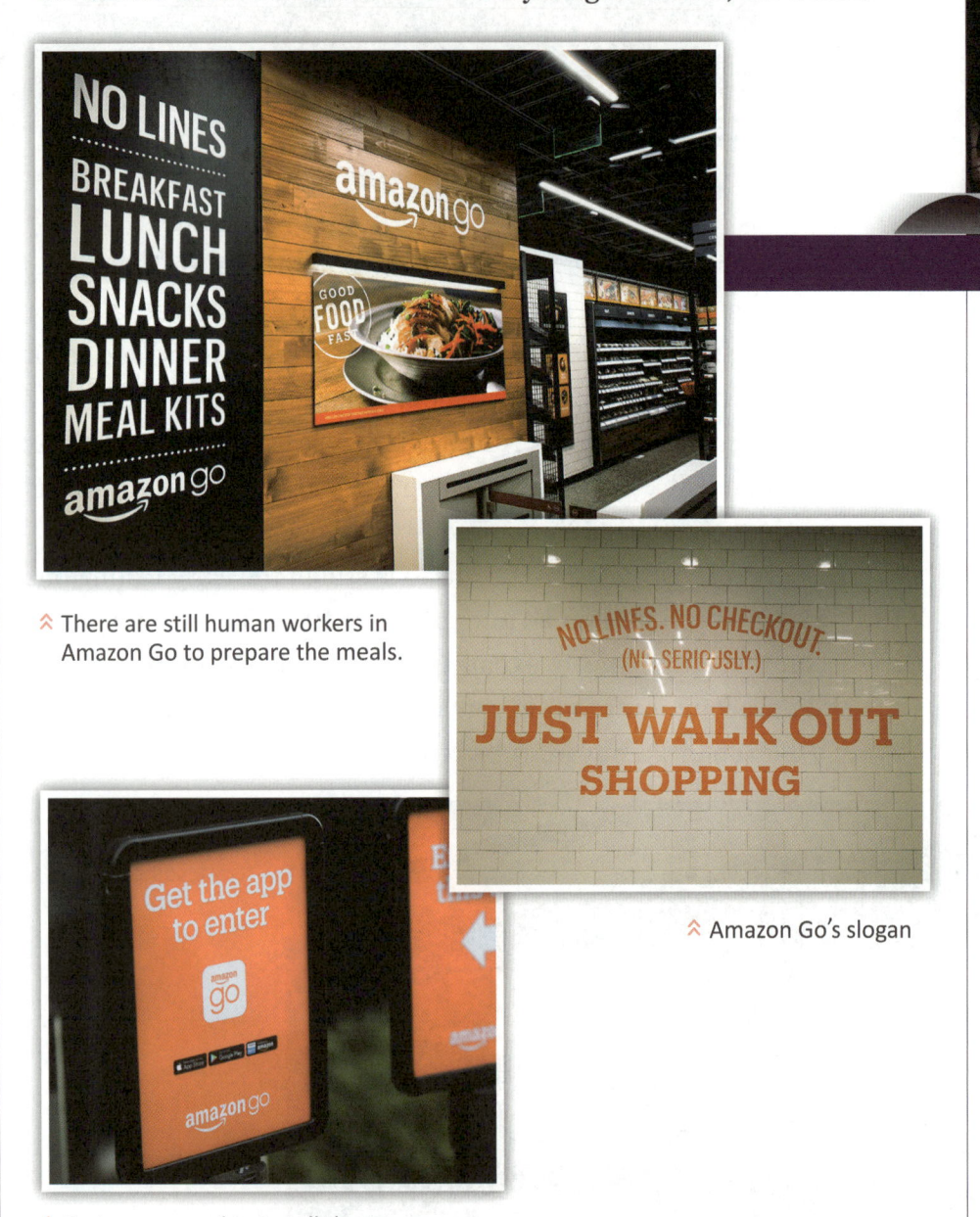

⌃ There are still human workers in Amazon Go to prepare the meals.

⌃ Amazon Go's slogan

⌃ Customers need to install the Amazon Go app to enter.

↑ the entrance and exit turnstiles at Amazon Go

Questions

_____ 1. Which of the following is a fact?
  a. Before long, Amazon Go stores might be as common as 7-Eleven branches.
  b. The sooner there's an Amazon Go in my neighborhood, the better.
  c. Right now Amazon Go is in the early testing phase.
  d. The stores offer a variety of delicious treats to nibble on.

_____ 2. Which of the following is an opinion?
  a. No one should stand in the way of progress.
  b. When customers leave the store, their Amazon account is charged.
  c. Amazon Go is a brick-and-mortar location that customers can visit.
  d. There are ready-to-eat meals for breakfast, lunch, and dinner.

_____ 3. Which of the following is a fact?
  a. Amazon Go is a revolutionary shopping concept from Amazon.
  b. You'll find basic groceries like milk and cheese at Amazon Go.
  c. You're definitely going to hear about Amazon Go in the future.
  d. What you buy at Amazon Go is the boring part.

_____ 4. What is the sentence in the second paragraph: "The stores sell kits with all the necessary ingredients for a full meal"?
  a. A fact.
  b. An opinion.

_____ 5. What is the sentence in the fourth paragraph: "There are plans to expand to as many as 3,000 stores by 2021"?
  a. A fact.
  b. An opinion.

>> historical monuments

44 The Secret of the Stones

1   Located near Salisbury in southern England, Stonehenge is a curious prehistoric monument that is also a favorite destination for awe-stricken tourists and archaeologists alike. It is famous for consistently captivating people's imaginations, as it raises many questions for which there are no answers.

2   Stonehenge is situated in the center of a nearly impenetrable compound of Bronze Age and Neolithic monuments, including hundreds of burial mounds. It consists of a henge, or circle, of megaliths, which are very large stones set vertically into the ground. The prehistoric people of the area built numerous henges for use in rituals, so Stonehenge probably served a spiritual or mystical purpose.

3   The first phase of Stonehenge's construction was the digging of a circular ditch roughly 100 meters in diameter with two entrances sometime around 3000 BCE. The earth removed to make the ditch was mounded just inside and outside of it, forming two banks.

≫ Stonehenge is a UNESCO world heritage site in England.

Seven Wonders of Britain

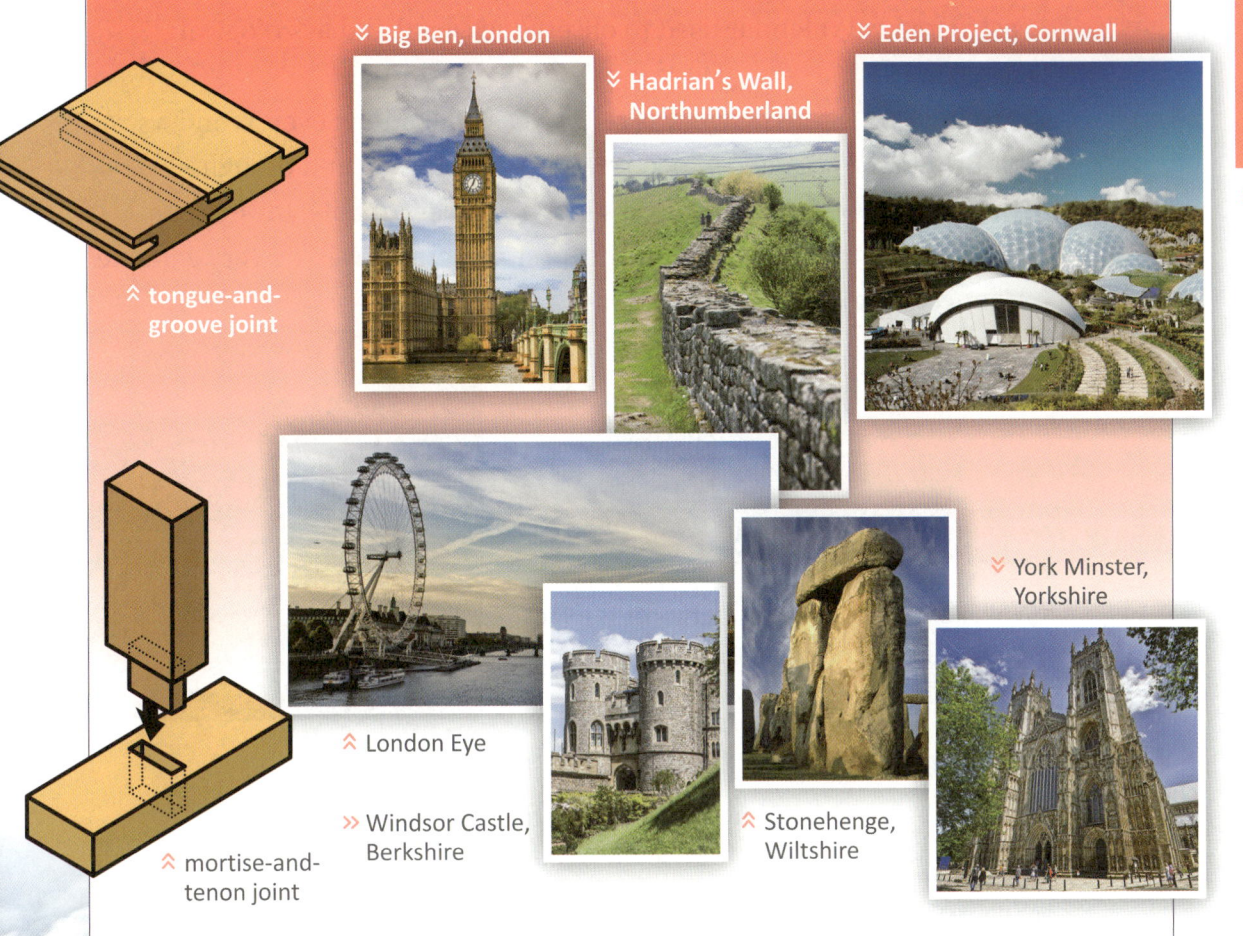

⌄ Big Ben, London

⌄ Hadrian's Wall, Northumberland

⌄ Eden Project, Cornwall

⌃ tongue-and-groove joint

⌃ mortise-and-tenon joint

⌃ London Eye

» Windsor Castle, Berkshire

⌃ Stonehenge, Wiltshire

⌄ York Minster, Yorkshire

4   Work on the henge itself started around 2500 BCE. Sixty huge stones, each nine meters long and weighing 25 tons, were most likely brought 32 kilometers south from a quarry at Marlborough Downs and assembled into a circle of 30 uprights and 30 lintels (the horizontal stones that lie on top of the columns). Both the columns and lintels were hammered smooth. The lintels were held in place by mortise and tenon joints, and connected to each other by tongue and groove joints.

5   People from all over the world are perplexed by the endurance and sheer magnitude of Stonehenge. How did prehistoric people transport such massive, heavy objects over what was then a great distance? Reference to research and a bit of imagination may allow us to conjure up some idea of the process, though it must have been incredibly difficult. Besides that, what was its function? Has Stonehenge been the site of UFO landings, as many believe? It was once a "certainty" that it had been used for sacrifices and ceremonies by the Druids, a mysterious ancient religious order, but that has been disproven. The prevailing idea now is that it was an advanced astronomical calendar used to observe seasonal and astrological events.

6   In 2002, Stonehenge was selected as one of the Seven Wonders of Britain. From any perspective, it is a fascinating and thought-provoking wonder. Many even say it has indescribable, mysterious powers. But for us, perhaps its deepest meaning lies in its very genuine connection to our early ancestors.

» 17th century depiction of Stonehenge

Questions

1. Which of the following statements is a fact?
   a. Stonehenge probably served a spiritual or mystical purpose.
   b. Stonehenge is located near Salisbury in southern England.
   c. Stonehenge's stones most likely came from Marlborough Downs.
   d. Stonehenge has been the site of UFO landings.

2. Which of the following statements is an opinion?
   a. Stonehenge is surrounded by Bronze Age and Neolithic monuments.
   b. Prehistoric people in southern England constructed many henges.
   c. The henge at Stonehenge started being built around 2500 BCE.
   d. Stonehenge is a fascinating and thought-provoking wonder.

3. Which of the following is NOT a statement of fact, based on the article?
   a. No one knows for certain why Stonehenge was constructed.
   b. Stonehenge was used for ceremonies by the Druids.
   c. The columns and lintels at Stonehenge were hammered smooth.
   d. People from all over the world are perplexed by Stonehenge.

4. Is the statement "Perhaps (Stonehenge's) deepest meaning lies in its very genuine connection to our early ancestors" a fact or an opinion?
   a. A fact.   b. An opinion.

5. Which of the following is a fact about Stonehenge?
   a. It is listed as one of the Seven Wonders of Britain.
   b. Everyone who sees it is awe-stricken by it.
   c. It was designed as an astronomical calendar.
   d. We don't know how the lintels on it are held in place.

> Plants have their own network to communicate with each other.

45 Welcome to the Wood Wide Web

1   In the 21st century, human beings can communicate with each other better than ever before. We pass messages and information to each other through networks of wires that span vast distances—otherwise known as the World Wide Web. When the Internet was invented, it was considered a true revolution in communication and connectivity. But as much as we'd like to congratulate ourselves on our genius as a species, we were not the first to create or use such a network. In fact, plants have been doing something similar for millions of years!

2   It's true—plants use their own version of the Internet to communicate with each other and share resources. They warn each other of threats, share nutrients with weaker relatives, and even perform "data dumps"—dumping their resources into the network when they get old or injured in order to support a new generation of plants. And it happens right beneath your feet.

« Fungi attach to a plant's root to gather water and nutrient from the soil.

3 It is all made possible by fungi. Most—almost 90% of plants, in fact—are in a symbiotic relationship with fungi. These fungi, which look like a mass of thin threads, attach themselves to a plant's roots and help it gather water and other difficult-to-obtain nutrients from the soil. The plant, in return, provides the fungi with carbohydrates. As these fungi spread out their "wires" underground, they come into contact with other "wires" and allow communication between plants. The result is the so-called Wood Wide Web!

4 That's pretty fascinating. But even more interesting is this: just like our own Internet, the Wood Wide Web has hackers! Some plants use their access to the network to spread toxic chemicals to neighboring plants in order to sabotage their competitors. Others, such as the phantom orchid, set up near a large tree, hack into the network, and steal its energy resources—just like a hacker stealing money from your online bank account!

5 The more we learn about how plants connect to each other, the more we need to rethink what exactly plants are. It is no longer useful to think of plants as single organisms. In fact, far better is to think of them as belonging to one large super-organism. And if we start thinking of plants in that way, we should probably start thinking of ourselves differently, too. With so much connectivity between us, are we still individuals, or simply parts of a larger, interconnected whole?

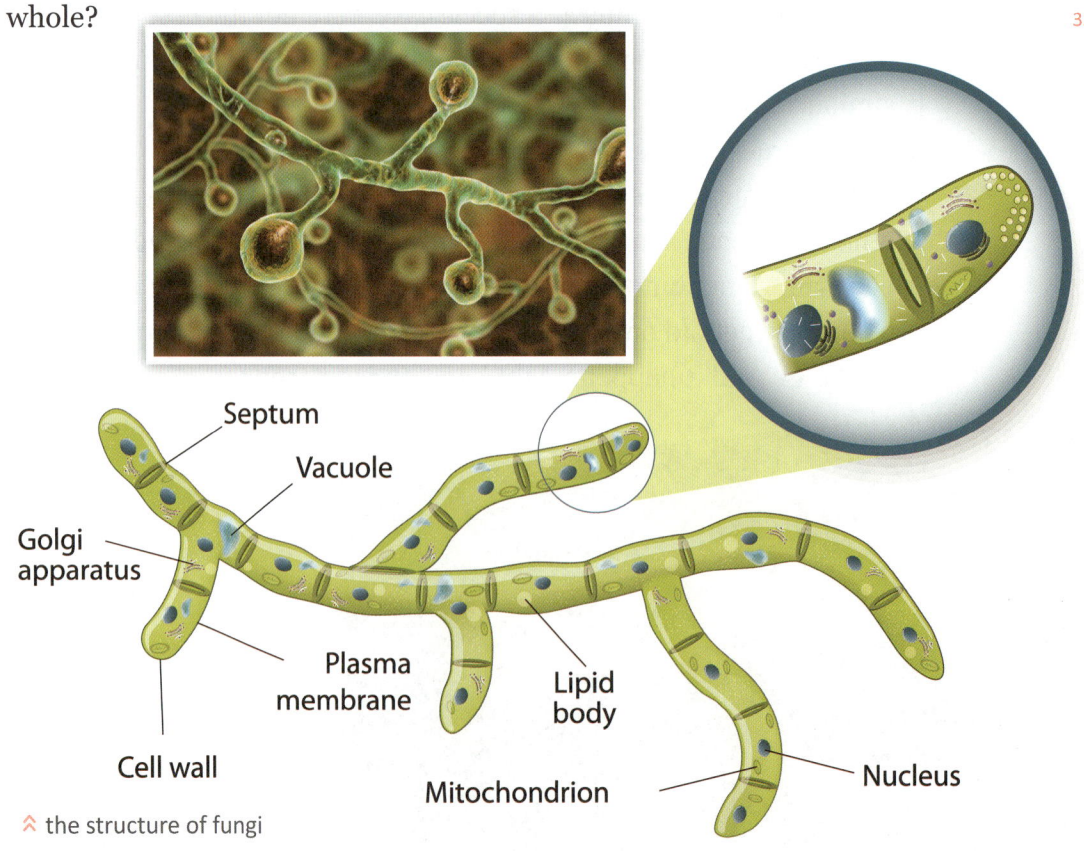

⌃ the structure of fungi

» Most fungi are inconspicuous because of the small size of their structures. (Wikipedia)

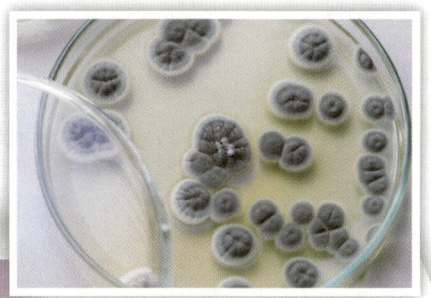

Questions

____ 1. Which of the following statements is a statement of fact?
   a. Human beings can communicate with each other better than ever before.
   b. Almost 90 percent of plants are in a symbiotic relationship with fungi.
   c. It is better to think of plants as one large super-organism.
   d. The existence of the Wood Wide Web is pretty fascinating.

____ 2. Does the sentence beginning "They warn each other of threats . . ." contain a series of facts or opinions?
   a. Facts.
   b. Opinions.

____ 3. Is the sentence "But even more interesting is this: just like our own Internet, the Wood Wide Web has hackers!" one of fact or opinion?
   a. Fact.
   b. Opinion.

____ 4. The author describes the phantom orchid as being "just like a hacker stealing money from your online bank account!" Is the author stating a fact or giving his opinion?
   a. Stating a fact.
   b. Giving his opinion.

____ 5. Which of the following sentences from the passage is a statement of opinion?
   a. "We pass messages and information to each other through networks of wires that span vast distances."
   b. "It is no longer useful to think of plants as single organisms."
   c. "Some plants use their access to the network to spread toxic chemicals to neighboring plants in order to sabotage their competitors."
   d. "The plant, in return, provides the fungi with carbohydrates."

⌄ Fungi may become noticeable when fruiting, either as mushrooms or as molds. (Wikipedia)

1-10 Review Test

>> *The Day the Earth Stood Still* movie poster

46 Is There Anybody Out There?

[1] In the 2008 movie *The Day the Earth Stood Still*, a question is posed: would a technologically superior alien race treat humans well, or would it treat us as more materially advanced people have treated primitive cultures, enslaving and slaughtering us? In the movie, the answer is ambiguous, but it seems most people believe that aliens would be benign. Perhaps this is because so many of us are anxious to make contact with extraterrestrial beings. We are not just listening for them; we're broadcasting messages to them. Is it insatiable curiosity, the demands of science, or a desire to solve the mysteries of the universe that makes us do this?

[2] The Search for Extraterrestrial Intelligence—SETI—is perhaps the world's most widely known acronym. Beyond simply using telescopes to watch stars, the SETI Institute aims radio antennas at specific areas of the sky and listens. The search began in earnest in 1960 with one channel and has been increasing in breadth and complexity ever since. Today, a single scanning device listens simultaneously to 250 million high-resolution channels and feeds the resulting data to computers loaded with powerful frequency-analyzing hardware. The computers sift through the random noise, searching for anything that appears unearthly.

[3] The project SETI@home outsources computer analysis to any volunteer with an Internet-connected computer. In March of 2003, SETI@home shocked the world by revealing that two volunteers had received potentially unearthly signals. While the results don't

necessarily mean anything, they are still exciting, and SETI@home continues to grow in both popularity and number of volunteers.

4   Active SETI, also known as METI (Messaging to Extraterrestrial Intelligence) is much bolder, and in the opinion of some scientists, such as the late Stephen Hawking, it is foolhardy. Hawking suggested that we "lay low," but in 2008 Bebo, then a social networking site, sent 501 of its users' messages to a "nearby" Earth-like planet, where they are due to arrive in 2028. Fortunately, there have been many scientific efforts to bridge the chasm of space with more intellectual content. However, their scheduled arrival dates are all much later than that of Bebo's transmission.

5   Thus far, the focus of the search for life in outer space has been almost exclusively on radio waves, because our current concept of physics is that nothing can surpass the speed of light. Therefore, with transmission times measured in decades and centuries, we might have to keep wondering until our communication technology breaks the light barrier.

« aliens

❖ SETI@home (cc by Namazu-tron)

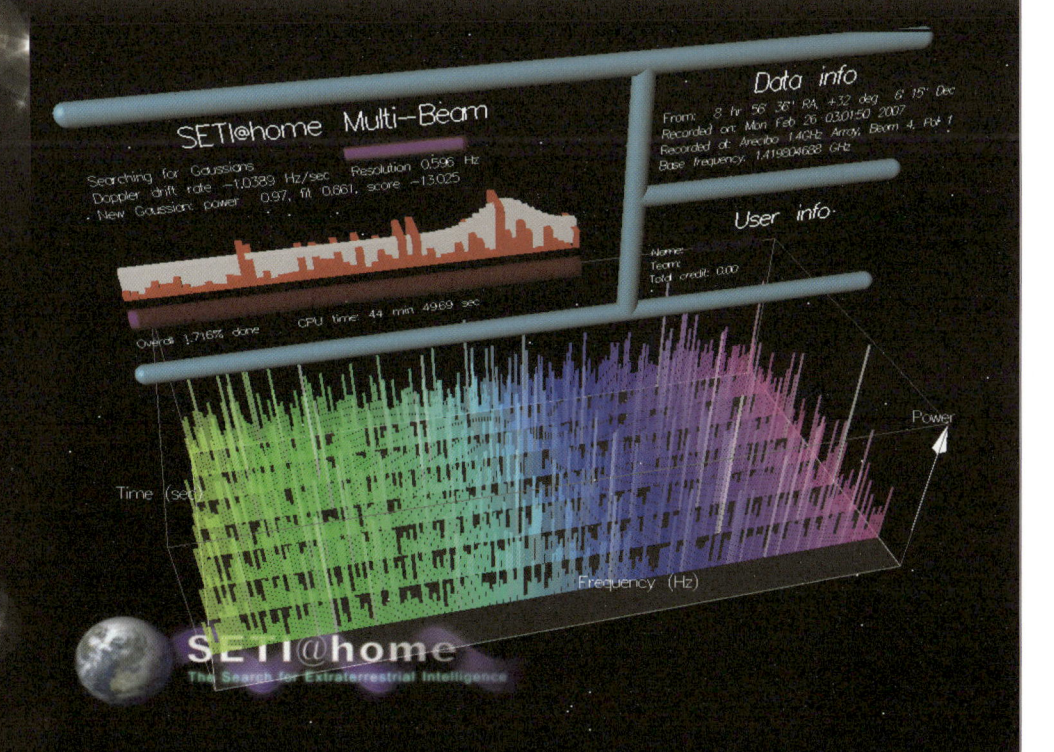

Questions

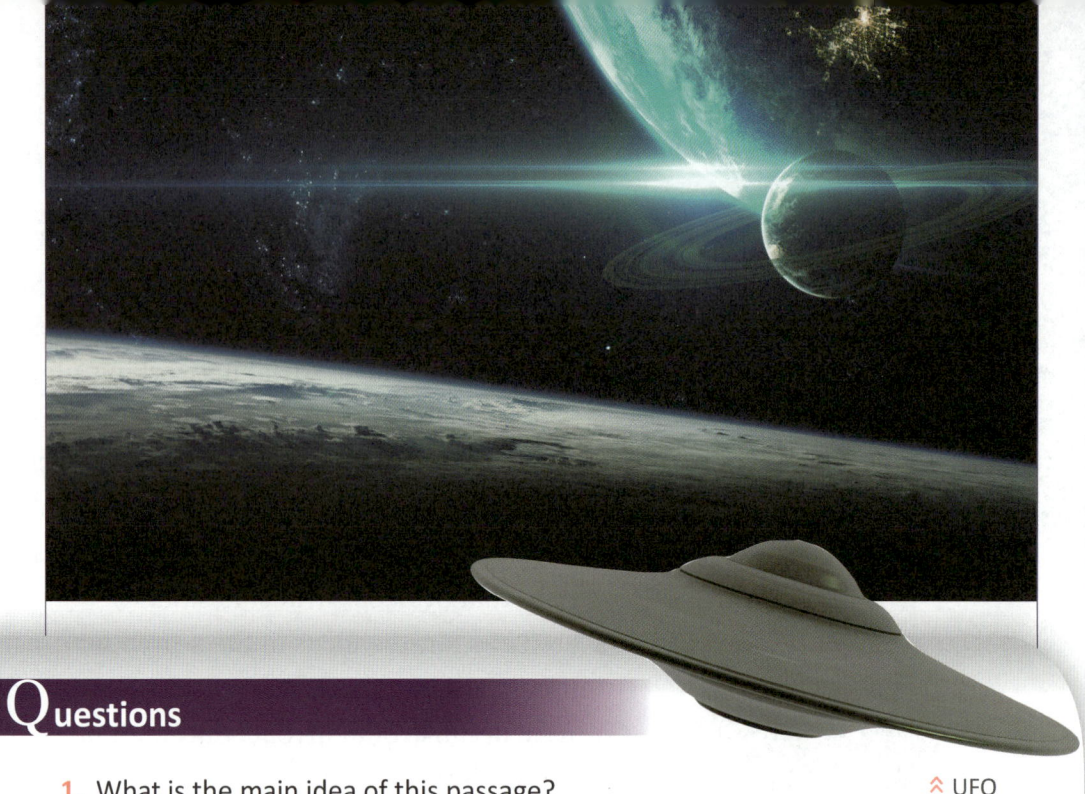

▲ UFO

____ 1. What is the main idea of this passage?
   a. *The Day the Earth Stood Still* is a good movie.
   b. The SETI Institute has grown a lot since 1960.
   c. No proof of extraterrestrial intelligence exists.
   d. Many people want to make contact with aliens.

____ 2. Which of the following statements is NOT true?
   a. SETI technology can listen to millions of radio channels.
   b. Stephen Hawking thought METI was a bad idea.
   c. Advanced cultures have treated primitive cultures badly.
   d. Bebo's message is traveling faster than the speed of light.

____ 3. What has the SETI Institute NOT done in its search for alien life?
   a. Listened to radio waves.
   b. Sent people to outer space.
   c. Observed stars with telescopes.
   d. Sent messages to other planets.

____ 4. What does the author suggest in the fourth paragraph?
   a. The Bebo transmission's content isn't very intellectual.
   b. No scientist supports the idea of messaging to outer space.
   c. Active SETI is a waste of time because of the distances involved.
   d. We are likely to receive messages from aliens within a few years.

____ 5. What is the author's purpose in writing this passage?
   a. To persuade readers to become SETI@home volunteers.
   b. To convince readers that no life exists on other planets.
   c. To tell readers the current status of the search for alien life.
   d. To make readers want to watch *The Day the Earth Stood Still*.

47 Kiss, Kiss, Hello!

1   If you have lived in Asia your whole life, you'll probably view kissing as something that is done only between lovers. You certainly wouldn't kiss a friend, not to mention someone you were meeting for the first time! Visit Europe or South America, however, and you are likely to see kisses being exchanged without a care between friends, acquaintances, and even near strangers as a common form of greeting or farewell.

2   Where does this tradition come from? Some speculate that the practice goes back to an old Catholic ritual of saluting fellow Christians with "a holy kiss," which may go some way to explain why the kiss greeting is so commonplace in the traditionally Catholic countries of South America and Southern Europe.

3   For those not used to these practices, traveling to a country where kissing is common can be a nerve-racking experience. What exactly are the rules? Who should I kiss? How many times? On the cheek or does it have to be the lips?

⌃ kiss greeting

Cheek kissing can be used as a form of greeting or farewell.

[4] Well, it's complicated. The rules are different almost everywhere you go. In much of South America, one kiss on the cheek is sufficient. In Mediterranean countries, such as Italy, Spain, and Greece, it's two kisses (one on each cheek). But in some countries, such as Belgium, Slovenia, Switzerland, and the Netherlands, you're expected to exchange three kisses!

[5] Here's how you do it: you start by leaning in and touching your right cheek to their right cheek, making a soft smacking sound with your lips. If more kisses are needed, repeat on the other cheek. There are always exceptions to the rule, however. In Italy, for example, you start with the left cheek rather than the right, and in the United Kingdom, kisses are often accompanied by a loud "mwah" sound. In terms of gender, kisses between women and between women and men are commonplace. Kisses between men are rarer but do happen in some places such as Argentina, Serbia, and Southern Italy.

[6] What to do, then, if you're caught by surprise by a social kisser? Think of it like dancing with a more experienced partner. Instead of tensing up, it's best to relax and let the other person take the lead. If you are unsure of how many kisses to give, two is usually appropriate, even in countries that commonly only use one. There really is no need to be nervous when visiting any of these countries. Just don't forget to pack your lip balm!

« Different countries may have different forms of greetings.

˅ Hand-kissing is also a form of greeting in some countries.

Questions

_____ 1. What is the article mainly about?
   a. How to be a better kisser.
   b. The custom of kissing as a form of greeting.
   c. How people from different countries kiss.
   d. The origin of kissing.

_____ 2. Which of the following statements is true, according to the article?
   a. In Italy, it's common to greet someone with one kiss on each cheek.
   b. In Belgium, when greeting someone you must kiss them only once.
   c. Kissing as a form of greeting can be traced back to the ancient Greeks.
   d. In the United Kingdom, you must remain absolutely silent when kissing someone.

_____ 3. What tone is the author trying to create in the third paragraph?
   a. Joyful.   b. Outraged.   c. Panicked.   d. Sentimental.

_____ 4. What is the fifth paragraph mostly made up of?
   a. Warnings.   b. Definitions.   c. Statistics.   d. Instructions.

_____ 5. Which of the following sentences contains an example of a simile?
   a. "Think of it like dancing with a more experienced partner."
   b. "If more kisses are needed, repeat on the other cheek."
   c. "The rules are different almost everywhere you go."
   d. "For those not used to these practices, traveling to a country where kissing is common can be a nerve-racking experience."

161

hawker center in Singapore

48 Food Worth Saving: Preserving the World's Culinary Heritage

1 When you think of a country's culture, the first thing that comes to mind is often the food. But in an ever-globalizing world where American fast-food chains like McDonald's and café chains like Starbucks continue to grow in popularity, some culinary heritages could one day be lost. Luckily, the UNESCO Intangible Cultural Heritage for Food is on a mission to preserve them. One of the most recent applicants is Singapore and its "hawkers," a special type of food vendor who serve affordable homemade food in large dining rooms where Singaporeans gather to eat and socialize. Let's find out what other unique culinary practices have already made the UNESCO list.

2 Traditional Mexican Cuisine

In Mexico, the growing and grinding of corn are ancient practices that are integral to reaffirming social ties and promoting sustainable living. This cultural tradition is thus good for society and the planet, too.

Mexican food, tacos

Turkish coffee

Coffee houses in Turkey serve as a community hub for people to socialize.

3 **Turkish Coffee Culture and Tradition**

The coffee houses in Turkey not only serve drinks but also serve as a community hub. Turkish coffee itself is a special type of strong black coffee made by mixing finely powdered coffee with water, slowly boiled until it froths. Sugar can be added to the coffee while it brews, and those who are used to Starbucks cappuccinos might want to ask for lots of it!

4 **Art of Neapolitan "Pizzaiuoli"**

The true art of pizza making originates in the city of Naples, Italy, where *pizzaiuoli* have, for generations, used a special technique to make dough. This includes spinning the dough up in the air and catching it—not as easy as it looks!

Italian pizza makers have special technique to make dough, which involves spinning the dough up in the air.

Neopolitan pizza

163

Beer is an important part of Belgium culture.   Belgian beer

5 **Beer Culture in Belgium**

The small Western European country of Belgium produces almost 1,500 types of beer, using a variety of methods. Beer is so much part of the culture here that there's even a beer-washed cheese!

6 **Kimjang, Making and Sharing Kimchi**

In South Korea, kimchi (preserved vegetables seasoned with spices and fermented seafood) is not just a staple of the diet but part of the glue that holds society together. Communities gather for *kimjang* season in late autumn to prepare and share large quantities of kimchi to get them through the winter.

7 It remains to be seen what other culinary practices will be added to the list, but one thing is for certain: the world would be a much more boring (and less delicious!) place if we lost any of these unique culinary delights.

Kimchi has been the bond of Korean society.

a variety of kimchi in jars

▽ Traditional Mexican cuisine emphasizes growing and grinding of corn.

Questions

____ 1. What is the main idea of this passage?
   a. We need to recognize and celebrate the best food cultures in the world.
   b. It is important to safeguard the world's most valuable food cultures.
   c. Globalization is ruining food culture because fast food is so popular now.
   d. Singaporean hawker culture should be recognized by the UNESCO list.

____ 2. Why is traditional Mexican cuisine good for the planet?
   a. It strengthens social relationships among farming communities.
   b. It is a plant-based diet consisting mainly of corn and very little meat.
   c. It is a cultural practice which has existed for many generations.
   d. It uses ancient practices which are not harmful to the environment.

____ 3. At the end of the third paragraph, what does the author use to catch the reader's attention?
   a. A joke.
   b. An interesting fact.
   c. A strong opinion.
   d. A metaphor.

____ 4. What is the overall purpose of this passage?
   a. To talk about the problems of globalization.
   b. To celebrate the world's culinary heritage.
   c. To recommend what world food to try.
   d. To list the five best cuisines around the world.

____ 5. Which of the following is NOT true about Neapolitan *pizzaiuoli*?
   a. They are from Naples, where pizza originally comes from.
   b. They throw the dough in the air in a circular motion and catch it.
   c. They have been making pizza this way for many years.
   d. They use a technique that is a lot simpler than it seems.

165

Warren Buffett (b. 1930)
(cc by Fortune Live Media)

49 The World's Most Famous Famous Investor

Tap Dancing to Work is a retrospective collection of Fortune articles on Warren Buffett.

1 At six years old, Warren Buffett was no average child. While other children were playing games, Warren was buying six-packs of Coca-Cola from his grandfather's store for 25 cents and selling the individual bottles for five cents. At age 11, he bought a company's stock (for the first time) at $38 a share. They dropped to $27 a share, but he steadied his nerves and waited. When the stock rose to $40 a share, he sold them and learned an important lesson about patience, because the stock's value continued to rise—to $200!

2 It's difficult to believe, but this boy genius from Omaha, Nebraska, did not want to attend college; Warren's father persuaded him to go anyway. When Warren learned that two well-known securities analysts taught at Columbia Business School, he enrolled in their post-graduate economics program. One of them, Benjamin Graham, shaped Buffett's investing future profoundly. The strategy he learned is simple: determine a company's actual worth by examining its financial data; if the value of its stock is significantly less than the company's value, it's a good investment.

3 Using this method, Buffett accumulated so much wealth that at one time he surpassed Bill Gates as the world's wealthiest man. In addition, when Mr. Buffett acquires a successful business, he uses his amiable interpersonal skills to communicate with the existing managers. His plan of "management" is not to interfere with the running of the company. Instead, he maintains a hands-off approach and allows its directors to retain ultimate decision-making powers.

4 Despite his legendary wealth, Warren Buffett continues to live in the same, modest home. He carries no cell phone, and has no computer. He drives his own car: a common Cadillac DTS. When he finally bought a private jet for $10 million (NT$322 million), he named it "The Indefensible," for he had frequently been critical of other executives' extravagant purchases.

5 Buffett has long been helpful to charities by auctioning his possessions and time, and donating the money received. However, Buffett's largest philanthropic gesture met with some uncertain press. After he donated 83% of his money to the Bill and Melinda Gates Foundation, it was revealed by the *LA Times* and other reputable news sources that some of the Foundation's activities had glaring conflicts of interest. However, overall, the Gates Foundation appears to be sincere in its mandate and will provide an honest distribution of Warren Buffett's fortune.

⌄ Buffett and former president Obama at the Oval Office, 2010

>> Bill and Melinda Gates
(cc by Kjetil Ree)

Questions

_____ 1. What's the main idea of the passage?
   a. The Bill and Melinda Gates Foundation is sincere in its mandate.
   b. Warren Buffet is a genius investor who started young.
   c. Benjamin Graham taught Warren Buffett everything he knows.
   d. Warren Buffet is known around the world for his generosity.

_____ 2. What is the basic strategy that helped Warren Buffet accumulate so much wealth?
   a. Never use a cell phone or a computer.
   b. Patience is the most important thing; never sell your stock early.
   c. Always have a hands-on approach toward a company's management.
   d. Identify gaps in a company's stock value and financial data.

_____ 3. Which of the following is NOT true about the first stock that Warren Buffet ever bought?
   a. He bought it at $38 a share.
   b. He was 11 years old when he bought it.
   c. He sold it at $200 a share.
   d. At one point, the stock dropped to $27 a share.

_____ 4. Which of the following is Benjamin Graham probably known as?
   a. "The Father of Value Investing."
   b. "The Obstacle of Omaha."
   c. "The Hateful One."
   d. "The Bankruptcy Baron."

_____ 5. What's the author's purpose in the first paragraph?
   a. To offer a personal opinion.
   b. To express doubts.
   c. To present different examples.
   d. To provide a historical background.

▽ Hideko Yamashita

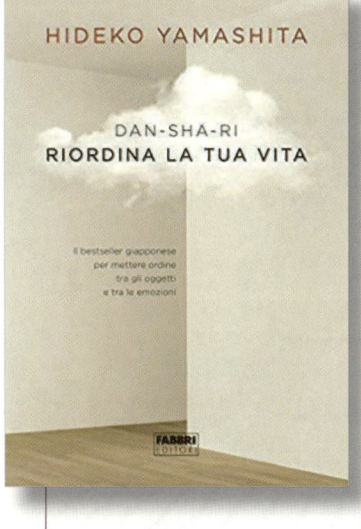

≫ *Dan-Sha-Ri* written by
Hideko Yamashita

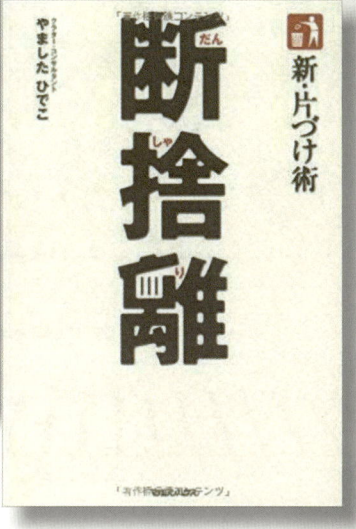

50 Declutter Your House, Declutter Your Heart

1   Almost all of us in the modern era are suffering from a disease: the disease of excess. We fill our houses with clothes we never wear, gadgets we never use, books we never read. Being able to amass more and more goods has for a long time been a signifier of one's success. But have you ever stopped to consider that filling your home with unused, unappreciated items may be cluttering up your soul as well as your abode?

2   That's exactly how Hideko Yamashita—the Japanese writer responsible for starting the *danshari* movement—felt when, during a stay at a shrine, the shrine master threw away all her belongings and left her with only two sets of clothes. Suddenly, she felt at peace: she had decluttered not only her home but her heart as well. From there, she formulated the principle of *danshari*—a word made up of three *kanji* meaning "refusal," "disposal," and "separation"—and decided to share it with the world.

3   Practicing *danshari* is simple: you refuse to bring unnecessary possessions into your life; you throw away any existing clutter from your living space; and you separate yourself as much as possible from your desire for material possessions. In fact, in many ways *danshari* is similar to a centuries-old Zen Buddhist philosophy that was once highly influential in Japan known as *wabi*. According to one Zen

⌃ The practice of danshari is to have a minimal amount of possessions in life.

master, *wabi* means to be satisfied with a little hut, a room of two or three tatami mats, and a dish of vegetables picked in the neighboring fields. It is the art of appreciating the lack of things, rather than the having of things.

4 With such familiar cultural roots, it's perhaps unsurprising, then, that the idea took off so rapidly in Japan. But *danshari* has been rapidly gaining popularity in the West, too, as people, inspired by the examples set by *danshari* practitioners, fight to reclaim something of the simplicity lost in their own highly materialistic lives. An example of a *danshari* practitioner is the writer Fumio Sasaki, also a popularizer of the movement. Despite his success, Sasaki lives in a small room that houses all of his 150 possessions. According to Sasaki, practicing *danshari* has helped him lose weight, become more proactive, and most importantly, feel grateful for what he has—all things that many caught up in modern consumerism aspire to.

5 Perhaps it's time to count those possessions of yours and decide for yourself whether a little *danshari* might not do you a world of good, too.

« *Danshari* means "refusal," "disposal," and "separation." (cc by 地底深山)

Questions

1. Which of the following sentences from the article contains a cause-and-effect relationship?
   a. "We fill our houses with clothes we never wear, gadgets we never use, books we never read."
   b. "In fact, in many ways *danshari* is similar to a centuries-old Zen Buddhist philosophy that was once highly influential in Japan known as *wabi*."
   c. "According to Sasaki, practicing *danshari* has helped him lose weight, become more proactive, and most importantly, feel grateful for what he has."
   d. "It is the art of appreciating the lack of things, rather than the having of things."

2. How does the author end the article?
   a. By warning the reader of an impending threat.
   b. By suggesting a course of action to the reader.
   c. By summarizing the content of the passage.
   d. By providing a watertight conclusion.

3. Which of the following statements is TRUE, according to the article?
   a. *Danshari* is completely unknown in the West.
   b. *Danshari* was invented by Zen Buddhist monks.
   c. The word *danshari* is made up of four Japanese kanji.
   d. *Danshari* shares many similarities with *wabi*.

4. Which of the following comes closest to describing the author's tone in the first paragraph?
   a. Frustrated.   b. Amused.   c. Detached.   d. Wonderstruck.

5. Which of these statements from the passage shows the author's bias?
   a. "Almost all of us in the modern era are suffering from a disease: the disease of excess."
   b. "With such familiar cultural roots, it's perhaps unsurprising, then, that the idea took off so rapidly in Japan."
   c. "From there, she formulated the principle of *danshari* . . . and decided to share it with the world."
   d. "According to one Zen master, *wabi* means to be satisfied with a little hut. . . ."

Wabi is the art of appreciating the lack of things.

Unit 2

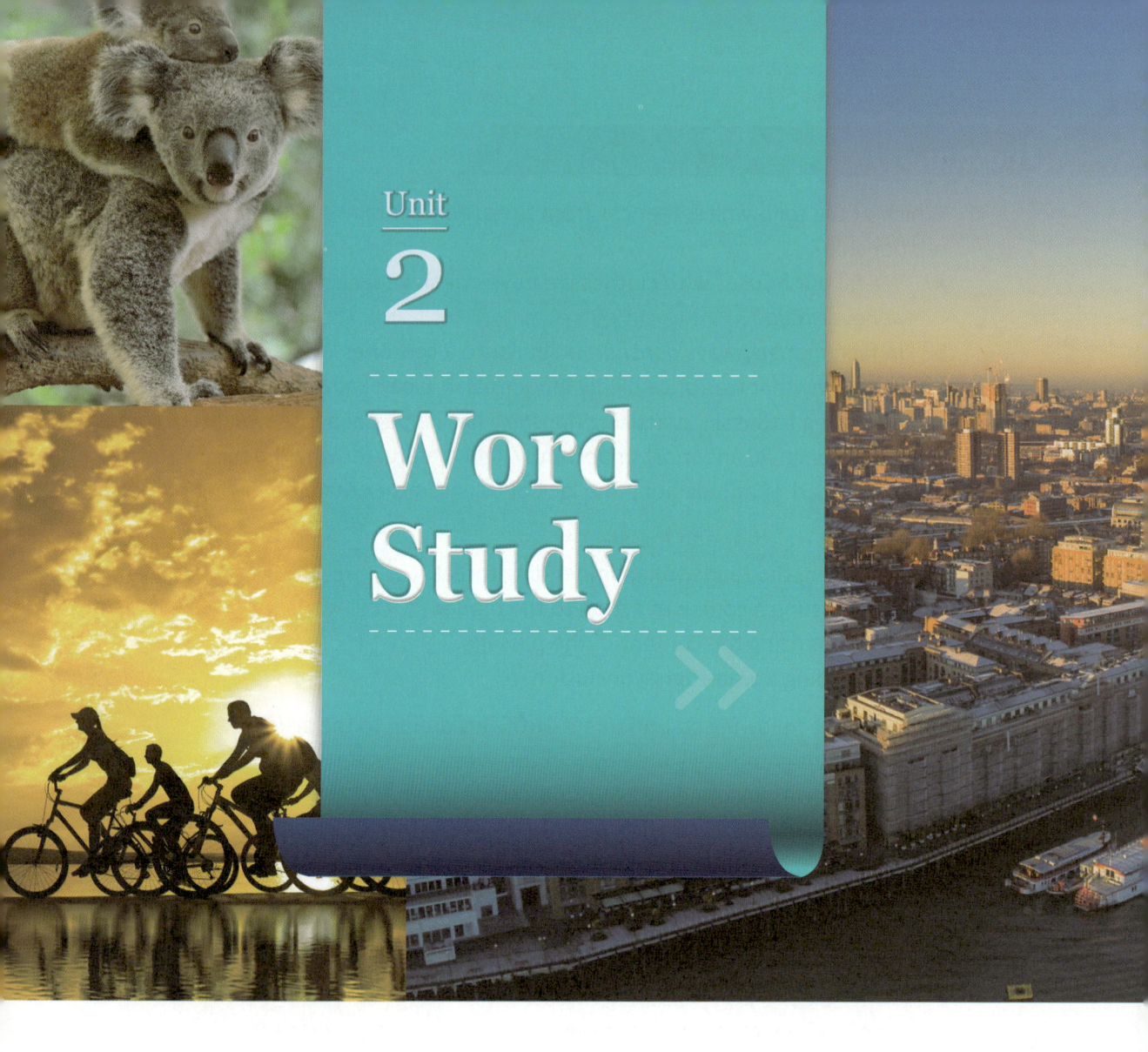

Word Study

2-1 Synonyms (Words With the Same Meaning)

2-2 Antonyms (Words With Opposite Meanings)

2-3 Words in Context

2-4 Review Test

Unit 2
Word Study

With so many words in the English language (nearly a million by some estimates), memorizing the meaning to every single one is an almost impossible task. But as your knowledge of English grows, you'll notice that many words share similar meanings. In addition, you'll see that clues to the meaning of any problematic word can be found in the sentence or paragraph that surrounds it.

By the end of this unit you'll have the skills to tackle any difficult word you come across. Being able to identify and use these words will make you not only a fluent reader but also a better writer and speaker.

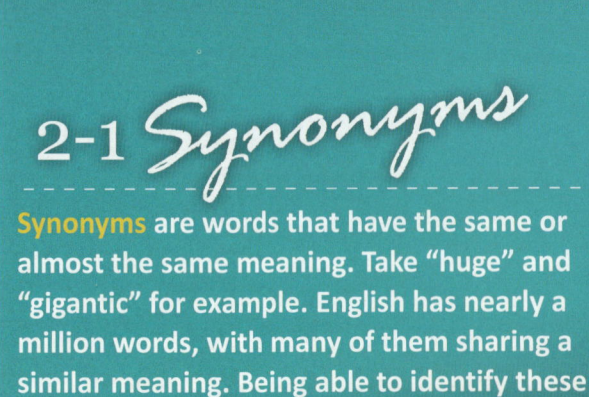

2-1 Synonyms

Synonyms are words that have the same or almost the same meaning. Take "huge" and "gigantic" for example. English has nearly a million words, with many of them sharing a similar meaning. Being able to identify these words is a vital skill for improving your reading comprehension.

▲ flag of Northern Ireland

▲ the English Protestant King William (1650—1702)

51 Ireland: A Troubled History

[1] While "The Troubles" in Ireland are **conventionally** said to have taken place over 30 years from the 1960s to the 1990s, they actually began centuries ago. It's nearly impossible to understand what The Troubles are unless you look back to the beginning of it all.

[2] History tells of the Battle of the Boyne in 1690, a conflict between Protestant England's King William and Catholic Scotland's King James over the Irish, Scottish, and English thrones. King William was victorious, and this began Protestant **domination** in Ireland. An **extensive** area in the north was settled

▲ the Scottish Catholic King James (1685—1688)

174

⌃ Battle of the Boyne in 1690

by English and Scottish Protestants, leaving Ulster, one of Ireland's northernmost provinces and whose population was largely Catholic, isolated from the rest.

3   Division between Catholics and Protestants grew during the 1800s due to differences in their standards of living. While the north enjoyed economic success, the south, which was mostly Catholic, remained poor because Anglican Protestants were the biggest, richest landowners. Growing dissension **transpired** in the early 1900s, when the majority of Irish Catholics wanted freedom from Britain. The Irish Protestants didn't want to live in a nation where most of the citizens were Catholic, so they formed militant groups over it. To foster peace, the 1920 Government of Ireland Act was enacted by Britain, dividing Ireland into two parts. The legislation was only supported by the Ulster Protestant population; the southern Catholics wanted full independence above all.

4   In 1921, an Irish Free State was created as the result of the Irish War of Independence between the Irish Republican Army (IRA) and British forces. The Free State was composed of three counties in Ulster and 23 counties in the south. The rest of Ulster, six counties, was named "Northern Ireland."

5   In the 1960s, Londonderry and Belfast saw **tremendous** outbreaks of violence. Many bombings and riots by both the IRA and Protestant paramilitary groups lasted into the 1990s. The hostilities during this period of time are known as "The Troubles." Over 3,600 people died in spite of attempts at peaceful resolutions.

Tony Blair, prime minister of the United Kingdom from 1997 to 2007

6   In July, 2005, the IRA put a stop to all militant activity, ending their long campaign for unification, and in May, 2007, Northern Ireland was granted local government within the United Kingdom. Prime Minister Tony Blair said, "Look back, and we see centuries marked by conflict, hardship, even hatred among the people of these islands. Look forward, and we see the chance to shake off those heavy chains of history."

volunteers of the IRA during the Irish War of Independence

Questions

_____ 1. Which of the following is closet in meaning to **conventionally** in the first paragraph?
   a. Dangerously.
   b. Traditionally.
   c. Slowly.
   d. Intellectually.

_____ 2. "King William was victorious, and this began Protestant **domination** in Ireland." Another word for **domination** in the second paragraph is _____.
   a. control
   b. negotiation
   c. retreat
   d. exploration

_____ 3. "An **extensive** area in the north was settled by English and Scottish Protestants." What is an interchangeable word for the way **extensive** is used in the second paragraph?
   a. Worthless.
   b. Uneven.
   c. Expensive.
   d. Broad.

_____ 4. Which of the following is most similar to the word **transpired** in the third paragraph?
   a. Halted.
   b. Arranged.
   c. Occurred.
   d. Broke.

_____ 5. The fifth paragraph describes how Londonderry and Belfast saw **tremendous** outbreaks of violence. Which of the following defines the word **tremendous** the way it is used here?
   a. Immense.
   b. Intermittent.
   c. Occasional.
   d. Tranquil.

» Northern Ireland

↑ crop circles in England

52 Crop Circles: A Worldwide Enigma

1   A design appearing quickly and secretively in a field of corn, barley, wheat, or similar crop, formed by the breaking down to the ground of these plants, is a crop circle. Sometimes they are also made by the etching of soil in dry, winter fields or in newly plowed ground. Vivid photographs, as well as colorful videos, have been published, but seeing a crop circle in person by air or from a hilltop, and perhaps walking through it, is the ultimate experience. Crop circles are a big tourist draw for this reason, with most being located in England.

2   The name "crop circle" was given because the first pattern was a circle. They have since "matured" to include straight lines of geometry, curved lines, and **flourishes** that make one think of outer space orbits and calligraphy. Some appear to have messages; others look like drawings and exquisite works of art; still others depict mathematical symbols.

⌃ crop circles in the Southwest

3   Where do these **enigmatic** designs originate from? There is one thing we *do* know for sure: crop circles have been around for a very long time. Although modern crop circle discoveries began in the 1970s, the phenomenon is said to have existed as early as the 7th century. The circles tend to be man-made; researcher Colin Andrews estimates that around 80 percent of crop circles are the direct result of human activity. In one of the most famous cases, two men, Doug Bower and Dave Chorley, confessed that they had been secretly making hundreds of crop circles in Southampton, England, in 1991.

⌄ crop circles in Slovakia

4 Yet the Bower-Chorley **deceit** doesn't explain the crop circles formed before and after they were active. It also doesn't provide an explanation for the thousands of crop circles that have appeared in other countries throughout the world. Are they the work of extraterrestrial beings? Many enthusiastically say: "Yes!" Others point to the possibility of **severe** weather like ball lightning or tornados. Some yet combine the two theories, raising the possibility that paranormal forces are *controlling the weather*. How else, they ask, could something like ball lightning produce such exquisitely intricate patterns?

5 Whether they're the result of a hoax, alien **conspiracy**, or natural phenomena, everyone can agree that crop circles are a highly compelling research topic. To say they're "interesting" is a gross understatement; studying crop circles is so engrossing that it can easily become an obsession!

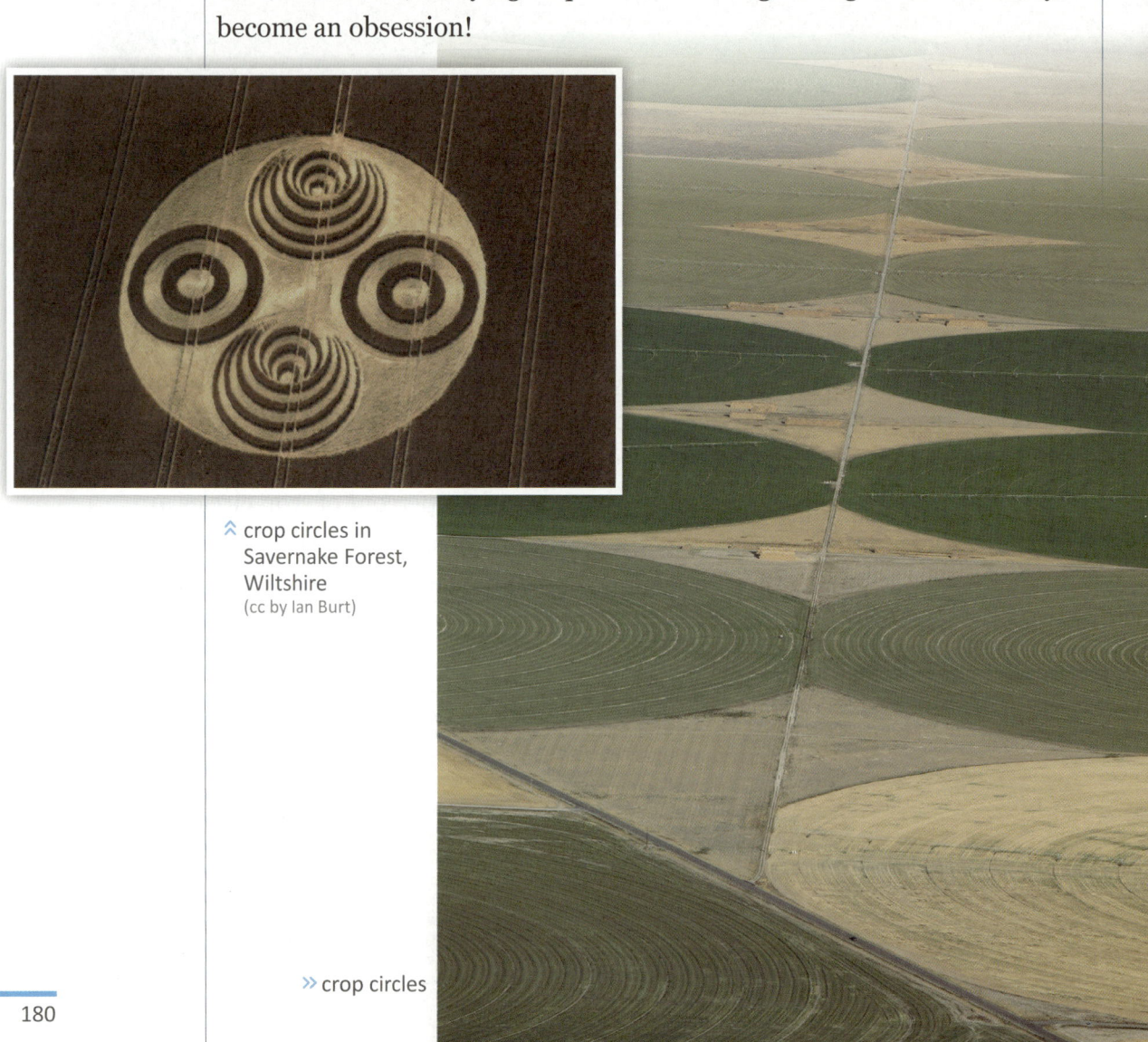

⌃ crop circles in Savernake Forest, Wiltshire
(cc by Ian Burt)

» crop circles

180

↑ crop circles in Switzerland

Questions

1. What is an interchangeable word for the way **flourish** is used in the second paragraph?
   a. Alteration.
   b. Quirk.
   c. Slash.
   d. Angle.

2. Which of the following can replace the word **enigmatic** as it is used in the passage "Where do these **enigmatic** designs originate from"?
   a. Puzzling.
   b. Original.
   c. Hateful.
   d. Enlightening.

3. Which of the following is closest in meaning to **deceit** in the passage "Yet the Bower-Chorley **deceit** doesn't explain the crop circles formed. . . ." located in the fourth paragraph?
   a. Surprise.
   b. Data.
   c. Apology.
   d. Trickery.

4. "Others point to the possibility of **severe** weather. . . ." Another word for **severe** in the fourth paragraph is _____.
   a. common
   b. extreme
   c. gradual
   d. constant

5. **Conspiracy** can be used to describe an organized plan to carry out a harmful action. Which of the following can replace the word **conspiracy** in the final paragraph?
   a. Group.
   b. Hazard.
   c. Plot.
   d. Commotion.

› Bruce Lee
(1940—1973)

53 Bruce Lee: From Trailblazer to Legend

1 Bruce Lee is a legend that nearly everyone in the world recognizes. Although no longer living, he is still the martial arts master to whom all others are compared. He is a world-famous movie star, a cultural icon, the creator of Jeet Kune Do, and the hero of many.

2 Although Bruce Lee had appeared in more than 20 films by the time he was 18 years old, it wasn't until he played the character Kato in the American television show *The Green Hornet* that he began to rise in popularity. The show was on the air for only one season, but in Hong Kong he had become a star, and the show was mostly referred to as "The Kato Show." Lee, however, was dissatisfied with playing supporting roles.

3 In 1971, at 31 years old, Lee acted in his first starring role as Cheng Chao-an in the hugely successful movie *The Big Boss*, which **propelled** Lee to stardom throughout Asia. This film was immediately followed by *Fist of Fury* in 1972, which broke all of the records that *The Big Boss* had just broken.

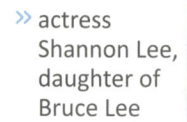

› actress Shannon Lee, daughter of Bruce Lee

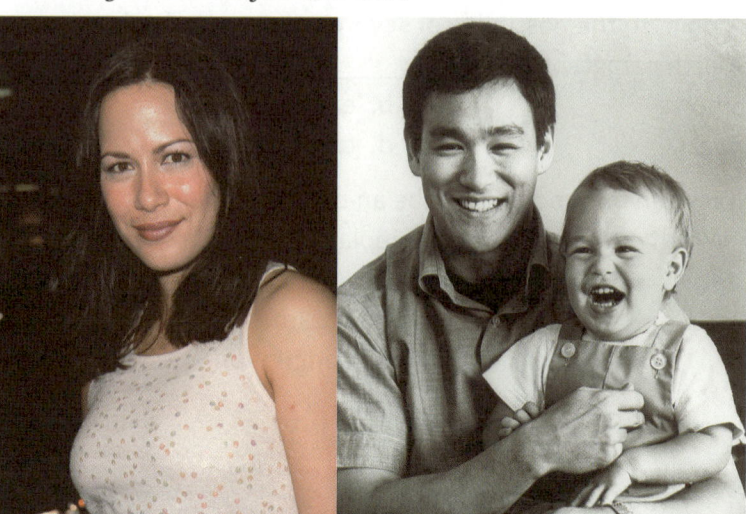

‹ Bruce Lee with his son Brandon in 1966

182

Fist of Fury (1972)

The Big Boss (1971)

Way of the Dragon (1972)

4 That same year, Lee renegotiated with Golden Harvest studio to become the writer, director, star, and fight choreographer of *Way of the Dragon*. This time, he also brought fame to American martial artist Chuck Norris in the movie's legendary, **climactic**, fight-to-the-death scene.

5 To the Chinese, those with whom he shared ethnicity, Bruce Lee was much more than a movie star—he was a **symbol** of national pride. In his movies, Lee often included scenes that showed him rising up against prejudices directed against the Chinese. For example, in *Fist of Fury*, Lee beat up a man and smashed a sign that **likened** Chinese people to dogs.

6 Combining the most useful parts of dozens of disciplines, Lee created Jeet Kune Do. He emphasized "the style of no style" to convey his rejection of overly **structured** and thus weaker methods. Two years before his death, Lee closed his schools, permitting only private instruction of his legacy.

7 Lee's final movie, *Enter the Dragon*, earned him celebrity throughout the United States and Europe, but most unfortunately, he did not live to see it. Six days before the movie's debut, despite having been in perfect physical condition, Bruce Lee mysteriously died. *Enter the Dragon* continues to earn accolades and praise more than 40 years after its release.

Bruce Lee (right) played Kato in the television show *The Green Hornet*.

Bruce Lee (1940—1973)

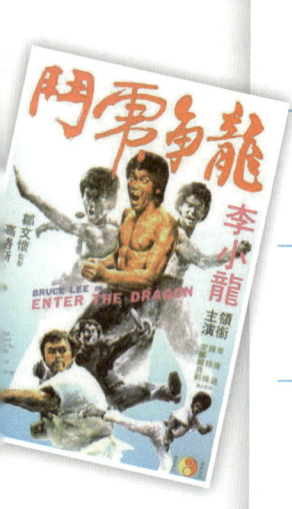

Questions

_____ 1. "... *The Big Boss*, which **propelled** Lee into stardom throughout Asia." Another word for **propelled** in the third paragraph is _____.
   a. launched   b. isolated   c. avoided   d. exploded

_____ 2. What is an interchangeable word for the way **climactic** is used in the fourth paragraph?
   a. Original.   b. Sudden.   c. Ultimate.   d. Permanent.

_____ 3. Which of the following is closest in meaning to **symbol** in the fifth paragraph?
   a. Figure.   b. Remnant.   c. Language.   d. Calculation.

_____ 4. Which of the following is the most similar to the word **likened** in the fifth paragraph?
   a. Praised.   b. Compared.   c. Supposed.   d. Enjoyed.

_____ 5. **Structured** is a good word to describe something that is highly organized and well-defined. Which of the following can replace the word structured as it is used in the passage?
   a. Haphazard.   b. Ornate.   c. Inconsistent.   d. Systematic.

« *Enter the Dragon* (1973)

« statue of Bruce Lee on the Avenue of the Stars in Hong Kong

184

↑ a simulation image of a plane crash

54 How to Survive a Plane Crash

1   It's a nightmare scenario many of us have considered before: that sharp and sudden lurch, the smell of smoke in the cabin, and the screams of frightened passengers throughout the plane. But the realities of air travel have never aligned with the **pervasive** anxieties that live in our collective consciousness. US travelers are three times more likely to die from lightning than they are from a plane crash, and they are 19 times more likely to die from an auto collision. Even in the unlikely event of a plane crash, some 95% of the passengers can be expected to survive the ordeal, according to data compiled by the US National Transportation Safety Board in a landmark 2001 study. Yet none of this means that travelers should be totally **complacent** when flying. Even though air travel is generally quite safe, in the off chance you're faced with a calamity in the clouds, it's still possible to take the burden of survival into your own hands.

2 Here are some safety measures that could help save your life:

Plan Ahead	Don't wear loose clothes or clothes made from flammable or synthetic materials, and avoid wearing uncomfortable shoes like high-heels.
Environmental Awareness	Listen to the guidelines read by the flight attendants, and read the safety information provided. Note where the exits are, particularly the closest one, because there is often limited visibility during a crash.
Smoke Inhalation	Wet a piece of fabric to cover your mouth and nose to avoid smoke inhalation. It is not advisable to stay low, because you might get trampled by other passengers.
Safety Belts	The seat belts on air crafts have buckles, not push-buttons. Do not panic and forget to unbuckle the belt when you must. Before impact, make sure your belt is pulled as tightly as you can make it.
Follow Instructions	Be prepared to listen carefully to the crew's instructions, and follow them. If they appear dazed, do not waste time—move forward on your own.
Forget Your Personal Possessions	Don't try to save your possessions. It is critical to have your hands free to use when needed.

⌃ emergency exit in the aircraft

⌃ Read the safety information provided on board.

⌃ safety belt

⌃ carry-on luggage

3   Remember that most deaths result from smoke **inhalation** and/or burns from the fire, and that with proper action, most of these deaths can be avoided. There's no need to get too worried about air travel—just be prepared, and enjoy the trip!

Pay attention to the guidelines read and demonstrated by the flight attendants.

Questions

1. **Pervasive** is a good word to describe something that can be found nearly everywhere. Which of the following can replace the word **pervasive** as it is used in the first paragraph?
   a. Concentrated.
   b. Sparse.
   c. Prevalent.
   d. Random.

2. "Yet none of this means that travelers should be totally **complacent** when flying." Another word for **complacent** in the first paragraph is _____.
   a. casual
   b. annoyed
   c. fearful
   d. organized

3. ". . . because there is often limited **visibility** during a crash." Which of the following is closest in meaning to **visibility** in the passage?
   a. Brevity.
   b. Clarity.
   c. Sincerity.
   d. Rarity.

4. Which of the following is the most similar to the word **dazed** in the passage?
   a. Stunned.
   b. Depressed.
   c. Enraged.
   d. Ecstatic.

5. What is an interchangeable word for the way **inhalation** is used in the final paragraph?
   a. Generation.
   b. Interruption.
   c. Intake.
   d. Observance.

» a pop-up store of Coca-Cola in Romania to celebrate its 100th birthday

55 Here Today, Gone the Next

1 Temporary retail is not a new idea by any stretch of the imagination: Halloween shops, Christmas markets, and village fairs have been appealing to our sense of "here today, gone tomorrow" since time immemorial. But in the last two decades, bigger companies have begun to see the potential in this **ephemeral** style of retail, too, setting up temporary stores—known as pop-up shops—that use their short-lived nature to boost sales. Indeed, pop-up shops are causing something of a modern retail revolution.

2 It started in the late 1990s, with an event held in Los Angeles called The Ritual Expo, which aimed to bring together the coolest underground fashion brands for a one-day hipster-friendly shopping experience. It wasn't long before larger fashion brands began to catch on to, and cash in on, the idea of using short-term shopping experiences to build their profiles with a young, cool target audience.

3 **Fast-forward** to today, and everyone is getting in on the trend, from tech giants such as Google and Amazon (who set up pop-ups to allow people to try out their new gadgets) to Michelin-starred restauranteurs and beauty gurus.

4 Why is this kind of retail so valuable for brands and businesses? In an age where e-commerce is dominating the marketplace, having permanent **brick-and-mortar** stores just isn't the most ideal option any more, particularly with rent for commercial spaces skyrocketing. However, existing

« a pop-up food and drink experience outlet in London

188

in a physical space still has its advantages. Pop-up stores are an excellent way to launch a new product or to generate brand awareness, giving customers the feeling that they are trying something new or having a unique experience—something that Millennials, a key market demographic, are strongly drawn to.

5 But pop-up shops don't just have to be the domain of big brands—small, up-and-coming businesses can take advantage of the trend, too. For any young go-getter who feels daunted by the prospect of having to invest in **costly** long-term rent for a store space, a pop-up shop is an ideal alternative, since it requires only a fraction of the investment. Furthermore, starting out as a pop-up can be a fantastic way for a young artist, chef, or designer to experiment with their products, test the market, and get people talking about their brand.

6 The stores themselves may be here today and gone the next, but with so many advantages for both established brands and up-and-coming **entrepreneurs**, the pop-up trend is most certainly here to stay.

⌄ Halloween shop is a form of temporary retail.

⌄ a Marvel pop-up store (cc by kyu3)

Questions

_____ 1. What is another word for **ephemeral** as used in the first paragraph?
   a. Friendly.   b. Temporary.   c. Unique.   d. Modern.

_____ 2. The verb **fast-forward** at the beginning of the third paragraph could be replaced by which of the following?
   a. Erase.   b. Jump.   c. Reverse.   d. Record.

_____ 3. Which of the following words could replace **brick-and-mortar** in the fourth paragraph?
   a. Physical.   b. Digital.   c. Profitable.   d. Novel.

_____ 4. Which of the following is an alternative word for **costly,** as used in the fifth paragraph?
   a. Exorbitant.   b. Affluent.   c. Invaluable.   d. Profuse.

_____ 5. In the final paragraph, the author says that pop-up stores have "advantages for both established brands and up-and-coming **entrepreneurs**." What word could he have used instead of **entrepreneurs**?
   a. Employees.   b. Investors.   c. Businesspeople.   d. Customers.

2-2 Antonyms

Antonym is another way of saying "a word with an opposite meaning." Good and bad, big and small, hot and cold—all of these are antonym pairings. Sometimes, finding an antonym can be very easy. At other times, it can be a little challenging. Remember to always check the surrounding context for potential clues.

56 Why Do We Forget Things?

1   When it comes to having a perfect memory, it seems that we humans must have some flaws in our blueprints! Why don't we remember everything that we want to? It can be frustrating and **disheartening**. Sometimes, it can even **damage** our self-esteem or make others think less of us. Truly, we are all forgetful. If we weren't, we wouldn't keep diaries or hire secretaries, and the Blackberry would never have been invented! However, recent research suggests that forgetting may, in fact, be a necessary and important function of our brain.

2   Most of us have vivid memories of our lives from about age three up until the present. These are stored in what we call our long-term memory. What about before age three? Sigmund Freud is credited with the discovery that we forget most of our early childhood. Psychologists disagree on what causes this **amnesia** and have been investigating it since Freud's time. One very sound theory, resulting from experiments with toddlers, is that the absence of linguistic ability at the time of an event stops us from being able to describe it to others. The memory exists in the mind, but words were not associated with it when it happened;

» Sigmund Freud (1856—1939)

190

« amnesia

therefore, it doesn't become part of one's adult autobiography. There are some exceptions, but these are rare.

3 The other type of memory, short-term memory, is what we are usually referring to when we say, "I forgot." Experts say that you can keep about seven things in your memory at once for up to three days. During that time, you may forget something in order to put something else in its place. In fact, some researchers now argue that forgetting is **essential** because the biological goal of one's memory is not **preserving information** but rather helping the brain make good decisions. Recent findings suggest that we actually sometimes actively forget things to make space for new, more useful memories. It's a bit like a computer running a program that wipes data off your hard drive. A simple way to test your short-term memory is to look at a list of 20 words for a minute or two. You will discover that you cannot remember more than about seven of them and that they are the ones at the beginning and end of the list, since your mind has judged them to be more important than those in the middle.

Questions

☆ toddler

_____ 1. Which of the following means the opposite of **disheartening**?
    a. Exciting.   **b.** Encouraging.   **c.** Disappointing.   **d.** Relieving.

_____ 2. The author writes that not being able to remember everything can sometimes **damage** self-esteem. Which of the following means the opposite of **damage** in this context?
    a. Fill.   **b.** Push.   **c.** Boost.   **d.** Gather.

_____ 3. When someone has **amnesia**, he or she does NOT _____.
    a. forget   **b.** remember   **c.** believe   **d.** know

_____ 4. Which of the following has the opposite meaning of **essential** that would completely change the idea the author is trying to convey in the last paragraph?
    a. Worthless.   **b.** Vital.   **c.** Invaluable.   **d.** Treasured.

_____ 5. Which of the following situations means the opposite of **preserving information**?
    a. Saving a document on your computer.
    b. Archiving some papers in you drawer.
    c. Locking your passport in a safe.
    d. Destroying a confidential document.

Forty million tons of electronic waste is thrown out every year.

57 Is Your Smartphone Destroying the Planet?

Modern people tend to throw away old devices once there are newer and shinier models.

1 Consumer electronics like smartphones and tablets have us locked in a cycle of **perpetual** replacement. Every year a new model comes out, one that is faster, prettier, and more functional than the last. Many of us succumb to the allure of new and shiny products, and we end up buying them.

2 But what happens to the old model?

3 Tragically, it probably ends up in a landfill, contributing to the 40 million tons of electronic waste that is thrown out every year. In case you were wondering, 40 million tons translates into 800 laptops being thrown out *every second*.

4 It is not just the amount of electronic waste, or "e-waste," that is the problem. The nature of this kind of waste is especially **ruinous** to both human health and the natural environment. Electronic items like monitors, televisions, and computers contain harmful substances like mercury, lead, arsenic, and selenium. These substances can seep into the soil and poison **fertile** land and water sources. They can also harm the health of workers whose job it is to clean up or recycle e-waste. Overall, some 70 percent of the United States' toxic waste is from discarded electronics.

5 The burden of e-waste is unfairly distributed across the world. Up to 80 percent of e-waste from the United States ends up in landfills in Asia and Africa. The same is true of e-waste from Europe, which is usually shipped to Africa. Once the e-waste gets there, it is picked through by workers who try to recover precious metals like gold and silver from the old electronics. These workers can get very sick doing

e-waste landfill

192

their job because they lack safety equipment and techniques. Some of them are as young as 12 years old, and all of them are woefully underpaid, making an average of US$1.50 a day.

6   In a perfect world, all of our discarded electronics would be recycled in a safe and **just** manner. But as it stands, only around 12.5 percent of e-waste is recycled. What can we do in the meantime? The answer is simple: fight the urge to upgrade. The longer we use our devices, the less e-waste we produce (and incidentally, the more money we save). If you must upgrade, then try to find someone who can use your **outdated** device. Either that or find a certified recycling service that uses best practices.

7   We can turn the e-waste crisis around, and can do it one smartphone at a time.

↑ E-waste worker is dismantling toner cartridges in the landfill.
(cc by baselactionnetwork)

Questions

_____ 1. Which of the following has the opposite meaning of **perpetual** in the first paragraph?
   a. Temporary.   b. Significant.   c. Boring.   d. Eternal.

_____ 2. When something is **ruinous**, it is NOT _____.
   a. sudden   b. irreversible   c. beneficial   d. confusing

_____ 3. When something is not **fertile**, it is _____.
   a. rich   b. barren   c. bountiful   d. old

_____ 4. Which of the following has the opposite meaning of **just** in the sixth paragraph?
   a. Unfair.   b. Original.   c. Dangerous.   d. Innovative.

_____ 5. Which of the following has the opposite meaning of **outdated** in the sixth paragraph?
   a. Expensive.   b. Ugly.   c. Rare.   d. Current.

» biofuel

˅ bus running on soybean biodiesel

58 Biofuels

[58] **1**   With **oil prices rising** and concerns about global warming increasing, modern biofuels—fuels processed from plant matter—have in recent years become a much-**touted** alternative to traditional fossil fuels.

2   Bioethanol, produced primarily from fermenting corn and sugar cane, and biodiesel, produced from oil crops such as rapeseed, palm, and soybean oil, can effectively substitute for gasoline and diesel, respectively, in road vehicles. These alternatives are already in use around the world: much of the petrol **available** in the United States is blended with bioethanol; in Brazil, bioethanol processed from sugarcane has been used for decades to run cars; and biodiesel is widely used in Europe. Car exhausts, as is well known, are a major source of carbon dioxide, the main greenhouse gas that causes global warming. Plants, however, absorb carbon dioxide as part of their food cycle, so any carbon dioxide that gets produced by burning biofuel will have previously been taken from the atmosphere by the plants used to grow it. It seems like the perfect carbon-neutral solution!

3   Unfortunately, it's not that simple. The process of growing and extracting fuel from these crops itself takes a lot of energy—most of which still comes from burning fossil fuels. Therefore, it's often the case that producing biofuel uses more energy than the biofuel itself creates. Further, many argue that these biofuel crops—corn, soybeans, etc., all of which are **edible**—could be put to better use as a food source than as fuel. Conservationists add that clearing the extra land needed for growing these biofuel crops would mean large areas

« Palm oil can be used to produce biodiesel.

194

of rain forest being destroyed. This would, of course, be disastrous for many endangered plant and animal species.

4   In order to **reduce** our dependence on petroleum, the International Energy Agency wants biofuel to account for a quarter of the world's demand for transportation fuel by the year 2050. Currently, we are a long way from reaching this target, and innovation is necessary to make achieving this goal possible.

5   The most likely solution for the future is to produce biofuels not from food crops but rather from grasses and saplings, which can be grown easily on land not used for food farming. If these plants can be turned efficiently and cheaply into biofuel—and some recent discoveries involving fungal bacteria prove that it can—the resulting product would be far more environmentally friendly than the previous generation of biofuels. With such an **abundant** source of carbon-neutral fuel at our fingertips, fossil fuels could truly be made a thing of the past.

« bioethanol plant in France

Questions

1. Which of the following has the opposite meaning to **touted**, as used in the first paragraph?
   a. Envied.   b. Refused.   c. Delayed.   b. Discouraged.

2. Which of the following words is an antonym of **available**, as used in the second paragraph?
   a. Unfashionable.   b. Unusable.
   c. Unobtainable.   d. Unstable.

3. Which of the following could NOT be described as **edible**?
   a. A raw carrot.   b. A poisonous mushroom.
   c. A cooked chicken.   d. A slice of processed ham.

4. Which of the following has the opposite meaning to the word **reduce**, as used in the fourth paragraph?
   a. Increase.   b. Diminish.   c. Reassure.   d. Moderate.

5. Which of the following is an antonym of **abundant**, as used in the final paragraph?
   a. Economic.   b. Fruitful.   c. Natural.   d. Scarce.

Earth night view from space with city light

59 Blinded by Too Much Light

1 For those of us who live in a big city, seeing the night sky full of stars, with the Milky Way spanning the heavens like a bright silver river, is something that can only be done on visits to the remotest countryside. In cities and towns across the world, the sheer number of electric lights that fire up after the sun goes down creates a blanket of ambient light that effectively blots out the stars and reduces the majesty of the night sky to a dull, **uninspiring** glow.

2 But the loss of this natural wonder isn't the only downside to urban light pollution. More and more studies are proving that a brightening night sky has negative effects on areas such as human health, animal behavior, the environment, and even our safety after dark.

3 For example, light trespass, which is when streetlights or a neighbor's lights shine into your home, can cause serious disturbances to your body's natural sleep-wake cycle, contributing to **anomalies** in hormone production, cell function, and brain activity. Nocturnal animals, too, are under threat from this unwelcome light, as most need darkness to effectively hunt and mate.

» Too many street lights may reduce visibility rather than increasing it.

˅ Nocturnal animals need darkness to effectively hunt and mate.

[4] But isn't having bright light at night necessary for our safety? After all, we all know the dangers of walking home in the dark or driving on poorly lit roads. In fact, **contrary to** popular opinion, having too much lighting at night actually reduces visibility rather than increasing it. The glare from uncovered lights can be so bright as to be blinding and make it difficult for our eyes to naturally adjust to the darkness. In darkness, the acuteness of our night vision increases with every minute. However, if our eyes are constantly being assaulted by bright lights, any dark areas outside that light becomes almost impenetrable, making them excellent hiding places for anyone wanting to cause you harm.

[5] Of course, this is all not to mention the billions of dollars and masses of energy that are wasted each year in providing these unnecessary and often harmful lights. How much good could we do to the environment if we relied instead on our eyes and the occasional flashlight?

[6] While **reforming** our usage of street lights is something only local governments can implement, taking small intermediary steps such as removing or covering unnecessary lights around your home will itself do wonders for the nighttime ambiance of your neighborhood. And remember, if you can get rid of enough light pollution, you will be rewarded—with a skyful of **luminous** stars!

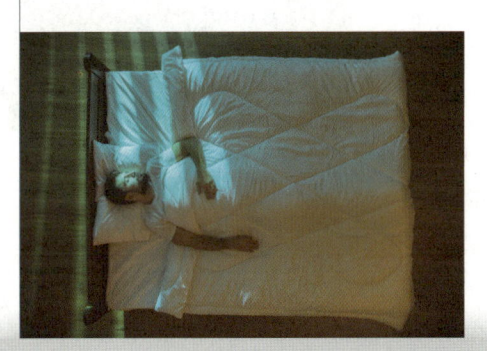

« Light trespass can disturb our natural sleep-wake cycle.

Questions

1. Which of the following words has the opposite meaning to **uninspiring**, as used in the first paragraph?
   a. Multicolored.   b. Dreary.   c. Stimulating.   d. Upsetting.

2. Which of the following is the opposite of **anomaly**, as used in the third paragraph?
   a. Regularity.   b. Exception.   c. Inconsistency.   d. Abnormality.

3. Which of the following phrases has the opposite meaning to **contrary to**, as used in the fourth paragraph?
   a. Entirely different to.   b. In accordance with.
   c. In relation to.   d. Unrelated to.

4. Which of the following has the opposite meaning to **reform** in the final paragraph?
   a. Maintain.   b. Adjust.   c. Abandon.   d. Downgrade.

5. Which of the following can NOT be described as **luminous**, as it is used in the final paragraph?
   a. The sun.   b. A street light.   c. A rainbow.   d. A candle.

60 Saving Up for the Future

1 Whether it's because they haven't found the right partner yet, or because they want to delay having children to focus on their career, many women are deciding to freeze their eggs for use at a future date. The technology, which involves **stimulating** egg production with fertility drugs, then harvesting the eggs, freezing them, and storing them for several years, allows women to retain the option of having a family when they are older, even though their fertility may have significantly fallen by that age.

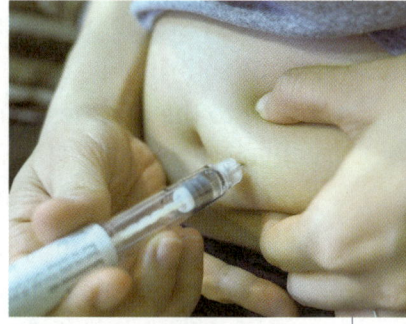

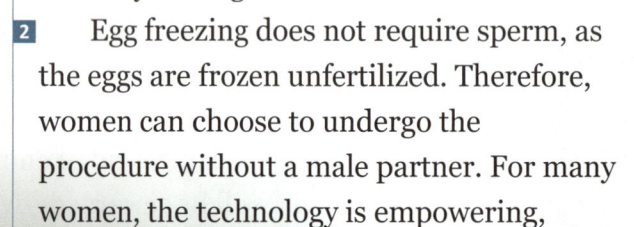

2 Egg freezing does not require sperm, as the eggs are frozen unfertilized. Therefore, women can choose to undergo the procedure without a male partner. For many women, the technology is empowering, allowing them to design their own future without the input of a man. When they feel ready, their eggs can be **thawed** and fertilized with sperm from their partner or a donor and implanted in their uterus. It is easy to see how this is considered more preferable than having children in your early twenties when you may not be ready for the responsibility and cost of raising a family.

3 However, having a store of frozen eggs at one's disposal does not guarantee pregnancy. For those who choose to use their eggs later in life, the chances of becoming pregnant after implantation can, depending on the age the woman was when her eggs were frozen and her age on **implantation**, be lower than 30 percent.

4 Furthermore, freezing one's eggs in the first place is far from cheap. One round of ovarian stimulation

≪ stimulating egg production with a fertility drug

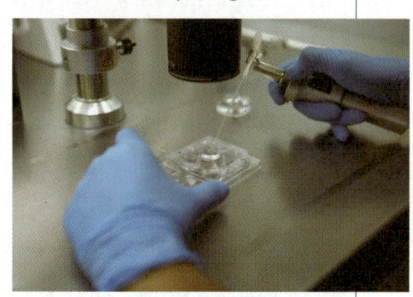

≪ the process of artificial insemination in an IVF clinic

≪ Many women decide to freeze their eggs for use of future pregnancy.

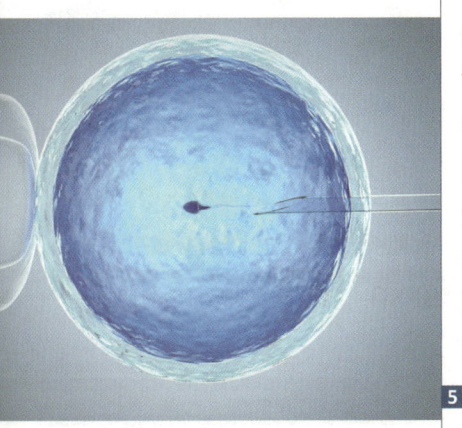

costs thousands of US dollars, and on top of that there are also annual storage fees and the cost of future fertility treatment to take into account. It is so expensive that most women are forced to take out loans to afford it. This, coupled with the fact that the chances of a successful pregnancy later in life are so low, makes egg freezing a risky investment that seldom **bears fruit**.

 It is a sad fact, then, that despite the availability of egg freezing technology, choosing to delay having children until later in life still often comes at a great cost. For those women who wish to spend their younger years focusing on their careers or finding a suitable partner, the options remain frustratingly limited—either risk the possibility of future infertility or spend a lot of money on an alternative that is far from being **a sure thing**.

≪ a needle in an ovum for artificial insemination or in vitro fertilization

≪ Medical technology enables women to delay having children.

Questions

1. Which of the following means the opposite of **stimulating**, as used in the first paragraph?
   a. Reacting.   b. Advising.   c. Discouraging.   d. Provoking.

2. Which of the following words, also used in the article, is the opposite of **thawed** in the second paragraph?
   a. Considered.   b. Frozen.   c. Fertilized.   d. Fallen.

3. Which of the following means the opposite of **implantation**, as used in the third paragraph?
   a. Extraction.
   b. Division.
   c. Reconciliation.
   d. Repetition.

4. If something does NOT **bear fruit**, what does it do?
   a. It comes to nothing.
   b. It comes alive.
   c. It goes with the flow.
   d. It goes too far.

5. If something is NOT **a sure thing**, what is it?
   a. A definite.
   b. A judgement.
   c. A conviction.
   d. An uncertainty.

2-3 Words in Context

English words can have a variety of different meanings. For example, the adjective "fine" can be used to mean "acceptable," "thin," or "attractive." When you come across a potentially confusing word, it's important to examine the **context** to determine its meaning. Looking for **context clues** can also help you deduce the meanings of words that you are completely unfamiliar with.

» Amazon review
(cc by Gustavo da Cunha Pimenta)

61 Five-Star Fibs

1   Online shopping has taken off in a big way over the past decade or so, with more and more businesses cutting back on their **brick-and-mortar stores** and moving their sales online. Having so many options available at the click of a button, customers are increasingly depending on online reviews to reliably evaluate their potential purchases, preferring to put their trust in their fellow shoppers over company-generated marketing.

2   In order to stay competitive in the crowded online market, where a lack of good reviews (or even a lack of reviews) can mean a massive loss in sales, some companies are using dishonest means to **game the system**—writing, or employing others to write, fake reviews. The practice, called "brushing," often involves hiring an online reputation company, which then uses their large team of paid reviewers to positively comment on their client's products. Of course, it goes without saying that these "reviewers" have never bought and most likely never used said products before in their lives.

3   The sites of large online retailers such as Amazon and Taobao are **rife** with these fake reviews. In one particularly audacious case, a set of headphones by a small, relatively unknown brand was found to have over 400 five-star reviews, all of which had been posted on the same day!

4   The consequences contributing to this fakery can be severe, and guilty companies have been

» Some companies hire people to write fake reviews to game the system.

fined or banned from selling their goods on online platforms. However, there is a more serious consequence—the damage caused to a company's reputation. The lack of trust that exposed companies have triggered in their customers means that few will ever buy that brand again. Indeed, the danger of faking reviews is becoming even greater as customers are getting better at identifying bogus praise. And yet, some companies still persist in **rolling the dice**, the lure of higher sales numbers outweighing the risk to their credibility.

5 So how can you as a customer avoid falling victim to false information? There may not be any sure-fire way to do so, but generally speaking, try to pay attention to the more balanced reviews—ones that list both the pros and cons of a product. Consulting reviews from a range of sites, too, should give you a better idea of the general customer consensus. Unfortunately, in the age of fake reviews, anyone raving about a product needs to be **taken with a very large pinch of salt**.

Questions

1. What does the phrase **brick-and-mortar stores** mean in the first paragraph?
   a. Poorly designed stores.
   b. Stores selling building products.
   c. Physical, not online, stores.
   d. Stores selling secondhand goods.

2. In the second paragraph, the author writes that some companies are trying to **game the system**. What does **game the system** most likely mean?
   a. Abusing the rules to gain a more favorable outcome.
   b. Playing a harmless trick on someone for fun.
   c. Taking the rules seriously and playing fairly.
   d. Reveal the secret practices of others.

3. In the third paragraph, the author writes that many sites are **rife** with these fake reviews. Which of the following is an acceptable definition for **rife**?
   a. Strongly discouraged.
   b. Very popular with customers.
   c. Tending to disappear quickly.
   d. Widespread and largely unchecked.

4. In the fourth paragraph, the author writes that some companies persist in **rolling the dice**. What does he mean by this?
   a. They continue to take risks despite the consequences of being caught.
   b. They invest their profits in illegal businesses such as gambling.
   c. They find pleasure in doing something that others think of as wrong.
   d. They stop their activities out of fear of being discovered.

5. In the final paragraph, the author writes that anyone raving about a product need to be **taken with a very large pinch of salt**. What does it mean to **take someone with a pinch of salt**?
   a. To sit down for a discussion with someone over a home-cooked meal.
   b. To give someone respect due to their expertise in a particular subject.
   c. To make false claims about someone in order to blacken their name.
   d. To be suspicious of someone's claims because you think they're likely untrue.

African swine flu is highly contagious and can spread very fast.

African swine flu virus

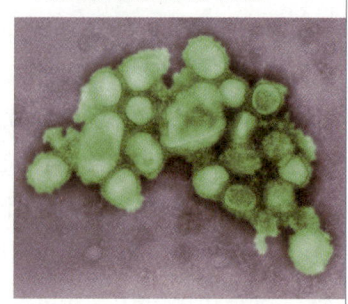

62 The Problem With Pork

1 The name says it all. African swine fever travels via pigs and is highly contagious. Luckily, humans can't contract the disease, which affects both wild and domesticated pigs and is also known as ASF and warthog fever. First documented in Kenya in 1921, the virus later spread through Africa, thus earning the name African swine fever. Clinical signs of this disease include high fever, lesions, elevated pulse and respiration rate, and redness on the ears, legs, and underbelly. Swine that contract the disease die within days of displaying the symptoms. The mortality rate can be as high as 100 percent. Pig farmers are forced to **dispose of** drifts, or groups, of infected pigs, making this not only a health problem for humans but also a serious economic issue.

2 ASF has developed into a global **predicament**. Countries such as Portugal, Spain, and Italy first encountered African swine fever in the late 1900s, and by the 1970s it had spread to the Americas. Recently, occurrences of African swine fever have been reported in parts of Asia, Europe, and Africa. Since 2014, Russia and its neighboring countries have reported over 355,000 cases of ASF. Globally, in 2018 alone, over 119,000 pigs were killed after being diagnosed with the virus. Also by April 2019, China faced huge economical setbacks, as a large outbreak caused the country to kill over 1,020,000 pigs. Currently, China is the largest producer of pork, but the recent spread of swine fever throughout the country threatens to drive the global price of pork up by

Swine that contract the disease die within days of displaying the symptoms.

swine flu detection with a thermal camera

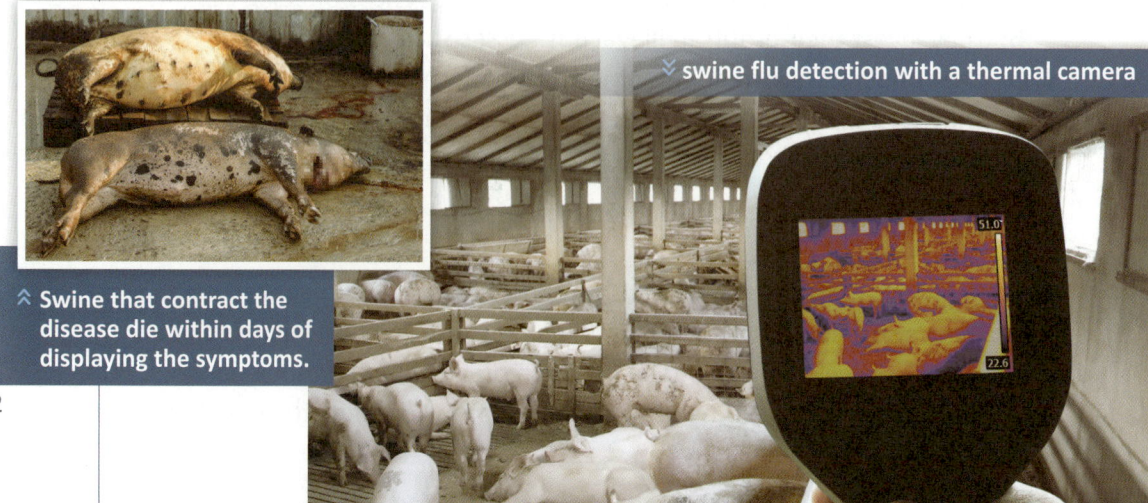

78%. With the pork industry losing money and national governments struggling to track and control the disease, ASF is proving to be an incredibly vexing issue. Depending on where you live, you may be out of pork!

3 Due to the disease's ability to spread rapidly and its potential to cause **devastating** economic damage, extreme measures are needed to eradicate **it**. To prevent the spread of African swine fever, many countries currently ban items from ASF-contaminated areas. Some countries even ban swill feeding (feeding pigs scraps of food), which can cause the disease to spread.

4 But there is hope. Portugal eradicated ASF in 1994 and Spain followed soon after in 1995. Both countries targeted ticks that were spreading the disease to drifts of swine. These countries now serve as an educational beacon of hope for other nations wishing to eradicate the scourge of African swine flu.

›› A country may be out of pork if ASF strikes.

Questions

1. What does **dispose of** indicate in the first paragraph?
   a. Pig farmers must keep a close eye on their pigs for signs of infection.
   b. Pig farmers have to kill pigs that have African swine fever.
   c. Pig farmers have to sell their infected pigs for cheaper than usual.
   d. Pig farmers are often forced to lie about the number of infected pigs.

2. At the beginning of the second paragraph, the author writes that "ASF has developed into a global **predicament**." What does **predicament** mean?
   a. A story that inspires happiness and joy in those who hear it.
   b. An event that has no obvious explanation or cause.
   c. A feeling of dread that something terrible is going to happen.
   d. A challenging or unpleasant situation that is hard to solve.

3. Which of the following is an example of something **devastating**, as the word is used in the third paragraph?
   a. An earthquake destroying a city. b. A firework exploding in the sky.
   c. A lion attacking a deer. d. A car overtaking another in a race.

4. What does **it** refer to in the third paragraph?
   a. An infected pig. b. Swill feeding.
   c. African swine fever. d. The lack of pork.

5. In the final paragraph, what does the author mean by "These countries now serve as an educational beacon of hope"?
   a. Portugal and Spain show just how difficult it is to successfully eradicate ASF.
   b. The information about how Portugal and Spain have handled ASF is misleading.
   c. Portugal and Spain are examples of how not to proceed in handling ASF.
   d. Portugal and Spain act as useful examples of how to solve ASF.

» mammoth

63
Giants of the Steppe

1   Throughout the great epochs of our planet's history, dramatic climate change has been the driving force for the genesis and extinction of countless species. Among **them** stands one of the largest mammals ever to have
5   walked the earth: the steppe mammoth. At the shoulder it was 4.7 m tall, and it weighed about nine metric tons. During the last ice age, it primarily grazed on the grasses, sedges, and rushes that grew in the steppe plains, which were characterized by extremes of temperature and little precipitation. The species is thought to have survived until as late as 11,000 years ago, which coincides with the
10 ending of the previous ice age, from which we are still warming.

2   To really appreciate just how prodigious this animal was, consider the facts about living elephants. **They** spend about 17 hours every day consuming 60 to 300 kilograms of food, drinking 60 to 160 liters of water, and dropping 140 to 180 kilograms of dung. The average mass of a modern elephant is 2.7 metric tons (for
15 females) to 5 metric tons (for males). Now double the amount of food, water, and dung to get an idea of how much bigger the steppe mammoth really was.

3   Besides the colossal size of the steppe mammoth, another identifying feature
20 is the tusks. **These twin marvels** are uniquely shaped in a recurve fashion and up to 5.2 meters long, making the beast instantly recognizable and easily distinguished from other mammoths. The thick fur that covered
25 it was of three different lengths and textures, with the longest measuring about 50 cm.

⌃ size comparison of a mammoth and human (cc by Kurzon)

204

4   It might occur to you **that** much more detail is known about this creature than fossils could possibly provide. That is because a few steppe mammoths have been found nearly intact, mummified (preserved by dehydration) in muddy ice shells; even the contents of the stomach remain. The unique circumstances of a late ice age helped preserve the organic material for thousands of years.

5   There is another factor that might have influenced the extinction of the steppe mammoth. It is the same one that now threatens their modern counterparts: human predation. Piles of fossilized mammoth bones have been found, indicating a likely early human encampment. Though long extinct, the steppe mammoth may have had a more dignified demise—they died for a reason and a purpose, unlike today's hunted elephants, which lie rotting on the ground with only their tusks removed.

Questions

1. What does **them** in the first paragraph refer to?
   a. The coming and going of various epochs.
   b. Species that rise and fall.
   c. Forces like dramatic climate change.
   d. The steppe mammoths.

2. What does **they** in the second paragraph refer to?
   a. Animals in general.
   b. Steppe mammoths.
   c. Modern elephants.
   d. The facts.

3. What is the author referring to when he says "**these twin marvels**" in the third paragraph?
   a. Tusks.
   b. Steppe mammoths.
   c. Food and water.
   d. Identifying features.

4. What does **that** in the fourth paragraph refer to?
   a. Some steppe mammoths have been found completely intact.
   b. The steppe mammoth went extinct 11,000 years ago.
   c. Fossils have provided some details about the steppe mammoth.
   d. An unexpectedly large amount of detail is known about the steppe mammoth.

5. What does the author mean when he writes that today's hunted elephants "lie rotting on the ground with only their tusks removed"?
   a. Elephants are killed for their tusks, not for food.
   b. Elephant corpses rot faster than other animals.
   c. Elephants are hunted more than steppe mammoths ever were.
   d. Tusks are an elephant's primary defense against hunters.

Mammoth VS Elephant

↑ comparison of a mammoth (left) and an elephant (right)

64 Did We All Come From Africa?

>> Scientists believe all humans originate in Africa.

1   Where did we all come from? How did humans populate the entire world? These are queries that people have had since time immemorial. Now, it seems as though science has finally come up with an answer.

2   In 2008, the *Journal of Science* published a report on a widespread investigation of the development of human diversity and migration. The investigation took place at the Stanford Human Genome Center at Stanford University, in California. The study's focal point was to determine genetic variations in nearly 1,000 people from 51 different populations. **It** has offered valuable insight into the growing worldwide curiosity about how we began as a species.

3   A major breakthrough came when researchers uncovered the biggest migration in the history of humankind: the very **first flights** out of Africa. The evidence lay hidden in the genes of the ancestors of those who originally walked its various pathways. Stanford scientists took countless DNA samples, which have an extremely high level of precision, and used them to group people according to their likenesses at 650,000 locations. Their findings suggest that humans first emerged from the areas that are now Ethiopia and Tanzania before going on to populate the rest of the world in various surges. This would seem to confirm the "out of Africa" theory that rose to prominence in the early 1990s.

4   Another international study has discovered that the Chinese did not come from "Peking Man," an early primate mammal that walked upright and is said to have been a human ancestor. Instead, the Chinese people came from early humans in Africa who progressed to China through South Asia about 100,000 years ago. The revelation, which came from a research group at Fudan University in Shanghai, amounted to further evidence that humans evolved from one origin, not many. The team **there** took 100,000 samples of DNA from people all over

« A study has discovered that the Chinese did not come from "Peking Man."

the world and determined that their lineage was from human families in East Africa 150,000 years ago. **Their descendants** began to leave 50,000 years later, some going to China and the rest moving elsewhere to inhabit the earth.

5   What is the significance of all of this? It can only mean that we are all members of the same human family. Regardless of each country's borders, **our differences are only skin deep**—a lesson to take to heart so that true love and harmony can flourish.

▲ human migration

Questions

1. What does **it** in the second paragraph refer to?
   a. The *Journal of Science* magazine.
   b. A DNA sample from one of 1,000 test subjects.
   c. Curiosity about the origin of humankind.
   d. The Stanford University study.

2. What are the **first flights** mentioned in the third paragraph?
   a. The first DNA samples taken in the Stanford study.
   b. The first mass movements of human beings.
   c. The first time the out of Africa theory was published.
   d. The first humans to ever exist.

3. What does **there** in the fourth paragraph refer to?
   a. Fudan University.   b. South Asia.
   c. East Africa.   d. Stanford University.

4. What does **their descendants** in the fourth paragraph refer to?
   a. The descendants of the early humans who settled South Asia 100,000 years ago.
   b. The descendants of the first people to reach China 100,000 years ago.
   c. The descendants of early humans in East Africa 150,000 years ago.
   d. The descendants of human families all over the world 150,00 years ago.

5. What does **our differences are only skin deep** in the final paragraph mean?
   a. Skin color was an important factor driving human migration in the past.
   b. Though our appearances might be different, we're all the same inside.
   c. Humans will always fight each other over differences in how we look.
   d. We have major differences that we'll never be able to resolve.

65 Born Survivors

▲ Tardigrades can survive for days in the vacuum of outer space.

1   They are only as big as the period at the end of this sentence, but tardigrades, also known as "water bears" due to their somewhat **ursine appearance**, are some of the hardiest creatures to ever exist on the planet. Plump-bodied, with eight peculiarly arranged claw-footed legs, tardigrades, usually live in sediment at the bottom of lakes or in other similarly wet environments. However, it's what happens when you take them out of their comfort zone that makes tardigrades special. When confronted with hostile environments, tardigrades become near indestructible, able to survive conditions that would kill a human almost instantly.

2   Experiments have shown that tardigrades can survive in temperatures as low as minus 200 degrees and as high as 148.9 degrees Celsius. They can withstand boiling liquids and pressures of up to six times the amount of pressure felt in the deepest parts of the ocean. They can endure immense doses of deadly radiation and survive for days in the **vacuum** of outer space. In fact, name any apocalyptic event **short of** the sun exploding, and tardigrades are more than likely to be able to survive it.

3   So how exactly are they able to perform these miraculous feats of survival? In short, they hibernate. Just as real bears hibernate to survive the harshness of the northern winters, these microscopic water bears also fall into a kind of "sleep" when their environment threatens their survival. By retracting their heads and legs and curling up into a dehydrated ball, tardigrades can reduce their metabolic activity to 0.01 percent of its normal rate. While hibernating, they produce a sugary gel and a large amount of antioxidants, which protect their vital organs, as well as other chemicals that help shield them from radiation and prevent the growth of ice crystals. They can stay in this hibernated state for years, sometimes decades, and all they need to become their old selves again is to be exposed to water. In fact, in

« tardigrades, also known as "water bears"

2016, scientists managed to revive two tardigrades that had been in this **death-like state** for 30 years!

[4] Unsurprisingly, then, scientists are eager to harness the tardigrade's uncanny survival abilities and use them to create hardier crops and longer-lasting medical supplies. The first steps have already been taken—one scientist isolated the gene that activates when tardigrades go into hibernation and used it to engineer a strain of yeast with a **tolerance** to drought that's 100 times more than normal.

[5] Tardigrades may be almost microscopic, but their potential to benefit humanity is clearly enormous!

> Tardigrades hibernate like a bear when they encounter threatening environments.

Questions

1. In the first paragraph, the author writes that the tardigrade have an **ursine appearance.** What is the meaning of the word **ursine**?
   a. Unusual or seldom seen.
   b. Repulsive to look at.
   c. Very difficult to describe.
   d. Bear-like.

2. In the second paragraph, the author writes that tardigrades have survived for days in the **vacuum** of outer space. What does **vacuum** mean in this context?
   a. A gap left by death of someone important.
   b. A space devoid of any matter.
   c. An electric device used to clean carpets.
   d. A state of isolation from outside influences.

3. "In fact, name any apocalyptic event **short of** the sun exploding, and tardigrades are more than likely to be able to survive it." What does the writer mean by **short of**?
   a. Rather than.   b. Worse than.   c. For example.   d. Not including.

4. What does the phrase **death-like state** in the third paragraph refer to?
   a. Hibernation.
   b. A freezing environment.
   c. A total lack of water.
   d. The deepest part of the ocean.

5. In the fourth paragraph the author writes that tardigrade genes have been used to increase yeast's **tolerance** drought. What does the word **tolerance** mean in this context?
   a. The capacity to endure pain.
   b. Sympathy for someone else's beliefs.
   c. The capacity to survive difficult conditions.
   d. The amount of variation permitted when measuring something.

2-4 Review Test

> Scammers keep coming up with fresh tricks to cheat unsuspecting people out of their money.

66 Scammers, Scammers Everywhere!

1 Scammers have been cheating unsuspecting people out of their money, whether through gambling hustles or confidence tricks, since the dawn of civilization. Nowadays, people spend most of their time on the Internet, so it's no surprise that scammers operate online, too. Infinitely adaptable, Internet scammers constantly **put fresh twists on** old scams, tripping up new and unsuspecting victims every day.

2 Though scams such as tricking people into buying fake goods or donating money to fraudulent crowdfunding campaigns are undeniably devious, falling for one will only mean you lose a relatively small amount of cash. However, other scams, known as phishing scams, are often far more **insidious**. Phishing scams specialize in acquiring your personal or financial information, which can lead to infinitely more serious consequences, such as identity theft or large-scale bank fraud. You may, for example, get an email from your bank asking you to verify your account details. The email will appear highly convincing, with the bank's logo, formal language, and an official-looking signature all present and correct. But it's all a **charade**, and you reply at your own peril.

[3] In fact, phishing scams are constantly evolving to fit in with the latest online norms and trends. The latest racket is for scammers to masquerade as celebrities and send messages to their "fans" inviting them to click on a link to win a special prize. Following on from this will be a series of questions or forms to fill out that will result in the scammer getting their deceitful hands on your personal info.

[4] Social media sites, too, are prime hunting grounds for data thieves. If you ever see someone posting a survey or chain-letter game where you are required to answer a series of innocuous-looking questions (e.g., "What was your first pet's name?" or "What was the first concert you ever went to?"), be very **wary** about replying. Why? Because whenever you set up a new password, you're often asked to provide a security question in case you forget and need to retrieve your password. If you play along with the scammer's game, you're potentially giving them access to your passwords by inadvertently handing them the answers to your security questions!

[5] Scammers are smart, so it is your job to be smarter. Stay **savvy**, sceptical, and ahead of the game by educating yourself about the latest scams. It's a tough world out there on the web. Take steps to ensure you don't become a victim.

⌄ Some scammers fake a real email from a bank to get personal information.

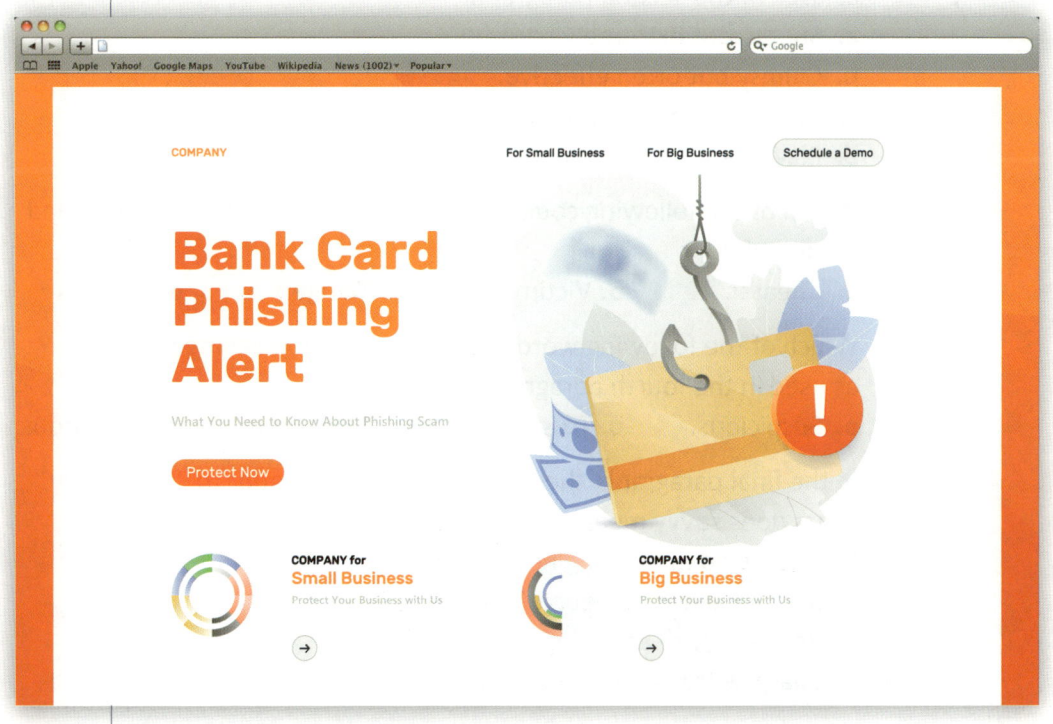

▽ phishing scams

Questions

____ 1. In the first paragraph, the author writes that Internet scammers constantly **put fresh twists on** old scams. What does he mean by this?
   a. Scammers find it easier to take advantage of older people than younger people.
   b. Scammers invent completely new scams on a daily basis.
   c. Scammers are always coming up with new variations of well-established tricks.
   d. Scammers often struggle to come up with new ideas on how to scam people.

____ 2. Which of the following is a suitable definition for the word **insidious**, as used in the second paragraph?
   a. Subtle, but extremely harmful.
   b. Clumsy but often effective.
   c. Incredibly easy to detect.
   d. Playful and often harmless.

____ 3. Which of the following could replace the word **charade** in the second paragraph?
   a. Cheater.   b. Victim.   c. Danger.   d. Scam.

____ 4. Which of the following words has the opposite meaning to **wary**, as used in the fourth paragraph?
   a. Suspicious.   b. Trustful.   c. Intelligent.   d. Humorous.

____ 5. In the final paragraph, the author advises the reader to "Stay **savvy**." What does **savvy** mean in this context?
   a. Interested in learning new information.
   b. Solitary, avoiding people's company.
   c. Ready to take advantage of others.
   d. Sharp-witted and aware of danger.

≫ Kizuna AI's YouTube channel
(Retrieved from https://www.youtube.com/channel/UC4YaOt1yT-ZeyB0OmxHgoIA)

▲ Kizuna AI in 3D
(cc by kyu3)

67 Virtually Famous

1   Kizuna AI and Shudu Gram are Internet celebrities. Kizuna is a YouTube vlogger, who entertains her viewers with a variety of kooky activities and has over 2.5 million subscribers to her channel. Shudu, on the other and, is a South African supermodel with over 170,000 followers on Instagram. What makes these two different from any other Internet celebrity? Kizuna and Shudu aren't made of flesh and blood, they are **made of 1s and 0s**.

2   The two are among a growing number of virtual social media celebrities that are **making waves on the Internet**, gaining huge fanbases, corporate deals, and celebrity endorsement offers. Some, like Kizuna, who is animated in the distinctive style of Japanese anime, are clearly not-human, while others—like Shudu—are far more realistic. They are created using 3-D modelling software and, in the case of the YouTubers, motion trackers and voiceover actors. Digital Instagram models are often the creations of a single digital artist, whereas an entire team—including script writers, directors, and visual effects artists—is needed to bring a VTuber to life.

213

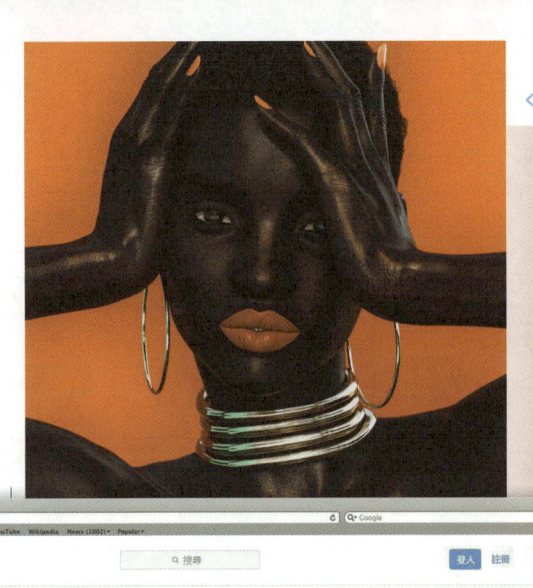

≪ ≫ Shudu Gram

⌃ Shudu Gram's Instagram page (Retrieved from https://www.instagram.com/shudu.gram/?hl=zh-tw)

⌃ Shudu Gram's creator, Cameron-James Wilson

3 So what is it that makes these "fake" Internet celebrities so popular? To answer this question, we must look back to 1970s Japan, a time when, due to slow economic growth, many Japanese developed a dissatisfaction with reality and a subsequent **embracement** of fictional, digital realities that has continued to this day. With Japanese culture becoming ever more popular in the West, an enthusiasm for and acceptance of the virtual world has followed closely behind.

4 But what about human Internet celebrities? How do they feel about this new trend? Many feel threatened and have **voiced** concerns that virtual YouTubers, who never get tired or demand payment, could take over the platform. Criticism has also been levelled against Shudu's creator, Cameron-James Wilson. Some point out that Shudu, who is portrayed as dark-skinned, may be taking opportunities that would otherwise have been offered to real dark-skinned models.

5   Wilson is confident that real-life models have nothing to fear. However, he does think that the increase in the role of digitalization in fashion, such as creating digital versions of real-life models in order to save on shooting cost, will ultimately change the industry. YouTubers, on the other hand, will soon have access to software that allows them to **morph** their own facial images into those of digital cartoons and animals in real time. Eventually, Wilson says, 3-D and humans will co-exist and benefit each other.

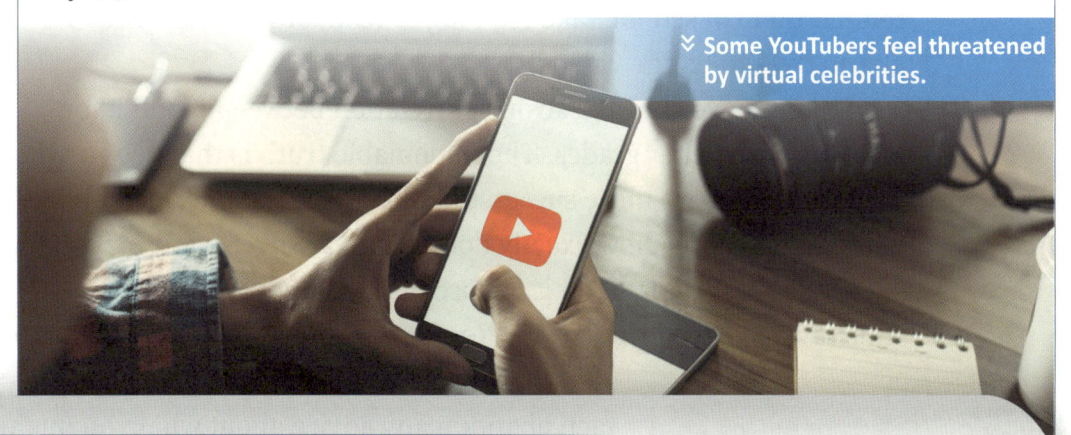

> Some YouTubers feel threatened by virtual celebrities.

Questions

1. What does the author mean when he writes that Kizuna AI and Shudu Gram are **made of 1s and 0s**?
   a. They earn an awful lot of money.
   b. Their success is very easy to understand.
   c. They have large fanbases that support them.
   d. They are created using computer software.

2. In the second paragraph, the author writes that a growing number of virtual celebrities are **making waves on the Internet.** What does he mean by this?
   a. Virtual celebrities are creating a big impression online.
   b. Virtual celebrities are popular with netizens who also like to surf.
   c. Virtual celebrities are dangerous and may cause harm to their fans.
   d. Virtual celebrities are a trend that will come and go.

3. Which of the following words could the author have used instead of **embracement** in the third paragraph?
   a. Acceptance.   b. Rejection.   c. Distrust.   d. Tolerance.

4. Which of the following has the same meaning as **voiced** in the fourth paragraph?
   a. Shouted.   b. Expressed.   c. Whispered.   d. Demanded.

5. Which of the following has the opposite meaning to the word **morph** in the final paragraph?
   a. Transform.   b. Modify.   c. Preserve.   d. Create.

68 Becoming a Bookworm

1   The entrepreneur Bill Gates famously gets through 50 books a year. How do you measure up? For many people, the idea of reading (almost) one book per week seems gloriously, impossibly indulgent; for others, regular reading simply isn't an attractive prospect. Books remind them of school, take too long to read, or feel like **dreary** alternatives to online videos.

2   Studies have shown a strong correlation between reading for pleasure and higher grades. The undeniable truth is that people who read for leisure are more successful in life—so if **this** is one of life's most useful habits, how exactly do we cultivate it?

3   The easiest thing to do is choose material that excites you. It's fine to **disregard the bestseller lists** and your friends' insistence that this or that book is "unputdownable." In fact, abandon any advice about what you ought to read, whether it's from peers or teachers. If you have a passion for fashion, read magazine articles. If your brain loves to wander through fantasy worlds, read comic books. If nonfiction leaves you cold, stick to novels. Reading tends to lead to greater and broader reading, so just read on with whatever material you have to hand.

Upheaval, by **Jared Diamond**. I'm a big fan of everything Jared has written exception. The book explores how societies react during moments of cris fascinating case studies to show how nations managed existential challen threats, and general malaise. It sounds a bit depressing, but I finished the about our ability to solve problems than I started.

Nine Pints, by **Rose George**. If you get grossed out by blood, this one prol you're like me and find it fascinating, you'll enjoy this book by a British jo personal connection to the subject. I'm a big fan of books that go deep on Pints (the title refers to the volume of blood in the average adult) was righ super-interesting facts that will leave you with a new appreciation for blo

A Gentleman in Moscow, by **Amor Towles**. It seems like everyone I know h joined the club after my brother-in-law sent me a copy, and I'm glad I did count sentenced to life under house arrest in a Moscow hotel is fun, cleve Even if you don't enjoy reading about Russia as much as I do (I've read ev Gentleman in Moscow is an amazing story that anyone can enjoy.

Bill Gates is famous for being a bookworm, and recommends his book list to the world every year.
(Retrieved from https://www.gatesnotes.com/About-Bill-Gates/Summer-Books-2019)

Studies show that people who read for leisure are more successful in life.

216

People tend to associate reading with school and textbooks.

4   A lot of people complain that buying books will break their budgets. Certainly, new books are not cheap, but you probably order three takeaway coffees per week without a second thought. That costs around the same as a paperback—and the book will be far more beneficial in the end! Research second-hand bookstores in your area. You can get **significant** discounts there, as well as finding rare treasures. And the best option of all is to visit a library, where knowledge is absolutely free.

5   Another thing you can do is have a book with you at all times. There's more dead time in your day than you might think. Riding the bus or train, waiting for your friend to show up or for the microwave to ping—these are all moments that you can use to dive into those pages! And this is a great technique for anyone with a short attention span, since five minutes of reading a few times a day quickly adds up. And you'll probably find yourself reluctant to put down a good book.

6   One final tip is to reduce that lethal screen time. Without the distractions of the virtual world, you're more likely to pick up a book. The advantage of the latter is that you can't mindlessly click away from what you're reading. So switch off your tablet, get hold of some inspiring reading matter, and go for it!

« Seizing the dead time during the day to read is good for people with short attention spans.

217

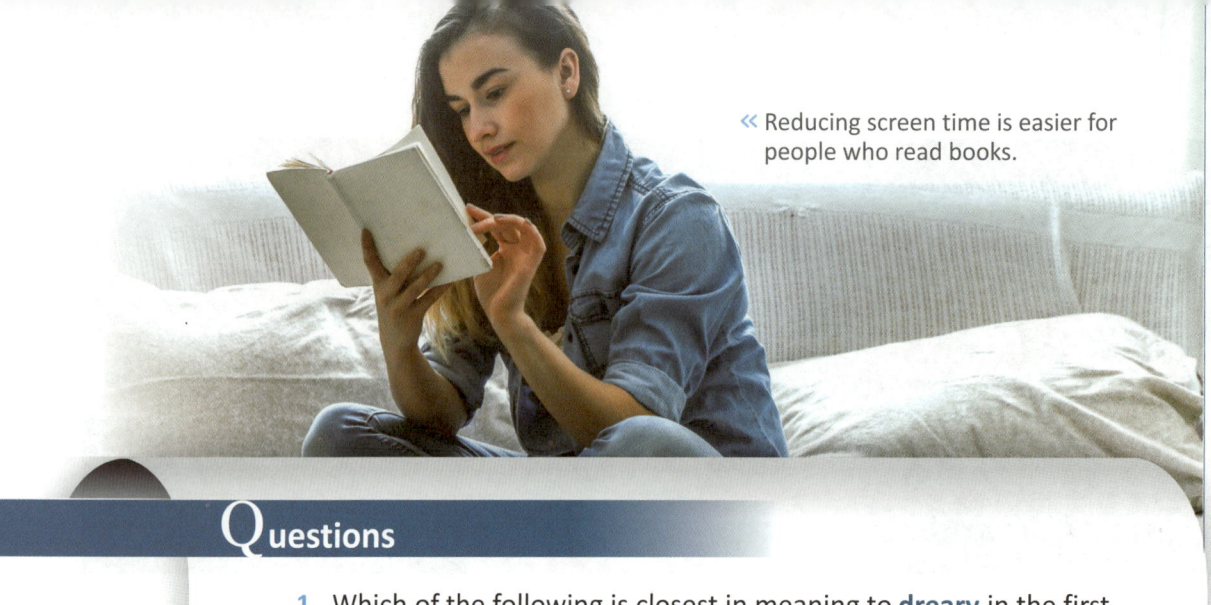

« Reducing screen time is easier for people who read books.

Questions

1. Which of the following is closest in meaning to **dreary** in the first paragraph?
   a. Tempting.
   b. Depressing.
   c. Encouraging.
   d. Fascinating.

2. What does **this** refer to in the second paragraph?
   a. The correlation between reading and higher grades.
   b. The habit of reading for pleasure.
   c. The importance of becoming successful in life.
   d. The finding of the undeniable truth.

3. Why does the author say **disregard the bestseller lists**?
   a. Some bestselling books are badly written.
   b. What interests the majority may not interest you.
   c. Large publishers can pay to put books on the list.
   d. Books on bestseller lists all tend to be similar.

4. Which of the following sentences uses **significant** in the same way as in the fourth paragraph?
   a. You and your significant other are both invited to the party.
   b. Steve Jobs is one of the most significant figures in modern history.
   c. If you invest smartly, you could earn a significant sum of money.
   d. The results of the study will be significant for anyone working in education.

5. When someone is willing to do things without hesitation, he or she is NOT _____.
   a. hopeful
   b. empathetic
   c. adaptable
   d. reluctant

69 Life Lessons From the Ancient Stage

>> Dionysus, the god of wine and fertility

1   Of the three types of drama (tragedy, comedy, and satire), tragedy is the one most closely associated with ancient Greece. The Greeks used the term to refer to plays involving gods, kings, and other heroic figures whose destinies changed for the worse as a result of their actions. In Aristotle's view, tragedy functioned as a catharsis – a means of purging the viewer of pity and fear.

2   Athens was **inarguably** the most significant city-state in Greece from around 550 to 220 BC, and performances of tragedies were important to Athenians. This was first made abundantly clear around 508 BC at a religious festival that honored Dionysus, the god of wine and fertility. The festival was called the City Dionysia, a major part of which was a competition to determine who would be the official playwright of the festivities. Thespis was the winner of the first such contest, and thus his name came to be closely connected with drama. He is also credited with having been the first dramatist whose characters spoke their lines rather than sang them. Theatrical performers are known to this day as thespians.

ⱽ ancient theater in Athens

3 Until the Hellenistic period began in 323 BC, tragedies were written solely to celebrate Dionysus. They were performed only once, so that now we know only those parts which were recalled clearly enough to be replayed when the performance of old tragedies became customary.

4 Perhaps the most **renowned** of all Greek tragedies is *Oedipus Rex*, or *Oedipus the King*. Written by Sophocles around 429 BC, it strikingly illustrates how humans cannot avoid destiny. In a complicated series of circumstances, King Oedipus murders his father and marries his mother without realizing it. Only in his pursuit of the truth, which will save his kingdom from a plague, does Oedipus learn to his horror what he has done.

⌃ Sophocles

⌃ Euripides

« *Oedipus and the Sphinx*

[5]   *Helen*, authored by Euripides in 412 BC, is another famous tragedy. It concerns the mythological character Helen, daughter of Zeus, who was both loved and hated for her beauty. This led to wars in which many lost their lives.

[6]   Interestingly, the word "tragedy" is derived from the Greek words *tragos* (goat) and *oide* (ode, or song), so its literal meaning is "goat song." One possible explanation for this is that Dionysus had followers and attendants who were half human and half goat. The origin of the term becomes a bit more understandable when you consider the Greek mythology that surrounds it.

Questions

1. What does "a means of purging the viewer of pity and fear" mean in the first paragraph?
   a. A way of instilling pity and fear in the viewer.
   b. A way of eliminating the viewer's feelings of pity and fear.
   c. A way of writing plays about pity and fear.
   d. A way of making the viewer laugh at pity and fear.

2. Which of the following words could replace **inarguably** in the second paragraph?
   a. Possibly.   b. Definitely.   c. Occasionally.   d. Suitably.

3. What does "determine who would be the official playwright of the festivities" mean in the second paragraph?
   a. Celebrate the person chosen to write the festival's drama.
   b. Learn more about drama from popular playwrights.
   c. Choose the best play from a series of performances.
   d. Decide who would be allowed to write the drama for the festival.

4. In the third paragraph, what does "tragedies were written solely to celebrate Dionysus" mean?
   a. Dionysus was the main character in all tragedies.
   b. Dramatists wrote plays they thought Dionysus would like.
   c. Tragedies were happy stories involving celebrations.
   d. Tragedies were only written for Dionysus's festival.

5. Which of the following words means the opposite of **renowned** in the fourth paragraph?
   a. Unknown.   b. Famous.   c. Simple.   d. Ancient.

˄ Our stomach is a flexible organ, and sugar stimulates this reflex.

70 Deceptive Digestion

1   You've just finished your meal—mountains of mashed potatoes, an enormous steak, piles of vegetables, all coated in a rich gravy. You couldn't possibly eat another bite. But then someone suggests dessert—"**The chocolate cake looks to die for!**"—and suddenly you feel you might just have some space left after all.

2   This phenomenon, known as "dessert stomach," has tormented diners and frustrated dieters for as long as ending our meals with a sweet little something has been common practice. But the reasons behind this dinnertime quirk are actually very well understood. A large part of it is down to what's known as sensory specific satiety—or "getting bored with your food" **in layman's terms**. After finishing a large plateful of one type of food, your senses have had enough. What once enchanted you is now dull and uninteresting. However, when the dessert menu arrives listing all those appealing dainties, your interest picks up and your brain encourages you to eat for the pleasure of experiencing new and pleasant flavors.

3   Usually, if you have just eaten a **substantial** meal, your stomach will already be full. But the stomach is a flexible organ, able to relax and make room for more food when necessary. Sugar, it turns out, stimulates this reflex, so after just a few bites of your ice-cream sundae, your stomach, having been triggered to relax, won't feel so full any more. This allows you to consume the whole bowl, despite feeling just a few minutes ago as if you were about to burst.

˄ "Dessert stomach" is a phenomenon that has tormented diners and frustrated dieters.

[4] The sensation is only temporary, of course, and after you are done with your dessert, your stomach will once again feel uncomfortably full, leaving you **sluggish** and unable to move without discomfort for some time after. Of course, the additional danger here is that because of dessert stomach, we often overindulge at mealtimes, adding additional and unnecessary calories to an already high-calorie meal.

[5] But there is a way that we can use this phenomenon to our advantage. If, for example, instead of eating a whole dessert yourself, you shared it with several friends, you would trigger your stomach to relax but avoid filling it to the point of discomfort. In other words, you'd leave the meal feeling less full and thus more comfortable, having also both **alleviated** your sensory boredom and avoided too many unhealthy calories. Your digestive health—and waistline—will be a lot better for it.

Questions

_____ 1. What does the author mean by the phrase **The chocolate cake looks to die for**?
   a. Eating the cake will likely kill you.
   b. The cake looks extremely delicious.
   c. The cake is too big for one person to finish.
   d. The cake is overly expensive.

_____ 2. What does the phrase **in layman's terms** most likely mean?
   a. Written using a dry, academic style.
   b. Said with enthusiasm and conviction.
   c. Phrased simply so that everyone can understand.
   d. Heavily edited so that anything offensive has been removed.

_____ 3. Which of the following has the opposite meaning to **substantial**, as used in the third paragraph?
   a. Light.   b. Heavy.   c. Unhealthy.   d. Nutritious.

_____ 4. Which of the following has the opposite meaning to **sluggish**, as used in the fourth paragraph?
   a. Delighted.   b. Easy-going.   c. Frustrated.   d. Energetic.

_____ 5. Which of the following could replace the word **alleviated** in the final paragraph?
   a. Intensified.   b. Relieved.   c. Altered.   d. Misused.

223

Unit 3
Study Strategies

3-1 Visual Material

3-2 Reference Sources

In this unit, we will introduce you to two important strategies: interpreting visual material and using reference sources. Visual material graphically represents data such as statistics and figures in a way that is easy to understand. Reference sources, on the other hand, are things that help us locate information quickly and efficiently. This unit will give you the skills you need both to analyze graphical representations of data effectively and to find desired information quickly.

By the end of this section, your reading comprehension will no longer allow you merely to understand, interpret, and criticize a text; it will also allow you to effectively navigate the vast world of information that is out there.

3-1 Visual Material

Information comes in many forms, and sometimes it can be difficult to convey using words. This is where **visual material** can come in handy. **Visual material** uses pictures and graphics to convey information. It includes **charts**, **tables**, and **maps**. If used properly, it can make complex information easy to understand.

71 Bar Graph:
A Concerning Road Safety Record

1   Taiwan is well-known for being one of the safest countries in the world and is often ranked among the world's top five law-abiding countries. Rates for violent crimes are extremely low, as are those for theft. But there is one area that is a blot on Taiwan's otherwise impeccable record—road safety. Even a casual glance at some of Taiwan's road accident statistics is enough to cause a prospective driver to sweat. Roughly 300,000 traffic accidents occur in Taiwan each year.

2   The island's city roads packed with speeding scooters create particularly fertile conditions for accidents. Though the number of fatalities has fallen in recent years, hundreds of people still die each year as a result of careless driving. It's undeniable that if the island's reputation as a safe-haven is to be maintained, Taiwan's culture of dangerous driving must see some dramatic improvement.

3   The page below are two bar charts that give you some idea of the state of road safety in Taiwan. A bar graph displays information as colored bars of different lengths, making it easy to compare data quickly. The first graph displays data from five different countries, including Taiwan; the second includes data from Taiwan only.

Scooters go down the Taipei bridge during rush hour in the morning.

Unit 3 Study Strategies
3-1 Visual Material

> Speeding scooters are the main cause of accidents.

The Form of Transportation Being Used by Sufferers of Fatal Road Accidents in 2014

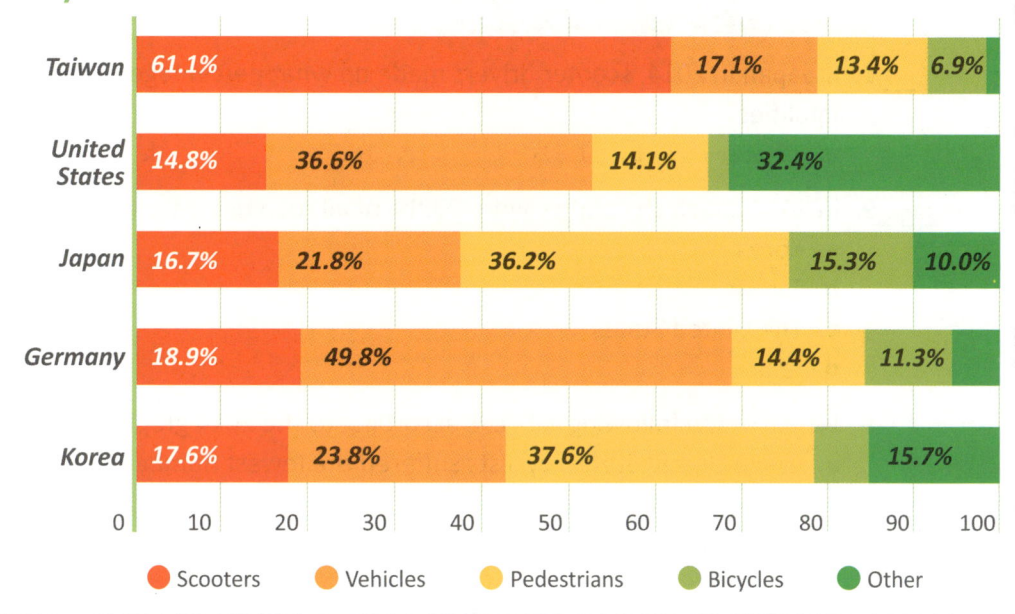

Country	Scooters	Vehicles	Pedestrians	Bicycles	Other
Taiwan	61.1%	17.1%	13.4%		6.9%
United States	14.8%	36.6%	14.1%		32.4%
Japan	16.7%	21.8%	36.2%	15.3%	10.0%
Germany	18.9%	49.8%	14.4%	11.3%	
Korea	17.6%	23.8%	37.6%		15.7%

(scale: 0 to 100)

● Scooters ● Vehicles ● Pedestrians ● Bicycles ● Other

Ages of Those Responsible for Causing Fatal Road Accidents in Taiwan, 2015

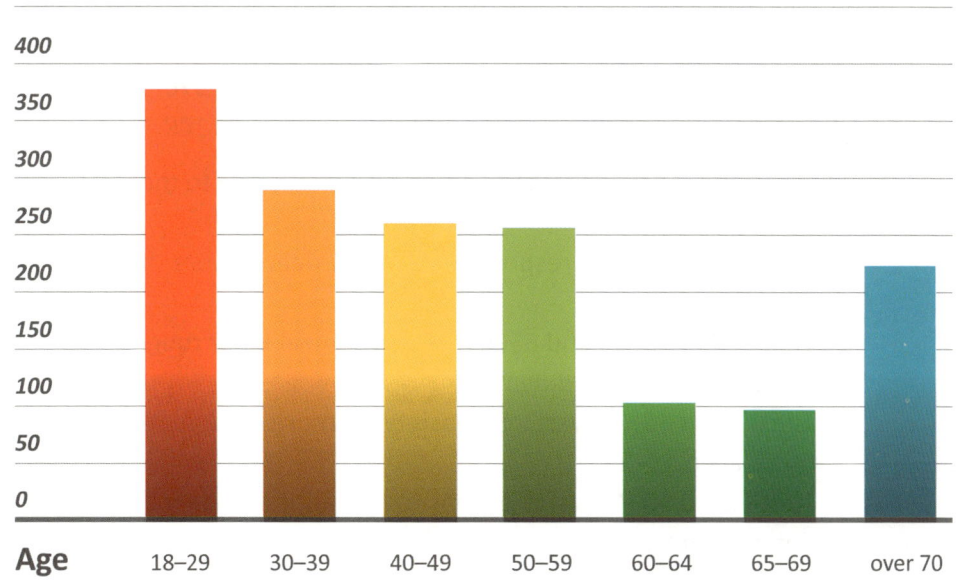

Age	18–29	30–39	40–49	50–59	60–64	65–69	over 70

(y-axis: 0 to 400)

» A policeman is recording the details of a traffic accident involving a scooter.

Questions

1. In Japan in 2014, scooter drivers made up what percentage of road fatalities?
   a. 18.9%
   b. 21.8%
   c. 16.7%
   d. 32.4%

2. In 2014, in which country were 23.8% of all road deaths car drivers?
   a. Korea.
   b. Taiwan.
   c. The United States.
   d. Japan.

3. Which of the following is FALSE according to the 2014 graph?
   a. In the United States, cyclists suffered the fewest number of fatal road accidents.
   b. In Germany, the most common way to die on the road was driving a car.
   c. In Taiwan, 13.4% of those killed on the road were pedestrians.
   d. In Japan, the number of car driver deaths was double the number of pedestrian deaths.

4. In Taiwan in 2015, how many road deaths were caused by those aged between 40 and 59?
   a. Approximately 500.
   b. Approximately 370.
   c. Approximately 250.
   d. Approximately 100.

5. Which of the following statements is TRUE according to the 2015 graph?
   a. The age group most responsible for road deaths were those aged 70 and over.
   b. Those aged 60–64 and 65–69 were responsible for roughly the same number of road deaths.
   c. Those aged 30–39 were responsible for more road deaths than those aged 18–29.
   d. Those aged 40–49 were responsible for approximately 100 road deaths that year.

People in Asia are living longer, and the number of older people will continue to grow.

72 Line Chart: Asia's Ticking Time Bomb

1 There is a crisis in Asia. Due to young people having fewer children and older people living longer, by the year 2060, over a third of the population in many Asian countries could be made up of over 65s.

2 One serious consequence of this trend is that the brunt of the financial burden of caring for this elderly population will fall on young people's shoulders. Of course, the larger the ratio of elderly to young, the more unsustainable this financial burden becomes.

3 Another is that as the active workforce shrinks, so will these countries' economies. Even now, there is an increasing pressure for the elderly to retire later than in previous generations, with some working even into their 70s. For many, taking an early retirement has become nothing more than a fantasy.

4 The line graph on the next page illustrates the growing share of elderly people in four Asian countries and projects those figures into the future. A line graph shows how something has changed or will change (usually over a period of time). If the line goes up, that signals an increase; if down, a decrease.

» The elderly have to retire later than in previous generations.

∧ Caring for the elderly population will fall on young people's shoulders.

Water Stress by Country: 2013

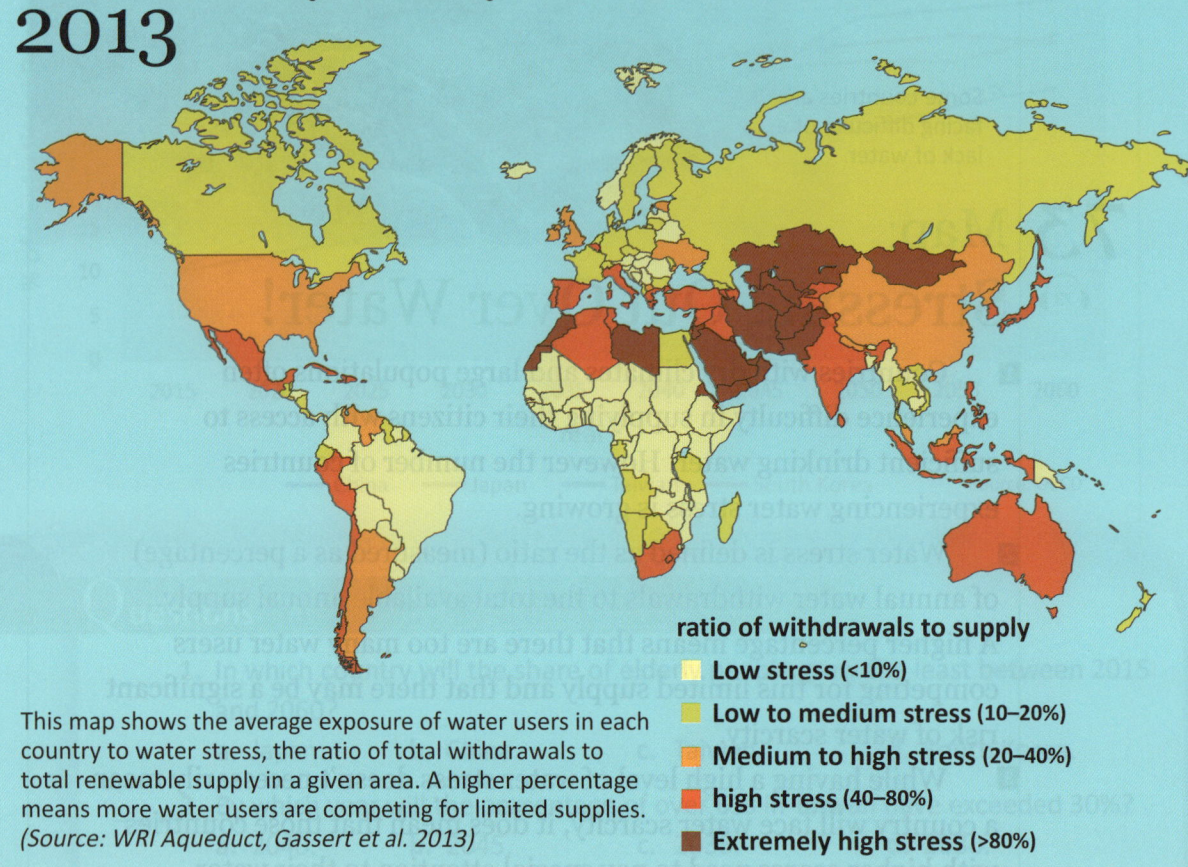

This map shows the average exposure of water users in each country to water stress, the ratio of total withdrawals to total renewable supply in a given area. A higher percentage means more water users are competing for limited supplies.
(Source: WRI Aqueduct, Gassert et al. 2013)

ratio of withdrawals to supply
- Low stress (<10%)
- Low to medium stress (10–20%)
- Medium to high stress (20–40%)
- high stress (40–80%)
- Extremely high stress (>80%)

Questions

_____ 1. In which of the following countries is the level of water stress expected to stay the same between 2013 and 2040?
   a. United States.   b. China.   c. Australia.   d. Japan.

_____ 2. What was the level of water stress in China in 2013?
   a. Extremely high.   b. Low.   c. Medium to high.   d. Low to medium.

_____ 3. Which of the following statements is TRUE?
   a. Japan's water stress level will increase by 2040.
   b. In 2013, Australia's water stress level was the same as China's.
   c. The United States' water stress level will go from high in 2013 to extremely high in 2040.
   d. In southern Africa, more countries will experience high water stress in 2040 compared to 2013.

Water Stress by Country: 2040

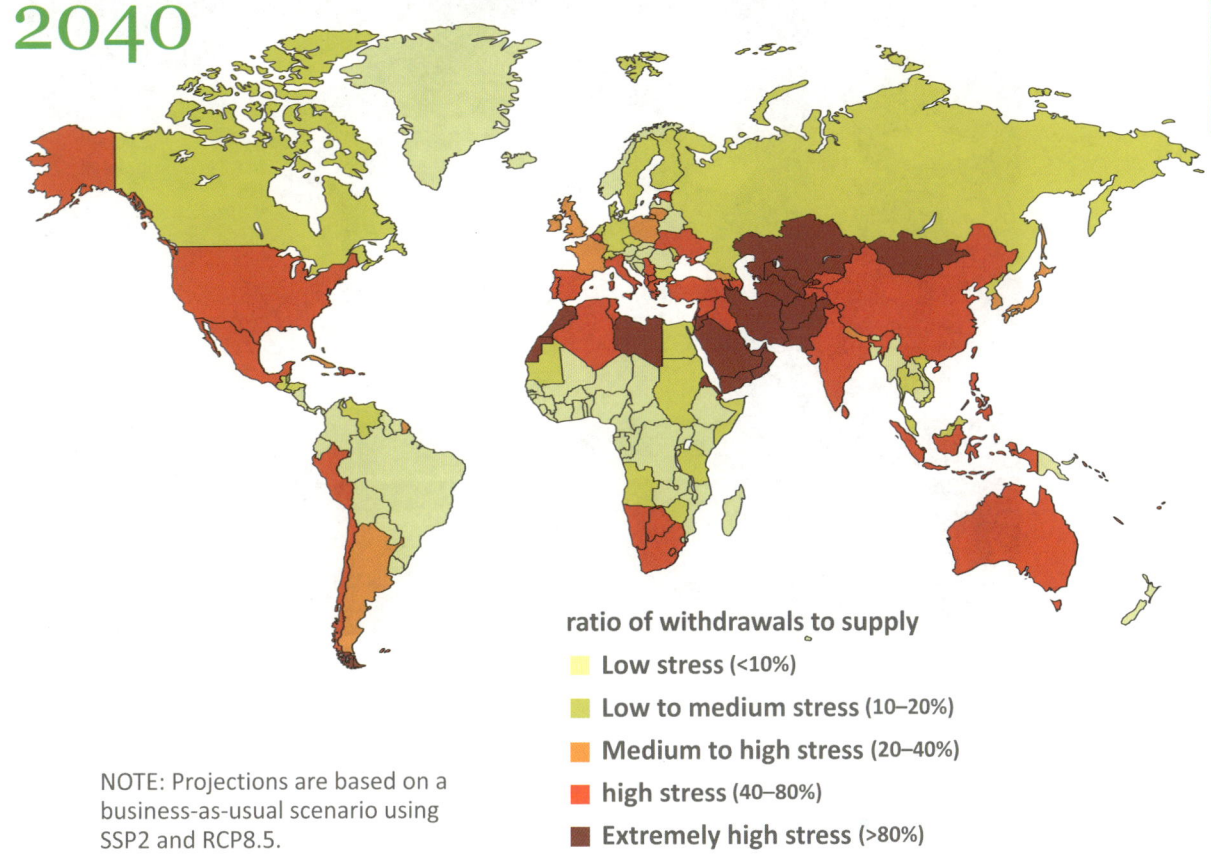

NOTE: Projections are based on a business-as-usual scenario using SSP2 and RCP8.5.

ratio of withdrawals to supply
- Low stress (<10%)
- Low to medium stress (10–20%)
- Medium to high stress (20–40%)
- high stress (40–80%)
- Extremely high stress (>80%)

_____ 4. Which of the following countries will have the lowest level of water stress in 2040?
   a. Canada.   b. Brazil.   c. United Kingdom.   d. Russia.

_____ 5. Which of the following statements is FALSE?
   a. In 2040, most of South America will be experiencing extremely high levels of water stress.
   b. In 2040, Canada will be experiencing low-to-medium water stress.
   c. In 2013, China experienced less water stress than India.
   d. The level of water stress experienced by New Zealand is going to fall by 2040.

⌃ Working out is a key to losing weight, but not the most vital one.

74 Pie Chart: Get Your Priorities Right!

1   Most of us know that diet and exercise are the two things you need to focus on if you want to lose a few pounds. Eating healthy foods is important, but probably the most vital element to cutting weight is working out. The only way to really burn those calories is by training hard in the gym. And while we all know a good night's sleep is important for our physical and mental health, it is not really a priority when trying to lose weight. Instead of getting a full night's rest, it is far better to get up early and hit the gym. Right?

2   Wrong! According to fitness experts, these commonly held priorities are completely topsy-turvy. Take a look at the pie charts on the next page. Pie charts are circular charts divided into slices, with each slice representing a percentage of a whole. The chart on the left shows the way most people prioritize sleep, nutrition, and working out when trying to lose weight. The chart on the right shows the way you should be prioritizing those three elements if you want to lose weight effectively.

Priorities For Fat Loss
@dancudes

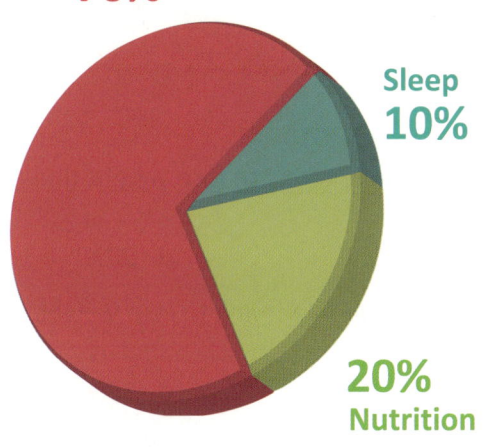

What most people are doing
- Working out 70%
- Sleep 10%
- Nutrition 20%

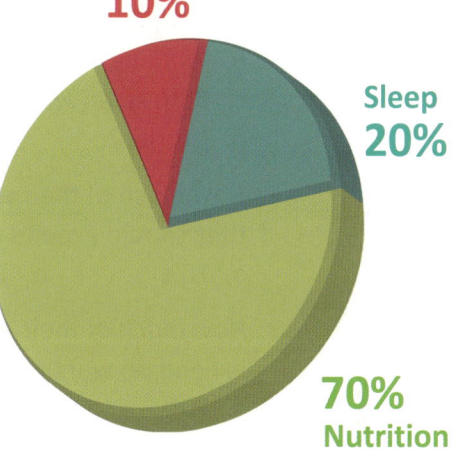

What they should be doing
- Working out 10%
- Sleep 20%
- Nutrition 70%

> Nutrition is actually what people should pay attention to if they want to lose weight.

Questions

____ 1. What is the most important element for losing weight according to the pie charts?
   a. Sleep.
   b. Working out.
   c. Both sleep and working out equally.
   d. Nutrition.

____ 2. How much of their efforts do most people trying to lose weight think they should expend on working out?
   a. 70%   b. 10%   c. 20%   d. 50%

____ 3. How much of their efforts should most people trying to lose weight expend on working out?
   a. 70%   b. 10%   c. 20%   d. 50%

____ 4. In what order of importance do most people trying to lose wright put these three elements?
   a. Nutrition, sleep, working out.   b. Sleep, working out, nutrition.
   c. Working out, nutrition, sleep.   d. Nutrition, working out, sleep.

____ 5. Which of the following is true?
   a. Working out is more important than people think.
   b. Nutrition is not as important as people think.
   c. Sleep is twice as important as most people think.
   d. Sleep is actually the least important element.

« Sleep is more important than working out if the goal is to lose weight.

▽ Students can experience the school atmosphere by attending a summer program.

75 Schedule/Timetable: Try Before You Apply

1 When deciding which university to apply to, making the correct choice is vital—after all, it is where you are potentially going to spend the next several years of your life! To ensure that you and the university are a good fit, it is always best to check out any university in person before you apply. This is often doubly important if, like an increasing number of Taiwanese students, you plan to attend university abroad.

2 Consequently, many universities offer short summer programs for international students in order to give them the opportunity to try out the university before making their final decision. Students attending these courses can experience the university's unique atmosphere and study practices, get accustomed to the local environment and culture, and speak personally with current staff and students. The programs will often include workshops that help students successfully navigate the application process when the time comes.

3 On the next page is part of the schedule for a two-week summer program at the University of Oxford. Schedules (or timetables) are tables that show which classes and activities happen each day and during which time period they take place. By understanding a timetable, you'll know exactly what's going on and when so that you won't miss out on any of the fun!

Oxford Summer Programme

Week 1

	Sunday	Monday	Tuesday
Breakfast		A variety of breakfast options served in the college dining hall.	
Morning Session	Day of arrival – Check in after 2 p.m.	Welcome & orientation	University application system: Personal statement (3 hours)
		University introduction (incl. Oxford college system) with college tour	
Lunch		A selection of hot and cold food options served in the college dining hall.	
Afternoon Session		Oxford walking guided tour	Academic elective (3 hours)
		Academic elective (2 hours)	
Dinner	A selection of hot and cold food options served in the college dining hall.		
Evening Activities	Games: Ice-breaker	Party "Welcome to Oxford"	Shakespeare theatre performance

Questions

1. What will the programme attendees be doing on Wednesday morning?
   a. Sightseeing in London.
   b. Visiting the university library.
   c. Attending class.
   d. Studying in their rooms.

2. Which of the following is TRUE about Saturday?
   a. The attendees will study their academic elective in the afternoon.
   b. The attendees will not eat lunch in college.
   c. In the evening, the attendees will watch a play.
   d. The students will visit the Botanical Gardens before lunch.

3. On which day will the attendees NOT study their academic elective?
   a. Thursday.   b. Friday.   c. Saturday.   d. Wednesday.

» the University of Oxford

Source: Summer In Oxford

Wednesday	Thursday	Friday	Saturday
Day out in London London walking tour (incl. Big Ben, the Houses of Parliament & London Bridge)	Academic elective (3 hours)	Academic elective (3 hours)	Academic elective (3 hours)
Packed lunch	A selection of hot and cold food options served in the college dining hall.		Packed lunch
Visit to the London Dungeon & the London Eye, river cruise	Oxford Castle guided tour	Bodleian Library guided tour & visit to the University Church Tower	Oxford University Botanical Gardens guided tour
	University interview workshop (2 hours)		Free time in the city centre
Study time	British sports	Evening talk: Student life at Oxford University	Quiz night

_____ 4. When will the attendees learn how to develop their university interview skills?
   a. Friday morning.
   b. Thursday afternoon.
   c. Thursday evening.
   d. Friday afternoon.

_____ 5. Which of the following statements is FALSE?
   a. The attendees will learn about the Oxford college system on Monday morning.
   b. After lunch on Thursday, the attendees will visit Oxford Castle.
   c. On Saturday evening, the college will organize a quiz for the attendees.
   d. On Tuesday evening, the attendees will watch a play by Oscar Wilde.

239

3-2 Reference Sources

We live in a world of boundless information. Encyclopedias, travel guides, the Internet, newspapers, cookbooks—all are valuable warehouses of knowledge. But finding specific information in such vast repositories can be tricky. That's where indexes, search engines, listings, and similar tools come in handy. By learning how to navigate these collections, a world of information will soon be at your fingertips!

˄ Celebrity chef Gordon Ramsay has his own TV show to teach haute cuisine.

76 Table of Contents: Teaching Haute Cuisine to the Masses

1 Able to create taste sensations and culinary wonders, great chefs have always been figures of admiration, though for much of history they remained mysteriously hidden away in smoky kitchens. The television age, however, took chefs out of their highly exclusive restaurants and set them right into our living rooms. Curious amateur cooks around the world began to tune in to watch TV chefs like Julia Child and Fanny Craddock teach the art of haute cuisine.

2 Several decades later, TV chefs enjoy the kind of celebrity status usually reserved for Hollywood actors. With so many eager home cooks itching to learn how to cook like their favorite chef, the cookbook market has exploded, too. Each celebrity chef now has their own cookbook (or several) in which they share their favorite recipes and techniques.

3 On the next page is the table of contents from a cookbook by a well-known chef. A table of contents is found in the front of a book after the title page, and it lists the book's contents in order of their appearance. As well as the book's chapters, the table of contents also includes other functional and incidental sections, such as the index or acknowledgments.

CONTENTS

CONVERSIONS	8
PREFACE BY JEFFREY STEINGARTEN	11
INTRODUCTION: A NERD IN THE KITCHEN	13
WHAT'S IN THIS BOOK?	17
THE KEYS TO GOOD KITCHEN SCIENCE	21
WHAT IS COOKING?	28
ESSENTIAL KITCHEN GEAR	34
THE BASIC PANTRY	74
1. EGGS, DAIRY, and the Science of Breakfast	83
2. SOUPS, STEWS, and the Science of Stock	175
3. STEAK, CHOPS, CHICKEN, FISH, and the Science of Fast-Cooking Foods	277
4. BLANCHING, SEARING, BRAISING, GLAZING, ROASTING, and the Science of Vegetables	403
5. BALLS, LOAVES, LINKS, BURGERS, and the Science of Ground Meat	483
6. CHICKENS, TURKEYS, PRIME RIB, and the Science of Roast	563
7. TOMATO SAUCE, MACARONI, and the Science of Pasta	669
8. GREENS, EMULSIONS, and the Science of Salads	763
9. BATTER, BREADINGS, and the Science of Frying	845
ACKNOWLEDGMENTS	917
INDEX	919

Questions

1. In which chapter would you most likely find the recipe for a cheese burger?
   a. Chapter 3.   b. Chapter 2.   c. Chapter 5.   d. Chapter 6.

2. If you'd like to learn about how to cook soups, which page should you turn to?
   a. 83   b. 175   c. 481   d. 761

3. Which section should you turn to if you wanted to find the names of people who helped the author write his book?
   a. Index.
   b. Acknowledgments.
   c. Conversions.
   d. Introduction.

4. On what page would you find information about the tools you need to cook properly?
   a. 34   b. 11   c. 74   d. 17

5. In which chapter would you find information about the best methods of cooking vegetables?
   a. Chapter 9.   b. Chapter 8.   c. Chapter 1.   d. Chapter 4.

» Kingfisher

77
Index:
Keep Your Eyes on the Skies

1   Birdwatching as a hobby began in the early 20th century, after binoculars made it possible to identify birds without shooting them first. Relatively inexpensive to pursue, it soon became well-accepted as an accessible and rewarding hobby for anyone interested in the natural world.

2   Anyone can be a birdwatcher. All you need is a pair of binoculars and a field guide to help you correctly identify each bird. With over 10,000 species of birds in the world, the latter in particular is vital. Many species of birds appear very similar but can be told apart via minor differences, such as their body size or beak shape—all of which should be detailed in your guide.

3   Should you want to look up a particular bird, consult the index at the back of your guide. An index is an alphabetical list of names/subjects along with the pages on which they are mentioned. In the index on the next page, birds are listed alphabetically by family, with variant species listed alphabetically within those families. For example, the grouse family has two entries, the black grouse (*Grouse, Black*) and the red grouse, listed below it.

≪ Birdwatching only requires a pair of binoculars, thus making it a hobby rather inexpensive to pursue.

Questions

_____ 1. On what page of this bird guide would you find information about the pintail?
   a. 40
   b. 60
   c. 220
   d. 21

_____ 2. How many species of owl are featured in this book?
   a. Three.
   b. One.
   c. Five.
   d. Four.

Grebe, Black-necked 16
Great Crested 14
Horned 17
Little 15
Red-necked 15
Slavonian 17
Greenfinch 222
Greenshank 98
Grouse, Black 70
Red 69
Guillemot 118
Black 119
Gull, Black-headed 104
Common 111
Glaucous 108
Great Black-backed 109
Herring 107
Lesser Black-backed 106
Little 105

Harrier, Hen 56
Marsh 56
Montagu's 56
Hawfinch 224
Heron, Grey 26
Purple 26
Hobby 67
Hoopoe 137

Jackdaw 208
Jay 205

Kestrel 64
Kingfisher 135

Kite, Black 55
Red 55
Kittiwake 110
Knot 88

Lapwing 86
Lark, Crested 143
Shore 142
Wood 144
Linnet 220

Magpie 204
Mallard 37
Martin, House 146
Sand 146
Merganser, Red-breasted 52
Merlin 65
Moorhen 76

Nightingale 160
Nightjar 127
Nutcracker 202
Nuthatch 198

Oriole, Golden 212
Osprey 62
Ouzel, Ring 167
Owl, Barn 128
Little 130
Long-eared 130
Short-eared 130
Tawny 128
Oystercatcher 80

Partridge 72
Red-legged 73
Peewit 86
Peregrine 66
Petrel, Storm 21
Pheasant 74
Pigeon, Wood 122
Pintail 40
Pipit, Meadow 148
Rock 151
Tawny 150
Tree 149
Plover, Golden 84
Green 86
Grey 85
Kentish 82
Little Ringed 82
Ringed 82
Pochard 43
Ptarmigan 69
Puffin 121

Quail 74

Rail, Water 76

_____ 3. Which of the following statements is NOT true?
   a. To find information about the hoopoe, turn to page 137.
   b. Information about the grey heron and the purple heron can be found on the same page.
   c. The grebes can be found on pages 20–25.
   d. There are more species of gull than grouse featured in this book.

_____ 4. Which species of plover is NOT featured in this book?
   a. The green plover.
   b. The Kentish plover.
   c. The ringed plover.
   d. The long-billed plover.

_____ 5. Which species of lark would you find in this book?
   a. The shore lark.
   b. The horned lark.
   c. The black-tailed lark.
   d. The desert lark.

78 Menu: Start Your Day the Right Way

1 You've probably heard the old adage "breakfast is the most important meal of the day" countless times, yet many of us still maintain the bad habit of skipping this early meal. There is, however, a lot of wisdom in that old saying. At night, the body uses a substantial amount of energy to repair and replace damaged cells. So, when you wake up, your body is very much in need of refuelling.

2 In fact, research has shown that those who make breakfast their largest meal of the day are more likely to have a lower body mass index (BMI) than those who get the majority of their calories later in the day. Among other benefits, filling up on breakfast makes you feel less hungry throughout the day (therefore lowering your overall calorie intake).

3 If you are planning to eat out for breakfast, pay close attention to the menu. Modern menus usually include plenty of information that will help you choose the most suitable breakfast. Facts such as the number of calories and ingredients are all listed alongside the price, helping you choose the very best breakfast to start your day!

›› biscuits and gravy

Breakfast Additions

Slice of Bacon
(cal. 90) **$4.29**

Sausage
(cal. 240) **$4.29**

Toast
(cal. 100) **$2.75**

English Muffin
(cal. 270) **$2.79**

Biscuits and Gravy
(cal. 510) **$4.29**

Bowl of Oatmeal
(cal. 200) **$4.29**

Questions

1. Mike won't have a chance to eat lunch, so he wants to fill up as much as possible at breakfast. What should he order?
   a. Jimmy's Kid's Breakfast.
   b. A Special Omelette.
   c. Jimmy's Classic Breakfast.
   d. Eggs Benedict.

2. Jessie wants to add a bowl of oatmeal to her order of Eggs Benedict. How much more will she have to pay?
   a. $4.29
   b. $9.99
   c. $14.29
   d. $5.70

⌃ English muffin

Breakfast Menu @ Jimmy's

Served until 12 noon

Big Breakfasts

Jimmy's Classic Breakfast
Three fried eggs, two slices of bacon, two sausages, and two buttermilk pancakes, served with crispy hash browns.
(cal. 2190)
$11.59

Jimmy's Vegetarian Breakfast
Three fried eggs, three vegetarian sausages, and two buttermilk pancakes, served with crispy hash browns.
(cal. 1910)
$11.59

Jimmy's Kid's (small) Breakfast
Suitable for children – and adults with a smaller appetite. One fried egg, one slice of bacon, and one sausage, served with crispy hash browns. (cal. 920)
$7.59
★ Vegetarian option also available (cal. 730)

⌃ Omelette

Eggs

Special Omelette
Beef, spinach, mushrooms, tomato, onions, and cheddar cheese. (cal. 1590)
$10.99

Vegetable Omelette
Mushrooms, broccoli, tomatoes, red and green bell peppers, and Swiss cheese. (cal. 800)
$10.49

Eggs Benedict
A toasted English muffin, topped with ham, poached eggs, and Hollandaise sauce, served with crispy hash browns. (cal. 970)
$9.99

---

3. Sam is on a special diet and needs to keep his breakfast under 1000 calories. Which of the following can he order?
   a. Jimmy's Kid's Breakfast plus a slice of toast.
   b. The Vegetable Omelette plus a slice of bacon.
   c. Eggs Benedict with biscuits and gravy.
   d. A Special Omelette.

4. Tara does not eat meat. Which of the following can she order?
   a. Jimmy's Kid's Breakfast.
   b. Special Omelette.
   c. Eggs Benedict.
   d. Jimmy's Classic Breakfast.

5. Which of the following is TRUE about Jimmy's Vegetarian Breakfast?
   a. It is over 2000 calories.
   b. It comes with a serving of toast.
   c. It includes two pancakes.
   d. It comes with scrambled eggs.

79 Internet: Sharpening Your Search Skills

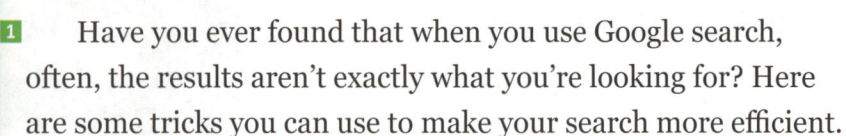

1 Have you ever found that when you use Google search, often, the results aren't exactly what you're looking for? Here are some tricks you can use to make your search more efficient.

2 First, you can use the tabs beneath the search box (Images, News, Videos, and so on) to filter your search so that only the specific type of results show up on the results page.

3 You can also use quotation marks to tell Google to search for the exact phrase rather than provide results for each individual word. For example, "Midnight in Paris" will search for the movie of that title rather than information about 12:00 a.m. and the city of Paris.

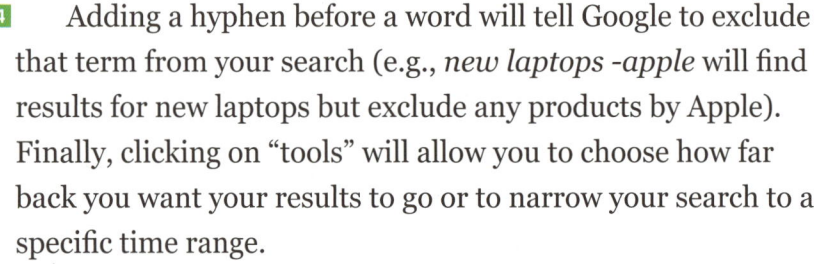

4 Adding a hyphen before a word will tell Google to exclude that term from your search (e.g., *new laptops -apple* will find results for new laptops but exclude any products by Apple). Finally, clicking on "tools" will allow you to choose how far back you want your results to go or to narrow your search to a specific time range.

5 I'm very interested in Elon Musk—the South African billionaire behind innovative projects like the space exploration company SpaceX and Tesla, the electric car manufacturer. Here's a search I recently performed on this person.

⌃ Tesla founder Elon Musk

Questions

1. What can you infer about the writer's intentions from this search?
    a. He's not interested in reading about Musk's company Tesla.
    b. He wants results from up to a year ago.
    c. He wants to view images of Elon Musk.
    d. He wants results about the perfume ingredient known as musk.

2. On which of these sites would you NOT find information about Musk's space exploration company, Space X?
    a. www.mirror.co.uk
    b. www.thesouthafrican.com
    c. hypebeast.com
    d. socialketchup.in

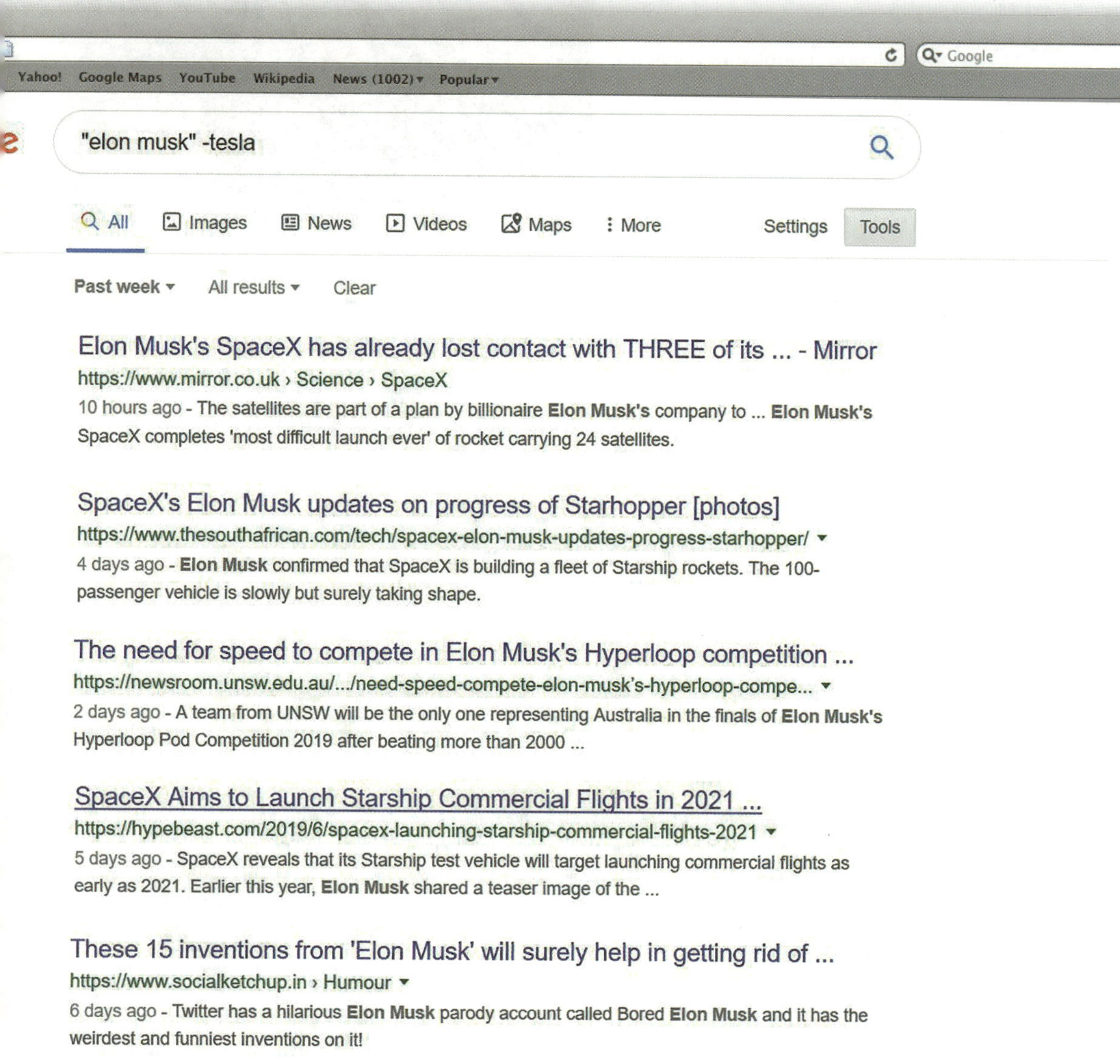

| Yahoo! | Google Maps | YouTube | Wikipedia | News (1002)▼ | Popular▼ | | Google |

"elon musk" -tesla

All | Images | News | Videos | Maps | More | Settings | Tools

Past week ▼   All results ▼   Clear

Elon Musk's SpaceX has already lost contact with THREE of its ... - Mirror
https://www.mirror.co.uk › Science › SpaceX
10 hours ago - The satellites are part of a plan by billionaire **Elon Musk's** company to ... **Elon Musk's** SpaceX completes 'most difficult launch ever' of rocket carrying 24 satellites.

SpaceX's Elon Musk updates on progress of Starhopper [photos]
https://www.thesouthafrican.com/tech/spacex-elon-musk-updates-progress-starhopper/ ▼
4 days ago - **Elon Musk** confirmed that SpaceX is building a fleet of Starship rockets. The 100-passenger vehicle is slowly but surely taking shape.

The need for speed to compete in Elon Musk's Hyperloop competition ...
https://newsroom.unsw.edu.au/.../need-speed-compete-elon-musk's-hyperloop-compe... ▼
2 days ago - A team from UNSW will be the only one representing Australia in the finals of **Elon Musk's** Hyperloop Pod Competition 2019 after beating more than 2000 ...

SpaceX Aims to Launch Starship Commercial Flights in 2021 ...
https://hypebeast.com/2019/6/spacex-launching-starship-commercial-flights-2021 ▼
5 days ago - SpaceX reveals that its Starship test vehicle will target launching commercial flights as early as 2021. Earlier this year, **Elon Musk** shared a teaser image of the ...

These 15 inventions from 'Elon Musk' will surely help in getting rid of ...
https://www.socialketchup.in › Humour ▼
6 days ago - Twitter has a hilarious **Elon Musk** parody account called Bored **Elon Musk** and it has the weirdest and funniest inventions on it!

_____ 3. If you wanted to find only current-affairs articles about Musk, what could you click on?
   a. More.   b. News.   c. Videos.   d. Tools.

_____ 4. On which site would you find the most recent news about Musk?
   a. www.thesouthafrican.com   b. hypebeast.com
   c. www.mirror.co.uk   d. newsroom.unsw.edu.au

_____ 5. What would you find if you clicked on the link to www.thesouthafrican.com?
   a. The latest images of Musk's starship project.
   b. Funny ideas for Elon Musk-style inventions.
   c. News updates about SpaceX's recent satellite launch.
   d. Details of Musk's plan to begin offering commercial space flights by 2021.

» More and more people are becoming YouTubers to make money.

80 Data Flow Chart: How to Make Money From Social Media

1 It is not uncommon these days for people to spend several hours of each day on social media and video streaming sites. Some might consider this a waste of time, but if you understand how the system works and are willing to put in the effort, you can in fact make yourself a decent income from these sites.

2 Most online revenue comes from advertisements that appear alongside your content, and while it was once true that companies exclusively wanted big celebrities with millions of followers to promote their products, nowadays brands are increasingly seeking creators or "influencers" with smaller, niche audiences and highly engaged followers.

YouTube Data-Flow Diagram

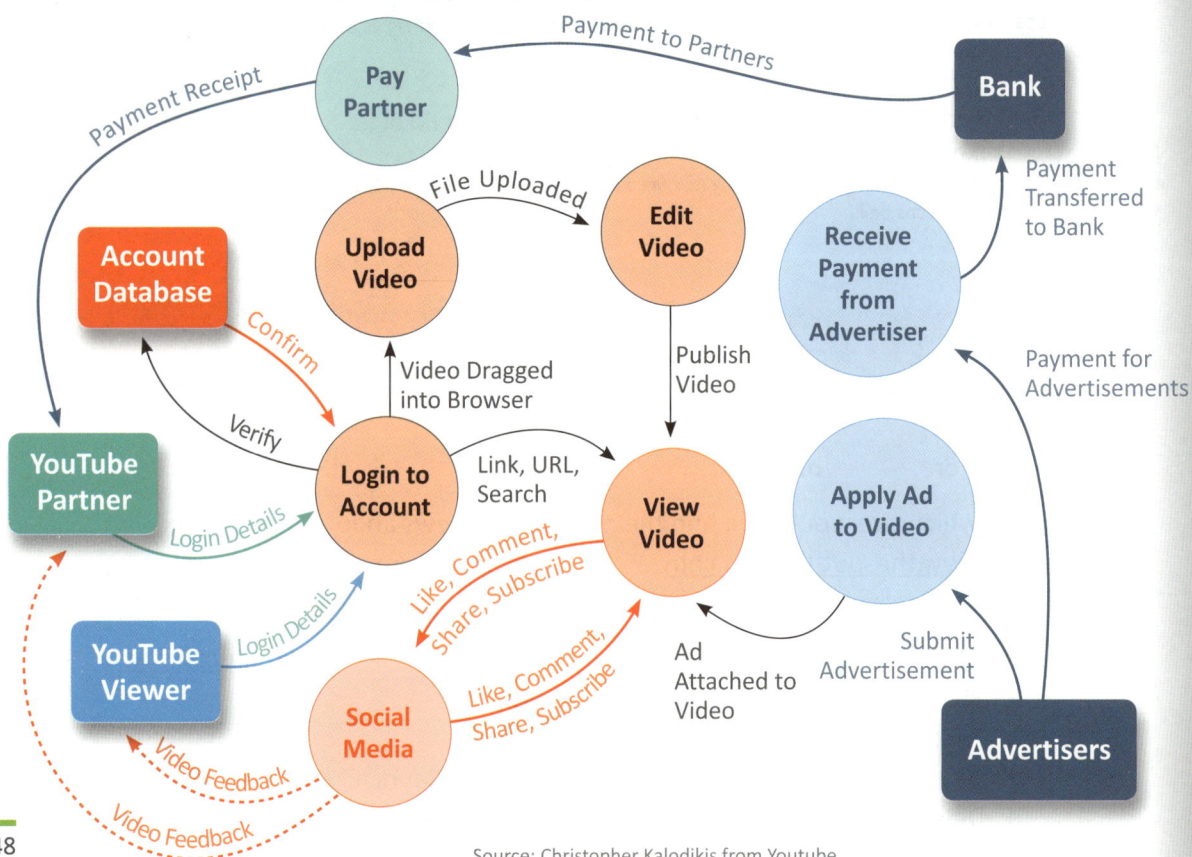

Source: Christopher Kalodikis from Youtube

248

YouTube's channel report on number of views.

[3] In the case of YouTube, anyone can make or upload a video, but if you attain a certain number of subscribers, you will be able to apply to become a YouTube partner, gaining access to features that allow you to more effectively monetize your created content.

[4] To help you understand how a company like YouTube works, it can be helpful to refer to a data-flow diagram. A data-flow diagram makes the workings of companies like YouTube clearer by graphically representing the flow of data into and around their information system.

Questions

____ 1. According to the diagram, what is the difference between YouTube partners and YouTube viewers?
   a. YouTube partners get paid but YouTube viewers don't.
   b. YouTube partners can upload videos but YouTube viewers can't.
   c. YouTube partners do not have to log in to YouTube, but viewers do.
   d. YouTube partners get feedback from YouTube's social media functions, but viewers don't.

____ 2. After YouTube partners or YouTube viewers log in to their accounts, what happens to the login data?
   a. It is transferred to the bank.
   b. It is sent to the account database to be verified.
   c. It is sent to YouTube Partners in the form of a receipt.
   d. It is attached as an ad to a YouTube video.

____ 3. What can YouTube partners and viewers NOT do?
   a. Watch videos.   b. Edit their videos.
   c. Attach ads to their videos. d. Upload videos.

____ 4. What data flows from advertisers to YouTube?
   a. Video feedback.   b. Advertising media and payments.
   c. Payment receipts.   d. Likes and comments.

____ 5. Which of the following is TRUE, according to the diagram?
   a. Advertisers pay YouTube partners directly.
   b. YouTube partners are able to upload videos by dragging them into their browser.
   c. YouTube partners are able to upload videos before logging in.
   d. The bank receives payments from YouTube partners.

Unit 4

Final Review

4-1 Final Review

Unit 4 Final Review

4-1 Final Review

Now that you're familiar with a variety of reading and word skills, not to mention some important study strategies, it's time to put them to the test. Unlike in previous units, you'll no longer be faced with just one type of skill per article; now you'll be faced with the challenge of having to apply several different skills to each individual text.

   Use these review units to see how much you've progressed and how much you've learned from the study units. Try to do these tests under exam conditions, and then analyze your strengths and weaknesses. This will give you a good idea of which areas you need to work on in the future.

4-1 Final Review

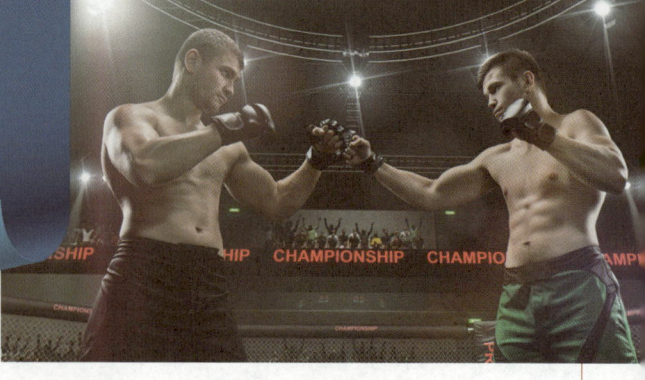

81 Get in the Cage!

MMA fighters only wear shorts and padded fingerless gloves.

[1] A knee to the head followed by the crack of broken bones; the crowd roars; a fighter falls, his blood staining the mat. These are the sights and sounds of mixed martial arts, one of the most violent and popular combat sports of our modern era.

[2] The sport, commonly known by its abbreviation, MMA, pits two highly skilled fighters against each other inside an eight-sided metal cage and allows them to duke it out using techniques from any martial art they choose, whether it be boxing, wrestling, judo, jujitsu, karate, or any other forms of hand-to-hand combat.

[3] Wearing only shorts and padded fingerless gloves, fighters are constrained by only a handful of rules. No headbutting, eye-gouging, biting, hair-pulling, or groin attacks; no strikes to the throat, spine, or back of the head, and no kicking or kneeing an opponent in the head once he is on the ground. Otherwise, pretty much anything goes. And the incredible skill and adaptability required of its fighters, not to mention the physical risk they undertake each time they step into the cage, make the sport a thrilling viewing experience for its devoted fans, particularly when compared to other, more rigorously regulated combat sports such as boxing.

[4] While the roots of mixed martial art combat can be traced back to the ancient Greeks, the story of modern MMA begins in Brazil in the early 20th century with a combat sport known as *vale tudo*—"anything goes." In the 1990s the sport debuted in the United States, in a tournament christened the Ultimate Fighting Championship (UFC), which later developed into the leading

padded fingerless gloves

MMA fighters are constrained only by a handful of rules.

promotional organization of MMA events, with well over 200 main events having taken place at the time of writing.

5   However, though the initial UFC events drew large TV audiences, the sport's brutality had many comparing it to human cockfighting and calling for an outright ban. Starting in 2001, after a change of ownership, the UFC introduced a new set of rules, including new weight classes, round and time limits, official fouls, which would help make MMA acceptable to a wider audience. While the sport remains incredibly dangerous, bloody, and violent, it's this process of civilization that has allowed it to thrive in the mainstream and become recognized as a legitimate sport. However, with such fierce fighters and notoriously unpredictable matches, it is unlikely that the sport will ever truly be tamed.

⌃ MMA fighters compete against each other in an eight-sided metal cage.

Questions

1. Which of the following best encapsulates the main idea of the article?
   a. MMA's roots can be traced back to the ancient Greeks, but the modern version originated in Brazil.
   b. In MMA, fighters can use a wide variety of martial arts to attack their opponent.
   c. MMA is a violent but exciting sport that has become incredibly popular in recent years.
   d. MMA is a brutal sport that has been compared to human cockfighting.

2. Which of the following can be inferred from the article?
   a. MMA is more dangerous than boxing.
   b. MMA is more popular than boxing.
   c. Fans of boxing don't tend to like MMA.
   d. Boxing requires more skill than MMA.

3. How does the author create interest in the first paragraph?
   a. By providing a vivid description.
   b. By providing a shocking statistic.
   c. By making a humorous comment.
   d. By invoking a shared experience.

4. By saying "it is unlikely that the sport will ever truly be tamed," what is the author comparing MMA to?
   a. A wild animal.
   b. A violent storm.
   c. A fast car.
   d. A perilous mountain.

5. What tone does the author take towards MMA fighters?
   a. One of disapproval.
   b. One of pity.
   c. One of disappointment.
   d. One of awe.

82
A Monument to Flops and Failures

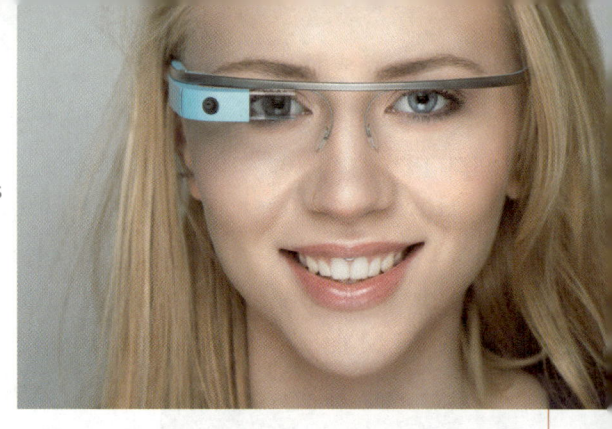

» Google Glass

[1] Failure—we all fear it, and when it happens to us we often wish we could bury our failures in the sand, never to be confronted with them again. How would you like it, though, if your biggest blunders were immortalized in a museum for all to see? The Museum of Failure in Helsingborg, Sweden, does just that. It takes all the biggest commercial flops from modern history and puts them on display—from Google's failed attempt at creating the smart spectacles Google Glass, to Coca Cola's disastrous Diet Coke-and-coffee mixture, Blak.

[2] All manner and levels of failure are represented: Some products, like Bic's "For Her" pen—designed to "fit comfortably in a woman's hand"—were doomed to fail from the start and stand as a lesson for anyone trying to shift products through cynical, manipulative marketing. Others are products that just couldn't keep up with the times, such as Sony's Betamax, a video tape format introduced in 1975 that was quickly made obsolete by VHS, or more recently, Blockbuster rental DVDs, made redundant by online streaming.

[3] There are examples of companies being completely and laughably unaware of their target audience (such as the Harley Davidson perfume—launched by the motorcycle manufacturer in 1996). Still others, such as Apple's Newton Messagepad—a device that could take notes and send faxes—were clearly steps towards something greater and which played a key role in developing revolutionary devices—in this case, the iPhone.

[4] In some cases, the museum is more of a celebration of innovation and creativity than a lampooning of failure. Instead of burying these commercial bombs, the museum shines a light on these brave, if imperfect, attempts at creating something new and exciting, in the hope that others will see them and perhaps be inspired.

[5] The message behind the museum is clear—failure does not have to be a negative, and it may indeed be a necessary step in achieving something spectacular. After all, the museum makes it abundantly evident that the most successful companies of our age—Amazon, Google, and Apple—are no strangers to failure and have lost billions of dollars on products that were almost there, but not quite. True innovation is being prepared to take a huge risk, fail miserably, and despite that failure, try again.

Questions

- Blak, Coca Cola's Diet Coke-and-coffee mixture
  (cc by Rob Durdle)

- Bic's "For Her" pen

- Betamax video cassette

- Sony's Betamax videorecorder

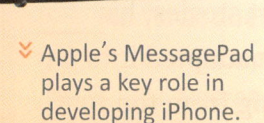

- Apple's MessagePad plays a key role in developing iPhone.

_____ 1. Which of the following is TRUE according to the passage?
  a. Harley Davidson's perfume was a surprise success amongst motorcycle fans.
  b. Sony's Betamax was quickly made redundant by the rise of DVDs.
  c. Apple's Newton Messagepad was an important step in the development of the iPhone.
  d. To date, Amazon has never developed a product that has failed commercially.

_____ 2. According to the passage, what does the Museum of Failure hope to achieve with its exhibits?
  a. It hopes to dissuade creators from putting their products on the market.
  b. It hopes to encourage people to campaign for the re-release of these failed products.
  c. It hopes to warn people against wasting their money on products that might become obsolete.
  d. It hopes to inspire people to take risks and not be afraid of failure.

_____ 3. Which of the following sentences does NOT contain biased language?
  a. "Instead of burying these commercial bombs, the museum shines a light on these brave, if imperfect, attempts at creating something new and exciting. . . ."
  b. "Others are products that just couldn't keep up with the times—Sony's Betamax, an analogue video tape format introduced in 1975, for example."
  c. "Some products . . . were doomed to fail from the start, and stand as a lesson for anyone trying to shift products through cynical, manipulative marketing."
  d. "There are examples of companies being completely, laughably unaware of their target audience. . . ."

_____ 4. Is the final sentence—"True innovation is being prepared to take a huge risk, fail miserably, and then, despite that failure, try again"—one of fact or opinion?
  a. Fact.   b. Opinion.

_____ 5. How does the author structure the second paragraph?
  a. As a series of contrasting examples.
  b. As series of steps in a process.
  c. As a series of events in chronological order.
  d. As a series of statistics used to prove a point.

255

84 The Shining Spoils of War

[1] Diamonds that are mined in places where there are wars and human rights abuses are called conflict diamonds. Some of these come from the Democratic Republic of the Congo (DRC), and the perpetrators of human rights abuses there are military organizations, including the Armed Forces of the DRC and the Democratic Forces for the Liberation of Rwanda. These groups, under various names, have been fighting in the Congo and battling over its rich natural resources for more than a century. Heinous crimes against humanity are fueled by their greed for the country's wealth, with mass rape—sometimes of children—being employed as a means to drive fear into local communities and keep residents away from mines and other places the militants want to control. Profits from diamond sales helped finance the Second Congo War (officially 1998-2003, though conflicts in the country are still ongoing), and some of the fighting was, and is, actually over control of diamond, gold, and other mines.

[2] Many international efforts to remedy the exploitation of Africans in the center of the continent are being made, as global awareness of their plight grows. Most attempts, however, are inadequate, and some may in fact be perpetuating the DRC's sorry state of affairs rather than rectifying it. There is a great focus, for instance, on the Democratic Forces for the Liberation of Rwanda, but very little attention is paid to Uganda, which has been charged with looting and crimes against humanity in the Congo by the International Court of Justice. Rwanda has likewise **played a starring role** in United Nations

⌄ diamonds

« Congo

reports for looting in the Congo and maintaining the state of conflict there.

3   The advertising of diamonds as symbols of love and joy contrasts sharply with the violence and misery which actually surround their production. This goes beyond rebel groups, the fight for control over mines, and the purchase of war supplies with the resulting profits. We must also consider the involvement of financial institutions, major diamond retailers, transport companies, traders, and smugglers. Nor can we forget about the countless diamond miners who seek—or are forced—to earn a living from their work. That work is difficult, dirty, unsafe, and unhealthy, and leaves them and their families in a state of abject poverty. All of this is especially troubling when you consider the true value of the stones the miners unearth and the accordingly vast opportunities to increase their meager earnings.

↟ Congolese National Army

Questions

_____ 1. What is the main idea of this passage?
   a. The Democratic Republic of the Congo is a dangerous country.
   b. The world is not doing enough to help people in central Africa.
   c. Something we view as a luxury often has a very dark side.
   d. You can make a lot of money by investing in African diamonds.

_____ 2. Which of the following statements is NOT true?
   a. People have been fighting in the DRC for a long time.
   b. All the conflict diamonds in the world come from the DRC.
   c. International efforts to help the DRC are rarely effective.
   d. Diamond miners in the DRC make very little money.

_____ 3. How does the author end this passage?
   a. With a personal recollection.   b. With an expression of outrage.
   c. With a humorous example.   d. With a statement of sad irony.

_____ 4. The phrase **played a starring role** in the last sentence of the second paragraph is an example of what?
   a. A simile.   b. A metaphor.   c. Hyperbole.   d. Alliteration.

_____ 5. In the passage, the author displays a bias against what?
   a. Militant groups in the DRC.   b. The advertisement of diamonds.
   c. The United Nations.   d. Central African people.

259

▼ Superfoods are particularly high in nutritional density.

85 🎧

The Superheroes of the Food World

1   Not all foods are created equal. Like the heroes in comic books, some foods have superpowers. These "superfoods" are particularly high in nutritional density, providing a **substantial** amount of our recommended daily vitamins, minerals, and antioxidants—natural molecules that help decrease the risk of health conditions like heart disease, cancer, and strokes.

2   Several foods are common recipients of the title: blueberries, for example, are high in fiber and vitamin K, goji berries in vitamins C and E, and acai berries in both amino acids and antioxidants. Soybeans contain natural compounds that can help reduce your cholesterol and prevent age-related memory loss. Green tea contains **potent** antioxidants that reduce inflammation and help prevent cancer. Leafy green vegetables, such as kale and spinach, are all rich in vitamins A, C, E, K, and B, as well as containing minerals such as iron, magnesium, potassium, and calcium in abundance.

3   However, these so-called superfoods are not immune to being manipulated by food sellers. In fact, nutritionally speaking, there is no such thing as a superfood. The label was invented for marketing purposes in order to influence health-conscious buyers and sell products. While they may be rich in certain nutrients, foods labelled as superfoods are certainly not miracle cures for diseases.

4   As a result of such cynical advertising, many consumers have unrealistic expectations of superfoods, and are convinced that if **they** add one or two of them to their diet, they'll become immune to disease and stay in the pinnacle of health forever. The truth is, superfoods are not able to cancel

⌃ blueberries

⌃ goji berries

⌃ acai berries

out the effects of an otherwise poor diet and lifestyle, no matter how enthusiastic the label on the packaging may be. While eating these superfoods as part of a healthy, balanced diet will certainly benefit your health, consumers must learn to manage their expectations and understand that there is no single food that holds the key to good health or disease prevention.

5 What can consumers do, then, if they want to reap the benefits of these foods? First, **take a holistic approach to your diet**, rather than a piecemeal one, by remembering that a handful of blueberries isn't going to do anything if you are eating fast food for breakfast, lunch, and dinner. Secondly, view the term superfood with some skepticism. Take the time to learn about what exactly is so super about the superfoods you are choosing and decide if they're truly worthy of the label.

> Leafy green vegetables contain minerals such as iron, magnesium, potassium, and calcium in abundance.

Questions

1. Which of the following words could replace **substantial** in the first paragraph?
   a. Considerable.   b. Useless.   c. Intermediate.   d. Enduring.

2. Which of the following has the opposite meaning to the word **potent**, as used in the second paragraph?
   a. Mighty.   b. Overpowering.   c. Ineffective.   d. Tedious.

3. In the third paragraph, the author claims that **superfoods are not immune to being manipulated by food sellers.** What does he mean by this?
   a. Food sellers often highlight how superfoods can help boost the body's natural defenses.
   b. Food sellers often refuse to eat the foods they label as superfoods on their advertising.
   c. Food sellers themselves often don't know what the word "superfood" actually means.
   d. Food sellers often take advantage of the label "superfood" to sell more products.

4. What does **they** refer to in the fourth paragraph?
   a. Consumers.   b. Superfoods.   c. Food sellers.   d. Antioxidants.

5. In the final paragraph, what does the author mean by "**take a holistic approach to your diet**"?
   a. Do more research about the foods you consume.
   b. Give up on dieting altogether.
   c. Transform your diet as a whole.
   d. Take advice only from a qualified nutritionist.

86 The Woman Who Invented Science Fiction

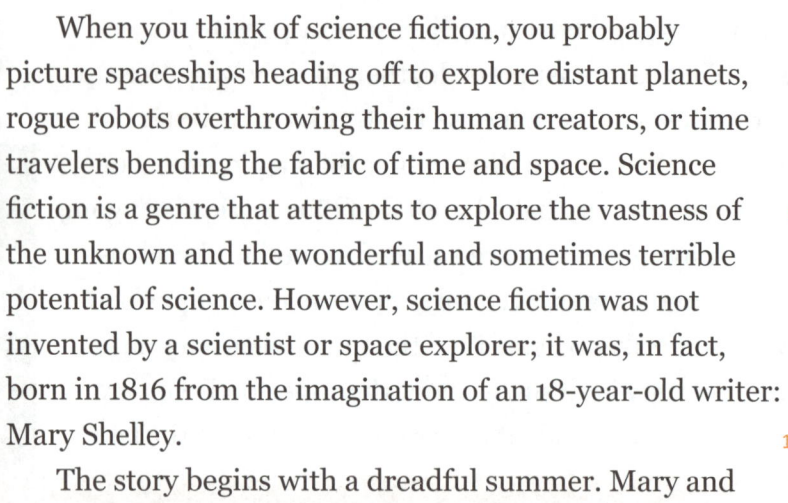

[1] When you think of science fiction, you probably picture spaceships heading off to explore distant planets, rogue robots overthrowing their human creators, or time travelers bending the fabric of time and space. Science fiction is a genre that attempts to explore the vastness of the unknown and the wonderful and sometimes terrible potential of science. However, science fiction was not invented by a scientist or space explorer; it was, in fact, born in 1816 from the imagination of an 18-year-old writer: Mary Shelley.

[2] The story begins with a dreadful summer. Mary and her husband, the poet Percy Shelley, were spending June at Lake Geneva, Switzerland, along with their friends George Byron—another famous poet—and his physician, John Polidori. One evening, in an attempt to pass the time while the rain continued to pour outside, Byron suggested they all write their own ghost story. Mary quickly busied herself with thinking of a tale which, she later wrote, would "speak to the mysterious fears of our nature, and awaken thrilling horror—one to make the reader dread to look around, to **curdle the blood**, and quicken the beating of the heart."

[3] The story she penned was *Frankenstein*—an **account of a scientist who builds a monster from the stitched-together parts of stolen corpses** and then brings it to life with electricity. Though many now think of *Frankenstein* as a horror story—in the same realm as *The Wolf Man* or *Dracula*—it is, in fact, pure science fiction. Unlike the aforementioned monsters, Frankenstein's creature is a product of science, not the supernatural.

[4] Those who have only seen film adaptations of the novel would be forgiven for thinking Mary Shelley's creation to be somewhat **cartoonish** or overly theatrical. However, the original novel is a bold and fearless exploration of themes such as the ethics of creation, the pursuit of knowledge, and the transgression of the natural order, all of which

↥ Mary Shelley (1797–1851)

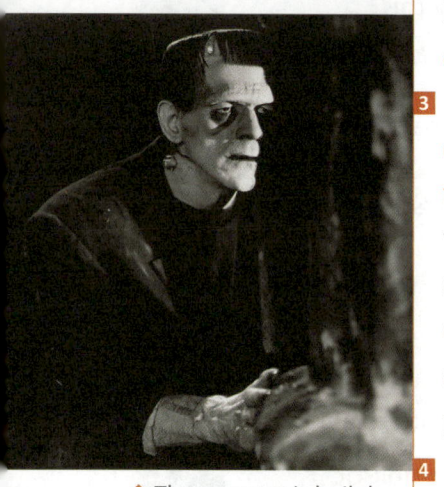

↥ The monster is built by Dr. Frankenstein from stitched together parts of stolen corpses.
(cc by Insomnia Cured Here)

are themes that modern science fiction constantly battles with. Shelley's legacy can be seen in the works of the prolific science fiction writer Isaac Asimov, in particular his collection concerning robotics, *I, Robot* (1950), in movies such as *Blade Runner* (1982) and *Ex Machina* (2014), and indeed any work that deals with artificial beings being brought to life by science and the possible **repercussions** of that act.

⟨5⟩ So the next time someone tries to tell you that science fiction is not for girls, you can confidently point them to Mary Shelley, who laid the very foundations upon which **the entire genre** is built!

› Isaac Asimov

» *Frankenstein* written by Mary Shelley (cc by CHRISTO DRUMMKOPF)

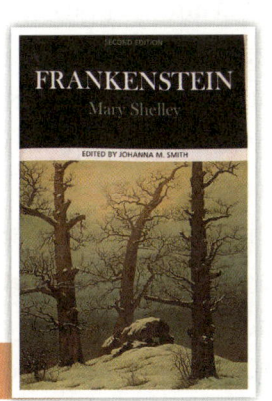

Questions

____ 1. What is meant by the phrase **curdle the blood**, as used in the second paragraph?
  a. To inspire vengeful thoughts.
  b. To severely frighten or disgust.
  c. To prompt poetic writing.
  d. To alleviate boredom.

____ 2. "The story she penned was *Frankenstein*—an **account** of a scientist who builds a monster from the stitched-together parts of stolen corpses. . . ." Which of the following uses the word **account** in the same way as this sentence?
  a. At the end of each month, I have to do the accounts for the entire business to see how much money we've made.
  b. I gave the police a detailed account of what had happened during the robbery.
  c. He was unable to access his account because he had forgotten his password.
  d. The car was extraordinarily expensive, but as money was of no account to him, he bought it outright.

____ 3. Which of the following has the opposite meaning to **cartoonish** in the fourth paragraph?
  a. Realistic.   b. Humorous.   c. Heartfelt.   d. Meaningless.

____ 4. Which of the following is a suitable definition for the word **repercussions**, as used in the fourth paragraph?
  a. The unexpected consequences of one's actions.
  b. A loud ringing or echoing sound.
  c. Compensation in the form of monetary payment.
  d. The unexpected loss of a loved one.

____ 5. What does **the entire genre** refer to in the final paragraph?
  a. Frankenstein's monster.
  b. The summer of 1816.
  c. Mary Shelley's imagination.
  d. Science fiction.

263

87 Cactus: The Ultimate Desert Survivor

1 Deserts and steppes are harsh environments where only very specialized plants and animals are capable of survival. While temperatures can soar to as high as 45 degrees Celsius during the day, they can also drop below freezing at night, since there is no water vapor in the atmosphere to hold in heat (by the greenhouse effect). Rainfall is less than 25 cm (250 mm) per year, if it rains at all.

2 This **impossible situation** has caused the cacti, the resident tree populations, to evolve some very interesting attributes to the point that people usually don't even think of them as being trees. The organism has been **rebuilt from the ground up**. The root systems are usually exceptionally wide, shallow, and highly saline to allow the most water absorption in the least amount of time. For example, a full-grown Saguaro cactus can absorb 3,000 liters of water in 10 days. Because the big, broad, flat leaves have become thin, sharply pointed protective spines, it is the trunk and branches that carry out the **indispensable** process of photosynthesis.

> Many cacti live in extremely dry environments.

3   Cacti are also covered with a wax that seals in moisture, and they normally have long, deep creases or ribs running along most or all of their length. These creases allow for a great amount of swelling to occur when rains do come, so that enough water can be stored to keep it alive for years without rain.

4   That which lies **beyond the reach of the naked eye** is the plant's breathing and chemistry. Cacti do the equivalent of holding their breath during daylight hours. The pores that allow transpiration, called stomata, close when the sun is out to prevent excessive water loss. At night, the pores open and allow oxygen, carbon dioxide, and water vapor to pass through. Since photosynthesis cannot happen in the dark, the carbon dioxide is stored as malic acid, which is commonly found in unripe fruit. When the sun rises, the stomata close again, and the cactus performs photosynthesis using the stored carbon dioxide. If one tasted the pulp from a cactus at sunrise it would taste sour, and at sunset it would taste sweet.

⌃ Cacti have long, deep ribs.

⌃ Cacti have thin, sharply pointed, protective spines.

5   Even the general shape of the cactus is an advantage. It has very few branches, and all structures tend toward cylindrical and spherical shapes, which maximize the ratio of volume-to-surface-area in order to more easily protect water reserves. Surviving so well with so many unique **adaptations**, the cactus has become the most recognizable symbol of desert life.

265

Questions

____ 1. What does the **impossible situation** in the second paragraph refer to?
   a. How cacti are sometimes considered to be trees.
   b. The moderate temperatures where cacti grow.
   c. The harsh environmental conditions of the desert.
   d. The challenges that result from the unique root system of cacti.

____ 2. What does **rebuilt from the ground up** mean in the second paragraph?
   a. Everything about it has changed.
   b. Rescued from a near-death situation.
   c. Able to survive in some of the harshest environments.
   d. Extremely rare and hard to find.

____ 3. What is a word with the opposite meaning to **indispensable** in the second paragraph?
   a. Replaceable.
   b. Predictable
   c. Valuable.
   d. Forgettable.

____ 4. What does the author mean by **beyond the reach of the naked eye** in the fourth paragraph?
   a. It is very obvious.
   b. It is confusing.
   c. It is unexpected.
   d. It cannot be seen.

____ 5. What is an interchangeable word for the way **adaptations** is used in the final paragraph?
   a. Arrangements.
   b. Weaknesses.
   c. Modifications.
   d. Characteristics.

↑ A guardian is protecting access to an oil well set on fire by Isis.

88 Isis: The Rise and Fall of a Global Terror Network

1   If you have turned on the news any time in the last decade or so, you are likely to have heard the names Isis, IS, ISIL, or Daesh. All of these are different names for one of the most terrifying and violent organizations of recent times: the group calling itself Islamic State.

2   From the destruction of ancient buildings and cultural artefacts, to public executions of ethnic minorities, homosexuals, journalists, and charity workers, to shocking terrorist attacks around the world, Islamic State has gained global infamy for its many actions in the last decade. But what does it really want? Where did it come from? And what is its future?

» a propaganda video of Isis
(cc by Alibaba2k16)

⌄ Flag of Islamic State of Iraq

267

3 Islamic State began as a splinter group of Al-Qaida in the chaos and violence following the American invasion of Iraq. Up to that point, Al-Qaida were seen as the most dangerous extremists in the region, having claimed responsibility for the September 11th attacks. But in 2006 Islamic State of Iraq (ISI) was born, and over the subsequent years it separated completely from Al-Qaida and spread into a global terror network even more terrifying than **that once feared group**.

4 By 2014 ISI claimed that it had formed a caliphate, a new land governed by sharia law, and their name was officially changed to Islamic State (or Isis). The group wanted Muslims all over the world to join the caliphate and wage an all-out war against the non-Muslim world. In Iraq and Syria Isis took over more and more land and held many towns and cities under a brutal regime where basic freedoms were restricted and people who did not follow the group's fundamentalist form of Islam were punished violently.

5 The Isis reign of terror became truly global after a wave of attacks in cities around the world. The attacks were often carried out by small terrorist cells or even **lone wolves** who pledged allegiance to Isis before publicly killing themselves and scores of innocent civilians.

6 So what is next for Isis? **The good news** is that, as a military force, it has been **hugely depleted**, with much of the land it once held lost to US backed Iraqi forces. However, as the deadly Easter Sunday attack in Sri Lanka recently showed, as long as there are individuals willing to kill themselves and others in the name of the group, it will remain a great threat to the peace and stability of the world.

>> the streets of the former Isis capital

« A woman escaped abuse from Isis in a refugee camp.

Questions

_____ 1. When the author says that "Islamic State has gained global infamy for its many actions," what does this mean?
   a. Its actions are not as well-known around the world as one would expect.
   b. Its actions have become notorious all around the world.
   c. Its actions are supported by many other countries in the world.
   d. Its actions have helped it to gain a lot of international respect.

_____ 2. Who does **that once feared group** refer to in the third paragraph?
   a. Islamic State of Iraq.
   b. Al-Qaida.
   c. The Americans.
   d. The Iraqis.

_____ 3. The author speaks of **lone wolves** killing themselves and others in the name of Isis. Which of the following can replace the phrase **lone wolf**?
   a. Terrorist cell.
   b. Terror group.
   c. Guerilla army.
   d. Individual attacker.

_____ 4. What does **the good news** in the last paragraph refer to?
   a. Isis is becoming a strong military force.
   b. Iraqis lost their land to the United States.
   c. Isis has lost much of the power it once had.
   d. The United States has declared a war against Isis.

_____ 5. Which of the following is the opposite of **hugely depleted** as used in the final paragraph?
   a. Greatly increased.
   b. Slightly improved.
   c. Greatly reduced.
   d. Largely removed.

269

89 Table and Bar Chart: A Shift in Belief

[1] Humanity's belief in gods has been one of the great constants of our species, existing in one form or another for tens of thousands of years. However, which religion dominates among the many available faiths is something far more mutable. Currently the religion with the largest number of followers is Christianity; however, as birth rates in non-Christian countries remain high while those in Christian countries continue to fall, Christianity will soon fall into second place.

[2] In addition, the number of non-believers and those unaffiliated with any religion also continues to grow in Europe and in the United States (traditionally Christian regions), further lowering the number of future Christians. Over the next 30 years, 106 million are predicted to leave the Christian faith, while only 40 million are expected to convert to it. Though in 2050, Christianity will still maintain its position as the world's number one religion, by 2070, it is estimated that Islam will have far outstripped it.

[3] The table and bar chart on the next page demonstrate this trend. The table contains information on the number of each religion's followers in both 2010 and a projection for 2050. The bar chart shows the population for these religions in 2015 in billions to one decimal place.

▽ The number of Christians is expected to drop over the next 30 years.

Size and Projected Growth of Major Religious Groups

	2010 Population	% of World Population in 2010	Projected 2050 Population	% of World Population in 2050	Population Growth 2010–2050
Christians	2,168,330,000	31.4%	2,918,070,000	31.4%	749,740,000
Muslims	1,599,700,000	23.2%	2,761,480,000	29.7%	1,161,780,000
Unaffiliated	1,131,150,000	16.4%	1,230,340,000	13.2%	99,190,000
Hindus	1,032,210,000	15.0%	1,384,360,000	14.9%	352,140,000
Buddhists	487,760,000	7.1%	486,270,000	5.2%	-1,490,000
Folk Religions	404,690,000	5.9%	449,140,000	4.8%	44,450,000
Other Religions	58,150,000	0.8%	61,450,000	0.7%	3,300,000
Jews	13,860,000	0.2%	16,090,000	0.2%	2,230,000
World total	6,895,850,000	100.0%	9,307,190,000	100.0%	2,411,340,000

Source: The Future of World Religion: Population Growth Projections, 2010-2050
(https://www.weforum.org/agenda/2016/05/fastest-growing-major-religion/)

Number of people in 2015, in billions

⌄ Christians are the largest religious group in 2015.

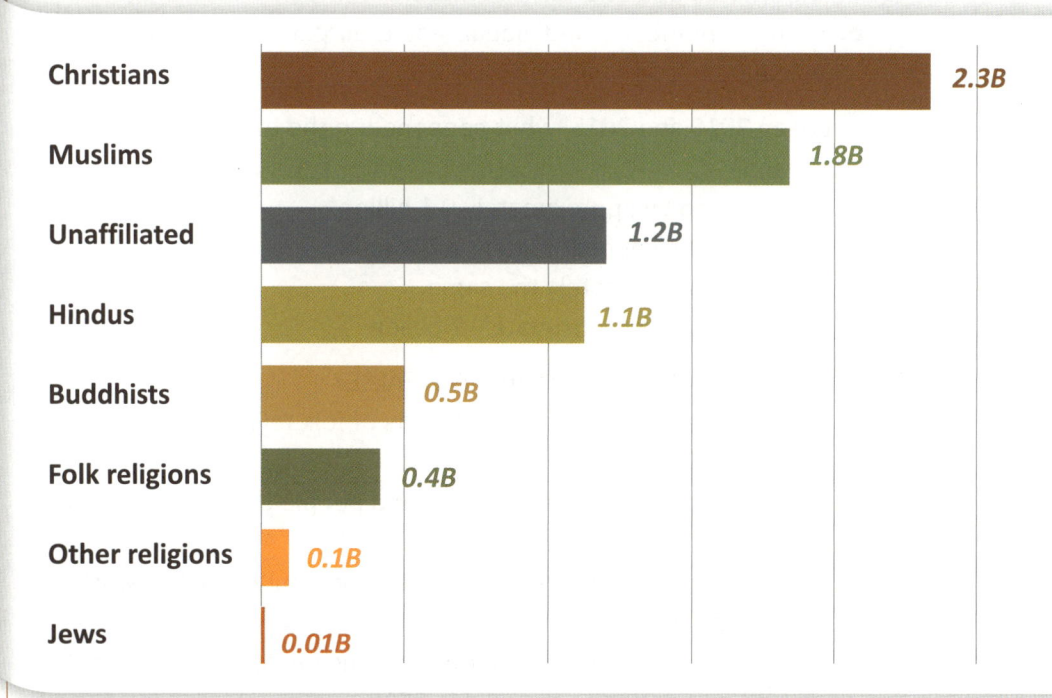

- Christians: 2.3B
- Muslims: 1.8B
- Unaffiliated: 1.2B
- Hindus: 1.1B
- Buddhists: 0.5B
- Folk religions: 0.4B
- Other religions: 0.1B
- Jews: 0.01B

Source: Pew Research Center demographic projections "The Changing Global Religious landscape"
(https://www.pewresearch.org/fact-tank/2017/04/05/christians-remain-worlds-largest-religious-group-but-they-are-declining-in-europe/)

Questions

_____ 1. In 2050, what is projected to have happened to the Buddhist faith?
   a. It will have gained over 3 million followers since 2010.
   b. It will have gained a 2% share of the world's population in followers since 2010.
   c. It will have lost nearly a million and a half followers since 2010.
   d. It will have become the religion with the fewest number of followers.

_____ 2. According to the table, how many Hindus will there be in the world in 2050?
   a. Nearly 3 billion.
   b. Half a billion.
   c. Over 1.3 billion.
   d. Almost 16 million.

_____ 3. Which of the following describes what will happen to the number of those unaffiliated with any religion by 2050?
   a. The number of individuals will increase, but their percentage of the whole population will decrease.
   b. Both the number of individuals and their percentage of the whole population will increase.
   c. The number of individuals will decrease, but their percentage of the whole population will increase.
   d. Both the number of individuals and their percentage of the whole population will decrease.

_____ 4. Between 2010 and 2015, what happened to the total number of Christians?
   a. It decreased by approximately 0.1 billion.
   b. It increased by approximately 0.2 billion.
   c. It stayed approximately the same.
   d. It increased by approximately 2 billion.

_____ 5. Which of the following statements is FALSE?
   a. In 2050, there will be more followers of folk religions than there were in 2010.
   b. In 2015, there were fewer unaffiliated people than there were in 2010.
   c. In 2050, Hindus will make up a greater percentage of the world's population than Jews.
   d. In 2050, Christians will make up the same percentage of the world's population as they did in 2010.

> Lots of modern people rely on plastic forms of payment, such as credit cards or debit cards.

90 List: Debit or Credit?

1 In an increasingly cashless world, most of us now rely on some form of plastic, such as a debit or a credit card, to make our daily purchases. The difference between these two types of cards is simple: with a credit card, all your purchases are paid for by your bank, with the expectation that you will pay off your debt to the bank at a later date, whereas with a debit card, the money is subtracted (or debited) directly from your current bank balance. There are obvious advantages to both, but for many who are concerned about overspending or getting into debt, a debit card is the preferred option.

2 When using a debit card as your primary card, it is important to keep a sharp eye on your bank balance. You can do this via paper bank statements, or by logging into your online banking account. You can also set up a system with your bank to receive a warning when your balance gets too low, thus making overspending even less of a likelihood.

3 On the next page is the monthly bank statement for John Mitchell. A bank statement lists all of the transactions an individual has completed during a particular time period, including withdrawals (paid out), transfers, and deposits (paid in), along with their changing bank balance.

MÖBIUS BANK

JOHN MITCHELL
1566 DURHAM ST. REPTON COUNTY
M6K 1V4

CHECKING ACCOUNT STATEMENT

Date	Description
2019-10-01	Payroll Deposit - GREENHOUSE MEDIA
2019-10-02	ATM Withdrawal - NATION BANK
2019-10-05	Transfer to Savings Account No. 345234558
2019-10-05	Payment to - WILLIAM BRIGGS (Description: Rent)
2019-10-07	Visa Purchase - MUSIC ONLINE
2019-10-10	Bill Payment - NATIONAL ELECTRIC CO.
2019-10-13	Bill Payment - STREAM WATER CO.
2019-10-13	Visa Purchase - THE BOOK WAREHOUSE
2019-10-17	Cheque Deposit - Cheque No. 45634567
2019-10-18	Payment to - MARTIN RICHARDS (Description: Fixing Broken Faucet)
2019-10-19	Bill Payment - POWERON GAS CO.
2019-10-23	Visa Purchase - GOLDEN DRAGON RESTAURANT
2019-10-23	Bill Payment - SWAN TELECOM
2019-10-24	ATM Withdrawal - FIRST BANK
2019-10-27	Visa Purchase - GOODFOODS SUPERMARKET

» Card users can also use online banking to track their transactions.

Statement Period
2019-10-1 to 2019-10-31

Account No.
554563567

Page: 1 of 1

Ref.	Paid out	Paid in	Balance
5657		2700	3234.43
3421	500		2734.43
7890	500		2234.43
2233	750		1484.43
7788	66.99		1417.44
2322	154.75		1262.69
1123	23.44		1239.25
8878	58.56		1180.69
3564		1000	2180.69
5519	50		2130.69
6788	40.98		2089.71
7890	35.52		2054.19
9876	40.32		2013.87
4454	500		1513.87
9903	150		1363.87

Questions

____ 1. How much does John spend on rent each month?
   a. $500   b. $750   c. $1000   d. $154.75

____ 2. When did John pay his electricity bill this month?
   a. The 10th.   b. The 13th.   c. The 24th.   d. The 5th.

____ 3. How much income did John receive this month?
   a. $3700   b. $1000   c. $3234.43   d. $1363.87

____ 4. Which of the following statements is FALSE?
   a. John made two ATM withdrawals this month of $500 apiece.
   b. On the 7th of the month, John spent $66.99 buying music online.
   c. John paid his gas bill on the 19th of the month.
   d. John ended the month with more money than he began.

____ 5. Which of the following can we correctly infer from John's bank statement?
   a. John's landlord's name is Martin Richards.
   b. John is employed at a company called Greenhouse Media.
   c. John's water heater broke this month.
   d. John saves $500 each month.

TRANSLATION

Unit 1 閱讀技巧

關於理解內文的技巧，光是瞭解各語詞的意義仍稍嫌不足。必須具備各種不同的閱讀技巧，才能真正讀懂作者所試圖傳達的訊息。當然，看懂一段文章的字面意義是重要的起步，但除此之外，還要能會意字裡行間的弦外之音，也就是分析各要點之間的關係、理解因果關係，以及預測文中所述事件的結果。

更進一步來說，你必須要能看出作者遊說的技巧和其本身的偏見，還能明辨事實與意見。本單元所介紹的閱讀技巧，將有助你培養上述能力。

1-1 歸納要旨

文章主旨並非總是顯而易見，因此當閱讀時，別忘了在心裡提問：「作者想要傳達的重點是什麼？」此外，文章除了具有整體主旨之外，每段內容也有其中心思想，只要清楚每段內容的重點，即可藉此了解整篇文章的意思。

1. 有聲詩的魅力　P. 14

詩作一般給人的印象，就是列出行段字句的印刷品，但詩作其實不侷限於紙本形式。事實上，綜觀人類歷史，詩作常以宏亮吟誦於群眾面前來呈現。節律、類疊和押韻等修辭技巧，據說是為了有助於詩人創作方便記憶的詩句所演變而來。隨著寫作文化崛起且形成通俗習慣，吟詩般的口述傳統便逐漸式微。不過，美國到了 1980 年代，興起一股讀詩競技風潮，讓詩詞表演的樣貌重獲新生，至今人氣仍然居高不下。這就是所謂的「尬詩擂臺」！

尬詩擂臺的制度，是由來自芝加哥的建築工人兼詩人——馬克‧史密斯所創。他認為現代詩愈來愈偏學術路線而顯得沉悶。史密斯希望建構一個氣氛較為輕鬆自在、又能直接與觀眾互動的平臺。以尬詩擂臺的制度而言，主持人會選出擔任該場競賽評審的觀眾。每一位詩人表演完畢後，每位評審就會進行評分。得分最高者可晉級至下一回合繼續對戰，直到分出最終贏家的勝負。

尬詩擂臺上各種語調、表演風格和吟詩方式之豐富，讓每場賽事充滿獨一無二的驚喜。有些詩人運用激動的抑揚頓挫，快速轉換各種音量和口氣。有些人選擇以肢體語言傳達詩作的意義，運用精心編排且具有張力的動作，甚至是舞蹈。詩作主題偏向政治以及種族、性別、歧視等具有爭議的題材，非常容易引起現場觀眾的情緒共鳴和聲援（對於詩人取得技壓對手的優勢來說十分重要）。

不過，尬詩擂臺的某些批評聲浪，認為這種譁眾取寵的表演風格是一大詬病。因為競技式的回合賽，讓尬詩擂臺成為一種運動而非藝術形式。不過，某些詩評認為，那些對紙本詩集和在靜肅廳堂讀詩感到沉悶乏味的人，尬詩擂臺是一個能讓詩人放聲吼叫、向世人唱出詩作的管道。更棒的是，臺下觀眾能以即時起鬨或歡呼的方式附和，讓詩人與觀眾之間形成充滿詩意的互動氣氛，這都是紙本文字不可能如法炮製的特色。

2. 飢餓的小小汪星人　P. 16

恭喜領養新小狗！但你很快就會發現，幼犬雖然超級可愛，卻時常處於爆餓狀態。身為一個負責的寵物主人，你一定會想為狗狗供應含有各種適當必需養分的食物，才能讓狗狗成長為健康開心的成犬。

不過，這樣的想法不一定正確，因為照本宣科的準備充滿豐富養分的超級狗食，不見得是正解。許多狗狗基於品種或體型的緣故，會有某些健康方面的風險。因此，牠們發育時需要特定的養分均衡，才能抵禦潛在的危險病症。舉例而言，大型犬是罹患骨骼與關節毛病的高危險群，尤其是攝取過多鈣和鉀的大狗。只有購買專為自己飼養犬種所設計的狗食，才能確保狗狗吃下最理想分量的營養。

許多新手狗爸媽常被幼犬的食量嚇到。因為幼犬的成長期集中在出生後的五個月內，因此需要充裕的熱量來滿足剛開始的快速成長期——食量可能會是相同品種成犬的兩倍。不過，隨著狗狗長大，食量也要隨之調整，只要參考多數狗食品牌隨附的餵食表即可。那麼該持續多久呢？幼犬的這種特殊飲食法必須持續，直到他們長至九成的成犬體重。小型犬也許可於九個月內達標，大型犬則需要將此特殊餵養方式延續至一歲半。

不過，雖然幼犬媲美大食怪，他們很樂意掃空眼前的任何食物，但請務必小心別餵養過量。八至十週大的健康幼犬，如果看似體型纖瘦，是極其正常的一件事。過多的體脂肪反而對狗狗不利，如果不減少食量，很有可能會演變為肥胖症。如果正確餵養狗狗，可明顯觀察到狗狗充滿活力、毛皮厚實亮澤、糞便成形且呈棕褐色。而上述指標均表示狗狗攝取了茁壯所需的養分。

3. 領薪公民　P. 18

有一種新政策概念，開始席捲世界各地而蔚為風潮。無論是以「基本收入」、「全民基本收入」、「公民收入」、甚至是「自由紅利」來稱呼此政策，基本理念均不變：也就是無論公民就業與否，每個月均可獲得特定金額的收入。

很多人也許心想：「不勞而獲就能拿錢？什麼瘋理論……但我贊成。」

雖然有些人認為全民基本收入（簡稱 UBI）的論點顯得很極端，但這樣的概念其實是源自於全球經濟發生了最根本性的改變。世界各地的許多工廠已藉由自動化機器人來取代傳統人力。人工智慧突飛猛進的發展，意味著下一個被淘汰的族群將會是白領階級。工作機會變得愈來愈少，絕望的求職者激烈競爭僅存的職缺，終將導致低薪與高度貧窮的結果。

而全民基本收入的政策彷彿一線曙光。其用意不見得要取代工資，而是不無小補的概念。舉例而言，如果每位公民每個月可獲得美金 500 元，就能兼職工作，又不會危及自己的整體經濟狀況。還能讓更多人從事屬意的工作，例如小型創業或追求藝術理想，而非因現實需求才不得已就業。

理論上，UBI 政策具有幾項顯著的優點。例如縮短貧富差距，讓低收入戶和中產階級可以獲得更多的收入，藉此刺激消費並促進經濟發展。最後，政府能因此簡化或撤除過往專為貧戶制定的福利計畫，有效節省時間和預算。

不過，UBI 政策亦有缺點。最令人無法忽視的是執行此類計畫的成本。美國國家經濟研究局的一項研究指出，此政策如果一年發放 12,000 美元，會讓政府多出 3 兆美元的巨額預算。UBI 政策亦無法取代像健保這類預算龐大的政府計畫。

然而，從臺灣到英國，這概念在全球的年輕世代與政府間引發相當多的話題與討論。加拿大和芬蘭已經嘗試於某時限內執行此類政策，而印度政客則大力提倡以 UBI 改善農村的貧窮問題。UBI 的支持者希冀隨著時間的推進，能讓更多人聽到他們的心聲。

4. 讓心情自然變好　P. 21

憂鬱症是最讓人心神耗弱的常見疾病之一，影響世界無數人。從暫時無法跳脫悲傷的情緒，到長期感覺失落、喪志、氣憤及／或哀傷等需要治療的臨床病症，都是憂鬱症的表現範疇。

目前已有許多抗憂鬱的藥物，多數患者的服藥效果很好。不過，仍有部分飽受憂鬱之苦的人，不希望承擔副作用或用藥上癮的風險。有時會需要花上好一段時間，醫師才能為個別病患找到適合的抗憂鬱藥物。

幸好研究顯示，自然療法可以是有效治療輕度憂鬱症的替代方案。更棒的是，在尋求精神科醫師的協助之前，可先試試自然療法，因為醫師有可能會直接採取較極端的治療方式。

以下列舉幾項可改善憂鬱傾向的自然療法：

1. 運動量充足。運動能提高大腦中的血清素分泌量，而血清素能改善心情。
2. 維持健康的飲食習慣。營養對心理健康的影響程度舉足輕重。請攝取新鮮蔬果，並補充適量的維他命與礦物質。
3. 避免酒精飲品。雖然許多人會借酒澆愁，但酒精本身就是一種抑鬱劑。長期下來，會加劇情緒負能量。

4. 拓展朋友圈，多花點時間與朋友相處。摯友愈多，愈不容易感到憂鬱。此外，也請拉近與家人的距離。向信任的對象分享自己的感受極為重要。

5. 擔任志工。當你不再將重心放在自己身上，就難以持續處於憂鬱狀態。此外，你也能藉機意識到其他人也有自己要面對的問題。幫助對方度過難關，會讓自己充滿正能量。

6. 從事自己擅長的事物，讓自己生活充實。看見自己的成就後，你自然會神采奕奕，提升自信心。

7. 放輕鬆、冥想，還有睡眠要充足。冥想能舒緩緊繃的神經。放鬆休息是擁有平穩心境的不二法則。

8. 寫日記。日記能追蹤你憂鬱的來龍去脈，藉此觀察導致憂鬱的原因。在憂鬱症左右你之前，先拿回主控權。

　　許多維持健康心理的關鍵，同時也有助於生理健康。不過，如果你發現自己仍然無法回到正常的開心狀態，事不宜遲，絕對要尋求專業人士的協助。

5. 一夜好眠的教戰守則　P. 24

　　我們的身體每天晚上必須仰賴充足的睡眠才能恢復活力。否則白天昏昏欲睡，對工作、學業、人際關係和社經地位都會帶來負面影響。本文將提供一些容易執行的一夜好眠教戰守則。

　　有時徹夜輾轉難眠的元凶很單純：那就是身體的生理時鐘紊亂。原因有可能是生活作息改變，例如進入新的職場環境，身體需要一段調適時間。也可能在你需要寶貴睡眠之前，做了過度激烈的運動。雖然每天運動 30 分鐘有益健康，但千萬要避免睡前才運動！

　　心理過勞和運動一樣，會讓你過於清醒而整夜盯著天花板。避免在床上處理公事或看電視，反之，要幫自己安排睡前兩小時的心靈平靜時間。許多人會嘗試的一招就是寫日記，也就是寫下你隔天可能會面臨到的問題與壓力，而不是讓這些事徹夜徘徊在腦海裡而睡不著覺。

　　別忽略了睡前的沐浴儀式。睡前約 90 分鐘去淋浴或泡個熱水澡，甚至是先去個桑拿浴。體溫會在洗澡時升高，但到了睡覺時間就會慢慢降下來，讓你擁有放鬆身心的深層睡眠。還有睡前別忘了如廁，避免半夜跑廁所。

　　另一項重點就是避免會使消化系統紊亂而令人難以入睡的食物。食物過敏症會導致消化不良和腸胃不適的問題，吃太飽可能會導致睡眠呼吸中止症。若下午攝取到咖啡因，可能會讓人失眠，因為人體無法有效代謝。此外，睡前也別喝酒，否則會造成淺眠問題。理想的情況是睡前幾小時食用少量的高蛋白食物，例如一小盤鹹餅乾夾花生醬。此方法能幫助必需胺基酸 L- 色胺酸，來分泌控制睡眠的褪黑激素。

1-2 找出支持性細節

　　一篇好文章，一定會以事實、統計數據和其他證據為基礎，堆砌出作者想要表達的主旨。這就是「支持性細節」，因為此類資訊能「佐證」作者的論點。因此，倘若你想撰寫講述俄羅斯嚴寒程度的文章，最佳的輔助細節資訊就是氣溫統計數據。

6. 惡魔來敲門的日子　P. 26

　　孩童總是對潛伏於黑暗中的怪獸感到害怕。他們的恐懼大多來自反應過度的想像力。但對日本北部某地區的孩子而言，這樣的威脅卻非常真實。

　　除夕，是秋田縣男鹿市的孩子們最需要繃緊神經的一天。因為隨時隨地都會有一群喧鬧的惡魔亂入家裡。惡魔到訪後，會大吼著：「這裡有沒有壞孩子啊？」而懼怕的小孩們，來年就會乖乖聽話。

　　這其實是男鹿市一項歷史悠久的民俗傳統，讓所謂的「生剝鬼」造訪當地孩童。而生剝鬼是由穿戴手工精緻獸角面具和蓑衣的年輕男子所扮演。

　　就如同許多的農村傳統一樣，隨著日本經濟於第二次世界大戰後蓬勃發展，生剝鬼的習俗卻遇到瓶頸。由於遷居大都市求學和就業的人數增加，使得男鹿市的年輕人所剩無幾。沒有年輕人的帶動，自然沒有小孩可嚇，也沒有能夠嚇人的生剝鬼演員。1989 年，男鹿市尚有 120 組生剝鬼表演團體，到了 2015 年卻只剩下 85 組。

幸好近年來，生剝鬼習俗已有東山再起的跡象。原因其一在於聯合國教科文組織，將此民俗列入「無形文化遺產」，進而吸引了外界的重視。其二是男鹿市想方設法讓外國遊客體驗生剝鬼習俗。

要將生剝鬼習俗與現代觀光業接軌，其實會遭遇某些現實面的特殊挑戰。雖然男鹿市有許多不同的文化活動都需要搭配生剝鬼表演，但是像生剝鬼於除夕夜拜訪兒童的習俗，卻難以結合觀光。因為拜訪範圍超過 80 個社區，且生剝鬼團體的拜訪路線不定。不過，仍有適合遊客體驗的其他節慶活動，例如二月的柴燈祭，表演重點在於拿著柴燈下山遊行的生剝鬼。柴燈祭近年來大受歡迎，於 2019 年吸引了 7,600 名遊客，超越 2018 年 6,100 人的紀錄。

地方政府有意透過觀光業來保存生剝鬼的傳統，希望好好延續此原創人物的精髓。所有人都對此作為樂觀其成，大概只有精神受創的男鹿市孩童會抗拒到底吧！

7. 從塗鴉到嘻哈　P. 30

許多人認為街頭塗鴉是一種破壞公物的行為，世界各地均有法律禁令。不過，多數人不了解的是，塗鴉文化其實早已行之有年。以史前時代來說，洞穴壁面常刻劃野生動物和集體狩獵的圖像。隨著文字的演進，人類開始在巨石、碑塔與石壁上鑿刻公告與個人訊息。內容包括可放牧性畜的範圍、追思悼文、愛情宣言，甚至是流鶯廣告。此類早期塗鴉的時間，最早可追溯至西元前八世紀，且中東地區、希臘以及羅馬帝國的許多地區都可見其蹤影。

英文「graffiti」一字源於義大利文「graffiato」，意指「刻劃」。這些刻劃出來的陳述及符號，能讓我們一窺過往的文明概況與其生活形態。其實仔細深究，也許會發現即使經過數世紀，人類想在街頭向大眾傳遞訊息的天性並沒有太大的改變，如同現今的塗鴉藝術家，也是用著一樣的手法。

許多塗鴉藝術家會背負罵名，不過真正的現代塗鴉之父則是別名為「玉米麵包」的藝術家德瑞爾・麥卡瑞。1960 年代晚期的費城，麥卡瑞展開他傳奇性的「簽名塗鴉」，他在各大建築、火車與公車上，畫出極具個人風格的簽名。這樣的塗鴉簽名開始蔓延至世界各地，成為風靡全球的文化現象。

塗鴉形同饒舌和霹靂舞，都是活躍的嘻哈文化之一。創意雲集的嘻哈環境，以塗鴉和舞蹈等藝術性質的對尬元素，有助於降低貧民區的幫派暴力，因此獲得肯定。雖然塗鴉競賽有時會以政治或當地敵對勢力為主題，卻是不需透過暴力、讓年輕人安心表達自我的方式。有些年輕人極為細膩的塗鴉傑作，幾乎能夠贏得所有人的青睞。

現今塗鴉藝術家與其作品的價值已獲得重視，因為某些都市願意大費周章，設置方便拆除的塗鴉專用臨時牆面。與此同時，如雨後春筍般的都會小型企業，則善用街頭藝術家的技能，創作廣告用途的吸睛壁畫。

8. 無論貧富甘苦　P. 33

世界各地的婚禮習俗大相逕庭，多數新人會依循自己家鄉的嫁娶傳統。不過，歷史悠久的婚俗文化，近年來卻逐漸標新立異。因為新人希望婚禮更有自己的風格，而非只是迎合禮俗期望。

長裙襬拖地的白色禮服搭配頭紗，是一般人心目中的西方新娘形象。不過，這兩樣服飾配件的起源與涵義，卻顛覆多數人的想像。頭紗和長禮服可追溯至古羅馬時代。當時的新娘必須全身包裹紅紗，象徵退散惡靈的意義。一直到 1840 年才有白色婚紗的概念，因為維多利亞女王很喜歡白色，才在自己的婚禮上穿著白色禮服，並非是為了象徵純潔。西方新郎方面，有時仍以燕尾服和領結赴重要宴會，但其實任何深色西裝均適宜。雖然教堂是歐洲與美洲文化舉辦婚禮的熱門場所，但只要是新人心中認定的任何重要場地皆可。

許多婚俗十分重視首飾配件。亞美尼亞人的婚禮前夕，婆家必須將裝有頭紗、婚鞋、香水、珠寶與其他可能需要的實用物品，以精美的禮盒包裝送至新娘的娘家。捷克新娘會在婚禮戴上伴娘所做的迷迭香花環，來象徵愛情與智慧。而印度婚禮的新人則會互換花串。

新人的未來是另一項重要的考量。中國人格外注重，雙方會根據新人的生辰八字與生肖來慎選婚禮日期，以確保結縭後恩愛有福氣。而荷蘭婚禮的某項習俗，則是在婚宴現場擺放一座「許願樹」，讓賓客在「葉片」上寫下恭賀新人未來的祝詞。而德國新人在婚禮舉行之前，需砸碗摔盆再一起清理，象徵共同做好面對人生試驗的準備。

至今許多婚禮仍保有上述習俗。但自行撰寫誓詞、設計婚禮儀式、量身訂製這件人生大事的新人亦大有人在。而多元成家的趨勢與日俱增，勢必會帶來許多截然不同的婚禮傳統。無論每個人決定在何時何地「執子之手，與子偕老」，相信新人與賓客都能為這場喜宴創造難忘的回憶。

9. 腦力邂逅體力的運動　P. 36

常言道，異性相吸。沒想到，新興的西洋棋拳擊運動，竟然同理可證此格言。

西洋棋拳擊結合了兩種極端的人類潛能領域：智力和運動能力。如此違背自然的組合，想當然耳是出自天馬行空的突發奇想。1992年，法國藝術家恩奇・畢拉在他的漫畫創作《寒冷赤道》中，描繪一場世界西洋棋拳擊冠軍爭霸賽。到了2003年，荷蘭籍的伊皮・華比殊從該部漫畫得到靈感，在現實世界中催生了此項運動，還建立了世界西洋棋拳擊組織（簡稱WCBO）。

西洋棋拳擊的規則十分簡單。以輪流對戰西洋棋和打拳擊的方式，進行11回合，每回合計時三分鐘。西洋棋賽局占六回合，意指每位選手各有三回合、總計九分鐘的下棋時間。選手只要擊倒、將殺對方，或由裁判評斷獲勝者，均可贏得比賽。如果某選手下棋的時間超過規定，對手亦可贏得勝利。

有些人認為西洋棋拳擊賽只不過是個噱頭，大家真正想看的是選手從西洋棋桌起身後互毆的場面。不過某些人卻認為，輪流進行不同賽事的遊戲規則，反而是極為獨特的挑戰。假設選手在西洋棋回合落後，就可在拳擊回合奮力擊倒對手。另一方面，如果消耗太多體力在拳賽，就會難保清晰思緒進行下棋回合。

無論西洋棋拳擊有何迷人之處，觀眾顯然對此運動興致盎然。第一屆賽事於2003年的阿姆斯特丹舉辦，超過一千名好奇的觀眾入場。而第一個西洋棋拳擊俱樂部則在隔年成立於柏林。截至2019年，此項運動已成為國際賽事，WCBO的會員遍布中國、伊朗、義大利、俄國、德國、墨西哥、西班牙和美國。此運動在印度尤其熱門，至少有10個一級行政區成立相關協會。而且受歡迎的程度男女通吃，有三分之一的印度西洋棋拳擊手是女性。那麼西洋棋拳擊熱到底會延燒至什麼程度？熱衷此運動的支持者相信，有朝一日必能晉身為奧運項目。

10. 帝王的國度　P. 39

坐落於北京天安門廣場北邊的故宮博物院，堪稱全球占地最廣、現存最龐大的木造宮院建築。故宮博物院的宮殿不下980座，面積超過72公頃，更見證了明清兩朝皇帝執政500年的歷史。故宮另一個廣為人知的中文名稱是「紫禁城」，意指「門禁森嚴的紫色之城」。所謂的「紫色」，代表的是紫微星（西方稱之為北極星），也就是玉皇大帝的天宮住所。而皇帝既然貴為「天子」，所居住的宮殿自然等同紫微星的凡間化身。「門禁森嚴」則是因為沒有皇帝的允許，任何人均不得擅自出入。

如今，紫禁城不僅門戶大開，還歡迎世界各地的遊客與學者參觀。每年估計有1,500萬至1,600萬的人潮湧入欣賞故宮的藝術與建築古物，只要向中國官方購買門票，沒有皇帝的許可一樣能入內。因此，故宮博物院被聯合國教科文組織列為世界文化遺產，絕對當之無愧。

紫禁城最主要的施工期介於1406年與1420年。據說超過一百萬名工人，包括十萬名技術精湛的工藝師傅，均成為建造紫禁城的苦力。工人至鄰近礦場開採大理石，並從全國各地運來不計其數的珍貴木材與其他建材。

紫禁城的主色是象徵帝王之家的黃色。宮內裝潢同樣多以黃色為主，屋頂均鋪設黃色琉璃瓦（除了文淵閣和太子寢宮外）。連最重要的大殿，地板鋪設的都是黃色「御窯金磚」。

紫禁城分為外朝和內廷。中國 14 位明朝皇帝與 10 位清朝皇帝於外朝治理國家大事，與后妃皇子居住於內廷。而清朝末代皇帝溥儀，則因 1924 年的政變而被驅逐出宮。1933 年，日本入侵中國，導致無數宮內文物珍寶被倉促撤往安全的藏匿處。雖然第二次世界大戰結束後，部分文物已回到北京故宮，但有許多文物漂流至台灣，陳列於台北國立故宮博物院。

1-3 作出推論

「推論」技巧意指運用已知資訊來猜測未知的人事物。舉例而言，如果朋友開門時看似怒氣沖沖，你會猜測事有蹊蹺或有事發生。作者同樣會以推論方式，來提點讀者相似的情境。

11. 一窺水晶球　P. 42

雖然每個人都會好奇自己的未來，有些人卻迫不及待、求助於命理師來一窺究竟。算命或稱「占卜」，可說是全球蓬勃發展的行業，而且常與許多宗教文化密不可分。正因如此，算命在各種社會風俗裡，占日常生活很大的比重。

不過，歐洲卻反其道而行。教會與政府於數世紀以前，宣稱算命是一種罪行，至今仍有部分地區以法律嚴禁算命。因此，算命不是一個大眾推崇的職業和行為。美國的主流宗教秉持著同樣看法。但是不論貧富、不分問題類型，喜歡算命的人何其多，這樣的現象還真是令人吃驚。畢竟，星座不也是一種算命形式嗎？

算命的方法衍生自文明的根源。宣稱能未卜先知的人，其實是承襲前人衣缽，並且就地取材，使用當時的可用資源。而歐洲、北美洲與南美洲所採用的部分算命法包括塔羅牌、茶渣占卜術、看手相以及水晶球占卜術。

亞洲的許多占卜術源自於中國的「算命」觀念。最廣受歡迎的一派，就是「生辰八字」。此命理學是運用一個人的出生年、月、日和時間，排出所謂的四柱命盤，而每一柱裡各有一對天干地支。因此四柱共有八種干支，形成「八字」此名稱。

而非洲最傳統的算命法，就是丟擲骨頭、石塊、貝殼、皮繩或木片等「卜卦」方式。這類算命法具有若干解卦類型，例如：丟擲不同標記的物體後，記住落下的順序，根據標記或物體是否互相碰撞來解卦；或是丟擲具有旅行、懷孕等象徵意義的一組骨頭或物品。

想當然爾，不管是哪一種算命方式，其實都極具爭議。難怪科學研究得出的結論是：占卜術不可能存在，命理師不過是深諳肢體語言、以看似符合當下情境、實則做出籠統陳述的專家罷了。

12. 野化動物的解套辦法？　P. 45

看到備受呵護的健康毛小孩，與飼主在家開心相處，是多麼令人暖心的畫面。不幸的是，全世界保守估計，有三億左右的龐大數量貓狗流浪在外，甚至是「野化」——意指在街頭繁殖出來的後代，或是長期沒有接觸人類而害怕與人類互動。以往為了控管流浪／野化動物的數量，世界各地常以不人道的殘忍方式撲殺。

幸好到了現代，多數國家均視上述做法為野蠻行為。不過，我們仍需靜心思考，該如何種人道措施來減少流浪動物的數量。尤其是流浪狗很容易成群結黨，威脅到社區的安危。

目前大眾普遍接受的解決之道就是「誘捕、絕育、放生」計畫（簡稱 TNR）。此計畫顧名思義，先誘捕流浪動物、進行結紮，再將牠們放回自己的地盤。經過一段時間後，流浪／野化動物的數量就會因為無法繁殖而自然降低。野化動物愈少，愈能減輕流浪動物之家為了解決過度擁擠問題而施行安樂死的壓力，同時增加獲救動物再次找到飼主的機會。再者，動物如果缺乏性慾（尤其是狗狗），侵略性格會改善許多，進而減少衍生的問題。許多國家的 TNR 計畫均由政府贊助或資助，野化動物數量明顯下滑的效果十分顯著。

不過，身為寵物飼主的我們，同樣能透過各種正面管道，來為此問題帶來解套貢獻。第一，確保自己的寵物已結紮，避免不幸走失後，寵物在外失控繁殖而增加野化動物的數量。第二，幫寵物植入晶片。假使寵物走失，才能很快並安全地找回寵物。第三，終生照顧寵物。如果基於任何因素而無法繼續飼養，請務必為寵物找到另一個合適的家。無論是何種情況，萬萬不可將寵物棄於街頭不理。如果遵循上述步驟並支持當地的 TNR 計畫，我們想讓流浪貓狗擁有歸宿的目標已不遠矣。

13. 當影子籠罩恆星　P. 48

當月球運行至太陽和地球之間，月球的影子就會落在地球上，而位處此影子地帶的任何人，就會暫時看不見太陽。我們稱此現象為「蝕」，而日蝕在歷史上常被視為神秘、壯觀的天文奇景，甚至是帶有惡兆的意味。

西元前七世紀，享有盛譽的希臘詩人阿爾基羅庫斯，描寫希臘神話裡的眾神之王宙斯，讓白晝變成了黑夜。而中國古代則視日蝕為不祥異象，因為中國人相信這是龍吞日的緣故。對當時的人民而言，著實是令人惶恐不安的景象呀！

不是每個人都能幸運見證日全蝕，因為必須視地點或在恰當大氣條件下的時間點而定。事實上，必須具備天大的好運氣，才能目睹日全蝕。不過，雖然月球比太陽小約 400 倍，卻因太陽距離地球也有將近 400 倍的距離，而讓我們以為它們看起來一樣大，因此能讓月球看似完全遮蔽太陽而形成日蝕。

還有所謂的月蝕，則是因為地球運行至太陽和月球之間，使得地球的影子落在月球上。月球之所以具有亮度，是因為反射太陽光。但發生月蝕時，地球卻會擋住太陽光。有時月蝕現象成形的過程中，會讓月球蒙上一層略紅的陰影而有「血月」的別稱，在許多文化裡甚至會與魔法聯想在一起。

雖然日蝕和月蝕都不常見，不過每年仍在少數地區可以至少看見兩次日蝕。不常發生的原因在於，地球繞行太陽的軌道固定，但月球繞行地球的軌道卻不然。月球的繞行軌道傾斜且緩慢偏移，所以並非以直線模式行經地球和太陽之間，

即使這三種天體均進入促成日／月蝕的位置，亦需取決於月球軌道的傾斜度是否有成一直線。日蝕和月蝕的原理相同：只要太陽、月球和地球連成一線，位居中間的天體就會產生影子。當最外圈的天體運行至影子範圍，就會產生日蝕／月蝕現象。

14. 與眾不同的舞種　P. 50

「佛朗明哥」是一種形象鮮明的舞種。每個人的腦海裡，一定會浮現舞者雙手高舉過頭、隨著吉他音樂節奏踩腳的舞步畫面，而舞者的表情更是充滿情緒張力。最重要的是，佛朗明哥與鬥牛一樣，均為西班牙的文化特產。

不過，以我們目前所能考究到的資料而言，佛朗明哥的歷史其實比想像中的複雜。淵源可追溯至西元八世紀，相傳西班牙南部當時被非洲入侵者攻占。來自非洲的摩爾人引進了自己的樂器和舞種，並與後來到此落地生根的族群和平共處。源自印度西北部的羅姆人，就是在摩爾人之後，逐批遷徙至此安頓。兩大族群加上當地原有的基督徒和猶太人，揉合出不同的音樂傳統，造就了後世眼裡結合民謠與舞蹈的「佛朗明哥」。

一直到 18 世紀末，此舞種才被冠上「佛朗明哥」的名稱。數百年來，音樂搭配舞蹈的此傳統，不過是生活的一部分，常見於結婚典禮或朋友聚會。浪漫主義於 18 世紀末蔓延後，佛朗明哥頓時爆紅。主打佛朗明哥表演的咖啡廳如雨後春筍般開張，更成為了上流社會熱衷的餘興節目。1939 年，獨裁的佛朗哥掌權後，更下令讓佛朗明哥成為西班牙的國舞。他藉由佛朗明哥來推動觀光產業，卻同時壓榨當初創造此舞蹈的羅姆人。

佛朗明哥的跨文化特性至今仍然存在，且進化到風靡全球的程度。世界各地的年輕人紛紛來到西班牙拜師學藝，有些人還回到家鄉發揚光大。即使佛朗明哥在西班牙已逐漸式微，這些舞者仍支持當地的舞蹈老師與學院，甚至在海外帶動了成立舞蹈班的熱潮。例如日本的佛朗明哥舞蹈學院已經超越西班牙本地的數量。

也許是這樣的活躍度，讓佛朗明哥如此令人著迷。在塞維爾習舞的英國學生茵卡・格雷斯表

示：「佛朗明哥是一種表達豐富情感的舞蹈，無關它的血脈背景。」雖然佛朗明哥源自於西班牙，卻已於全球文化占有舉足輕重的推崇地位。

15. 麻雀般的啾鳴聲　P. 53

超夯的桌遊「麻將」，源自 19 世紀末左右的中國，而中國人亦稱之為「麻雀」。必須由四名玩家，透過狀似骨牌的 144 張精美象牙色麻將牌來對戰。遊戲目的在於湊出幾組相似花色即可獲勝，也就是所謂的胡牌。完整的麻將套組包含一對骰子、計分幣以及讓玩家可以整齊擺放麻將牌、避免對手偷看牌面的麻將立架。

雖然麻將的起源不明，但有一說是由孔子於西元前 500 年左右所創。因為相傳最早出現麻將的時間地點，均與孔子周遊列國宣傳學說的紀錄不謀而合。而由紅中、青發、白板組成的三元牌，象徵孔子宣揚的仁、誠、孝等元德。孔子亦愛鳥成癖，這也說明了麻將有「麻雀」別稱的由來。不過，許多歷史學家認為，麻將其實是衍生自清朝盛行的紙牌遊戲。目前歷史最悠久的麻將牌組約為 1870 年製，但最早出現麻將文獻紀錄的時間卻是十年之後。

麻將已流傳至日本、韓國與越南等眾多亞洲國家。各國與臺灣一樣，均視麻將為融入在地玩法特色的博弈遊戲。美國人 J.P. 巴布考克於 1920 年左右，將麻將帶入西方世界。在巴布考克專為說英語的玩家精心制定遊戲規則與完整的術語後，麻將竟成為風靡美國的餘興活動。如此永垂不朽的麻將甚至與科技接軌，搖身一變，成為接龍形式的網路遊戲。

1998 年，中華全國體育總會為麻將運動制定標準化的競賽規則（也就是所謂的「國標麻將」），來與非法賭博的麻將玩法切割。這種新式「衛生麻將」的原則，在於打牌全程不賭不菸不酒。採用組隊競賽的方式，強調麻將正式歸類為團體運動。世界麻將協會於 2005 年成立，2007 年於中國成都舉辦第一屆世界麻將錦標賽。從此以後，麻將世錦賽成為定期舉辦的運動項目，來自全球各地的選手紛紛前來參加。

1-4 釐清寫作技巧

作者通常會想盡辦法呈現妙趣橫生與主題清楚的作品。例如運用各種技巧、文字和措詞，編排出起承轉合的文章結構，吸引讀者的注意力。為了辨識出此類技巧，你必須要能夠系統化的解構分析文章，以便看出作者寫作風格的巧思。

16. 歐洲的實驗　P. 56

歐盟創辦以來已超過六十年，歐洲歷經悠久又腥風血雨的歷史後，終於在前所未有的祥和繁盛之中度過一段平靜時光。歐盟的自由流通政策，讓五億人口享有在 28 個會員國任意居住、求學與就業的權利。而單一市場制度，使歐盟成為全球最為強大的貿易霸主。

不過，隨著規模持續擴大，歐盟逐漸無法滿足許多重要會員國的需求。再者，高度官僚的體系與繁複的決策程序，依舊讓許多會員國無所適從與充滿挫折感。

更糟糕的是，歐盟以雄心壯志進行的單一貨幣實驗「歐元」，使得受到 2008 年金融海嘯重創的會員國，經濟成長率仍不見起色，不滿的情緒逐漸高漲。以希臘為例，其他歐盟會員國得不斷協助希臘紓困債務。而義大利與西班牙等其他國家，因為財政壓力而採取緊縮措施，希望振興經濟頹勢，預防貨幣崩潰。歐盟境內經濟分歧的情況，更加深了會員國之間的怨懟。

2015 年發生移民危機後，歐盟出現了更大的裂痕。此事件起因在於成千上萬名伊拉克與敘利亞的難民，為了逃離衝突而欲湧入歐洲。雖然德國願意收容移民，但其他國家卻保持緘默。德國試圖強迫其他國家接納難民之舉，埋下了彼此敵對的心結。更使許多歐盟國家，產生了支持排外主義與民族主義的聲浪。

由於移民議題及無法掌控自身法律所產生的憤怒情緒，導致英國人民於 2016 年公投通過永久脫歐決策。曾以共享歐洲和平昌盛目的而團結一致的歐盟，如今卻愈來愈難與會員國取得共識。

歐盟的未來走向尚未明朗。其實歐盟一直是成功體制的表率，透過各種治理方式，為曾經四分五裂的歐洲帶來和平與經濟穩定。但近年來的事件卻證明了歐盟美中不足。如果能大力改革並且管理透明化，歐盟或許能妥善處理造成會員國歧異的問題。偉大的歐盟實驗是否能證明自己可成功永垂不朽，仍有待觀察。

17. 凍結之地　P. 59

冰河係指會移動的大量冰流，且至少存在於地球一百年至上百萬年。冰河範圍占地球表面的0.5%，因為經年累月的積雪而形成所謂的積雪區。

由於積雪區歷經多次融雪再凍結的過程，因此構成冰河外層的塊雪樣貌。而陳年積雪最後會形成十分緻密的淡藍色大型冰晶。

雪崩、冰雨和風吹流，都是保持冰河狀態的重要因素。侵蝕、消融、蒸發、崩落或因為斷裂而突然一分為二，都會減少冰河雪層。而最常見的兩種冰河則為大陸冰河與山谷冰河。

冰河本身的質量足以受到地心引力的牽引而移動。冰河可緩慢流經山谷與山腰，且通常出現在高緯度與高海拔地區，才能在冬季補足夏季所流失的雪量。雖然多數冰河都位於南北極附近居多，但除了澳洲以外，其他大洲均有冰河蹤影。

那麼冰河地形是如何生成呢？答案就是磨蝕作用。冰河底層的岩屑硬度、該區域的含水量以及冰河的冰層厚度，都是關鍵要素。如果岩屑硬度大於下方岩石，就會明顯磨損岩石。水一樣具有侵蝕作用，因為能夠加快冰河的移動速度。偏厚的冰層會產生高壓，導致周遭陸地自然變形。

冰河對土地利用的方式具有極大的影響力。歷經冰河活動的土地，會因為質地一致且富含沉積礦物，更能成功栽種作物。具有大量砂土與碎石的冰河地區，則是開採道路用沙石與水泥的現成來源。冰河沉積層亦可貯存地下水、泥煤與天然氣。

然而全球冰河卻面臨迅速消融的危機，堪稱最明顯的全球暖化指標。地球上約有198,000條冰河，蘊含全球將近70%的淡水。截至目前為止，多數冰河過去一百年來已削減不少，融冰率從1990年代中葉開始迅速攀升。如此寶貴的淡水來源，可能終將面臨消失殆盡的末日。

18. 破解人類基因密碼　P. 62

想像一下，未來的人類與現今人類相較下，免於罹病煩惱且能青春永駐、延年益壽、體力智力更強大靈活的光景。現代的先進基因編輯技術確實有可能締造這樣的未來——也就是更改活體的特定部分DNA。不過，雖然人類基因編輯技術充滿眾多令人興奮的可能性，很多人卻擔憂，如果在沒有警覺、謹慎的狀態下進行，這場美夢很快就會轉為夢魘。

基因工程以往常有不夠靈活、效率差且需要驚人天價的風評。不過，一直到2010年代初期，CRISPR-Cas9基因編輯技術崛起，它比其他現有技術的速度更快、要價更親民、更能準確執行且更具效率。科學家迫不及待把玩這項新技術，各種動物實驗成果豐碩——例如肌肉發達的超級狗狗、可愛的迷你豬、不會罹病的山羊等等。然而，每個人的腦海裡都盤旋著一個問題：該如何將CRISPR-Cas9應用於人類身上。此編輯技術能去除有害基因，甚至將防止罹病、提升骨骼強健度和心臟耐用度等有益健康的特點輸入新生兒的基因。

許多國家擔憂有心人濫用此項技術，紛紛制定人類基因編輯方面的嚴苛規定。有些國家則較為寬鬆。2018年11月，一位中國研究人員宣稱，他成功編輯兩名新生兒的DNA，降低他們感染HIV病毒的風險。此新聞震驚全球醫界，引起人類基因編輯醫學倫理的論戰，尤其是針對未出世寶寶的部分。

此技術變相在鼓勵金字塔頂端的人獨享「設計寶寶」的權利，已是不爭的事實；然而，更大的隱憂在於我們不確定基因編輯可能產生的副作用以及是否安全。改變一種基因往往不只有一種效果。看似有益的編輯方式，卻可能造成無法預料的其他問題。舉例而言，某些兔子因為基因改造，可產生精實肌肉，舌頭卻同時變得肥大；基因改造後的山羊，雖然能長出更長的喀什米爾羊毛，卻會在胎兒時期發育過大而無法讓母羊自然產。

雖然以科學背景和倫理道德而言，人類基因體的編輯充滿複雜爭議，但這似乎是人類不可避免要面對的未來。我們僅能盡人事，希望在基因編輯的發展過程中，不要犯下過多錯誤。

19. 太空發財夢！ P.64

1848 年，加州發現了金礦，於是超過 30 萬人湧入加州，希望一夕致富。如今，經過將近 200 年的時光，又有一股新的淘金熱潮即將席捲而來。只是地點不再是加州的山坡，而是浩瀚的太空。大家鎖定的目標，就是漂浮在無垠宇宙的成千上萬顆小行星。因為這些來自太空的巨石，滿載著鐵、鎳、白金與黃金等貴金屬。

許多大公司已開始打算利用這項未開發的太陽系資源，投入龐大的研發資金。大家也許會納悶，這樣的投資真的值得嗎？我們來看一下數據便知道：目前繞行地球附近的小行星，估計有 18,000 顆左右。某些小行星所含的白金量，超過地球史上開採出的白金總量，相當於價值上兆美元的貴金屬；某些小行星所含的鐵與鎳，則足以供地球使用三千年。名為「靈神星」的小行星，擁有一千京美元價值的鐵礦。相較之下，目前地球上的所有貨幣現值換算下來不過約 75 兆美元。

此外，小行星採礦之舉不僅能解決地球的資源短缺問題，還可能成為人類將到太空殖民的關鍵。開採可做為太空船燃料的資源，同時在太空設立補給站，能大幅增強我們造訪其他星球的能力。舉例而言，如果我們能在中途補給燃料和維生用品，登陸火星將不再是難事。許多專家的確相信，小行星採礦是實現永久太空開發計畫的唯一辦法，必須奠定此基礎才能開創未來的太空產業。

雖然這樣的想法看似科幻小說的情節，但其實小行星採礦行動可能遠比大家預計的要更快啟動並運作。有些公司已經打算最快於 2030 年付諸實行。雖然小行星採礦行為對人類未來社會的實際影響程度仍難以準確預測，但唯一能確定的——願意在太空一擲千金的投資者，所得到的報酬率將超乎想像！

20. 選擇操之在己！ P.66

2018 年 12 月，於網飛 Netflix 平台播出的黑暗科幻電視影集《黑鏡》，發布最新一集特別篇「潘達斯奈基」，全球影迷無不議論紛紛。原因在於，與觀眾無法掌控劇情的多數電視影集不同，「潘達斯奈基」允許觀眾即時決定故事的走向和結局。

由觀眾選擇劇情的發展，並非是史無前例的點子。1980 年代和 1990 年代，十分盛行《選擇你自己的冒險之旅》系列叢書。每一頁的末端，就會看到要求讀者選擇劇情的指示（例如進入山洞或探索叢林）。讀者只要翻閱至對應的頁碼，就能繼續閱讀故事。這種互動式的遊戲書具有多種結局，能讓讀者／玩家閱讀千遍也不厭倦，每次都能體驗不同的故事情節。

電玩遊戲開始蓬勃發展後，此類互動式的書籍就逐漸從主流市場退燒。雖然有很多人想將這種概念轉化至電視劇，但當時的科技仍望塵莫及——直到「潘達斯奈基」的上映。如今，「選擇你自己的冒險」概念可打造出潛力無窮的影集：例如由觀眾引導警探打擊恐怖犯罪的神祕謀殺劇；可選擇主角該情歸何處的浪漫喜劇；或是選擇以何種方式讓一群青少年在鬼屋存活一晚的驚悚劇。各種劇情將可永無止盡的神展開。

不過，製片公司急於製作互動式電視影集其實另有目的，也就是為了蒐集數據資料。以「潘達斯奈基」為例，影集剛開始是要求觀眾幫主角選擇早餐該吃哪一種穀片。儲存此類選擇數據後，能讓廣告公司更精準判斷產品的目標市場。觀眾的選擇亦呼應自己的個性——例如所選的是較為激進或較為暖心的行為？所有抉擇均可彙整為個人側寫資料，無論是介紹或推薦各種產品服務，廣告公司均可根據此資料而擬定量身訂製的行銷策略。耐人尋味的是，我們看似在娛樂世界得到更多的主控權，實際上卻是將更多的掌控權交到收集資料的大公司手上，讓他們藉此控制我們的視聽內容與消費方向。

所以，你願意踏入互動式的娛樂產業革命嗎？選擇與否，操之在己……

1-5 瞭解譬喻性語言

作者會運用**譬喻性的語言**來觸動讀者的感受或令人在腦海中產生畫面，讓讀者留下深刻印象。本單元會呈現幾種下列譬喻性語言。

明喻會以「like」（像）、「as」（如）或「than」（比……還……）等字比較兩者，例如「她的心比石頭還硬」。**隱喻**會更直接比較兩者，並且將兩者畫上等號，例如「她擁有一顆鐵石心腸」或「全世界就是一座大舞台」，因此表達效果比明喻更強烈。

擬人法意指將無生物的物體賦予人類特質，例如「太陽漫步於天空」。**成語**屬於不能照字面意思解讀的片語，其意義與拆解各字來看不同。例如「To let the cat out of the bag.」和貓咪一點關係也沒有，真正的意思為「洩漏祕密」。

最後，**誇飾法**意指加油添醋的誇張表達方式，例如「我已經告訴過你一百萬遍了！」

21. 凝聚全球力量的事件 P. 68

小行星的定義到底是什麼？有些人認為小行星等同於彗星或「流星」，其實兩者的結構大相逕庭。科學家相信，太陽系形成初期，受到木星引力干擾而無法藉由碰撞來形成行星的殘留物質，就是所謂的小行星。太陽系裡有成千上萬顆小行星，所有小行星的體積加總約為月球的一半大。最大的穀神星，直徑將近 1000 公里，其實已符合矮行星的資格。火星與木星之間遍布「小行星帶」，光是穀神星就占了小行星帶總質量的三分之一。

另一方面，流星體基本上是太空中的礫狀碎片，雖然接觸地球大氣層後，通常會燃燒殆盡，但仍有例外。如果有人在錯的時機處於錯的地點，不巧碰上進入大氣層的流星體，一樣會喪命。

雖然多數小行星大多安分地漂浮於火星和木星之間，但是「近地小行星」卻離地球近在咫尺。目前科學家認為，尚無任何「小行星」會對人類造成威脅。這是一則喜訊，因為即使小行星長度僅 300 公尺，一旦撞擊地球，可能會讓地球整整一年籠罩在冬季狀態中；如果是長度一公里的小行星撞擊地球，則會造成無法言喻的全球性毀滅。

2009 年 3 月 4 日，美國太空總署（簡稱 NASA）發布某小行星於上週一和地球擦身而過的消息。名為「2009 DD45」的這顆小行星，運行方向竟然離地表約 78,000 公里。這樣的距離僅是某些電信人造衛星與地表距離的兩倍，真要深究的話，造成災難的可能性很大。

「2009 DD45」的大小約與 1908 年撞擊西伯利亞的小行星相同，當時摧毀了 2000 平方公里的森林──等於比倫敦更大的面積！更令人不安的是，科學家僅於該小行星行經地球前的 48 小時察覺其蹤影，且撞擊程度堪稱一顆核彈爆炸的威力。我們還不能放下戒心，因為「2009 DD45」仍有可能受到地心引力的牽引而返回。

近地小行星最令人恐懼的原因在於我們束手無策。因為這樣一股純粹出自大自然的肆虐威脅，完全超越任何國家首領或科學家的能力所及。因此，一名 NASA 小行星專家認為此類潛在撞擊，會成為「凝聚全球力量的事件」。

22. 磚牆引發的戰役 P. 71

所有宗教均有聖地的概念，意指舉行特殊儀式慶典或紀念重要事件的地點。不過，有一處聖地卻無法維持各宗教「和平共處」的狀態，反而成為武力衝突之處。那就是耶路撒冷的哭牆。

哭牆其實只是猶太第二聖殿西牆的一小部分，是由大希律王於公元前 19 年所拓建。「哭牆」一詞於 19 世紀首度出現於英國文獻，此字詞源自於猶太人如送行者般沿著牆面，邊走邊啜泣哀悼聖殿於公元 70 年遭摧毀的傳統。相繼出現的基督教和伊斯蘭帝國，限制或完全禁止猶太人接近哭牆。一直到 1920 年開始的英國政府託管時期，才立法徹底整修哭牆。

接下來的十年時間，猶太人與阿拉伯人在哭牆所有權方面的爭端已到臨界點。阿拉伯人深信當年先知穆罕默德於夜間騎著神獸布拉克，飛往耶路撒冷落地時，就是將神獸栓於哭牆內。除了曾為套綁布拉克韁繩之處，哭牆更是伊斯蘭第三大聖地「阿克薩清真寺」的一部分。穆斯林深信先知穆罕默德從麥加騎著神獸布拉克抵達後，為後續前來的祈禱信徒帶路。清真寺的部分結構直接建於第二猶太聖殿遺址，被穆斯林視為耶路撒冷最神聖之地。

而猶太人則是堅持，哭牆（猶太人稱「西牆」）是躲過羅馬帝國維斯巴辛皇帝拆除命運，倖存下來的部分第二聖殿遺跡。他們到此哀悼人民所受的苦難，祈求福報或指引。雖然某些人認為此地是所謂的「究極聖地」，也就是應當保存十誡約櫃之處，但實為聖殿地基的擋土牆結構。

近年來，哭牆儼然成為超級熱門的景點。前三任教宗裡，有兩位教宗造訪此地。而前美國總統歐巴馬於 2008 年為參選宣傳造勢時，同樣到此一遊。此外，穆斯林和猶太人各有進入哭牆範圍的限制。而兩大宗教長期以來視為聖潔的這塊寸土必爭之地，將持續分化彼此，而非團結共處。

23. 人物剖析——追求原始主義的畫家
P. 74

保羅・高更生於 1848 年的巴黎，堪稱後印象派年代舉足輕重的藝術家之一。他的創作囊括無數油畫、雕像、素描、版畫、金屬雕刻作品和陶器。他備受推崇的傑作，包括《布道後的幻象》（1888 年）以及《沙灘上的大溪地女人》（1891 年）。

1871 年至 1882 年，高更一邊以證券經紀人為主業，一邊涉獵藝術領域而飛黃騰達。但是巴黎股市崩盤後，瞬間為這兩項事業劃下句點。高更與丹麥籍太太和五名子女短暫居住於哥本哈根後，於 1885 年返回巴黎。自從 1873 年他便以作畫為興趣，現在則決定將藝術做為事業重心。他的許多朋友都是畫家，包括後印象派大師畢沙羅、塞尚、莫內和梵谷。

成為後印象派畫家後，確實讓高更嘗到一些成功的甜頭，但他對於歐洲藝術抄襲與墨守成規的風氣感到失望。1887 年，高更暫居加勒比海的馬提尼克島，儘管不時罹患痢疾和瘧疾，他仍因為重拾繪畫熱情，創作了十幾幅油畫。

回到法國後，高更煥然一新的作畫風格與題材（馬提尼克原住民的日常生活），獲得藝術圈和買主的好評。為了繼續在異地尋覓靈感，高更於 1891 年前往大溪地。接下來的兩年，高更大量創作油畫與雕像，甚至娶了一名 13 歲的大溪地原住民女孩為妻。他的藝術品風格逐漸變得更具原始民族風與鮮豔色彩，甚至善用宗教圖像。

如同候鳥的他，於 1893 年返回巴黎，繼續以玻里尼西亞人作為油畫和雕像的創作主題。然而作品卻普遍不被看好，因此，他不得不接受朋友的金援，在 1895 年再次搭船前往大溪地，殊不知就此訣別歐洲。

接下來的六年，高更在大溪地的首都帕比堤創作雕像和油畫，希冀拓展買主市場。他於此時期完成最享譽盛名的畫作《我們從何處來？我們是誰？我們向何處去？》（1897 年至 1898 年），可惜他的健康狀態卻逐漸走下坡。1901 年，他因為堅信大溪地已不再「原始」，而前往馬克薩斯島安頓，希望滿足自己追求原始靈感的野心。1903 年，卻因罹患梅毒而去世，享年 54 歲。

24. 舉步維艱 P. 78

西元前 486 年，薛西斯繼承了父親大流士的波斯王位。當時的波斯帝國版圖，已鯨吞了三分之二的世界，僅剩歐洲倖免。對波斯人而言，希臘是通往歐洲的入口。大流士曾試圖征服希臘，卻在馬拉松吞下了著名的敗戰。薛西斯繼承了父親的抱負，決心一抹父親的失敗紀錄。

薛西斯花了六年的時間，籌備史上規模最大的軍隊，兵力預估十萬人甚至超過百萬人。另一方面，當時的希臘卻是一盤散沙、無心作戰的狀態。每座城邦都擁有自己的政府律法，缺乏互通有無的團結力量。有些希臘城邦甚至彼此交戰。

儘管如此，這是一場破釜沉舟的戰役。因此斯巴達國王列奧尼達，率領 1,200 人來迎戰波斯大軍。另一座希臘城邦則派出約 6,000 名士兵。如此微不足道的兵力，準備鎮守「溫泉關」此狹窄山口，與龐大的波斯軍隊對峙。波斯軍隊彷彿陷入瓶頸，漏斗狀的關口地形限制了可作戰的人數。希臘兵力儘管寥寥無幾，卻無法被包圍。

雖然斯巴達的軍隊兵力薄弱，但每位士兵卻是從七歲開始接受軍事訓練，從未從事過其他職業。他們是當時世上最重裝備戰武力的戰士，每一個人身上均穿戴銅製護胸盔甲，攜帶鍍銅的實心橡木盾牌、短劍以及裝有鋼製矛頭的 2.4 公尺長矛。不過，造就他們作戰熱忱的主因，並非是訓練或配備，而是他們極欲爭取自由的理想。

當希臘叛徒告知薛西斯一條包抄希臘士兵的小徑，深知寡不敵眾的列奧尼達，將多數的盟軍遣返家鄉，希望減少死傷。雖然薛西斯的軍隊確實包抄了所剩無幾的希臘士兵，卻得用漫天箭雨的作戰方式擊潰誓死奮戰的敵軍，最終才拿下溫泉關。

斯巴達士兵全軍覆沒，沒有留下任何足跡，留在人們記憶中的只有那兩天浴血奮戰的精神。如同他們手中的盾牌一樣，斯巴達士兵就擋在歐陸與冷酷西征的波斯軍隊中間抗戰。溫泉關戰役著實成為歷史上極具意義的戰事之一。

25. 下一個愛因斯坦？ P.82

身為第一代美籍古巴裔的莎賓娜・帕斯特斯基，土生土長於芝加哥郊區。年僅二十幾歲的她，顯赫的履歷可能會使許多年長的學者無地自容。她於哈佛大學完成物理博士學位，並獲封為「下一個愛因斯坦」。偉大的科學家史蒂芬・霍金，甚至引用她的論文。在一個傳統由男性主導的學術領域裡，帕斯特斯基猶如年輕女性的典範，鼓勵她們投入科學，在此領域占有一席之地。

她在九歲上過飛行課後，就此點燃科學魂。這樣的熊熊熱情，隨著年歲增長而有增無減。13歲時，她成功建造一架飛機，甚至單獨試飛。不過，她的求學之路並非一帆風順。帕斯特斯基於 16 歲申請提早入學哈佛大學和麻省理工學院（簡稱 MIT），卻被拒絕。不過，事隔多月，兩名 MIT 教授看到她在 YouTube 上傳的造飛機紀錄片時，無不瞠目結舌。他們肯定帕斯特斯基的潛力，為她開放入學名額。而她只用三年的時間，就以亮眼的 5.00 學業成績平均點數畢業於 MIT。

滿腔工程師熱血的帕斯特斯基，原本是以服務於太空公司、建造太空船為志向。但在 MIT 就學期間，她卻因為想了解飛行原理，而一頭栽入物理的世界。往後幾年，她以「破解我們每天習以為常的物理現象」為樂，逐漸進入最為繁複的科學領域。她開始研究黑洞、引力、空間時間的本質，目的在於了解宇宙運作的奧祕。

大家一定會納悶，帕斯特斯基究竟如何在這麼短的時間內，擁有如此驚人的成就。她的天文智商無疑是主因，但促使她成功的另一個重要因素，就是她鋼鐵般的意志。帕斯特斯基能以異於常人的方式來避開所有分心事務。她從不交男友、不菸不酒、也從來不玩任何社群媒體，甚至連智慧型手機也沒有。藉由全心全意的投入，才能在多數人仍游移不定的年紀，在科學界掀起浪潮。

1-6 明瞭作者目的和語氣

作者寫作皆有目的，可能是提出自己的論點、呈現重要議題，甚或只是想娛樂讀者。為了達到其寫作目的，作者會調整文中的字彙和資訊，來符合文章所欲呈現出的語氣。

26. 星夜榮光 P.86

徹夜流瀉於冷冽星空的北極光

令人震懾卻從未顯露召喚之意的光芒

救贖了將亡帝王與英雄

——W.E. 艾頓

這是蘇格蘭詩人威廉・艾頓於 19 世紀所寫下的看法，著實讚頌了至高榮耀的北極光情景。彷彿舞動光影與多變色彩的壯麗北極光，有時看似高掛晶耀星空的布幔。堪稱令人驚嘆的自然奇景之一，北極光的英文名稱取自羅馬曙光女神「歐若拉」（Aurora）以及希臘文的「北風」（boreas）。而最廣為人知的英文名稱則是「northern lights」。

不過，許多北極光粉絲卻不曉得，知名的北極光其實還有分身出現於南半球，也就是南極光。而原文「australis」一字則出自拉丁文「南邊的……」。

北極光與南極光的籠罩範圍為 60 公里至 600 公里的地球表面，只要是在北半球與南半球的地磁極地區裡，均可欣賞到此美景。北極光橫跨了西伯利亞北部、阿拉斯加、加拿大的哈德森灣以及挪威北部。加拿大與美國北部經常可見北極光，尤其是在春分和秋分時節，因為地軸的傾斜角度距離太陽剛好不偏不倚。如果是在極端活躍期，甚至可於美國南部見到北極光的蹤影。而南極光僅出現於南半球的南極洲、南美洲與澳洲的高緯度地區。

即使是在能以高科技進行研究的現代，仍有許多人疑惑如此嘆為觀止的天然景致從何而來。美國發明家暨政治家班傑明·富蘭克林，竟是公開發表極光理論的第一人。他認為北極和南極地區凝結的水氣強化了電荷，而極光就是電荷濃度變高的結果。

不過，真正的答案其實更加繁複。目前的研究顯示，極光是由進入地球大氣層的太陽帶電粒子碰撞空氣分子後所形成。這些粒子困在高於地表的輻射帶，因為本身的磁場而散布於極區。碰撞空氣分子後產生的發光現象，成為了壯觀的巨幅彩色光幕。我非常幸運曾親眼目睹北極光。我向讀者保證，宛如星夜榮光的極光奇景，確實能讓人打從心底，對絕美地球所能產生的天然景象深深讚歎不已。

27. 大醉一場　P. 90

德文的「Prost」意指「乾杯」，如果想參加全球最盛大的啤酒派對「十月啤酒節」，一定要學會這個字。

十月啤酒節源自 1810 年的德國慕尼黑，是為了慶祝王儲路德威希王子（後來繼位成為國王路德威希一世）與泰瑞莎公主的婚禮。這對皇室佳偶親切地邀請慕尼黑的市民前往婚禮接待場所共襄盛舉，狂歡時間竟為期 16 天。德國人因而得到靈感，打算每年都在同一個時期舉辦類似節慶。儘管名稱是「十月啤酒節」，但多於九月開跑，於十月的第一個週末結束。

無論如何，十月啤酒節儼然成為全球規模最大的盛事，每年有超過六百萬人前來朝聖。比人數更令人印象深刻的是飲用的啤酒量。2018 年，為期短短 16 天的十月啤酒節，就創下喝掉 750 萬公升德式冰啤酒的紀錄。慶典上供應的是特地為此節慶所釀的「十月啤酒節啤酒」，並以加大尺寸的玻璃德式啤酒杯盛裝。而搭配的傳統小吃包括德式香腸、烤雞、起司麵、燉牛尾以及發酵高麗菜絲所製成的德式酸菜，還有大量供應啤酒節最著名的德國軟式蝴蝶扭結麵包。

啤酒節以搭起大型帳篷的方式，為成千上萬的民眾供應各種餐飲。事實上，光是一頂帳篷就能同時容納超過 8,000 名的賓客！2018 年，會場為飢腸轆轆來參加派對的人供應將近 28 萬條香腸、55 萬隻烤雞和 124 隻烤牛！

在參與人數如此踴躍、商機無限的情況下，十月啤酒節已不再是專屬於德國的活動了。世界各國依著該國國情而推出自己的十月啤酒節版本。墨西哥市的德裔墨西哥人，會為慶典設置遊樂園與手工藝市集。巴西的布魯美瑙則以 18 天的音樂熱舞，讓巴西人向德國祖先致敬。美國則有上百場十月啤酒節的慶典，規模最大的場地位於俄亥俄州的辛辛那提。

十月啤酒節對臺灣而言仍是相當新穎的點子，不過當地德國業者已觀察到臺灣人對此節日的熱情迴響。這項德國味濃厚的傳統仍持續延燒全球，誰能料想得到下一個歡慶地點會在哪裡落腳？

28. 貓癡天堂島　P. 94

愛貓人士到了日本，一定會像小孩到了糖果店一樣興奮。貓神社、幸運招財貓、Hello Kitty 凱蒂貓、貓咖啡廳等元素隨處可見，彷彿全國上下都熱愛喵星人。不過，有些日本地區，甚至將這樣的狂熱無限上綱。日本共有 11 座的「貓島」——這些離島的貓隻數量大多超越居民人口，絕對是貓奴的終極朝聖景點。

最享譽盛名的貓島就是青島，從日本南岸搭乘渡輪 30 分鐘，即可抵達這座 1.6 公里長的島嶼。青島區民約 20 人，但是喵星人卻超過 100 隻，經常蜷縮於島上的廢棄建築，或在港口出沒捕魚。青島照片在網上瘋傳之後，造訪青島的遊客人數因而激增。但青島其實不適合觀光，因為完全看不見汽車、飯店、餐廳甚至是販賣機的蹤影，而且目前的居民多為捕魚維生的老年人。當初將貓隻帶來青島的用意是為了控制徘徊在漁船邊的鼠患。但隨著該島人口逐年下降，貓群就此喧賓奪主。

不過，貓島逐漸受到重視且大受歡迎的現象，卻帶來了問題。以相島這個小貓島為例，遊客帶來餵養上百隻當地貓群的豐富食物，使得貓隻過度大肆繁殖。貓群之間因而產生壓力、暴力與疾病，甚至因為島上過於擁擠，常為了爭奪領土而死亡。

因此，雖然愛貓人士此生必去的景點就是貓島，但也要謹記於心，盡可能降低觀光所帶來的負面影響程度。雖然許多貓島現已實施「誘捕、絕育、放生」計畫來控制貓隻數量，但遊客一樣要善盡職責。無論喵星人那讓人融化的可愛眼神多麼令人難以抗拒，遊客務必避免餵食島上貓隻！唯有如此，才能確保貓島維持遊客與喵星人共享的天堂勝地狀態。

29. 別相信你的所見所聞　P.97

根據維基百科的說法，都市傳說意指「深植本地流行文化的現代版民間故事，通常由帶有驚悚或幽默元素的虛構故事所組成。」某些都市傳說根本是蓄意嚇人的恐怖故事，例如清楚描述政府陰謀、罪犯攻擊等警告。有些則屬於繪聲繪影的荒謬故事，目的是製造令人吃驚的效果。都市傳說也許有真實事件為基礎，但經年累月下來，卻會演變為怪誕成分居多的迷思。

「都市傳說」一詞可追溯至 1960 年代晚期，網路的誕生促使都市傳說的數量和類型如雨後春筍般增加。最常見的兩則就是「電子郵件稅」和「克雷格・雪格的故事」。電子郵件稅的傳說裡，描述美國郵政即將針對每封電子郵件課徵五分錢的稅金，以彌補郵資虧損。因為現代人已不再使用郵政系統寄信，而是透過電子郵件。克雷格・雪格的傳說剛開始是真的。這名罹患惡性腦瘤的英國小男孩，想藉由發起連鎖信活動的方式，打

破金氏世界紀錄。雖然後來已公布他於 1991 年痊癒的消息，但到 2013 年底，他仍收到上千封的信件和名片。

當然，有很多人之所以受到都市傳說的影響，是因為耳根子軟，容易受到奇幻故事的吸引而無法自拔。為了找出可靠真相，許多都市傳說調查團體就此因應而生。兩個最廣為人知的就是 Snopes.com 網站，以及電視節目《流言終結者》。Snopes 網站通常侷限在研究的部分，但《流言終結者》卻進行許多有趣的實驗，來求證新舊迷思的真偽。

不過，有些都市傳說太有說服力，導致政府甚至為此立法。其中一個例子就是「一邊加油一邊使用手機會引爆燃油」的誤解。消防局的測試與其他實驗，均證明這是不實說法。最有可能的元兇，是民眾接觸金屬油槍時所產生的靜電。

無庸置疑，都市傳說會繼續滲透我們的文化、型塑我們的世界。然而，儘管我們出於本能地受到聳動資訊的吸引，但力求真相的求知者也許能將我們拉回真實世界。

30. 斜槓效應帶來的榮景　P.100

現在的就業性質，已經出現重大轉變。過往的工作模式，大多是畢生任職於同一公司、完成千篇一律的職務、仰賴一樣的技能。如今，許多公司就如同一年四季般來來去去。想想看，社群媒體經理人（譯註：俗稱「小編」）與手機 APP 設計師等熱門職業，15 年前都還不存在呢！

現代的工作者同樣需要轉變，否則就會有被遠遠拋在後頭的風險。而「斜槓效應」就此興起。「斜槓效應」此名詞，是由擔任《紐約時報》專欄作家的前律師瑪西・艾波赫所創。意指許多現代工作者，屬於擁有多重技能與身分的斜槓族。例如艾波赫就以「作家／演說家／指導老師」自居。

斜槓效應適用於各種情境。可用來表達轉換職場跑道的人，例如記者轉行當社工。亦可代表身兼數職的自由業工作者，例如作家／編輯／翻譯師。更廣義來說，還能用來表達因應現代生活而生的不同身分角色，例如總裁／媽媽。或指晚

上追求攝影等創意技能、白天則靠不相干工作維生的人。這類族群也許有天可以只靠藝術過活，但在成功之前，仍需要一份維持家計的收入。

在這個新經濟時代，哪些技能最寶貴呢？首先也是最重要的就是適應能力。想要具備斜槓條件，必須能以彈性應對的態度，面臨不同人生階段的角色變化。以「活到老，學到老」觀念來精進自我的人，必能成長茁壯，反之則將面臨被淘汰的風險。

然而，這樣的新經濟趨勢卻有顯著的缺點。因為斜槓效應在某種程度上，反映的是職涯愈來愈不穩定的徵兆。我們不一定真的「想要」另闢新事業，而是「不得已」才這麼做。況且，原本長年任職於單一公司所能享有的健保與退休金等福利，亦愈來愈罕見。

不過，斜槓人生還是有不少優點。年輕人可追求自己熱衷的事物，經過時間的洗鍊累積新技能。培養創意才華之餘，又不會讓自己陷入經濟困頓的泥沼。所以，大家還在等什麼呢？趕緊加入斜槓族的行列！

1-7 理解因果關係

事出必有因，所導致的行為或事件就是一種**結果**。因果之間的關係有時顯而易見，有時卻幾乎不著痕跡。為了更清楚理解因果關係，請仔細觀察具有因果意味的用字，例如「因此」（therefore）、「所以」（as a result）或是「因而」（consequently）。

31. 擺脫使用塑料的習慣 P. 104

縮減塑料使用量的宣導警語，大家已耳熟能詳。問題不在於缺乏環保意識——而是塑膠生活用品實在太氾濫。現在大家需要的是可輕鬆替代塑料、價格又親民的實用建議。

沒錯，你或許已經帶著棉製購物袋上超市（已有超過 90 個國家追隨孟加拉於 2002 年施行環保政策的腳步，開始禁用塑膠袋，或需付費才能使用），甚至是攜帶自己的隨行杯到咖啡店且拒用塑膠吸管。但如果真想貢獻一己心力，該是時候擴大減塑作為了。

回想一下你上次逛超市的情景。有多少你採買的雜貨都有塑膠包裝？加工食品（例如糖果、洋芋片和泡麵）是元凶，但連香蕉或稻米等原形食物都採用塑膠包裝。所以，將一堆塑膠容器裝滿棉製購物袋，有何意義呢？下次你到超市、麵包店或獨立商店採買時，請自備保鮮盒、保鮮罐以及收納布。

還可用天然物品來取代市售的清潔產品和美妝品。試著混調清水和白醋，來替代刺激性的家用清潔劑。擺脫小包面紙、瓶瓶罐罐的沐浴乳和體香劑，改用棉製手帕、香皂和小蘇打粉。小蘇打粉確實有效，還能加入薰衣草等精油來增添宜人香氣。無氣味的小蘇打粉還能洗碗，光亮的乾淨程度媲美市售洗碗精。

那麼廚房的常見用品該怎麼辦？現今許多所謂的「不沾鍋」，通常都具有鐵氟龍塗層。經過加熱的此塑料塗層，會釋放有毒化學物質。因此，請回歸老一輩所用的金屬鍋具。也請抗拒廉價塑料餐具的誘惑，因為使用壽命絕對不長。請投資可持續使用數十年的優質木製勺匙和金屬器皿。

不過，真正令人驚恐的是，從茶包到口香糖等許多產品，都含有看不見的塑料。你沒聽錯，為了擁有清新口氣，你其實咀嚼的是塑膠。（零廢料的替代方案，就是效法印度人常吃的茴香籽。）上述無法消化的「塑膠微粒」最防不勝防。不過，只要盡量改變整體生活習慣，購物的時候多三思，就能逐漸學會選購有益地球的產品。

32. 文靜的四種表現 P. 108

你會比較偏好以哪種方式打發週六晚上的時間呢？是參加能認識許多新面孔的派對，還是坐在電視前享用牛奶和餅乾呢？如果你比較想去派對，你很有可能個性外向，參與交際活動反而讓你精神抖擻。如果你選擇宅在沙發上，也許你的個性比較內向，需要獨處的時間來自我充電。

過去人們對內向性格帶有「輕度交際障礙」的印象。個性內向的人，會強迫自己跨出家門，來避免被取笑和冠上「無趣」的頭銜。幸好，大家現在多能體諒個性內向只是一種不同的性格，而非缺陷。現今對內向性格的研究和描述，比以往多很多。現在的專家甚至認為，內向性格不是只有單一「特徵」，而可劃分為四種類型。

第一種內向性格是指交際方面。交際型內向者不太願意花時間與人為伍。與傳統定義不同的是，交際型內向者不是厭惡人群或永遠堅持獨處。他們只不過希望擁有重質不重量的深層友情。一旦交際內向者能與你自在相處，說不定還會和你聊上好幾個小時！

第二種類型是思考型的內向者。與交際型內向者不同，思考型內向者不介意人山人海的環境。他們會接受自己感興趣的邀約場合，到場後就開始沉浸在自己的思維。他們很有想像力，許多作家和藝術家都擁有這類性格。

第三種類型可能是最棘手的──焦慮型內向者。焦慮型內向者大多時候確實不喜與人相處，因為擔心自己的表現會失準。即使是回到家，還是會重演與人互動時的變調表現。焦慮型內向者有時會被這樣極為艱難掙扎的性格所折磨。

最後一種類型為謹言慎行的內向性格，這類人喜歡在發言或有所行動前沉思一番。雖然在激辯場面裡，會顯得文靜，但不表示他們聽不懂或不感興趣。謹言慎行內向者比較慢熱，就像早晨氣溫偏低時，開車前需先暖車一樣。

你是否發現自己是其中一種的內向者呢？如果是的話，心理醫師認為，你應該接納這樣的內向性格！當比較外向的朋友們以你的內向個性做文章時，請藉機教育他們。誠如蘇珊‧坎恩在其著作《安靜，就是力量：內向者如何發揮積極的力量！》所言：「別將內向性格視為需要被治癒的缺陷……用你喜歡的方式打發閒暇時間，而不是順應世俗的看法。」

33. 惱人的地牛翻身　P.111

上千年來，我們有充分的理由相信，動物能預知地震。雖然未經科學證實，不過此類預言現象包括蜂群慌張竄離蜂巢、母雞停止下蛋、鯰魚狂暴游動，貓狗與籠中鳥變得明顯焦躁不安。

以野生動物為例，新聞報導指出，2008年中國四川大地震發生前三天，綿竹市的街上突然出現上千隻蟾蜍。地震發生後，造成兩千名市民罹難。地震當天，距離震央約965公里的武漢市動物園，斑馬開始以頭部焦慮撞門、大象發狂甩動象鼻，而白天通常都在睡覺的獅子與老虎，則在籠內來回踱步。地震發生前五分鐘，動物園裡的孔雀更發出尖銳叫聲。

諸如此類的例子早已出現於人類歷史。西元前373年，歷史學家以文字記錄了希臘赫里克市發生地震的前幾天，成堆的蛇群、黃鼠狼、老鼠和蜈蚣相繼離去。地震發生後，隨之而來的海嘯就此湮滅這座城市。

上述動物到底有何感知能力仍是未解之謎。某些論點認為，牠們比人類更能提早感受到地表的微小震動、注意到天然氣外洩，或能聽見地震與火山爆發前發出低於人類聽力頻率範圍的「超低頻音」。動物亦能駕輕就熟的利用地球磁場來辨別遷徙方向。因此，據說動物可察覺電磁場異動引起的電子信號，因而對於即將發生的地震有所警覺。

美國地質調查局聲明，地震與動物出現特定行為模式之間並無恆久不變的關連性，因此無法取得確鑿證據。同樣地，美國的地震學家也抱持存疑的態度。他們指稱動物隨時可能基於飢餓、守護地盤、面對掠食者或是交配季等因素而表現出怪異行為。不過，仍有其他研究人員對此觀點鍥而不捨。他們持續追蹤此類新奇證據，尤其是容易發生地震的日本、印度與中國等地。期許累積下來的經驗，有朝一日能成為準確預測地震的寶貴技術，進而拯救上百萬條生命。

34. 充滿熱忱使命感的人物 P.114

　　馬丁・路德・金恩二世是最備受推崇的 1960 年代美國民權運動鬥士。他生於 1929 年的喬治亞州亞特蘭大市，原名為麥可・金恩。五歲時，父親為了向宗教改革運動的創始人致敬，幫他改名為馬丁・路德・金恩。金恩彷彿受到此名的精神感召，一樣熱血勇於擔起服務人群的使命感。

　　金恩生長於種族隔離的南部，種族歧視一直是他早年生活最首要的問題。19 歲以優異成績自大學畢業，爾後前往柯羅澤神學院鑽研宗教。1954 年，他成為浸信會牧師，隔年取得波士頓大學的神學博士學位。金恩認為教會應許了他「強烈想為人群服務的信念」，因此希望透過布道這樣一個「受人敬重的力量，來傳播社運等各種理想」。

　　金恩開始重視種族和宗教議題的緣起，始於他與氣味相投的各路人士所建立的關係。其中一人就是身兼教育家、人權領袖與波士頓大學神學家的霍華德・瑟曼。他向金恩傳授了聖雄甘地非暴力社運的箇中道理。金恩曾表示，他「深信……非暴力抗爭是受壓迫的族群，最強而有力能去爭取正義的武器……」

　　1957 年，金恩協力創辦「南方基督教領袖會」（簡稱 SCLC）。SCLC 帶頭主辦以破除種族隔離為理念的遊行，並且致力保障黑人的投票權與勞動權。金恩離世前，一直是 SCLC 的靈魂人物，曾因參與該會的多次社運活動而遭逮補。

　　1963 年「為就業和自由朝華府進軍」的大遊行期間，金恩在林肯紀念堂面對約莫 25 萬的群眾，發表了舉世聞名的「我有一個夢想」演講。17 分鐘的演說堪稱史上最勵志的致詞之一。

　　1964 年，金恩因為以非暴力抗爭美國種族偏見的壯舉，榮獲諾貝爾和平獎。SCLC 專攻的人權運動，也因此促成 1964 年民權法案與 1965 年投票權法案的立法。

　　1968 年 4 月 4 日，金恩為聲援黑人公共衛生清潔工而前往田納西州孟非斯市，卻在下榻旅館的陽臺被槍擊暗殺。遇刺前一晚，他才剛發表著名演講「我曾站在巔峰」，向大家宣揚「……我們眾人終將踏入應許之地」。

35. 擁有超級敏感的靈魂 P.118

　　我的朋友珍妮擁有一種超能力——她感受事物的深入程度超乎常人。她一進到某廳室空間，就能立即察覺當下氛圍。她能對任何人發揮同理心，就好像吸取了他人的感覺。她走在鄉間時，會注意到鳥叫聲、色彩的變化、很細微的溫度起伏差異。她是畫家，也是詩人，對於自身的經歷和想法有很深的感觸。她每晚都會進入栩栩如生的夢境。珍妮就和全世界 15% 的人類一樣，是所謂的「高敏感族群」（簡稱 HSP）。

　　HSP 的大腦運作模式與多數人不同。HSP 體內的特定基因，會影響大腦對神經化學物質的反應方式、大腦特定神經元的活躍程度，以及大腦特定區塊對情緒刺激的敏感程度。也就是說，HSP 不僅對正面的情緒和生理感知具有強烈反應，對於壓力、痛苦和像噪音或不適衣著這類的負面刺激一樣感同身受。過度的負面刺激會讓 HSP 非常難熬，或因為某些情況而心神耗弱，但在相對不敏感的人眼裡，卻是再平常不過或是很容易忍受的情況。限時的考試、被批評、職場衝突、甚至是剛錄取新工作或升遷等事件，都可能讓 HSP 感到極為不適且很有壓力，甚至會覺得身體不舒服。過度頻繁經歷上述情況，都會使 HSP 遭受憂鬱或焦慮等心理疾病的折磨。

　　那麼，擁有如此高度敏感的體質，難道不是更像一種詛咒，而非擁有超能力嗎？不見得。HSP 可以運用一些方法來管理自己超級敏感的負面影響。

　　一般建議 HSP 可以減少環境中強烈刺激的來源，例如會發出噪音的家電、材質粗糙的家具或色彩鮮豔的壁紙。盡可能一次專注進行一種事務，避免產生難以招架的感覺。藉由寫作、油畫／水彩畫或素描來發揮創意，有助於清除思緒，改善想太多的習慣。關於忍痛程度低的部分，冥想可帶來明顯好處，幫助他們脫離任何負面的生理感知。

　　雖然 HSP 會是世上最懂你的超棒好友，但他們也需要被人照顧。因此，請為你生活中的 HSP 多著想一點，盡量體貼他們的需求。畢竟，有這些無微不至的敏感族群存在，就能讓這個社會變得更和平融洽。

1-8 分析寫作偏見

　　作者有其本身的歷練、看法和信仰。混為一談的時候，就會形成偏見，或是特定觀點。雖然有時難以看出作者的偏見，但可從作者的用字以及是否公平陳述兩造論點來窺見端倪。

36. 寵物至上　P. 122

　　曾淪為看家或捕捉害蟲用途的寵物，現已逐漸被視為家中的一分子。如果你和我一樣，對溺愛寵物感到樂此不疲，那麼你很可能是推動蓬勃寵物經濟背後的大戶。以寵物為主的產業來勢洶洶——尤其是亞洲，每年約以 **14%** 的速度在成長。

　　為了迎合經濟相對寬裕且人數逐漸增加的飼主客群，優質的寵物產品比以往更加唾手可得。加上飼主變得注重寵物的健康與飲食的品質，著重建立消費者信任感的品牌行銷手法顯得格外重要。以某些例子而言，本土寵物食品醜聞會使飼主捨棄本土品牌，寧願高價購買來自更高食品安全標準產地的寵物食品。只要攸關寵物的健康，飼主永遠不嫌麻煩。

　　的確，為了迎合龐大的新客群，許多公司爭相轉型，以便立足於現代化的市場。曾幾何時，我們都是前往本地的寵物店購物。如今電子商務當道，寵物經濟同樣被迫轉戰網路商店。不過，某些大型寵物產品品牌，仍缺乏強而有力的網路曝光率。不過像我這種偏好網路購物與宅配便利性、不想來回奔波寵物店的顧客，這類品牌如果仍想保有競爭力，最好是迎頭趕上。

　　而且不是只有寵物產品掀起熱潮。寵物美容、寵物 SPA 和寵物訓練等服務類型的利基市場，需求量也是超乎以往。這樣的趨勢雖然對寵物經濟有利，卻讓許多熱愛寵物的飼主不太認同。因為這類服務等於塑造了「寵物形同包包或珠寶，是飼主用來在社群媒體炫耀的物品」這種觀念，而非視為心愛的家人成員。

　　無論如何，對於什麼都想給寵物最好的我們而言，寵物經濟的繁盛彷彿是福音。雖然有些產品十分昂貴，但我們甘之如飴，因為我們就是沒辦法對寵物吝嗇。

37. 搶救剩食、變化菜色、享用盛食　P. 125

　　「不要暴殄天物！這世上還有人餓得沒飯吃！」想必很多人跟我小時候一樣，吃不下晚餐時，都會被吼這番話。我小的時候從未將這些話放在心上，但長大了解食物生產的更多內幕後，我才真正大開眼界。根據聯合國的統計，竟有 **30%** 全球生產的食物被白白浪費。這可是將近三分之一的統計數據，著實令人倒吸一口氣！

　　顧客偏好外觀精美的產品，因此許多「賣相不佳」的食物，還沒送進超市就先被丟棄。如此膚淺的我們，真該慚愧。畢竟，歪七扭八的紅蘿蔔和筆直的紅蘿蔔，煮熟後的味道不都一樣嗎？就算這樣的食物進得了超市，關店前沒賣出去的話，你覺得會發生什麼事？當然會基於「不新鮮」的理由而直接被丟到垃圾車，最終面臨焚化的命運。這種做法不僅浪費食物，也浪費金錢與能源，甚至對大氣層有害。光是想到這裡，就讓我氣得血壓飆高。

　　謝天謝地，總算有人挺身而出。許多國家的慈善機構，不眠不休的搶救可能會被丟棄卻完全可食用的食物。從餐廳、大賣場、農人市集所蒐集而來的剩食，通常會捐至食物銀行與遊民之家，讓清楚食物真正價值的人好好享用。事實上，我們都應該對剩食負責，而不是把責任推給遊民和飢民。如果餐廳顧客能改掉虛榮的習性，食物浪費的問題就能大幅改善。荷蘭一家名為「Instock」的機構，在剩食處理方面的表現值得激賞。該組織從荷蘭的 **160** 家生鮮超市收集剩食，做為旗下三家時尚餐廳其中一家分店的食材。他們希望藉由在高級餐廳環境下供應剩食的做法，能永遠洗清人們對剩食的負面印象。

　　我希望將來大家能夠居住在一個剩食不會葬送在焚化爐的社會。畢竟，消耗剩食的方法百百種，我們毫無理由浪費。

38. 唾手可得的便利生活 P.128

對臺灣人而言，7-11 的意義遠超過臺灣規模最大的連鎖便利商店。7-11 滲透臺灣人日常生活的歷史實在過於久遠，以致於大家可能都想不起來，自家附近的第一家 7-11 到底是什麼時候開張。

有誰不喜歡隨處可見的 7-11 進出方便、服務迅速、價格公道又一致的特色？琳瑯滿目的熟食可隨時微波，讓我們飽餐一頓；可直接到櫃臺繳納水電瓦斯費與停車費；透過店內機器，能購買客運車票、火車票和電影票，還能在旁邊的影印機列印、掃描和／或傳真文件。如果懶得跑「不便」的郵局一趟，還可以在此寄送與簽收包裹。身上現金如果不夠付款，走幾步路到店裡的提款機領錢即可。

7-11 的亮眼成就始於 1927 年，當時服務於德州達拉斯市「南方製冰公司」的喬‧C‧湯普森，決定於一般賣場未營業的週日和夜間時段，開始販售牛奶、麵包和雞蛋。湯普森最終買下南方製冰公司，並以開設販賣常見生活必需品的小型便利商店為目標。店名原本稱為「購物車商店」，因為顧客多以購物推車運走自己購買的商品。1946 年，湯普森將營業時間延長為早上七點至晚上十一點，同時更名為「7-11」來達到廣告效果。如今，店名維持不變，但門市已改為 24 小時營業。

截至 2018 年底，共有 67,480 家的 7-11 門市遍布於 17 個國家，臺灣門市就占了超過 5,200 家。近數十年來，該公司在亞洲區的發展突飛猛進，後來更由日本收購經營。值得一提的是，美國的 7-11 完全不像亞洲區的門市，提供各種應有盡有的額外服務，雖然我認為他們應該向亞洲門市看齊！

想當然爾，許多人希望加盟 7-11。新的加盟商可至當地訓練中心接受六週的教育訓練。結業之後，總公司會持續提供評估程序、定期新訊刊物、商務會議、安全性與保安資訊、免付費電話專線以及採購合作等支援。難怪 7-11 如此繁榮昌盛，除了是顧客眼中的無價之寶以外，更妥善照顧加盟同仁。

39. 想要按讚嗎？ P.131

幫認同的文章「按讚」，是多數社群媒體網友的直覺反應。到處按個讚，應該無傷大雅，對吧？事實上，這樣狀似無害的舉動，反而為資料探勘工具提供充足資訊，在罔顧你分享意願的情況下，建構你的完整個人檔案。

2013 年的一項研究顯示，電腦程式可找出看似不相干事物之間的關聯性，例如高智商與熱愛捲捲薯條之間的關係。資料探勘工具只要透過一個人在網路上的「按讚」行為，就能推算此人的各種相關資料。事實顯示，推算得出的資訊範圍十分廣泛，不僅僅是年齡、性別或政治立場等相對簡單的事物，還包括是否有藥物成癮問題、甚至是被調查對象的爸媽是否到他／她 21 歲以前都還會保持結縭狀態。光聽到這裡，就令人毛骨悚然！

多數現代人應該都有被廣告盯上的經驗，我們還沒與親朋好友分享自己的喜好，這些廣告似乎就已經對我們瞭若指掌。我曾經收到一些針對我想去歐洲旅遊的相關廣告，問題是我都還沒來得及向伴侶提到這個想法！如果廣告公司只需要輕鬆統計分析我們公開按讚的內容，就能擁有神奇預知能力般，清楚知道我們內心深處的慾望和想法，大家難道不覺得這樣很詭異嗎？

假使你不在意廣告公司對你知之甚詳，那如果換成是政府機關或惡意團體呢？萬一有心人不僅利用此資料影響你的購物選擇，還左右你對關鍵議題甚至是選舉投票的決定呢？

愈深入思考這個問題，愈會對上述的可能性感到不安。但我們是否能有因應的對策？前往隱私設定，取消第三方存取你個人資料的選項，也許能限制部分的危害。但事實上，社群媒體網站已經對資料剝削一事習以為常。真正能保護我們資訊安全的唯一辦法，就是保持網路零活躍的狀態。所以，請捫心自問一下：你的個人資料與你在社群媒體的曝光率相比，孰輕孰重？

40. 以植物改善全球暖化的妙計 P.134

　　撇除故意視而不見的懷疑論者不談，多數人現已接受全球暖化這個事實，而且對此議題憂心忡忡。再者，排山倒海而來的證據顯示，人類活動是導致全球暖化的元兇，尤其是釋放溫室效應氣體至大氣層的部分，這些氣體會困住太陽的熱氣並反彈至地球表面。對抗溫室效應氣體最有效的理想辦法，就是人類減少 50% 的碳排放量。然而，隨著全球人口不斷成長，這個數字可能有點天方夜譚。或許我們能以不同的解決角度切入問題點：那就是去除空氣中的大量溫室效應氣體，尤其是二氧化碳，並以安全的方式封鎖此類氣體。

　　能夠有效困阻二氧化碳的最大盟友之一就是植物。因為二氧化碳是植物養分循環的一部分，也就是從大氣中吸收二氧化碳來進行光合作用。大氣層的二氧化碳濃度逐漸升高，植物反而能更有效率地處理二氧化碳。成效較佳的光合作用能讓植物長得更壯碩，進而儲存更多碳量。如果植物的吸碳效率持續增加，很有可能抵銷人類產生的大量碳廢氣。但許多具有遠見的專家相信，植物吸碳效率增加的情形不會永無止盡，可能只會剛好打平，卻來不及拯救全人類死於高溫。

　　不過，還是有一絲希望。加州索爾克生物研究所的先驅研究人員，已著手試圖透過各種基因工程技術，來創造「理想植物」──也就是生長條件門檻低、可於根部系統儲存大量二氧化碳的植物。科學家在貌似芥末的阿拉伯芥這種植物上，鑑別出可促進發展更深層根部系統、增加根部質量、抗腐敗的基因。而科學家的當務之急，在於尋覓並啟用具有類似基因的農作物，例如玉米、小麥和稻米，才能讓此計畫的執行規模擴大至足以發揮影響力的程度。

　　根據上述研究人員的說法，幸運的話，這樣的解決之道應能在十年內問世。雖然屆時樹林的數量應當堪用，不過理想植物與負責該專案的科學家，或許就是人類的救星。

1-9 分辨事實或意見

　　多數文章的內容均含有事實和意見，因此分辨兩者間的差異相當重要。只要是能透過測驗、紀錄或文件來證明真實度的資訊，即屬於「事實」；「意見」則代表作者的信念或主觀評判。有時候「意見」看似「事實」，倘若無法證明其真實性，該資訊還是得歸類為「意見」。

41. 日本動畫大師 P.138

　　數位好萊塢大學創辦人暨《酷日本》的作者杉山知之認為，日本的可愛文化其實是從愛好自然和諧的心態演變而來。對他而言，「日本人欲透過可愛事物，來追求心靈上的平靜，以及逃離殘酷的現實」。才華洋溢的動畫導演宮崎駿，更是將此日本現代形象發揮淋漓盡致的箇中翹楚。他的奇幻故事意義深奧，生動的人物搭配精心布局的故事，多以反戰、愛的力量為主題，同時顧及社會、政治與環境議題等層面。此外，他以個人風格巧妙打造的動畫人物，與日本動畫著名的超大雙眼、鮮豔古怪髮色的角色不同，而是以日本傳統美學為基礎，呈現更符合現實比例的樣貌。

　　宮崎駿對藝術的熱愛形塑了他的人生。生於 1941 年 1 月 5 日的日本東京，宮崎駿在奇趣父母營造的溫暖家庭環境中長大。父親是宮崎航空興學的主任，母親則熱愛閱讀，常對普世通俗現象產生質疑。宮崎駿在父親的耳濡目染下，開始熱衷關於飛行的一切事物，並透過繪畫來抒發熱愛飛機的心情，進而培養了藝術才華。

　　父母的教養方式對宮崎駿造成潛移默化的影響，成為他打造長遠精彩事業的一大助力。除了擔任動畫電影的導演與製片人，宮崎駿更身兼編劇、人物設計師與吉卜力工作室（出品公司暨動畫工作室）共同創辦人的身分。1999 年，華特迪士尼的子公司「米拉麥克斯」，在美國發行他的《魔法少女》動畫電影，就此奠定他在西方國家無人不曉的地位。此外，《魔法少女》一直位居日本影史票房之冠，直到《鐵達尼號》上映後才被擠下寶座，更是首部獲頒日本電影學院獎「最佳年度映畫」的動畫。不過他至今最讓人念念不忘的電影，就是 2008 年推出的《崖上的波妞》。

他以水彩手繪動畫，而非使用電腦繪圖，因此呈現出討喜的美感。他最大的動畫成就是 2001 年上映的《神隱少女》，獲得奧斯卡最佳動畫片、日本電影學院獎的最佳電影，以及 2002 年柏林影展金熊獎等殊榮。

宮崎駿於 2013 年完成《風起》動畫後，宣布退休、不再拍片。但這樣一位創意鬼才不會甘於退隱過久的時間。有傳言指出，他已著手進行將於 2021 年發行的新電影。

42. 貫穿古今的故事精神 P. 142

《星際大戰》、《亞瑟王》的傳說、《哈比人》、《綠野仙蹤》、《哈利波特》系列以及希臘神話《奧德賽》這些故事有哪些共通點呢？它們確實都是讓許多讀者與觀眾著迷的精彩故事，但其實彼此還有更深層的連結。此類故事與歷史上其他無數的故事一樣，皆擁有相同的情節結構──那就是「英雄之旅」。

神話學家喬瑟夫・坎伯在他影響深遠的著作《千面英雄》（1949 年）首度提及，英雄之旅其實是古今中外著作常見的故事編排模式。此概念名稱也許不太耳熟能詳，但你絕對能從自己喜愛的故事中，一眼看出這種劇情套路。坎伯文中表示，最基本的英雄之旅架構，可濃縮為三大階段：「啟程」──英雄將熟悉的世界拋諸腦後；「考驗」──英雄歷經各種試煉，並證明自己的價值；「歸返」──英雄以勝利之姿返回家園。而坎伯更在此三大階段下，分析出十七種可能出現的情節元素。不過後輩學者也有提出自己的英雄之旅版本，僅與坎伯的原版架構稍有差異。多數故事至少會放入一些元素，但是最精彩的故事會包含大多的元素，即使有些會以不同的形式出現。

其中一個常見元素就是說服英雄接受「冒險召喚」的「先驅」人物。另一個是「越界」元素，意指英雄進入充滿奇特怪誕規定的夢幻王國（哈利波特第一次進入霍格華茲的魔法世界就是最好的例子）。最後一個英雄之旅常見的「苦難」元素，則是英雄因為對峙大反派而生死交關的情節。

不過，英雄之旅故事架構為何如此受歡迎？原因在於此類故事能與觀眾產生心理方面的深層連結，打動我們超越自己的意念，讓我們看見個人成長的可能性。這種常見的人性反應，就是英雄之旅架構廣受接納的原因，也因此成為強大的編劇工具。英雄之旅的故事彷彿是我們每個人基本生活歷練的寫照，劇情可橫跨文化與時間，即使原作者已不在人世，仍能流傳久遠。英雄之旅一直在探討生而為人的意義，想必作家／編劇無論有意或無心，依舊會沿用這樣的架構達千年之久。

43. 革命性的便利商店 P. 146

想像一下，走進商店、拿取所需物品後，直接離開而不需要找店員結帳。你沒聽錯，這不是犯罪行為，而是美國亞馬遜公司推出革命性的新購物形態概念。此無人商店名為「Amazon Go」，假使你尚未聽聞，別擔心，此消息絕對很快便家喻戶曉。

與亞馬遜享譽盛名的網路購物平臺不同，Amazon Go 是顧客可到訪的實體商店。店內販售各種解饞的可口零食，還有三餐都能有著落的熟食。麵包、牛奶、起司與巧克力等基本雜貨應有盡有。而熱愛烹飪的人，還能在店內找到已配好必要食材的全餐料理組合。

購物的部分雖然了無新意，但真正有趣的是付款方式！Amazon Go 的每位顧客必須在他們的智慧型手機安裝一個特殊 APP。顧客到店時，需使用 APP 才能進入門市，然後開始採買。只要顧客拿走一項商品，貨架上的重量感測器就會偵測品項身分，然後加入虛擬購物車。顧客如果放回商品，購物車一樣會自動刪除該品項。顧客離開門市時，費用會記在他們的亞馬遜帳戶。APP 會追蹤所有的購物紀錄，完全不需要使用現金或信用卡！

至 2019 年初為止，Amazon Go 仍在初期試營運的階段，僅分布於西雅圖、芝加哥與舊金山共 10 個據點。不過，亞馬遜公司預計在 2021 年前拓展到 3000 家門市。屆時 Amazon Go 也許會像 7-11 或全家便利商店般隨處可見。

有些人擔心 Amazon Go 與這類的先進科技商店會縮減人力就業機會。他們認為收銀員和銷售人員是最常見的兩大職務，少了此類職務，可能會造成大量失業問題。但這些人完全被誤導觀念。Amazon Go 據說仍需要部分人力的協助，例如備餐的廚師。大家不應該裹足不前，改變勢在必行。因為從網路購物問世後，我們就一直在面臨改變。因此，我認為 Amazon Go 愈早出現在我的社區愈好。

44. 巨石的祕密　P.150

位於英格蘭南部索茲斯柏立鎮附近的巨石陣，是一處奇特的史前遺跡，亦為遊客與考古學家帶著敬畏心情朝聖的熱門景點。巨石陣之所以出名，在於它帶來許多令人費解的謎團，讓人們想像力無限開展。

巨石陣是一個神祕的建築群，位在青銅器時代與新石器時代遺址內的中心點，此範圍還包括上百座墓塚。巨石陣是以龐大的石柱豎立於地表並圍成一圈的結構。居住該地區的史前人類有建造眾多儀式用石柱圈或木柱圈的習慣，因此巨石陣很有可能是宗教或神祕祭典方面的用途。

巨石陣工程的第一階段，在於挖掘直徑大約 100 公尺的圓形溝渠並設置兩個出入口，建造時間約公元前 3000 年。修建溝渠所挖出的泥土，堆於溝渠的內外，形成兩個路堤。

巨石陣圓環本身，則於西元前 2500 年左右開始興建。60 塊巨石各有 9 公尺長、25 公噸重，很有可能是從南邊 32 公里外的馬爾堡高地礦場所運來，以 30 塊石柱與 30 塊楣石（意指水平放於石柱上方的石塊）構成一個石圈。石柱與楣石均經過打磨而顯得光滑。楣石以榫眼和榫舌構造與下方石柱固定，楣石彼此之間則以槽榫接合構造相連。

世界各地的遊客，對於巨石陣的屹立不搖與龐大無不嘖嘖稱奇。史前人類到底是用什麼方法將如此巨碩重物從大老遠運過來？雖然透過研究資料與發揮一點想像力，能讓我們大致了解箇中原理，但這樣困難重重的任務還是令人驚嘆。除此之外，巨石陣到底有何功用？是否真如許多人所相信，是飛碟的降落地點？大家曾斬釘截鐵認為，神祕的古信仰德魯伊教曾以巨石陣做為獻祭儀式的神壇，但此說法後來已遭推翻。目前較普遍的論點，認為這是用於觀測季節與天象的先進天文年曆。

2002 年，巨石陣獲選列入英國七大奇景。從許多觀點而論，巨石陣是一個迷人又引人深思的遺跡。許多人甚至認為巨石陣擁有無法言喻的神祕力量。但對我們而言，巨石陣最深層的意義，也許是它為我們與老祖宗搭起了聯結的橋樑，讓我們能一窺歷史的面貌。

45. 歡迎來到植物界的全球資訊網　P.153

21 世紀的人類互通有無的方式超乎以往。我們透過無遠弗屆的「全球資訊網」，向彼此傳送訊息與資訊。網際網路問世時，堪稱通訊與上網方式的一大革命。儘管我們很想讚嘆自己身為人類的天才頭腦，但我們卻不是首創或率先運用此類網絡原理的物種。事實上，植物已經運用類似的生存模式達上百萬年之久！

沒錯，植物運用自己的「網際網路」來互相通訊和分享資源。它們會彼此警惕威脅狀況、和弱小旁枝分享養分，甚至是「大量匯入資訊」——也就是在自己老化或受傷時，將自己的資源大量匯入網絡，來支撐新一代的植物。這一切都默默地發生在我們的腳底下。

其實這得歸功於真菌。事實上，幾乎 90% 的植物均與真菌互為共生關係。看似大量細絲的真菌，會附著於植物根部，幫助植物吸收土壤中的水分與其他難以取得的養分；而植物則以碳水化合物來供給真菌。當真菌於地底下擴散菌絲，就會接觸到其他真菌的菌絲體，因此讓植物之間能互相溝通，進而構成了所謂的「植物界全球資訊網」！

真是太不可思議了。但更妙的是，植物界的全球資訊網和我們的網際網路一樣，會有駭客入侵的問題！某些植物會利用接觸網絡的機會，來向附近植物傳播有毒的化學物質，蓄意傷害競爭者。而其他像幻影蘭花這類植物，則會棲息在大樹旁，駭進植物網後竊取能源——這與駭客從你的網路銀行帳戶盜領存款如出一轍！

我們愈深入了解植物互相溝通的方式，就愈需要重新思考植物的定義到底為何。植物已不再是我們刻板印象中的單一有機體。實際上比較理想的角度，是將它們視為一個巨大的超級有機體。如果我們開始如此看待植物，也應該反思人類的定位。在我們彼此聯繫程度如此縝密的狀態下，我們究竟是個體，抑或歸屬於一個大型互聯總體的一分子呢？

1-10 實力檢測

46. 外星生命存在嗎？ P.156

2008 年的電影《當地球停止轉動》上映後，大家紛紛產生一個疑問：科技卓越的外星種族會善待人類，或是會待我們如同先進國家對待原始文明一般，奴役並屠殺我們？電影劇情對此問題的回應模稜兩可，但多數人似乎相信外星人會是良善的。也許就是基於這樣的想法，讓許多人急於想要接觸外星生物。我們不僅希望得到它們的音訊，更向它們廣播訊息。但是我們背後的動機，究竟是無盡的好奇心、科學的探索、抑或是想要解開宇宙謎團呢？

SETI——「搜尋地外文明計畫」，或許是世上最廣為人知的縮寫。不僅止於使用天文望遠鏡觀測星象的方式，SETI 更將無線電天線瞄準空中特定方位來收聽地外訊號。此類搜尋計畫於 1960 年代以單一頻道起步，爾後逐漸擴大搜尋的廣度與深度。如今，光是單一掃描儀器就能同時收聽 2.5 億個高解析度頻道，並將產生的數據輸送至搭載強大頻率分析硬體的電腦。電腦會過濾隨機噪訊，搜尋任何異於地球訊號的蛛絲馬跡。

SETI@home（在家搜尋地外文明）專案將上述電腦分析作業，外包給具備可上網電腦的任何志工。2003 年 3 月，SETI@home 專案表示有兩名志工可能接收到地外訊號而震驚全球。雖然搜尋結果不一定具有任何意義，卻仍讓人為之振奮。而 SETI@home 專案的人氣與志工人數均在持續成長。

而別稱為 METI（發送訊號至地外文明計畫）的主動式 SETI，作風較為大膽，但在已故的史蒂芬・霍金與部分科學家的眼裡，卻是魯莽之舉。霍金曾建議人類應當「低調行事」，但稱為「Bebo」的社群網站，卻於 2008 年傳送由用戶共同編撰的 501 則訊息至「鄰近」的類地球行星，預計 2028 年才傳送得到。幸好，已有許多科學機構致力傳送更具文明意義的訊息內容，希望彌補訊息斷層的不足。只不過，此類科學訊息的預計抵達日期，仍會比 Bebo 網站的訊息晚到很多。

截至目前為止，搜尋外太空生命的重心幾乎僅放在無線電波方面，因為我們現有的物理概念是沒有任何事物能超越光速。因此，在訊息傳送時間仍以數十載和數世紀為單位的情況下，除非我們的通訊科技有朝一日能跨越光速藩籬，否則我們依然得繼續揣測下去。

47. 親一下，說聲嗨！ P.159

如果你一輩子都住在亞洲，大概會將「親吻」視為戀人的專利。你肯定不會親朋友，更別提是初次見面的人！不過，前往歐洲或南美洲，你很有可能會看見朋友、泛泛之交、甚至是陌生人之間，不假思索的以親吻做為常見的打招呼或道別方式。

這樣的傳統從何而來？有些人推測此習俗可追溯至以「聖吻」向基督徒同袍致敬的舊式天主教儀式。某種程度上，似乎能解釋親吻禮儀為何在南美洲和南歐等傳統天主教國家如此常見。

對於不習慣這種社交禮儀的人而言，前往親吻如家常便飯的國家，可能會覺得十分傷腦筋。例如到底該遵循什麼樣的規矩？應該要親誰？該親幾次？親在臉頰還是一定要碰到嘴唇？

嗯，的確很複雜，因為每個地方都有不同的習慣。多數南美國家，只要在臉頰上親一下足矣。而義大利、西班牙和希臘等地中海國家，則需兩邊兩頰各親一下。不過像前往比利時、斯洛維尼亞、瑞士與荷蘭等國家，就要有親三下的心理準備！

方法如下：先傾身以你的右臉頰碰觸對方的右臉頰，嘴裡再輕輕發出啾一下的親吻聲即可。如果需要親更多次，只要換另一邊的臉頰重複上述步驟即可。不過，總是有例外的時候。以義大利為例，要先從左臉頰開始，而不是右臉頰；英國人的親吻禮儀則要大聲發出親吻聲才行。以性別來說，女性之間、男女之間的親吻禮儀很常見。男性之間的親吻禮儀則較為罕見，不過像阿根廷、塞爾維亞和南義大利確實有此習俗。

如果你對想向你行親吻之禮的人感到措手不及時，該怎麼辦？就當作是與資深的舞伴共舞。卸下緊繃心防、放輕鬆，讓對方主導即可。如果你不確定該親幾下，通常兩次最恰當，即使是多數時候只有親一下的國家也適用。所以，前往此類國家，真的不需要太緊張，只要別忘了帶上護唇膏就好！

48. 值得拯救的美食：保存世界料理文化遺產 P.162

只要聊起一國的文化，大家通常先想到的第一件事就是食物。不過，在麥當勞、星巴克這類美式連鎖速食店與咖啡廳在全球人氣高漲的情況下，部分料理文化的遺產很有可能就此失傳。所幸，聯合國教科文組織「無形美食文化遺產」的成立宗旨就是保存各國美食文化。近期申請的國家就是新加坡與其小吃攤販中心。這是一種將平價小吃攤販集中在大型用餐中心管理的特殊形態，更是新加坡人聚餐與社交的場所。讓我們一起來瞧瞧，還有哪些其他料理文化已名列聯合國教科文組織的保護名單。

傳統墨西哥料理：種植與輾磨玉米是墨西哥強化社會關係和推廣永續生活不可或缺的古法。因此，這樣的文化傳統有益於社會和地球。

土耳其咖啡文化與傳統：土耳其的咖啡廳不僅供應飲品，亦為社群聯絡感情的中樞。土耳其咖啡屬於先以開水調和細緻咖啡粉，再慢煮至沸騰起泡的特殊濃烈黑咖啡。煮製時可加糖，不過對於已經喝慣星巴克卡布奇諾口味的人，可能會需要很大量的糖才敢入口！

拿坡里披薩藝術：真正的披薩烤製藝術源自義大利的拿坡里市。當地披薩師傅代代相傳特殊的麵團揉製技術，包括空中拋接旋轉麵皮──看似簡單，其實不然！

比利時的啤酒文化：歐洲小國比利時竟然有辦法運用各種釀製法，生產將近1500種啤酒。啤酒根植於比利時文化之深，甚至連以啤酒洗浸的起司都有！

醃製與分享泡菜的「越冬泡菜文化」：泡菜（以各種辛香料與發酵海鮮調味的醃菜）不僅是南韓人重要的食物，更是凝聚社會向心力的橋樑。各社區居民會在秋末齊聚一堂，為越冬泡菜季做準備，醃製並分享可度過寒冬的大量泡菜。

還會有哪些料理小吃會名列榜上，著實令人拭目以待，但我們可以肯定的是：獨特的美味小吃如果失傳，將會是多麼枯燥乏味的世界！

49. 舉世聞名的投資人 P.166

六歲時的華倫‧巴菲特已非泛泛之輩。與其他仍在玩樂的孩子相比，巴菲特已經開始做生意，從祖父的商店買下 6 罐 25 分錢的可口可樂，再以單罐 5 分錢的價格轉賣出去。11 歲時，他首次買下某公司一股 38 美元的股票。跌至每股 27 美元後，他仍沉住氣等待時機，等攀升至每股 40 美元後，他全數賣出，結果卻學到了應當耐心等候的教訓，因為該股價後來竟持續攀升至 200 美元！

儘管難以置信，但這位來自內布拉斯加州奧馬哈市的天才，其實不想上大學，最後是在父親的勸說下才入學。巴菲特得知兩位知名證券分析師在哥倫比亞商學院授課後，主動申請經濟學（碩博）研究所。而其中一位班傑明‧葛拉漢，對於巴菲特未來的投資事業具有深刻的影響力。他習得的投資策略十分簡單：檢視財務數據即可判斷一家公司的實際價值；如果公司股價遠遠低於公司價值，就是一筆不錯的投資。

巴菲特運用此方法累積鉅富，甚至一度超越比爾‧蓋茲全球首富的地位。此外，巴菲特只要收購一家成功企業，就會運用親民的人際手腕，與目前的高階主管進行溝通。他的「管理」方針並非干預公司營運，相反地，他主張不插手策略，讓董事保有最終決策權。

儘管擁有傳奇性的致富人生，巴菲特仍然深居簡出。他沒有手機、沒有電腦，自駕常見的凱迪拉克 DTS 轎車。當他終於買了一架一千萬美金（3.22 億台幣）的私人噴射飛機，他將飛機命名為「自知理虧號」，因為他過去經常批評其他高階主管豪奢的消費行徑。

巴菲特長期以來，一直將拍賣個人物品與諮詢時間的所得捐助給慈善機構。然而，巴菲特出手最大筆的慈善作為，卻引來媒體爭議。他向「比爾暨梅琳達‧蓋茲基金會」捐出 83% 的個人所得後，《洛杉磯時報》與其他可靠的新聞來源，表示該基金會的一些活動有明顯的利益衝突。不過整體而言，蓋茲基金會應會克盡職守，公正地善用巴菲特的財富。

50. 居家環境與心境的斷捨離 P. 169

幾乎所有現代人都飽受一種通病之苦：那就是「物質過剩」的文明病。我們家中塞滿了不再穿戴的服飾、用不到的器具裝置、束之高閣的書籍。長久以來，累積愈來愈多的物品，似乎成為「一個人因為成功才能擁有這種物質生活」的指標。但大家是否曾靜下心來思考，居家環境充斥著毫無用武之地的物品，不僅在家寸步難移，心靈的空間也一樣雜亂無章嗎？

這就是發起「斷捨離」運動的日本作家山下英子，短暫居住於神社的感受。當時神主將她所有的隨身物品丟棄，只留下兩套衣物，她卻頓時感到平靜。因為她不僅只是清掃了居住環境，同時也為她的心靈清空一切雜念。於是乎，她建構了「danshari」原則——這是以日文的三個漢字「斷捨離」所結合而成的名詞，並與全世界分享這個理念。

斷捨離的修行很簡單：你必須斬斷生活中不必要的物慾、捨棄居家環境中過多的雜物、盡可能擺脫遠離對物質的慾望。事實上，斷捨離概念與曾經影響日本深遠的悠久佛教禪學「侘」十分相似。有位禪師曾說過，「侘」意指僅需一間小屋、在鋪有兩三張榻榻米的一間廳室裡，享用附近田野採摘而來的一盤蔬食，即可怡然自得的生活。這是一種「減法藝術」的欣賞角度，而非不斷在生活強加任何事物。

或許是文化基礎近似的緣故，因此不難想像斷捨離的概念何以迅速席捲日本。不過西方國家一樣蔚為風潮，因為受到許多斷捨離例子的啟發，

大家開始試著在過度物質化的生活中，找回那失去已久的簡約感受。而作家佐佐木典士則是實踐最為透徹、家喻戶曉的斷捨離狂人。儘管他已經擁有輝煌成就，卻仍住在個人物品僅有 150 件的小套房。佐佐木表示，施行斷捨離不僅讓他減重、變得更積極，最重要的是，他開始懂得感恩自己所擁有的一切——這些都是被困於現代消費主義的眾人所求之不得的收穫。

或許該是時候數一數你有幾件個人物品，試試看少許的斷捨離作為可否為你帶來一些收穫。

Unit 2 字彙學習

英語單字如此多（據估計將近一百萬字），要記住每個單字的意義幾乎是不可能的任務。隨著我們的英語知識增長，我們會發現其實很多單字的意義都相近。除此之外，我們也可以從前後句子或段落中，判斷出單字的意義。

在學完本單元之後，任何艱深的單字都將難不倒你。能夠辨識並運用這些單字之後，你不僅能閱讀無礙，亦能流暢地寫作和說英文。

2-1 同義字

同義字是意義完全相同或非常相近的單字，例如 huge 和 gigantic 就是同義字。英語擁有將近一百萬個字彙，其中許多單字的意義相近。如果能夠辨識這些同義字，將是增進閱讀理解能力的一大利器。

51. 愛爾蘭：動盪不安的歷史 P. 174

提及愛爾蘭的「動亂問題」時，一般是指 1960 年代至 1990 年代發生逾 30 年的事件，但這樣動盪不安的種子早已於上百年前萌芽。除非回顧一切的源頭，否則幾乎難以理解「動亂問題」的始末。

回到 1690 年，基督新教的英格蘭威廉國王與天主教的蘇格蘭詹姆斯國王，為了爭奪愛爾蘭、蘇格蘭與英格蘭的王位而起衝突，引發博因河戰役。威廉國王戰勝，愛爾蘭開始籠罩於基督新教

的統治之下。廣大的北部地區被英格蘭與蘇格蘭基督新教徒所占領，僅剩人口以天主教徒為主、位於愛爾蘭最北端的阿爾斯特省與世隔絕。

到了19世紀，由於生活水準的差異，導致天主教徒與基督新教徒之間愈發水火不容。愛爾蘭北部人民享受豐衣足食的生活，多為天主教徒的愛爾蘭南部人民，卻因為富可敵國的地主均為聖公會新教徒，生活依舊貧困。20世紀初，多數愛爾蘭的天主教徒希望爭取自由，脫離英國的統治，但愛爾蘭的基督新教徒不想居住在人民多為天主教徒的國度，因此組成自己的軍隊，雙方忍無可忍的歧異終於浮出水面。英國為促進和平，於1920年頒布「愛爾蘭政府法」，將愛爾蘭劃分為兩大區。但是僅有阿爾斯特省的基督新教徒支持這項立法，南部的天主教徒則希望完全獨立自治。

1921年，愛爾蘭共和軍（簡稱IRA）與英國武力引發愛爾蘭獨立戰爭後，「愛爾蘭自由邦」就此而生。自由邦是由阿爾斯特省的三郡與愛爾蘭南部的23郡所組成。而阿爾斯特省其餘六郡則成立「北愛爾蘭」。

1960年代，倫敦德里與貝爾法斯特的龐大暴動四起。由IRA與基督新教徒軍事團體帶頭的眾多炸彈暴亂事件，一直持續至1990年代。而此時期的雙方敵對情勢，就是所謂的「動亂問題」。儘管大家試圖以和平的方式解決這場紛爭，仍有超過3600人命喪於此。

2005年7月，IRA主動收手所有的軍事活動，結束長期以來欲統一南北的抗爭。2007年5月，大英帝國允許北愛爾蘭設立自治政府。首相布萊爾表示：「回顧過往，我們看見各島人民之間上百年來的衝突、紛爭、甚至是仇恨。前瞻未來，我們將看見擺脫歷史沉重枷鎖的契機。」

52. 麥田圈：遍布全球的世紀之謎　P.178

只要玉米田、大麥田、小麥田或類似作物的田地，神不知鬼不覺的迅速出現作物被壓倒在地所形成的圖形，就統稱為麥田圈。有時是冬季乾冷田地或是剛犁好的田地，會出現這類土壤蝕刻的圖樣。生動相片與精彩影片時有所聞，但親自從空中或山頂俯瞰麥田圈、甚至是步行穿越麥田圈，才堪稱終極體驗。麥田圈基於這樣的魅力而成為熱門景點，目前多數的麥田圈均位於英格蘭。

「麥田圈」一詞的由來，是因為第一幅圖樣為圓形。後來愈發「成熟」多變，開始出現令人聯想到外太空軌道和書寫筆觸的幾何直線、曲線與花紋。有些圖樣看似訊息，有些則像繪圖與精緻藝術品，甚至有些狀似數學符號。

那麼這些謎樣般的圖案從何而來？我們唯一能肯定的是：麥田圈存在於地表的歷史十分悠久。雖然我們於1970年代開始發現現代麥田圈，但據說此現象最早可追溯至七世紀。多數的麥田圈純屬人造的奇景，研究人員柯林・安德魯估計將近80%的麥田圈，都是人為蓄意打造。最出名的例子，就是道格・鮑爾和大衛・柯利坦承他們在1991年的英格蘭南安普敦，偷偷製造上百幅麥田圈。

雖然鮑爾和柯利的行為是場騙局，卻無法解釋他們此舉前後所出現的麥田圈。亦無法解釋其他國家所出現的上千幅麥田圈。它們是外星生物的傑作嗎？許多熱衷此道的人會給予肯定的答案。有些人則覺得可能是球狀閃電或龍捲風等極端氣候所造成的。另外有些人結合兩種理論，提出可能是超自然力量在掌控天候的說法。因為他們認為，如果不是這樣，球形閃電要怎麼產生如此精細又錯綜複雜的圖案？

無論麥田圈是造假的產物、外星人的陰謀或自然現象，大家一定都同意，麥田圈是非常值得研究的主題。以「耐人尋味」來描述麥田圈實在過於保守，因為麥田圈的研究領域很容易引人入勝而無法自拔！

53. 李小龍：格鬥先驅的傳奇故事 P.182

李小龍堪稱全球家喻戶曉的傳奇人物。雖已不在人世，他仍坐擁武術宗師的地位。他不僅是世界知名的電影明星、指標性的文化象徵、截拳道的創始人，更是許多人心目中的英雄。

雖然年僅 18 歲的李小龍，出演的電影已超過 20 部，卻是到美國電視影集《青蜂俠》中「加藤」一角，才真正嘗到走紅的滋味。儘管《青蜂俠》只播映一季，他卻成為香港人眼裡的大明星，甚至多數人暱稱該影集為《加藤秀》。不過，李小龍卻無法安於飾演配角的現狀。

1971 年，31 歲的李小龍首度擔綱賣座電影《唐山大兄》的男主角鄭潮安，瞬間成為亞洲巨星。1972 年緊接著上映的電影《精武門》，更是打破《唐山大兄》在影史上的所有紀錄。

同年，李小龍與嘉禾影業進行協商，擔任《猛龍過江》的編劇、導演、主角以及武術指導。他甚至在高潮迭起的傳奇世紀對決畫面裡，捧紅了美國武打明星查克‧諾里斯。

對於和李小龍流著相同種族血液的中國人而言，李小龍的存在不僅止於電影巨星——更多的是一種中國人的驕傲。李小龍的電影裡，經常出現他反擊一些對中國人固有偏見的橋段。例如《精武門》中，李小龍因為一塊「華人與狗不得入內」的告示，與他人大打出手並砸毀招牌。

李小龍集各式武術優點之大成而創立截拳道。他強調截拳道的哲學在於「無為而治」，以宣揚過於拘泥武術形式套路反而會自曝其短的理念。李小龍離世前兩年關閉了國術館，轉以私人傳授截拳道的方式教課。

李小龍的遺作《龍爭虎鬥》，讓他成為風靡美國與歐洲的名人。可惜他卻無法在有生之年目睹此盛況。因為在電影首映前六天，儘管身體健康狀態良好，李小龍仍神祕猝死。廣受好評的《龍爭虎鬥》上映至今超過 40 年的時間，世人仍對該片讚譽有佳。

54. 如何在空難中生還 P.185

我們很多人都曾設想過一個惡夢般的場景：飛機急遽傾斜，機艙裡瀰漫著濃煙的氣味，整個飛機上的乘客都在驚慌尖叫。然而，和我們集體潛意識中普遍存在的焦慮相提並論，現實的空中旅行從來都不是這樣。美國旅客被閃電擊斃的機率是空難的 3 倍、出車禍死亡的機率則是空難的 19 倍。美國國家運輸安全委員會於 2001 年發表了一項具有里程碑意義的研究，其中統整的數據顯示，即便是在不太可能會發生的空難事件中，也有大約 95% 的乘客可倖免於難。但這絲毫不代表旅客在飛行途中可以徹底地處之泰然。儘管空中旅行普遍很安全，但萬一在空中遭遇不測風雲時，生存的機會可能還得靠自己來掌握。

以下是幾項能夠幫您保命的安全措施：

事前防範：不要穿著寬鬆、易燃或合成材質的衣物，並避免穿高跟鞋等不舒服的鞋子。

對周遭狀況保持警覺：仔細聽空服員的指示並閱讀機上提供的安全資訊。務必留意出口的位置，尤其是最近的那一個，因為墜機時的能見度通常很有限。

吸入濃煙時：把布沾濕遮住口鼻以避免吸入濃煙。不建議保持低姿態，因您可能會被其他乘客踩踏。

安全帶：機上安全帶用的是扣環，不是按鈕。千萬不要驚慌，必要時別忘了解開安全帶的扣環。在撞擊前確保您的安全帶儘可能繫到最緊。

聽從指示：準備好仔細聽取並遵循機組員的指示。如果他們看起來不知所措就不要浪費時間——自己起身向前走吧。

忘掉您的私人物品：不要嘗試搶救您的財物。關鍵是要騰空雙手以備不時之需。

切記，吸入濃煙以及（或者）燒燙傷為主要死因，只要採取適當的行動就可以避免大多數的死劫。空中旅行並不需要太擔心——只要做好準備，享受旅程吧！

55. 曇花一現　P.188

暫時性的零售店，似乎已是江郎才盡、了無新意的點子：舉凡萬聖節商店、聖誕市集、主題博覽會等形態，自古以來給我們的印象就是「曇花一現」。但過去二十年來，大公司開始看出這種短線操作的零售潛力，因而設置暫時性的「快閃店」，利用期間限定的性質來推動業績。而快閃店確實帶來一場現代零售業的革命。

這樣的概念始於 1990 年代後期。當時洛杉磯舉辦一場名為「儀式」的博覽會，旨於網羅最為酷炫的各種地下時尚品牌。透過僅展售一天的方式，為嬉皮人士提供暢快購物的體驗。不久後，嗅到商機的時尚大牌紛紛跟進，利用短期購物體驗的模式，與年輕有型的目標族群接軌。

時間快轉至今日，大家都在追隨這股潮流，包括 Google 與亞馬遜等科技巨擘（設立快閃店來讓民眾試用電子新品），以及米其林星級餐廳與美妝達人品牌。

各大品牌與企業為何如此重視快閃店的價值？因為在這個電子商務主宰市場環境的年代，設置永久性的實體商店已不再是理想做法，尤其是店鋪租金水漲船高的情況下。不過，實體商店仍然有其優勢。快閃店非常適合用於發表新品或提高品牌曝光率，讓顧客有嘗鮮或獨特的購物體驗——而這樣的行銷手法，非常合千禧世代目標客群的胃口。

不過，快閃店不一定是大品牌專美於前的領域——新興的小型企業一樣可借力使力。對於想闖出一番天地卻又擔心長期高額店租負擔的年輕人來說，快閃店是最理想的替代方案，因為僅需一小筆的投資。再者，年輕藝術家、廚師或設計師如果以快閃店的模式，來實驗看看產品接受度、試一下市場水溫、同時造成話題，將會是最棒的事業起步方式。

快閃店本身或許是曇花一現，但對於發展成熟的品牌與初試啼聲的創業家而言，卻能帶來眾多優勢。因此快閃熱潮絕對會繼續延燒。

2-2 反義字

反義字是意思相反的單字，good 和 bad、big 和 small、hot 和 cold，這幾組都是反義字。有時候我們很容易辨別反義字，有時候則需要費點力。記得務必要從前後文當中，尋找可能的線索。

56. 我們為何忘事？　P.190

說到擁有完美的記憶力，我們人類的基因圖譜中看來必然有些缺陷！為什麼我們記不住所有想記的事情呢？這會讓人挫折和沮喪。有時候甚至會傷害到我們的自尊或者被他人看輕。說真的，我們所有人都很健忘。我們假使不健忘，就不必寫日記或聘秘書了，而黑莓機也永遠不會被發明出來！不過，近來研究指出，遺忘其實有可能是我們大腦必不可少的重要功能。

我們大多數人對約三歲起到現在的生活都有鮮活的記憶。這些被貯存在我們所謂的長期記憶中。至於三歲之前呢？西格蒙德・佛洛依德發現到，我們幾乎把幼兒期忘光光了。心理學家們對造成這種記憶缺失的原因抱持不同意見，並從佛洛依德時期開始就一直在研究。經由對蹣跚學步的幼兒進行的實驗，得到了一個非常合理的理論，那就是在事件發生的當下，我們因缺乏語言能力，無法向他人描述該事件。這段記憶存在我們心中，但因在事件發生時語言並未與之產生聯想，所以這些記憶不會成為我們成年自傳式記憶的一部分。當然也有一些例外，但這種情況很罕見。

另一種類型的記憶——短期記憶——就是我們通常在說「我忘了」時所提到的記憶。專家表示，你一次可以同時記住約七件事，長達三天。在這段時間內，你可能會忘記某些事情，好記住別的東西。事實上，當今有些研究學者主張遺忘是必不可少的，因為記憶的生理目標與其說是為了保存資訊，不如說是要幫助大腦做出正確的決策。近期的研究結果表明，我們其實有時會主動把事情忘掉，好騰出空間給新的、更有用的記憶。這有點像電腦在跑程式時會把硬碟裡的資料刪掉。有一個測試短期記憶的簡單方法，請花一兩分鐘看有二十個字的單字表。你會發現你最多只能記住其中的七個字,而且是單字表開頭或結尾的那幾個字,這是因為你的大腦判斷它們比中間的那些字更重要。

57. 你的智慧型手機正在摧毀地球嗎?
P.192

智慧型手機與平板電腦等消費性電子產品,已將我們禁錮於一個不斷汰舊換新的惡性循環裡。每一年都會有運算速度更快、外觀更精美且功能更強大的新機型上市。很多人會受光鮮亮麗的新產品吸引而天人交戰,但最後還是掏腰包買回家。

那麼舊機型該如何是好?

可悲的是,舊機型的下場大多是進入掩埋場,造成每年產生四千萬噸電子廢料的結果。如果你對四千萬噸不是很有概念,其實就形同每秒鐘丟棄 800 臺筆記型電腦的意思。

其實問題不只出在電子廢料的數量,電子廢料的性質對人體健康和自然環境具有毀滅性的傷害。螢幕、電視與電腦等電子產品,含有水銀、鉛、砷與硒等有害物質。此類物質會滲入土壤,毒害肥沃的耕地與水資源,亦會危害負責整頓或回收電子廢料的工人健康。整體而言,美國有 70% 的有毒廢料均來自廢棄電子產品。

但是世界各地的電子廢料重擔卻分攤不均。高達 80% 的美國電子廢料,最後都是送至亞洲與非洲的掩埋場。歐洲的電子廢料同樣運往非洲。電子廢料一抵達掩埋場,工人會從老舊電子產品中,挑揀可回收的金、銀等貴金屬。此類工人可能會因為缺乏安全設備與技術而產生嚴重的職業傷害。有些年輕工人甚至年僅 12 歲,而且工資低到不像話,平均一天僅賺 1.5 美元。

理想的情況下,所有的廢棄電子產品應該以安全正當的方式進行回收處理。但現實是,回收處理的電子廢料僅占 12.5%。那我們該如何應對?答案很簡單:忍住想要升級的衝動。我們使用電子裝置的時間愈久,愈能減少製造電子廢料(順便還能省下不少錢)。如果你一定得升級,那麼請試著找到適合使用你舊型裝置的對象,或是送往經過認證的優良回收服務商。

電子廢料危機仍有轉圜的餘地,就從一次僅使用一支智慧型手機開始做起吧。

58. 生物燃料
P.194

伴隨著油價上漲以及對全球暖化的日益關切,現代生物燃料(即從植物中提煉出來的燃料)近年來頗受吹捧,成了傳統化石燃料的替代品。

主要用玉米、甘蔗發酵製造的生質酒精,以及從油菜籽、棕櫚和大豆油等油料作物製造的生質柴油,可以分別有效地取代陸上交通工具所需的汽油和柴油。這些替代品(生質酒精與生質柴油)已在全球使用:在美國,市面上買得到的汽油大多都混合了生質酒精;在巴西,從甘蔗中提煉出來的生質酒精已被用於駕駛汽車數十年了;生質柴油則在歐洲被廣泛使用。眾所周知,車輛排放的廢氣是二氧化碳的主要來源,這是造成全球暖化的主要溫室氣體。然而,植物吸收二氧化碳本來就是食物鏈的一部分,所以生物燃料燃燒時所產生的二氧化碳都是之前植物為了生長而吸收的。這似乎是碳平衡的完美解決辦法!

可惜,事情並沒有那麼簡單。種植這些作物並從中提煉燃料的過程本身就需要大量的能源——其中絕大部分還是靠著燃燒化石燃料而來。因此,情況往往是,為了製造生物燃料用掉的能源比生物燃料本身所產生的能源還要多。此外,也有很多人主張,玉米、黃豆等生物燃料作物通通都能食用,作為食物來源比當燃料用更好。天然資源保育人士補充說,為了種植這些生物燃料作物就會需要開墾額外的土地,這意味著大片雨林將被摧毀。當然,這會對很多瀕臨絕種的動植物物種帶來災難性的後果。

為了降低我們對石油的依賴,國際能源署期望在 2050 年之前,生物燃料可以佔全球運輸燃料需求的四分之一。目前想要達成這個目標,我們還有很長的一段路要走,也必須創新才有可能實現這個目標。

未來最有可能的解決辦法還是提煉生物燃料,不過不是從糧食作物來提煉,而是從牧草和樹苗,這些植物在非食用作物的土地上很容易生長。如果這些作物能有效且便宜地轉化為生物燃

305

料（近期研究已證實加入真菌即可辦到），提煉出來的產品將遠比前一代的生物燃料更加環保。碳平衡燃料來源如此充裕且隨手可得時，化石燃料才能真正地成為往事。

59. 過多光害的夜盲問題　P. 196

對於居住在大都市的人而言，繁星夜空與劃破天際的耀眼銀河景象，只有在偏遠郊區才看得見。世界各地的城鎮，日落後的燈火通明，彷彿形成一片遮蔽星光的環境光毯，讓原本壯麗夜空該有的光芒黯然失色。

但是都會光害帶來的缺點，不是只有讓我們失去觀賞天然景觀的機會，愈來愈多的研究證實，明亮的夜空會對人類健康、動物行為、環境、甚至是入夜後的人身安全，造成負面影響。

舉例而言，街燈或鄰居家的燈光照射到自家的光侵擾問題，會嚴重干擾人體的自然（睡眠甦醒）生理時鐘，造成內分泌、細胞機能與大腦活動失調。而夜行性動物，同樣受到不速之客的光害威脅，因為多數夜行性動物必須在黑暗之中獵食與交配。

不過，夜間光線明亮，不是對人身安全比較好嗎？畢竟摸黑走路回家，或在道路光線不足的狀態下開車很危險。其實恰恰與普羅大眾的想法相反。夜間光線過於強烈，反而會讓人產生類似夜盲的反應，而非提高能見度。沒有遮罩的光線所產生的眩光，刺眼程度會遮蔽視線，使我們的雙眼無法自行調節到適應黑暗的狀態。原本我們身處黑暗環境中的每分鐘，夜視敏銳度都能隨之增加。但如果雙眼持續受到強光來襲的影響，就會無法看穿光源以外的任何暗處景象，形成有心人想傷害你的最佳藏匿處。

當然，更別提每年為了點亮不必要的有害光照，浪費了數十億元和龐大能源。如果我們僅需仰賴雙眼視力與空中偶爾出現的閃爍光源，是否能對環境更友善？

雖然改變街燈使用模式，只有當地政府才有辦法推行，但是移除或遮蔽住家附近不必要光照等舉手之勞，卻能對社區的夜間環境帶來不可思議的效果。切記，只要你擺脫足夠的光害，就能享有欣賞滿天星空閃耀的回饋！

60. 為未來存放　P. 198

不管是因為她們還沒找到適合的伴侶，或是她們想先專注事業、晚點再生孩子，現在有很多女性決定要凍卵，以備未來某天之用。這項技術將動用受孕藥刺激排卵、之後取卵凍卵再存放好幾年。這使女性得以在年紀漸長後仍還能選擇成家，儘管到時候她們的生育能力可能已顯著下降。

凍卵不需要精子，因為卵子冰凍時並未受精。因此，女性在沒有男性伴侶的情況下就能選擇動手術。對許多女人來說，這項技術使她們更加自主，無需男性參與也可以計畫自己的未來。等她們覺得準備好了，就能把卵子解凍，和伴侶或捐贈者的精子受精，然後再植入她們的子宮。顯然，與其在二十歲出頭，連自己或許都還沒準備好承擔養家的責任和開銷時就生小孩，凍卵被認為是較合適的作法。

然而，有了隨時可供運用的冷凍卵子保存著，並不能保證就能成功受孕。對於選擇在年紀老大之後再使用卵子的人，植入卵子後懷孕的機率可能低於 30%，這取決於凍卵當時以及植入卵子之時的年齡。

況且，把人的卵子冷凍本來就不便宜。每次刺激排卵動輒花費數千美元，此外還有每年的保存費以及未來生殖療程的花費都要列入考慮。費用高到大多數女性被迫去借貸才負擔得起，再加上未來成功受孕的機率如此之低，凍卵成為一項少有成效的風險投資。

然而，令人感傷的事實是，儘管有了凍卵科技可利用，選擇晚點再生兒育女的女性往往仍要付出龐大的代價。對那些想把青春花在事業上或尋覓合適伴侶的女性來說，選擇還是侷限得教人沮喪——不論是要冒著未來無法受孕的風險，還是得在非常不確切的替代方案上所費不貲。

2-3 依上下文猜測字義

英文單字可能有很多不同的意思，以形容詞「fine」為例，既可以指「可接受的」、「纖細的」，也可以指「有吸引力的」。當你遇到可能有爭議的單字時，一定要讀完上下文再決定字義。萬一你遇到完全陌生的單字，也可以從上下文來推斷字義。

61. 五星騙局　P. 200

由於有愈來愈多的商家削減實體店面的數量，轉往網路行銷，網路購物在過去十年左右的時間裡已有了大幅度地成長。只需按一下滑鼠按鍵就有這麼多選擇，致使消費者愈來愈依賴網路評價來好好評估自己想購買的東西，和店家所推出的行銷相比，他們更傾向於信任其他買家。

在競爭激烈的網路市場上，缺乏良好的評價（或甚至沒有評價）就意味著巨大的業績損失，所以為了保有競爭力，有些公司會用不正當的方式鑽制度的漏洞——自己或僱人寫假評價。這種所謂「刷評價」的作法，通常是僱用一家網路口碑不錯的公司，利用他們龐大的付費評論者對客戶的產品留下正面評價。當然，毫無疑問，這些「評論者」從未購買過，而且很可能從未用過這些產品。

亞馬遜和淘寶等大型網路零售商的網站上充斥著這些假評論。有一個特別誇張的案例中，一家相對不知名的小品牌推出的一組耳機，被人發現有超過 400 個五星評價，而且通通都是在同一天發文的！

造假的後果可能很嚴重，犯錯的公司會被罰款或禁止在網路平台上販售產品。但還有一個更嚴重的後果——對公司聲譽造成損害。公司被揭發後將在買家間失去信任，這表示當再次購買該品牌的人將所剩無幾。確實，評論造假愈來愈危險，因為買家愈來愈懂得怎麼分辨假好評。然而，有些公司還是堅持賭一把，畢竟業績成長的誘惑值得拿名譽去冒險。

那麼，作為買家的您，該如何避免成為假資訊的受害者呢？也許沒有什麼萬無一失的方法可以做到這一點，不過一般來說，可以試著去注意那些比較平衡、會列舉一項產品優劣的評論。從各種網站廣泛徵詢意見，也會讓您對一般買家的共識有更多的了解。可惜，在到處都是假評論的年代，只要有人對一項產品讚不絕口，就必須對其抱持著很大的保留態度。

62. 豬肉的問題　P. 202

非洲豬瘟顧名思義，屬於高傳染性的豬群疾病。幸好人類不會感染此疾病（別稱包括 ASF 與疣豬熱），只會波及野豬與家豬。首度爆發此疫情的紀錄始於 1921 年的肯亞，病毒最後肆虐全非洲，也因此得到「非洲豬瘟」之名。罹患此疾病的臨床症狀包括發高燒、各種器官病變、脈搏加快與呼吸急促，以及耳朵、四肢與下腹部泛紅。病豬出現上述症狀的幾天內就會死亡，致死率高達百分之百，豬農被迫撲殺受到感染的豬群。對人類而言，非洲豬瘟的問題不僅影響豬隻健康，更帶來嚴重的經濟風暴。

ASF 儼然成為全球聞之色變的難題。葡萄牙、西班牙和義大利均於 20 世紀晚期首次受到此疫情的侵襲，到了 1970 年代又延燒至美洲。部分的亞洲、歐洲與非洲國家，則於近期通報 ASF 捲土重來的消息。自 2014 年起，俄國與鄰國已通報超過 355,000 件 ASF 病例。光是 2018 年，全球確診患有豬瘟病毒而被撲殺的豬隻已超過 119,000 頭。截至 2019 年 4 月，中國爆發大規模疫情而撲殺超過 102 萬頭豬後，經濟就此受到重創。雖然中國目前仍是全球最大的產豬國，但遍布全中國的豬瘟疫情，卻使全球豬價上漲高達 78%。在養豬產業賠錢、各國政府仍在追蹤與控管疫情方面無之計可施的情況下，ASF 堪稱令人傷透腦筋的災難。視你居住的地方而定，或許已經吃不到豬肉了！

由於疫情傳播快速且可能對經濟帶來嚴重後果，因此需要採取可杜絕後患的極端措施。為了避免非洲豬瘟蔓延，許多國家目前已禁止 ASF 疫區製品入境。某些國家甚至禁止以餿水（廚餘）餵豬以防止疫情擴大。

不過疫情防治仍有希望。葡萄牙於 1994 年根除 ASF，西班牙則於 1995 年成功跟進。兩國以傳播病毒至豬群的壁蝨為控管目標。如今，希望消滅非洲豬瘟禍害的其他國家，均向上述兩國取經防疫措施。

63. 草原上的龐然大物 P. 204

綜觀地球歷史的輝煌時期，劇烈的氣候變遷一直是無數物種緣起緣滅的推手，包括曾於地球留下足跡的最大哺乳類動物：草原長毛象。從肩部算起，高度可達 4.7 公尺，重達九公噸。上一次的冰河時期中，在氣候極端和降水量微乎其微的大草原上，所生長的雜草、莎草與燈心草，都是草原長毛象的主食。草原長毛象一直存活至一萬一千年前才絕跡，恰與上一次的冰河時期因為暖化而結束的時間相符。而地球至今仍處於該時期遺留的暖化狀態。

要能真正體會此動物有多麼不同凡響，只要參考現今大象的相關數據即可。現代大象每天花上 17 個小時，攝取 60~300 公斤的食物、飲用 60~160 公升的水、解放 140~180 公斤的排泄物。而現代母象平均重約 2.7 公噸，公象重約五公噸。將現代大象的飲食與排泄物數據乘以雙倍，就能對草原長毛象的龐大外觀略知一二。

草原長毛象除了體型巨碩之外，另一個容易辨識的特徵就是象牙。成對的驚人象牙具有獨特的捲曲形狀，並可長達 5.2 公尺，能讓人一眼就輕鬆認出與其他長毛象的不同。身上的厚實毛髮具有三種不同的長度和質地，最長的毛髮約有 50 公分。

你也許會納悶，光是化石怎麼有辦法讓我們如此鉅細靡遺地了解此巨型生物。原因在於我們在泥濘冰殼中發掘的若干草原長毛象遺體，因木乃伊化（脫水保存）而幾近完好如初，連胃內容物都還在。上一次冰河時期的獨特環境條件，剛好將這些有機物質保存了上千年之久。

草原長毛象的滅絕可能另有原因，也就是現代大象所面臨的相同威脅：人類的追捕。成堆的長毛象骨骸化石出土後，顯示人類早期暫時群居附近伺機捕食的跡象。雖然早已絕種，但草原長毛象至少體現食物鏈的價值，以更有尊嚴的方式殞落。不像現今遭到獵殺的大象，因為人類強取象牙而棄屍荒野、任由腐化。

64. 我們都來自非洲嗎？ P. 206

我們都是從哪裡來的？人類是怎麼繁衍到整個世界的？這些都是人類自古以來就有的問題。現在科學似乎終於找到了答案。

《科學》期刊在 2008 年發表了一份研究報告，廣泛調查人類多樣性與遷徙的發展。這項研究是在加州史丹佛大學的史丹佛人類基因中心進行，其研究重點是從來自 51 個不同族群、近 1000 人當中調查其遺傳變異。全球都愈來愈好奇人類此物種起源的來龍去脈，而這份研究報告提供的觀點極具參考價值。

此研究之所以有重大的突破，是因研究人員發現了人類史上最大規模的遷徙：最初的遷離非洲之行。人類的先祖起初走上了不同的途徑，因而在其基因埋下了證據。史丹佛科學家拿到無數、精準度極高的基因樣本，根據其中 65 萬處相似性把人類分類。研究發現指出，人類最早出現在現今的衣索比亞和坦尚尼亞地區，之後才移居世界上其他高低不等的地方。1990 年代初期成為顯學的「非洲起源」理論，似乎也再次獲得證實。

另一份國際研究發現，華人並非來自「北京猿人」這種直立行走、被當作人類祖先之一的原始哺乳、靈長類，反而是來自非洲的原始人，從 10 萬年前開始，緩慢持續地經由南亞移動到中國。這個發現由上海復旦大學的研究團隊所提出，為人類從單一起源而非多起源演化的假說加添證據。該團隊從全球各地取來 10 萬人的基因樣本，推斷他們的血統來自東非 15 萬年前的人類族群。他們的後代子孫在 5 萬年後開始移動，有些到中國去，另一些則遷往地球其他地方居住。

上述有何重要的呢？這正是代表我們大家都是來自同一個人類家族的家人。沒有國之邊界，我們有的只是表面上的差異──記住這個教誨，才能讓愛與和平更普及。

65. 天生的生存高手 P. 208

牠們的體積只有這段句子後面的句點那麼大，但緩步動物（因外表像熊而被稱為「水熊蟲」）是地球上有史以來最頑強的一種生物。緩步動物的身體胖嘟嘟，有八條排列怪異的腳，末端有爪子，通常生活在湖底沈積物中或其他類似的潮濕環境裡。不過，緩步動物的特別之處，就在你把牠們帶離牠們的舒適區域後所發生的事。緩步動物在面臨險惡環境時，會變得幾乎無堅不摧，能在瞬間殺死人類的環境下生存。

實驗顯示，緩步動物可在最低攝氏負 200 度的低溫，到最高攝氏 148.9 度的高溫環境下生存。牠們可以承受沸騰的液體及高達海底最深處六倍的水壓。牠們能忍受致死的高劑量輻射，也能在外太空的真空中存活好幾天。事實上，隨便列舉一個除了太陽爆炸之外的世界末日事件，緩步動物很可能都有辦法活下來。

那麼，牠們究竟要如何實行這種神奇的生存技術呢？簡單來說，牠們會冬眠。就像真正的熊用冬眠熬過北方嚴峻的冬季一樣，這些極小的水熊蟲在環境會威脅到牠們的生命時，也會進入一種「睡眠」狀態。緩步動物會把頭和腳縮起來並蜷曲成一顆脫水的球，把代謝活動減少到只有平常的 0.01%。休眠時，牠們會分泌一種含糖的凝膠、以及大量的抗氧化物質來保護維生器官，同時也會製造其他化學物質，幫助牠們抵擋輻射並避免冰晶的形成。牠們能夠處在這種休眠狀態好幾年、有時候甚至長達數十年，而牠們只要接觸到水便能回復原狀。事實上，科學家在 2016 年，就曾救活兩隻過去三十年來一直處於這種死亡狀態的緩步動物！

於是，不出所料，科學家們渴望利用緩步動物不可思議的生存能力，用來創造出更頑強的農作物和更耐放的醫療用品。初步已有進展──一名科學家把緩步動物進入休眠時會活躍運動的基因分離，並用來製造出一株耐旱的酵母菌，其耐旱能力是一般正常的一百倍。

水熊蟲可能小到顯微鏡下才看得到，但牠們對全體人類的好處卻是龐大得顯而易見！

2-4 實力檢測

66. 騙子，無處不騙子！ P. 210

從人類有文明以來，無論是透過賭博還是設局，騙子就一直在欺騙沒有防備心的人把錢掏出來。如今人們把大部分的時間花在上網，所以網路上有騙子行騙也就不教人意外了。網路騙子的適應力強，不斷地在舊騙局上玩新招，每天陷害新的、沒有防人之心的受害者。

舉凡騙人買假貨或捐錢給假的眾籌活動等詐騙手法，無疑是不正當的手段，但儘管中招了，只會讓你損失一筆相對小額的現金。然而，其他被稱為網路釣魚的詐騙手段往往更為陰險。網路釣魚專門騙取你的個資或財務資訊，這可能導致極其嚴重的後果，像是身分被盜用或大規模的銀行詐欺。比如說，你可能會收到一封銀行寄來的電子郵件，要你核對帳戶細節。這封信看起來非常逼真，上面有銀行的商標、用語正式以及看起來像官方的簽名，應有盡有。但這全都是假象，假使回覆了就得自行承擔風險。

事實上，為了迎合最新的網路規範和趨勢，網路釣魚不斷地進化著。最新的詐騙手法是騙子偽裝成名人，發訊息給粉絲，邀請他們點擊一個連結以贏得特別大獎。接著會有一連串的問題和表格要填答，最後騙子就這麼把他們的個資騙到手。

社群媒體網站也是資料竊盜的一大狩獵場。如果看到有人張貼問卷或連鎖信訊息遊戲，要你回答一系列看似無害的問題（像是「您的第一隻寵物叫什麼名字？」或「您參加過的第一場演唱會是什麼？」，您一定要謹慎回答。為什麼呢？因為每當您設置新密碼時，通常會被要求提供一個安全問題，以防您忘記密碼而需要重新取得。如果您照著騙子的遊戲走，不經意地交出了您安全問題的答案，就可能給了他們機會存取您的密碼！

騙子很聰明，所以比他們更聰明是您的責任。保持頭腦清醒、抱持著懷疑的態度，透過了解最新的詐騙手法來掌握先機。網路世界很殘酷，採取行動才能確保您不會成為下一個受害者。

67. 虛擬名流　P. 213

絆愛和 Shudu Gram 是網紅。絆愛是 YouTube 上的影音部落客，用各種古怪行動取悅觀眾，她的頻道已有超過 250 萬人訂閱。Shudu 則是位南非超模，在 Instagram 上有超過 17 萬名追蹤者。是什麼讓這兩人有別於其他網紅呢？絆愛和 Shudu 都不是血肉之軀，而是由 1 和 0 的二進位系統所組成的。

有愈來愈多的虛擬社群媒體網紅在網路上引起了轟動，他們招來了龐大的粉絲群、企業合約和代言機會。這兩位就是其中之二。有些虛擬網紅（比如以日本動漫畫獨特風格創作的絆愛）很明顯就不是人類。但另一群網紅（像是 Shudu）就非常寫實了。他們是由 3D 建模軟體打造的，而在某些 YouTube 影片創作者的案例中，也會動用到動作捕捉器和配音員。Instagram 的數位模特兒通常是某位數位藝術家的作品，然而要讓一個虛擬的影音部落客（VTuber）活靈活現，就需要動員包括編劇、導演和視覺特效師在內的一整個團隊。

那麼，究竟是什麼讓這些「假」網紅紅起來的呢？要回答這問題，我們必須回顧 1970 年代的日本。當時由於經濟成長緩慢，很多日本人對現實有所不滿，轉而擁抱虛擬的數位真實，此一現象延續至今。隨著日本文化在西方世界愈來愈流行，對虛擬世界的熱愛和接受度也相伴而來。

至於真人的網紅呢？他們對於這種新趨勢又有什麼看法？很多人覺得受到威脅，並對虛擬網紅可能席捲平台表達了關切，因為這些角色永遠不會感到疲倦，也不會要求付費。批評矛頭也指向 Shudu 的創作者卡麥隆－詹姆士・威爾森。有人指出，被刻劃成深色肌膚的 Shudu 可能搶走一些機會，而這些機會原本可能會提供給深色肌膚的真人模特兒。

威爾森相信，真實世界的模特兒沒什麼好怕的。但他確實認為，數位化在時尚界的作用日益增加（像是創造出現實模特兒的數位版，以節省拍攝成本），最終將會改變這個產業。另一方面，YouTube 影音創作者很快就能用軟體，把自己的臉部照片即時轉換為數位卡通人物或動物。最終，威爾森說，3D 和人類終將共存共榮。

68. 成為書蟲　P. 216

創業家比爾・蓋茲每年要讀 50 本書的事蹟人盡皆知。你跟得上嗎？對許多人而言，差不多每週閱讀一本書就已經是很了不起的奢侈餘裕；有些人則根本無法對定期閱讀的概念產生興趣。因為書本會讓他們想起在校時期、覺得閱讀太花時間，或覺得比網路影片乏味許多。

研究顯示，以閱讀為樂的人往往擁有較高的成績。不可否認的是，將閱讀視為休閒活動的人，多為人生勝利組──因此，如果閱讀是最實用的生活習慣，那麼我們該如何培養呢？

最簡單的方法就是選擇能讓自己感興致的題材。你可以不用在乎所謂的暢銷書單，或是朋友堅持推薦「愛不釋手」的書籍。事實上，直接屏除同儕或老師所建議的必要讀物即可。如果你熱衷時尚，請閱讀雜誌文章；如果你喜歡神遊於奇幻世界，請閱讀漫畫書；如果你對紀實類書籍提不起興趣，巴著小說不放無妨。只要養成閱讀習慣，閱讀範疇通常會逐漸擴大，所以只要先從你感興趣的任何題材開始就好。

很多人抱怨買書會超出自己的預算。新書確實價格不斐，但你也許每週都會不假思索的外帶三杯咖啡，這樣的花費相當於一本平裝書──何況書籍能帶來更棒的報酬率！所以請研究一下你所處地區的二手書店，不僅能拿到超值折扣，還可挖到奇珍異寶。而最棒的替代方案就是前往圖書館，免費知識任君選擇。

另一種培養方式就是隨身攜帶一本書。因為你一天中的空檔時間比你想像的還要來得多。搭公車或坐火車、等朋友來或等微波爐熱好食物，都是能夠埋首閱讀的零碎時間！而且對於注意力短暫的人而言，堪稱絕佳的閱讀技巧。一次閱讀五分鐘，一天之內少量多次的累積成果會很可觀。你甚至會發現自己不太情願放下一本好書。

最後一招就是減少要命的上網時間。沒有虛擬世界的分心誘惑，愈有可能重拾閱讀興趣。實體書本的優點在於，你無法隨意點選而跳離當下的閱讀頁面。因此，請關閉平板電腦，感受一下勵志的實體讀物溫度，盡情享受閱讀的樂趣！

69. 古代劇場的生命教育 P.219

在悲劇、喜劇和諷刺劇這三種戲劇類型中，悲劇與古希臘的關係最緊密。希臘人常用「悲劇」這個字詞來代指含有神、國王和其他英雄人物的戲劇，這些人的行為造就了他們多詭的命運。在亞里斯多德看來，悲劇起了情緒抒發的作用，是祛除觀眾憐憫與恐懼的一種手段。

約莫從西元前 550 到西元前 220 年間，雅典無疑是希臘最重要的城邦，而對雅典人來說，悲劇的演出很重要。這一點最早可從約西元前 508 年的一個宗教節日上看出，這個節日是為了祭祀身為酒神和豐收之神的戴歐尼修斯。這節日被稱為「城市酒神節」（或譯作「城市戴神節」），其中一個最重要的環節就是戲劇演出比賽，決定誰能在這個節日成為官方的劇作家。狄斯比斯（Thespis）是首場比賽的優勝者，因此他的名字與戲劇密切相連。他也是第一個讓筆下人物把台詞說出來，而不是唱出來的劇作家。劇場表演者至今仍被稱為悲劇演員即為此故（譯註：thespian 即「狄斯比斯的」）。

一直到西元前 323 年希臘化時代展開前，悲劇向來只為歌頌酒神而寫。因僅演出一次，所以我們現在熟知的片段，是在古悲劇的演出成了慣例後，那些記得夠清楚、足以反覆演出的片段。

所有希臘悲劇中最著名的或許是《伊底帕斯王》。這本書是索福克勒斯約於西元前 429 年所著，書裡生動描繪了人類無法逃避免命運的處境。在一連串複雜的事件中，伊底帕斯王殺了自己的生父，然後娶了自己的生母，可是他本人卻對此一無所知。為了拯救王國不受瘟疫肆虐，伊底帕斯追查起殺害老國王的真兇，不料在追查真相的過程中，他驚恐地發現自己的所做所為。

歐里庇得斯於西元前 412 年所著的《海倫》是另一部膾炙人口的悲劇。它與神話人物宙斯之女海倫有關。人們對海倫的美貌既愛又恨，最終引發造成許多人喪生的戰爭。

很有意思的是，「悲劇」（tragedy）一詞源自古希臘語的「tragos」（山羊）和「oide」（頌歌或歌曲），因此它的字面意義是「山羊之歌」。對此，有一個可能的解釋是，戴歐尼修斯有個半人半羊的信徒兼隨從。以後看到某個字詞，仔細想想與之有關的希臘神話，這個字詞的起源就變得更容易理解了。

70. 靠不住的消化作用 P.222

你剛吃完飯——好幾坨的馬鈴薯泥、一塊巨無霸牛排和成堆的蔬菜，通通沾著濃郁的肉汁。你一口都吃不下了。但是有人提議吃甜點——「巧克力蛋糕看起來超誘人的！」——突然間，你覺得肚子裡還有那麼一點空間。

這種現象也就是俗稱的「甜點是另一個胃」。一旦飯後吃點甜點成為了一種常態，用餐的人會備感折磨、節食的人同樣也會受挫。但這種正餐後吃點甜點的怪癖其背後的成因其實非常好懂。其中很大一部分要歸結於所謂的「特定感官的飽腹感」，或者用通俗一點的話說就是——「你對食物感到膩了」。同一種食物吃了一大盤後，你的各種感官已經受夠了。一度讓你愛不釋手的東西現在乏味又無趣。然而，看到上頭滿是誘人小點心的甜點菜單送來，你對食物的興趣再度死灰復燃，你的大腦促使你去進食，來得到嘗鮮和吃到美味的樂趣。

通常在你剛剛吃完一頓大餐後，你的胃已經滿了。但胃是有彈性的器官，必要時能夠鬆弛並騰出空間給更多的食物。事實證明，糖會激發這種鬆弛反應，所以你吃下幾口冰淇淋聖代後，你的胃受刺激開始放鬆，就不會覺得那麼撐了。這樣你就能吃完一整碗的冰，即使幾分鐘前你還覺得自己彷彿要撐爆了似的。

這種感覺當然只是暫時的，而且在你吃完甜點後，你的胃又會再次撐得難受，讓你好一陣子懶洋洋的，一動就不舒服。甜點的胃當然還會導致另一種危險，我們經常會在用餐時過於放縱，在熱量已經很高的正餐上添加了多餘且不必要的卡路里。

不過，我們有個辦法可以利用這種現象得到好處。比如說，你不要自己吃完一整個甜點，而是和幾個朋友一起分享的話，你就能讓你的胃放鬆下來，但又不會吃到不舒服的程度。換句話說，吃完了這頓飯，你會感覺沒那麼飽，胃也會比較

311

舒服,既能減緩你的感官麻木,又能避免攝取過多不健康的熱量。這麼一來,對你的飲食健康還有腰圍,也會比較好。

Unit 3 學習策略

本單元將介紹兩種重要的閱讀技巧:如何**解讀影像圖表**和**利用參考資料**。影像圖表是將統計資料和數字等以**圖表**呈現,讓我們更容易理解。參考資料則是可以幫助我們迅速有效地找到資訊的工具。本單元將同時訓練你這兩種技巧,讓你能有效分析圖表資料,並且迅速找到資料。

讀完這個章節以後,你將不僅能讀懂、解釋和評論文本,亦能有效地探索浩瀚的資訊世界。

3-1 影像圖表

資料有許多種形式,有些難以用文字來表達,這時候就需要使用影像圖表來輔助說明。影像圖表運用了**圖片**和**圖表**來傳達資訊,包括了圖表、表格和地圖。運用得當的話,可以化繁為簡,使資料容易理解。

71. 長條圖:令人憂心的道路安全紀錄
P. 226

眾所週知,台灣是全世界最安全的國家之一,且常名列全世界最守法國家前五名。暴力犯罪率極低,竊盜率也是如此。但是,在台灣無可挑剔的紀錄上,卻有一個污點——道路安全。即使只是隨意瞄一下台灣的交通事故統計數字,也足以讓即將成為駕駛的人冷汗直流。每年台灣約發生三十萬起交通事故。

島上城市的馬路上滿是高速行駛的摩托車,更是發生交通意外的溫床。雖然近年致死率已下降,但每年仍有數百人因疏忽駕駛而喪命。無可否認的是,如果這座島嶼想維持安全避風港的名聲不墜,台灣的危險駕駛文化就必須進行翻天覆地的改革。

下頁兩張長條圖可以讓你對台灣的道路安全狀況有些概念。長條圖表達資訊的方式,是以長度不同的有色柱狀圖呈現,以方便快速地比較數據。第一張圖呈現包括台灣在內的五個不同國家的數據;第二張則只包含台灣的數據。

72. 折線圖:亞洲即將引爆的定時炸彈
P. 229

亞洲目前有項危機。由於年輕人愈來愈不生養子女,而老年人愈來愈長壽,因此到了2060年,許多亞洲國家中,三分之一以上的人口將超過65歲。

這個趨勢的嚴重後果之一,是照顧這些老年人口的財務重擔將落在年輕人肩上。當然,老年人口對年輕人口的比例愈高,就愈難支撐這個財務重擔。

另一個結果是,隨著活躍勞動人口減少,這些國家的經濟也跟著衰退。即使是現在,年長者面對比之前世代更晚退休的壓力有增無減,有些人甚至七十幾歲仍在工作。對很多人來說,早早退休已成為幻想。

下頁的折線圖說明四個亞洲國家老年人口逐漸增加的比重,以及對未來的預估值。折線圖說明某事物過去或未來的變化(通常是一段時間的數字)。線條往上表示增加;往下則表示減少。

73. 地圖:水資源短缺焦慮 P. 231

氣候乾燥、人口眾多的國家常面臨無法供應居民充足飲用水的難題。然而,遭遇水資源短缺的國家數量正逐漸成長。

水資源短缺的定義是指,年度取水量與年度供水量的比率(以百分比為計量單位)。百分越高表示有太多用水者爭搶有限的水供應量,而這可能是水資源短缺的顯著風險。

雖然,一國的水資源短缺程度高不必然代表該國將面臨水資源缺乏問題,但這的確代表那些比率較高的國家需要特別注意水資源保育與管理。

隨著全球暖化與人口持續增加,未來數十年,預料遭遇重大水資源短缺的國家數量將明顯上升。

以地圖呈現地理上的資訊通常使用記號和顏色呈現不同的數據。下頁二張世界地圖中，第一張顯示 2013 年各國的水資源短缺情況，第二張則預測 2040 年的狀況，顏色越深的國家表示水資源短缺的程度越高。

74. 圓餅圖：弄清楚你的優先順序　P. 234

我們大部分人都知道，如果想要減掉幾磅肉，飲食和運動是必須專注的兩件事。攝取健康的食物很重要，但減重最關鍵的因素很可能是運動。唯一能真正燃燒那些卡路里的方法是透過去健身房努力訓練。雖然我們都知道睡個好覺對我們的身心健康很重要，但在努力減重時，睡眠卻未必是優先事項。相反地，起個大早去健身房運動要比充足的睡眠更好，這樣對吧？

錯！根據健身專家指出，這些人們常有的優先順序觀念完全與事實相反。請看下頁的圓餅圖。圓餅圖是分成幾個部分的圓形圖，每部分代表在整體中所佔的百分比。左邊的圓餅圖顯示大部分人在努力減重時，將睡眠、營養和運動制定為優先次序。右邊的圖顯示，如果想有效減重，應該將圖中三個要素制定為優先順序。

75. 時程表：申請前先試讀　P. 237

在決定要申請哪間大學時，做出正確決定極為重要──畢竟，那是你未來可能要度過數年光陰的地方！為了確保你和大學合拍，申請前親自去看看任何一家大學，總是有益無害。如果你計劃出國去念大學，就像愈來愈多台灣學生那樣，這點就變得加倍重要。

因此，許多大學都提供國際學生短期的夏季課程，以便他們在做出最終決定前，有機會先試讀。參加這些課程的學生可以體驗大學的獨特氛圍與研究方式、適應當地的環境與文化，並和現有的教職員與學生親自談談。課程通常都有工作坊，幫助學生在申請時能夠成功過關。

下頁是牛津大學兩週夏季課程的部分課表。時程表（或課程表）是顯示每日課程與活動，以及在哪個時段進行的表格。了解課程，你可以確切知道課程進行的內容與時間，才不會錯過任何樂子！

3-2 參考資料

我們生活在一個資訊無垠的世界。百科全書、旅遊指南、網際網路、報紙、食譜等，這些都是知識的寶庫。但是，要在如此巨大的寶庫中找到特定的資訊可是一件很棘手的事。此時，索引、搜索引擎、節目表等類的工具就派得上用場了。只要學會怎麼瀏覽這些資料，知識的寶庫不久將垂手可得，任你遨遊！

76. 目錄：教授普羅大眾高級料理　P. 240

能創造味覺與料理奇蹟的卓越主廚一直是受人仰慕崇拜的對象，雖然在歷史上，他們大部分時候都神祕地隱身在煙霧蒸騰的廚房中。然而，電視時代把主廚從他們高度嚴防的餐廳中請出來，帶進我們的客廳。全世界充滿好奇心的業餘廚師開始收看像茱莉亞‧查爾德和芬妮‧克雷達克這樣的電視主廚教導高級料理的藝術。

數十年後，電視主廚享受著通常只有好萊塢演員能擁有的名流身分。由於有這麼多熱切的家庭廚師躍躍欲試，想跟自己最喜愛的主廚學習做菜，食譜書市場也隨之迅速擴大。現在，每位知名主廚都出版了自己的食譜書（或者出了好幾本），並在書中分享他們最愛的食譜和技巧。

下頁是一位知名主廚的食譜書目錄。目錄位在書的前面，在封面之後，目錄按出現的順序列出書的內容。除了書中的各章節，目錄也包含其他的功能性與附帶的部分，例如索引或謝辭。

77. 索引：注意看天空　P. 242

賞鳥這項嗜好始於二十世紀初期，在雙筒望遠鏡問世後，使得人們毋須開槍將鳥打下，就能辨識鳥類，便發展出此項嗜好。因為需要的花費相對不多，賞鳥很快就被對大自然有興趣的人，普遍視為一項門檻低且投報率高的嗜好。

任何人都可成為賞鳥人。你只需要有一副雙筒望遠鏡和一本圖鑑，幫助你正確辨認出每一隻鳥。由於全世界的鳥類超過一萬種，因此圖鑑更顯重要。很多鳥類看起來都很像，但可以透過小小的差異加以分辨，例如，牠們的體型大小或鳥喙的形狀——這一切應該都會詳述於你的圖鑑上。

如果你想查詢某種特定鳥類，可查閱圖鑑後面的索引。索引是一份按字母順序排列的名字／主題清單，上面還有它們出現的頁數。在下頁的索引裡，鳥類以科別的字母順序排列，科別內的不同鳥類再按字母順序列出。例如，松雞科有兩個條目，下面列有黑松雞和紅松雞。

78. 菜單：以正確的方式開始一天　P. 244

你很可能聽過「早餐是一天中最重要的一餐」這句古老的俗諺無數次，但我們很多人仍有跳過早餐的壞習慣。然而，這句古老的諺語裡藏著許多智慧。在夜裡，身體使用大量的能量來修補和替換受損的細胞。因此當你醒來後，你的身體非常需要補充能量。

事實上，研究顯示，早餐吃得最為豐盛的人，身體質量指數（BMI）更可能比在稍晚才攝取大部分卡路里的人低。其他的好處還包括，早餐吃飽會讓你在一天裡較不覺得飢餓（進而可降低你的整體卡路里攝取量）。

如果你打算出去吃早餐，要特別注意看菜單。現在的菜單通常列有許多資訊，有助你選擇最適合的早餐。像是卡路里數和成分這些詳細資料都列在價格旁邊，幫助你選出最棒的早餐，開始你的一天！

79. 網路：增強你的搜尋技巧　P. 246

你是否曾發現使用 Google 搜尋時，搜尋結果往往並未完全吻合你的搜尋項目？這裡有一些你可以運用的訣竅，讓你的搜尋更有效率。

首先，你可以使用在搜尋框下面的標籤頁（圖片、新聞、影片等等）過濾搜尋結果，如此一來，只有特定的結果會出現在結果頁面上。

你也可以使用英文引號要求 Google 搜尋精確無誤的語詞，而不是提供每個分開的字之結果。例如，輸入"午夜‧巴黎"會搜尋到這個電影標題，而不是關於午夜和巴黎這個城市的資訊。

在一個字之前加上連字號會告訴 Google，把這個字詞從你的搜尋結果剔除（例如，新筆電－蘋果，會搜尋新款筆記型電腦，但不包括任何蘋果公司的產品）。最後，點擊「工具」可讓你選擇的搜尋結果回溯到多久之前，或將你的搜尋結果限制在特定的時間範圍內。

我對伊隆‧馬斯克很感興趣——這位南非的億萬富豪推動了一些創新計畫，如太空探險公司 SpaceX，和電動車廠商特斯拉。以下是我最近搜尋此人的結果。

80. 數據流程圖：如何從社群媒體獲利
P. 248

現在的人每天花好幾個小時在社群媒體和影音串流網站上，是很常見的事。有些人也許認為這很浪費時間，但是，如果你了解這套制度如何運作且願意投入心力，其實可從這些網站上獲得可觀的收入。

大部分的線上營收來自在你的內容旁出現的廣告，雖然企業以往的確都只想找有數百萬追蹤者的大咖名人來促銷他們的產品，但現在的品牌愈來愈想找創作者或「網紅」代言，他們的追蹤人數較少，但卻為黏著度高的利基觀眾。

以 YouTube 來說，任何人都可以創作或上傳影片，但如果你的訂閱人數到達某個數量，你就能申請成為 YouTube 合作夥伴，並獲得使用某些功能的權限，讓你的創作內容帶來實際獲利。

為了幫助你了解像 YouTube 這樣的公司如何運作，參考數據流程圖很有用。數據流程圖以圖像表示數據如何流入和流經他們的資訊系統，讓像 YouTube 這樣的公司運作更清楚。

Unit 4 綜合練習

既然你們現在已經熟悉各種閱讀與字彙的技巧，還有一些重要的學習策略。那麼該是測驗的時候了。本單元與前幾個單元不同，不再是一篇文章只有一種技巧。現在，你面臨的挑戰是，你必須在每篇單獨的文本上，運用數種不同的閱讀技巧。

利用這幾篇複習的單元，看看自己有多大的進步，從之前的單元中又學到了多少。試著在模擬考試的情境下進行本測驗，然後分析自己的優缺點。這麼做能讓你知道自己將來需要在哪方面下更多的功夫。

4-1 綜合練習

81. 激烈的籠式擂臺！ P.252

膝蓋踢頭，緊接出現骨折聲；群眾嘶吼，格鬥選手倒地，血染擂臺。這就是現今最為暴力、熱門的綜合格鬥運動中的常見場景。

多以縮寫 MMA 代表的綜合格鬥運動，由兩名訓練有素的格鬥選手，進入金屬製的八邊形籠式擂臺對戰。雙方可任選拳擊、摔角、柔道、柔術、空手道或任何赤手空拳的格鬥武術來一分高下。

僅穿著短褲、戴上不露指頭的襯墊搏擊手套，選手需要遵循的規則屈指可數。禁止頭槌、戳眼、咬人、拉頭髮或攻擊下體；不能擊中喉嚨、脊椎或後腦勺；對手一旦倒地，就不能踢頭或用膝蓋頂頭。除此之外，雙方可盡情出招。選手需具備高超的技巧與適應力，還要承擔每次踏上籠式擂臺的安危風險。與規定較為嚴格的拳擊等格鬥運動相比，MMA 鐵粉享受的是更能讓腎上腺素激增的精采觀賽感受。

綜合格鬥運動的起源可追溯至古希臘，而現代 MMA 則始於二十世紀初的巴西「Vale Tudo」——意指「無限制格鬥」。到了 1990 年代，該運動首次登上美國，名為「終極格鬥錦標賽」（簡稱 UFC）的殿堂，該組織爾後演變為推動 MMA 賽事的主要單位。筆者編寫本文至今，已有超過 200 場的 MMA 大賽紀錄。

不過，雖然初期於電視播放的 UFC 賽事創下高收視率，但許多人認為 MMA 的殘暴程度相當於人類版本的鬥雞，因此呼籲相關單位徹底禁止此項運動。自 2001 年起，UFC 易主之後，引進全新的一套規定，包括新訂立的重量分級制度、回合數與時間限制、正式犯規原則，希望讓更廣大的觀眾接受 MMA。雖然此運動仍然極具危險性、血腥且暴力，卻也在文明化的過程中，成為蓬勃發展的合法主流運動。不過，以選手凶狠、比賽難以預測而惡名昭彰的情況來看，MMA 未來還是很難走向循規蹈矩之途。

82. 搞砸和失敗的紀念館 P.254

失敗——人人都害怕失敗，當它發生在我們身上時，我們往往希望可以用沙子埋葬我們的失敗，從此不用再面對它。但如果把你最大的錯誤永久地保存在博物館裡供人欣賞，你又怎麼看呢？瑞典赫爾辛堡的失敗博物館做的正是這件事。它把近代史上最大的商業失敗案例全都找出來陳列展示——從 Google 嘗試打造卻不成功的智慧型眼鏡 Google Glass，到可口可樂公司推出的災難性口味建怡可樂混合咖啡 Blak。

各式各樣各種程度的失敗全都被展示。有些產品打從一開始就註定失敗，比如 Bic 的「For Her」原子筆（旨在「舒適貼合女性的手」），對任何試圖以透過煽惑、刻意操作的行銷方式改變產品定位的人來說，這也是個教訓。有些產品就只是不再合時宜，像是 Sony 於 1975 年推出的 Betamax 錄影帶格式很快就被 VHS 淘汰了，或是比較近期的百視達 DVD 出租店也因為網路串流服務而變得多餘。

有些例子是企業完全可笑地不知道他們的目標群眾在哪（例如摩托車製造商在 1996 年開賣的哈雷戴維森香水）。還有一些產品，像是蘋果的牛頓 Messagepad（一種可用來記筆記和發傳真的設備），顯然是朝著更偉大的方向邁進，並且在開發革命性產品時扮演著關鍵角色——在蘋果的案例中指的是 iPhone。

與其說是嘲諷失敗，這間博物館在某些情況下反而更讚頌創新和創意。博物館沒有埋藏這些商業

315

炸彈，而是照亮這些儘管不完美卻勇於創造新鮮刺激的東西，希望其他人能看見，或許還能因此受到啟發。

　　成立這間博物館背後的寓意很明確——失敗不一定是負面的，而且很可能是達成驚人成就的必經之路。畢竟，這間博物館充分證明了，我們這個年代最成功的幾家公司——亞馬遜、Google和蘋果——對於失敗都不陌生，也為了這些和成功失之交臂的產品虧損了數十億美元。真正的創新是做好準備，去承擔巨大的風險、慘烈的失敗，並在失敗後再次嘗試。

83. 恐怖大師：史蒂芬・金　P.256

　　儘管史蒂芬・金本人否認有受到童年某一特定事件的影響，但人們不禁要問，是不是有件事催生了這位恐怖大師。他小的時候曾目擊朋友被火車撞死。此事對他造成的創傷之大，使得當年年幼的金壓抑到現在還是沒有這件事的記憶。在《有時候，他們會回來》短篇小說集中，他說到有人問他為什麼總是選擇寫恐怖故事，對此他回答說：「你為什麼認為我有選擇？」

　　金在校時就是一名狂熱的恐怖漫畫讀者，還會投稿文章到他大哥創辦的小報《戴夫報》。他也開始寫故事拿來賣給朋友，直到他的老師強迫他退錢。18歲時，《漫畫評論》為他出版了《我是一個青年盜墓者》系列。他在兩年後把短篇故事《玻璃地板》賣給了《驚嚇神祕故事》。

　　一直到1974年，他的第一本小說《魔女嘉莉》才被「雙日」出版社接受，金當時26歲，是一名老師，已婚。金的妻子塔比莎在垃圾桶發現小說的初稿，這才鼓勵他寫完。他收到一筆微薄的預支稿費，但這本小說卻大賣。

　　此後，金有豐富的作品產出——他寫了70多本書和無數的短篇小說；他的作品被改編成了64部電影，從1976年的經典之作《魔女嘉莉》到2017年的賣座電影《牠》。他的作品也成為超過26部電視節目的靈感來源，最近的是2018年的一部影集《城堡岩》。事實上，根據他的出版商的說法，讀者每年並不想閱讀同一個作者一本以上的書，而金有點太多產了。因此，金在1970、80年代時開始用筆名理查・巴克曼出版多餘的著作。但說真的，那些書大部分都讓人想睡覺，不值得一讀。

　　根據史蒂芬・金的官網所述，當他被問到為何而寫時，他給出很多典型多產作家都會給的回應：「答案相當簡單——我生來做不了別的事。我天生就是要寫故事的，我也愛寫故事。這就是我寫作的原因。我真的無法想像去做別的事情，也無法想像不做我現在做的事。」

84. 閃耀的戰利品　P.258

　　在戰爭或違反人權的地方開採的鑽石稱為衝突鑽石，其中有一些來自剛果民主共和國（DRC）。當地侵害人權的元兇是軍事組織，包括剛果民主共和國武裝部隊和盧安達解放民主力量。這些軍事組織以不同的名義在剛果民主共和國打了超過一個世紀的戰爭、爭奪當地豐富的自然資源。他們對國家財富的貪婪助長了令人髮指、危害人類的罪行。他們利用大規模性侵的手段——有時甚至連兒童也不放過——來恐嚇當地村落，讓居民不敢靠近礦藏以及武裝份子想要控制的地方。販賣鑽石的收益資助了第二次剛果戰爭（正式發生於1998到2003年間，儘管該國的衝突仍在持續），而當時甚或現在的一些戰爭，其實就是為了把持鑽石、黃金和其他礦藏而打。

　　隨著全球日益認識到這些非洲人的困境，國際間做出了許多努力，以彌補非洲大陸中部地區對他們的剝削。然而，大多數的嘗試卻都不夠好。其實有些努力與其說是撥亂反正，實際上有可能反而延續了剛果民主共和國的慘況。比方說，盧安達解放民主力量受到高度的關切，卻沒有多少人注意到烏干達，而烏干達已經被聯合國國際法庭起訴，被控在剛果犯下搶劫和危害人類的罪行。盧安達在聯合國的報告中同被列為主要參與者，在剛果民主共和國搶劫並延續該地的衝突情勢。

　　鑽石的廣告形象是愛情和喜悅的象徵，這和它生產過程中的暴利與痛苦形成了強烈的對比。這不僅限於叛軍、礦藏控制權的爭奪戰，以及用由此產生的收益所購買的軍需品。我們也必須考慮到金融機構、主要鑽石零售商、運輸業者、貿易商和走私者也都涉入其中。我們也不該忘掉無數的鑽石礦工，他們或主動或被迫挖礦謀生。這份工作艱難、骯髒、既不安全也不健康，使他們和家人處於極度貧窮的困境。在這一切當中，更讓人尤其不安的是，這些礦石的真正價值和商機如此龐大，把它們挖掘出來的礦工收入卻極其微薄的收入。

85. 食品世界的超級英雄 P. 260

食物並非都生來平等。有些食物像漫畫裡的英雄一樣具有超能力。這些「超級食物」的營養密度特別高，能為我們大量提供每日建議攝取的維生素、礦物質和抗氧化物，這些天然分子有助於降低心臟疾病、癌症和中風等健康風險。

有幾種食物經常贏得「超級食物」的頭銜：像是藍莓，它富含纖維和維生素K，枸杞則富含維生素C和E，巴西莓富含胺基酸和抗氧化物。黃豆含有天然化合物，有助降低膽固醇，預防與年齡相關的記憶衰退。綠茶具有強效的抗氧化物，可減緩發炎並有助防癌。綠色葉菜類像羽衣甘藍和菠菜均富含維生素A、C、E、K、B，還有豐富的鐵、鎂、鉀和鈣等礦物質。

然而，這些所謂的超級食物並不能倖免於食品業者的操作。事實上，就營養成分而言，並沒有超級食物這種東西。這項標籤是為了行銷目的而發明的，企圖影響在乎健康的買家並販賣產品。雖然有的食物可能富含某些營養素，但被貼上超級食物標籤的食物肯定不是治療疾病的靈丹妙藥。

在這類廣告的煽惑下，很多消費者對超級食物有著不切實際的期望，並相信如果吃飯時加個一兩樣超級食物，就能對疾病免疫，永遠保持在最棒的健康狀態。真相則是，無論包裝上的標籤再狂，超級食物並不能抵消不良飲食及糟糕生活型態的影響。雖然在健康均衡飲食之餘，吃這些超級食物作為補充確實有益健康，但消費者必須學習不要過分期待，也要理解到並沒有單一食物是保持健康或預防疾病的關鍵。

那麼，如果消費者想從這些食物得到好處，該怎麼做才好？首先，全方位檢視你的飲食，而非只看一餐，謹記如果你早午晚三餐都吃速食，一把藍莓也無濟於事。其次，對超級食物的說法抱持懷疑的態度。花點時間去了解你所選擇的超級食物到底有什麼超級之處，再判斷它們是不是真的配得上這個稱號。

86. 開創科幻小說的女子 P. 262

當你想到科幻小說時，腦海中浮現的很可能是前往遙遠行星探險的太空船、兇猛的機器人推翻人類創造者，或是時空旅人折彎時間與空間的結構。科幻小說是種文學作品的類型，嘗試探索科學的廣大未知與神奇，有時則是討論科學可怕的潛能。然而科幻小說並非出於科學家或太空探險家之手，事實上是誕生於一位18歲作家在1816年的想像：瑪麗·雪萊。

故事開始於一個糟透的夏季。瑪麗和丈夫詩人雪萊在瑞士日內瓦湖畔度六月的時光，同行的還有其他友人，包括另一位名詩人拜倫和他的醫生，約翰·波里道利。有天晚上，屋外持續下著傾盆大雨，為了打發時間，拜倫提議每個人寫下自己的鬼故事。瑪麗很快忙著構想一個故事，她後來寫道，這個故事會「觸動我們天性中的神祕恐懼感，喚醒令人戰慄的恐怖，並讓讀者不敢環顧四面，讓血液凝結且心跳加速」。

她寫下的故事是《科學怪人》，故事是一名科學家把從偷來的屍體上取下的器官縫在一起而創造出一個怪物，並利用電擊給它生命。雖然現在很多人認為《科學怪人》是恐怖小說，和《狼人》或《吸血鬼》屬於同一類，但事實上，它是純粹的科幻小說。不像前面提到的那些怪物，科學怪人是科學的產物，不是來自超自然的鬼怪。

那些只看過電影改編版的人，如果認為瑪麗·雪萊的作品有點卡通化或過於誇張，是可以被原諒的。然而，原版小說是對於如創造論的倫理學、知識的追求和違反自然法則等主題勇敢無畏的探索，這些都是現代科幻小說常爭論的主題。在多產科幻作家以撒·艾西莫夫的作品，尤其是他關於機器人學的系列作品《機械公敵》（1950）、電影《銀翼殺手》（1982）和《人造意識》（2014），都可看到雪萊的影響。的確，任何作品只要著墨透過科學賦予生命的人造生物，以及人造生物引發的負面影響，皆受到雪萊的影響。

所以，下次有人想要告訴你，科幻小說不適合女生看時，你可以自信滿滿地向他們指出瑪麗·雪萊女士，正是打下這整個文類基礎的人！

87. 仙人掌：沙漠的終極倖存者　P. 264

沙漠與乾草原是嚴酷的環境，只有非常特殊的動植物才能存活。雖然白天的氣溫可以飆升到攝氏 45 度，但由於空氣中沒有水蒸氣留住熱氣（造成溫室效應），夜晚的氣溫也可能降到零度以下。如果有下雨的話，全年降雨量也少於 25 公分（250 毫米）。

這種極惡劣的情況使得仙人掌這種原生樹種演化出一些非常有趣的特質，因而人們甚至常常不覺得它們是樹。整個生物體已徹底改造。根系通常分布格外地廣而淺，且含鹽量很高，好讓在最短時間內吸收最大量的水。例如，一株發育完全的巨人柱仙人掌可在 10 天內吸收 3,000 公升的水。因為，又大又寬又扁的樹葉已經變成薄而鋒利的保護尖刺，光合作用這樣必要的作用，便由樹幹和樹枝執行。

仙人掌表面也覆有一層蠟以鎖住水分，而且，從上到下的所有或是大部分的表面，都長著又長又深的皺褶或葉脈。這些皺褶在降雨時會大幅膨脹，因此可貯存足夠的水分，讓仙人掌在不下雨時，得以存活好多年。

肉眼看不到仙人掌的呼吸和化學作用。仙人掌在白天時等同於屏住呼吸。太陽出來後，氣孔會關閉，以避免流失過多水分。而氣孔是讓蒸發作用進行的毛孔。夜裡，毛孔會打開，讓氧氣、二氧化碳和水蒸氣通過。由於光合作用無法在夜間進行，二氧化碳被貯存為未熟水果裡常見的蘋果酸。當太陽升起，氣孔再度關閉，仙人掌利用貯存的二氧化碳進行光合作用。如果有人在日出時吃仙人掌的果肉，吃起來是酸的；而在日落時，味道則是甜的。

仙人掌就連一般的外觀也是種優勢。它的樹枝很少，整個結構偏向圓柱形和球形，讓體積／表面積比達到最大，以便能更不費力地保存水分。靠著這麼多獨特的適應作用生存，仙人掌已成為沙漠生活最具辨識度的象徵。

88. 伊斯蘭國：全球恐攻網路的興衰　P. 267

如果你在過去十年間曾打開新聞，你很可能聽過 Isis、IS、ISIL 或 Daesh 這些名字。這些全是近年來最恐怖暴力組織的不同名稱：即名為伊斯蘭國的團體。

伊斯蘭國過去十年的斑斑劣跡，已經讓該組織在全球惡名昭彰，其中包括了摧毀古代建築和文物，到公開處決少數民族、同性戀者、記者和慈善工作者，以及在世界各地發動令人震驚的恐怖攻擊。然它真正想要什麼？來自何方？未來又會如何？

伊斯蘭國是在美國入侵伊拉克後引發的混亂與暴力中，從蓋達組織分裂出來的小團體。在那之前，蓋達組織都被視為該地區最危險的極端組織，宣稱犯下 911 攻擊事件。但伊拉克伊斯蘭國（ISI）在 2006 年成立後，接下來幾年，它完全脫離蓋達組織，擴大為全球恐攻網路，甚至比那曾令人害怕的團體更駭人。

到了 2014 年，ISI 聲稱已組成哈里發國，這個新國度由伊斯蘭教法統治，並正式更名為伊斯蘭國（或 Isis）。這個團體想要全世界的穆斯林都加入哈里發國，並發動全面戰爭對抗非穆斯林世界。在伊拉克和敘利亞，伊斯蘭國佔領了愈來愈多土地，並殘暴統治許多城鎮和都市，限制人民的基本自由，不遵守該團體定義的伊斯蘭基本教義的人民，就會受到暴力懲罰。

在世界各國的城市受到一連串攻擊後，伊斯蘭國的恐怖統治變得真正全球化。攻擊行動通常由恐怖分子小團體或甚至是孤狼發動，他們在公開殺害許多無辜人民並自殺之前，都誓言效忠伊斯蘭國。

那麼，伊斯蘭國的下一步是什麼？好消息是，就軍事力量而言，它已大為衰竭，該國曾控制的許多土地都被美國支持的伊拉克軍隊收復。然而，從最近在斯里蘭卡發生的復活節死亡攻擊來看，只要還有人願意以這個團體的名義殺死自己和其他人，伊斯蘭國仍是全球和平和穩定的極大威脅。

89. 表格與長條圖：信仰的改變　P. 270

對神明的信仰一直是我們人類重要且亙古不變之事，並以某種形式存在數萬年之久。然而，現有的許多信仰中，哪一種宗教居主流地位，卻常變來變去。目前基督教是信徒人數最多的宗教。然而，由於非基督教國家的出生率居高不下，而基督教國家的出生率則持續下滑，因此基督教很快就會落居第二。

此外，歐洲與美國（傳統上信基督教）不信教和不隸屬於任何宗教者的人數也持續增加，進一步降低未來基督徒的數量。未來 30 年，預估有 1.06 億人會脫離基督教信仰，但預料只有 4000 萬人會改信基督教。雖然 2050 年時，基督教仍維持世界第一大宗教的地位，但到了 2070 年，預估伊斯蘭教的信徒人數會遠遠超越基督教。

下頁的表格和長條圖說明這個趨勢。表格包含每個宗教在 2010 年及 2050 年的預估信徒人數。長條圖顯示這些宗教在 2015 年的信徒數量，以十億人為單位，計算到小數點後一位。

90. 清單：簽帳卡或信用卡？　P. 273

在一個愈來愈不用現金的世界裡，我們大部分人的日常採購，現在都依賴某種形式的塑膠貨幣，如簽帳卡或信用卡。這兩種卡片的差異很容易分辨：使用信用卡時，你的所有採購皆由你的銀行先付款，預期之後你會付款給銀行清償債務；但是，使用簽帳卡時，消費金額是直接從你目前的銀行帳戶中扣除（或借記）。兩種顯然各有好處，但對許多擔心會超支或背負債務的人來說，簽帳卡是較好的選擇。

使用簽帳卡做為主要付款卡片時，盯緊你的銀行存款餘額就非常重要。你可透過紙本對帳單，或登入網路銀行帳戶查看餘額。你也可以透過銀行建立一套機制，餘額過低時會收到警告，如此一來，超支的可能性就更低了。

下頁是約翰・米契的每月對帳單。對帳單列出個人在某段時間內進行的所有交易，包含提款（支出）、轉帳和存款（存入），以及餘額的變化。

ANSWERS

Unit 1 Reading Skills

1-1 Main Idea

#	1	2	3	4	5
1	c	a	d	a	b
2	c	b	a	d	a
3	b	a	d	c	a
4	a	c	c	b	d
5	b	d	a	b	d

1-2 Supporting Details

#	1	2	3	4	5
6	a	d	c	c	a
7	c	d	a	c	c
8	c	a	d	c	b
9	b	d	c	b	a
10	d	b	b	a	c

1-3 Making Inferences

#	1	2	3	4	5
11	c	c	a	b	d
12	a	b	b	d	c
13	d	b	c	c	a
14	b	c	b	a	d
15	c	a	d	c	b

1-4 Clarifying Devices

#	1	2	3	4	5
16	c	a	b	a	c
17	d	b	b	a	c
18	d	b	a	d	c
19	a	b	d	a	c
20	c	a	d	a	c

1-5 Figurative Language

#	1	2	3	4	5
21	c	a	c	b	d
22	b	b	d	c	d
23	a	c	d	b	b
24	a	c	d	c	b
25	c	a	b	d	a

1-6 Author's Purpose and Tone

#	1	2	3	4	5
26	b	c	c	d	a
27	a	c	d	b	b
28	c	d	c	b	a
29	d	c	c	a	b
30	c	a	b	d	a

1-7 Cause and Effect

#	1	2	3	4	5
31	c	b	b	a	c
32	a	d	b	b	c
33	b	b	d	a	c
34	c	a	c	c	b
35	b	d	a	c	b

1-8 Finding Bias

#	1	2	3	4	5
36	c	a	c	c	a
37	b	d	a	c	c
38	d	c	c	a	b
39	c	b	a	c	b
40	a	c	a	d	a

1-9 Fact or Opinion

#	1	2	3	4	5
41	b	d	a	b	a
42	b	a	b	a	b
43	c	a	b	a	a
44	b	d	b	b	a
45	b	a	b	b	b

1-10 Review Test

#	1	2	3	4	5
46	d	d	b	a	c
47	b	a	c	d	a
48	b	d	a	b	d
49	b	d	c	a	d
50	c	b	d	a	a

320

Unit 2 Word Study

2-1 Synonyms

51	1. b	2. a	3. d	4. c	5. a
52	1. b	2. a	3. d	4. b	5. c
53	1. a	2. c	3. a	4. b	5. d
54	1. c	2. a	3. b	4. a	5. c
55	1. b	2. b	3. a	4. a	5. c

2-2 Antonyms

56	1. b	2. c	3. b	4. a	5. d
57	1. a	2. c	3. b	4. a	5. d
58	1. d	2. c	3. b	4. a	5. d
59	1. c	2. a	3. b	4. a	5. c
60	1. c	2. b	3. a	4. a	5. d

2-3 Words in Context

61	1. c	2. a	3. d	4. a	5. d
62	1. b	2. d	3. a	4. c	5. d
63	1. b	2. c	3. a	4. d	5. a
64	1. d	2. b	3. a	4. c	5. b
65	1. d	2. b	3. d	4. a	5. c

2-4 Review Test

66	1. c	2. a	3. d	4. b	5. d
67	1. d	2. a	3. b	4. b	5. c
68	1. b	2. b	3. b	4. c	5. d
69	1. b	2. b	3. d	4. d	5. a
70	1. b	2. c	3. a	4. d	5. b

Unit 3 Study Strategies

3-1 Visual Material

71	1. c	2. a	3. d	4. a	5. b
72	1. a	2. b	3. c	4. b	5. d
73	1. c	2. c	3. d	4. b	5. a
74	1. d	2. a	3. b	4. c	5. c
75	1. a	2. b	3. d	4. b	5. d

3-2 Reference Sources

76	1. c	2. b	3. b	4. a	5. d
77	1. a	2. c	3. c	4. d	5. a
78	1. c	2. a	3. b	4. a	5. c
79	1. a	2. d	3. b	4. c	5. a
80	1. a	2. b	3. c	4. b	5. b

Unit 4 Final Review

4-1 Final Review

81	1. c	2. a	3. a	4. a	5. d
82	1. c	2. d	3. b	4. b	5. a
83	1. c	2. b	3. c	4. d	5. d
84	1. c	2. b	3. d	4. b	5. a
85	1. a	2. c	3. d	4. a	5. c
86	1. b	2. b	3. a	4. a	5. d
87	1. c	2. a	3. a	4. d	5. c
88	1. b	2. b	3. d	4. c	5. a
89	1. c	2. c	3. a	4. b	5. b
90	1. b	2. a	3. a	4. d	5. b

英語閱讀技巧完全攻略 4

Success With Reading

二版

作　　者	Owain Mckimm / Connie Sliger / Zachary Fillingham / Richard Luhrs
協力作者	Laura Phelps (31, 32, 68) / Felix Norman (48, 56, 88) / Angela Carey (62)
審　　訂	Helen Yeh
譯　　者	劉嘉珮／蘇裕承／蔡裴驊
企畫編輯	葉俞均
編　　輯	賴祖兒／丁宥暄
主　　編	丁宥暄
校　　對	劉育如／黃詩韻／申文怡
圖　　片	Shutterstock
內頁設計	鄭秀芳
封面設計	林書玉
製程管理	洪巧玲
發 行 人	黃朝萍
出 版 者	寂天文化事業股份有限公司
電　　話	+886-(0)2-2365-9739
傳　　真	+886-(0)2-2365-9835
網　　址	www.icosmos.com.tw
讀者服務	onlineservice@icosmos.com.tw
出版日期	2024 年 08 月　二版三刷（寂天雲 Mebook 互動學習 APP 版）(0202)

郵撥帳號　1998620-0　寂天文化事業股份有限公司
訂書金額未滿 1000 元，請外加運費 100 元。
（若有破損，請寄回更換，謝謝）

版權所有　請勿翻印

國家圖書館出版品預行編目 (CIP) 資料

英語閱讀技巧完全攻略 (寂天雲 Mebook 互動學習 APP 版)
/ Owain Mckimm, Connie Sliger, Zachary Fillingham, Richard
Luhrs 著 ; 劉嘉珮 , 蘇裕承 , 蔡裴驊譯 . -- 二版 . -- [臺北市] :
寂天文化事業股份有限公司 , 2024.08 印刷 -
　冊 ;　公分
ISBN 978-626-300-271-5(第 4 冊 : 16K 平裝)
1.CST: 英語 2.CST: 讀本
805.18　　　　　　　　　　　　　　　　　113010927